Books by Lola White

Magic Matched

Betrothed
Married
Motherhood

The Double O Saga

Outrageous Offer
Audacious Audit

Motherhood

ISBN # 978-1-78651-339-7

Magic Matched

MOTHERHOOD

LOLA WHITE

Dedication

Thank you, Jennifer Douglas.

Chapter One

"Blood me as your heir." Silviu Lovasz let his magic rise and weave into the tone of his voice, sending it out with his words.

"Why should I?"

Mother Madeleine Davenold nearly blended in with her pillows, pale and frighteningly motionless. Only her eyes still held evidence of the fierce woman she'd been a week ago, before dark magic had infiltrated her defenses. A woman who prized the concept of Family above all else. Family was everything to the old lady.

Silviu had experience dealing with such a sentiment, however, having often manipulated the same driving emotion in his older brother. Influencing others was a talent Silviu wielded ruthlessly, and in Madeleine's weakened state, it would be easier than it had ever been before to gain a foothold.

"I will take care of them." Silviu pushed a little harder. "Trust me."

Silver light spread out over the woman's fragile skin, shimmering brightly before sinking in. Her eyes glazed. Silviu felt his magic meet the Davenold strength and slip through. With the dark spell poking holes in her resistance, Madeleine couldn't stand against him.

Burrowing deeper, his talent took hold as the woman's breathing turned ragged. Magic set down roots and reached farther. Silviu had a vision of tendrils curling out—only to meet a snarling black wall that surged up to reject the

5

influence with a violent expulsion.

Madeleine screamed softly, clutching her chest. Silviu was knocked back as the silver light retracted into his soul with a painful snap.

The dark magic had blocked his efforts.

The two witches stared at each other in grim astonishment. Madeline rubbed her chest with a shaking hand. "What was that?"

"Dark magic." Silviu refused to elaborate. There was no way he'd admit that he'd tried to gain influence over her. He rushed toward her to evaluate the damage he might have done.

Madeleine's pulse was weak but steady under Silviu's fingertips. The magic coursing through her veins was cool and smooth, nowhere near the raging river it used to be. There wasn't a trace of the dark magic energy that he'd felt, but that didn't mean it was gone.

"How do you feel?"

The old woman's eyes flashed with amusement. "Terrible."

"Then why do you look as if you're enjoying some private joke?"

Madeleine smiled. Her pale, papery skin stretched taut over her cheeks, lifting the sagging flesh until she appeared almost beautiful. A pang shot through Silviu's chest as he realized his betrothed would look like the Davenold Mother when she reached the same age.

Madeleine's voice was a thread of sound. "Because you've been doing all you can to save my life when it would be in your best interest to let me die."

Something inside him rebelled at the thought. "That's not quite true."

"I suppose you think I can still be of use to you."

Silviu closed his eyes and again searched for the spell draining Madeleine of strength and life. He couldn't find the origins, couldn't even feel its presence, but he could sense the changes within her. Every day she was weaker, every day a step closer to death.

"I expected to have your guidance when I joined the Council." Silviu released Madeleine's wrist and eased a hip onto the bed next to hers. "I haven't even been formally named to my Family's seat yet. I need your influence over others to further my cause."

"I doubt that." Her black eyes, still sharp with intelligence in spite of her ailment, narrowed. "You'll do just fine on your own."

"If I have to." Silviu's shoulder rose and fell as his mind busied itself with modifications to the plans that had been in place since he was four years old. "You taught me well, but it would be easier to have you at my side."

"You'll have Georgeanne."

He nodded, satisfaction racing through him at the old woman's simple statement. "Yes, you've trained her well, too."

Madeleine studied him for a long moment, a hint of suspicion in her eyes. Silviu met her gaze calmly, years of practice supporting his serenity in the face of such a thorough examination. His own father had a habit of watching him in the same manner.

"She knows how to handle herself in politics," Madeleine finally said. "I've made certain she was an asset to you and your rise to power. And vice versa."

"I know. We'll work together to achieve our goals. She'll cement your Family's influence over the other matriarchal houses and extend your reach over the patriarchal witches when I lead the combined covens."

"That was the plan."

A plan that had been concocted twenty-three years before, when the matriarchal Mother had agreed to betroth her infant granddaughter to the youngest son of a patriarchal coven. Reap and Bane were the rarest of witches — one with too much magic, the other with none. Silviu's Reap magic merged into the blocked Bane magic Georgie contained within her, making them the strongest Matched pair the world had ever known.

Silviu considered it their right to rule over the combined covens.

Legend suggested the pairing was able to join their talents into a force that could fell every witch before them. Together, Silviu and Georgeanne wielded a power that could pull each other back from the brink of death—a fact they'd learned when Georgie had nearly been injured by the same dark magic targeting the Davenold Mother.

"A thousand generations ago," Madeleine mused, "our community was torn apart by countless wars. The witches who walked the traditional, matriarchal path versus those who wanted to follow Fathers."

"I know the history very well," Silviu reminded her.

She frowned him into silence. "And when the war eventually dwindled down, they all saw how devastating it had been. To the world and especially to our community. The truce resulted in the Schism, Silviu. Motherhouses to one side of the divide, Fatherhouses to the other."

"With a High Seat to lead them all," he said impatiently. "A position you've held for half your life, a position I intend to hold for the rest of mine. What is your point?"

"You've been trained to take that position. Every tutor I sent to you and every burden your father heaped on your shoulders has all been to get you to the top of the covens' hierarchy." Madeleine's eyes flashed and a secretive smile played at the corners of her mouth. "But you won't get there without Georgeanne. Witches respect you, Silviu, but you are still a Lovasz."

"I can overcome that flaw. I know how others feel about my Family, but they also associate me with the Davenold coven. I've made damn sure of it."

Madeleine smirked. "When I step down from the High Seat, the Davenolds won't be eligible to reclaim it for a hundred years. Term limit laws were carved into stone and set with blood. Binding, for all time."

Silviu knew the restriction. Anything set with blood,

where the magic of a witch was concentrated in powerful doses, was unbreakable. "Yes, that's why you agreed to allow Georgeanne to take my Family name, rather than insisting on me taking yours, as is typical of matriarchal men."

"A Lovasz would be eligible to take the High Seat," Madeleine admitted. "It's just a shame that your grandfather's volatile blood runs through your veins. I wonder if the other covens will trust you enough to give you the position."

"You were supposed to help them understand that I would be a good choice."

"Was I?" Her brow lifted. "Whatever I have done has been for my granddaughter and my Family, not for you."

"It amounts to the same thing. My best interests are Georgie's too. Both of us need to occupy a place of power to protect ourselves."

Madeleine shifted on the pillows until she sat a little straighter. "You know how everyone will react if they find out she can break magic, if they learn how powerful you both are. Especially together."

"They'll dig out the pitchforks, light the torches and mob the castle gates, I know." Silviu looked away from the woman's shrewd gaze, but returned to it almost immediately. "Fear will prompt a few assassination attempts anyway. I'm prepared for it."

"Are you?" Madeleine's eyes turned cold. "I need my granddaughter in a position of power just so her life is *not* in jeopardy."

A position such as the Davenold Mother, the Council High Seat or the wife of the man who occupied the High Seat. Silviu already knew it and he'd had a similar conversation with the wily old woman a week ago in the Ngozi stronghold. He wished he could read Madeleine's thoughts to better anticipate her plans. She was even trickier than his father, who was more skillful at manipulation than most witches.

Madeleine's lips tightened. When she spoke, it was obvious from her tone that she'd rather hold on to her secrets and only shared them because her hand was being forced by the dark magic draining her of life. "I don't know if Georgeanne can hold the power of my bloodline. Her Bane imperviousness rejects every other magic but yours."

"Yes, we've discussed this already." Silviu's eyes narrowed.

"Two witches of myth and nightmares," she drawled. "Whatever will you do if you're not chosen for the High Seat?"

Silviu fought to keep his features impassive. "I'll challenge for it, if necessary."

"My boy, you still have much to learn."

He froze, facts rearranging themselves in his brain with lightning speed. Understanding was nearly instantaneous. "You think the witches are more likely to vote Georgie into the High Seat."

"She's perfect, don't you think? She's been actively involved in politics for both sides of the Schism for the past decade. She's fought shoulder to shoulder with witches persecuted in the Asian witch hunts. She's occupied the Davenold Council seat for three years now."

Silviu met Madeleine's cold stare. "You don't even know if she can take the Davenold Family power, and that's her bloodline. How do you expect her to take the combined magic of all the covens?"

"Do you really believe the covens would give a single witch all their magic to contain within them? That arrangement works inside familial bonds, but giving an outsider such authority would be unthinkable. Reigning over *all* the families, the High Seat is only able to access the power as it flows past."

"It flows through you, but doesn't reside inside you?" That was very different from his understanding of a Family's power—which was wholly housed within the Family leader, every witch of the bloodline contributing to its strength.

Satisfaction lit the old woman's face. "Georgeanne would be perfectly capable of filling the position. Perfect, *period*, considering what everyone believes her deficiency means for her talents."

"She's Bane. Others won't understand that my magic can unlock hers." Silviu's lips twisted. "They will believe she won't be able to use the magic of the High Seat."

Madeleine hummed. "That works in her favor, don't you think?"

"Before or after they try to kill her?" Silviu's heart raced in his chest at the mere thought. "When they discover what she can do, their fear will be boundless and unpredictable."

He knew everything legend could tell him about Bane witches along with everything Georgeanne herself had proven true. He'd learned that being Bane had distinct advantages, but Georgie's newly discovered talent would only increase the fear others felt for the so-called deficiency.

"I love my granddaughter. I love my Family. I chose you to protect them after I'm gone."

"You want me to protect them, but refuse to give me the means to do so!"

Madeleine took a deep breath. "I'm tired, Silviu. Leave me now."

"Blood me as your heir, Madeleine." He had to try, but he didn't dare send his magic out again.

"I will never blood a Lovasz man to lead the Davenold women. I would rather let the power choose its own heir from amongst my Family."

"And if it doesn't choose Georgeanne?" Silviu got to his feet but didn't move toward the door. "Your Family will go to war with itself."

"Then you'll protect her." Madeleine still managed to look authoritative, even with her eyelids drooping in exhaustion. "She's your weakness."

"She's my Magic Match. That's not a weakness, but a strength."

"Together, you will rise to lead the covens and Davenold Motherhood will cease to matter. I'll ask you what your father asked me, when he devised this crazy scheme. Who would value a different Family leader when the Council High Seat is of the Family?"

Silviu understood what the wily old woman meant. The High Seat ruled them all, and if Georgeanne held the position, the Davenolds would naturally look to her for leadership regardless of who their Mother actually was. Vasile Lovasz had counted on that very concept when he'd chosen to endorse his youngest son in his pursuit of power, rather than the rightful Lovasz heir.

Surrendering the field for the moment, Silviu did as he was asked when Madeleine repeated her command for him to leave. He paused at the door to add one last thought to the woman's plots and hoped his words would find fertile ground to grow in.

"Matches share power, Mother Davenold. Mine is Georgeanne's and hers is mine. The magic flows between us, so if you blood me as your heir, Georgie will still have access to the full force of your Family's strength."

Madeleine's weary eyes snapped open. Her words, when they came, tumbled through Silviu's head—until doubts and suspicions piled up. Especially as she was essentially on her deathbed.

"I'm counting on that," she told him.

Chapter Two

Georgeanne

"Do you really think this Family will ever follow a Bane Mother?"

Georgie came to a dead stop on the stairs as the husky voice floated up from the entry hall below. Gritting her teeth, she leaned over the balustrade and looked down to see her cousin, Suzette, smirking up at her. Georgie's palms itched to wipe the expression off the woman's face.

"A better question," Georgie stated clearly and calmly, "is why you think they would ever follow you."

Suzette's lips pulled into a thin line. "At least I have magic. You are nothing more than a defective bitch Madeleine took in out of sheer pity."

Heated anger slid over Georgie's nape. "If anyone garners pity in this Family, it's you."

"No, I am a true witch. I have power, and you have nothing. You're deformed, you poor thing."

Georgie discreetly wriggled her shoulders and slowly began to descend the stairs again. "This is exactly why no one likes you, Suzette. You pretend to be superior to everyone else, when you are nothing more than a substandard heir of the secondary Family branch."

"I am still heir to this branch," the woman purred. "Which is more than you've been promised, isn't it?"

Georgie flicked her gaze around the beautiful entry hall. The secondary branch of the Davenold Family boasted a gorgeous English estate that any woman would be proud to call home. Ancient and well-kept, it was filled with marble tiles and columns, priceless artwork and luxurious fabrics. One day, when Georgeanne's great-aunt Margaret died, it would all be Suzette's.

Georgie tried not to let that bother her.

Her jaw ached from the effort of her forced smile. "Margaret must be heartbroken that you're her only granddaughter. Right about now she would probably give anything to change the tradition of passing leadership down to the grandchildren. I can't say I blame her."

"Madeleine's the one wishing for the change," Suzette sneered. "Passing power to the grandchild is supposed to give longer, more stable reigns, but perhaps the old traditions *should* be abandoned, as neither you nor Christiana will inspire stability in this Family."

"And you think you will? Why do you think your grandmother is desperate for you to have children?" Georgie gripped the banister to keep from throwing herself over the rail and physically attacking her cousin. "So she can bypass your inheritance altogether."

Georgie saw a spark of pure rage in the woman's eyes. Suzette had been lectured on the subject of her childlessness repeatedly. As a whole, the Davenolds believed every witch of their bloodline had a duty to reproduce and, whenever possible, even went out of their way to find Magic Matches — another whose magic worked on the same frequency — so that more children could be born to the bloodline.

Defying the typical Family trait of growing more beautiful in anger, Suzette's cheeks turned a mottled pink and her lips pinched. "I will have children when I choose, and not a moment before."

"What are you waiting for, Suzette? Menopause?" Georgie didn't feel a flicker of remorse over prodding the vulnerability. "Aren't you afraid you'll be a little too old to have a baby? Aren't you afraid the magic will be faded by your age, creating a child as weak and defective as you accuse me of being?"

A shudder went through Suzette. Her pink face paled,

her lips disappeared as she pressed them tightly together. Her fists clenched so hard the lean muscles of her forearms visibly knotted beneath the lightweight sweater she wore.

Suzette's nostrils flared as she tossed her head. "I only need one child to pass on the magic."

"Mmm, it's probably best for our bloodline that you don't, though."

"You should take your own advice. You're Bane and your betrothed is a Lovasz." Suzette spat the surname as if it left a vile taste in her mouth—but she wasn't the only witch who said it that way. "You know, it's embarrassing the way you moon over that man."

Georgie clamped her lips against a denial. She certainly did not *moon* over Silviu, but she'd never show her cousin that her words had hit their mark. Reaching the bottom of the stairs, Georgie pretended a calm she didn't feel as she ambled toward her cousin. Suzette was a perfect example of the typical Family looks. Most Davenold women were petite and pretty enough, with a delicate jaw, dark hair and even darker eyes. Suzette was twenty years older than Georgeanne, a few inches taller and a little heavier, but their Family connection was clear to see.

It unnerved Georgie.

"The Lovaszes are a magically powerful Family, Suzette. I doubt you understand the benefits of having a strong man at your side, either in politics or in bed, but then, I suppose that's why you have no children, isn't it?" Suzette's lips cracked in an evil smile. "But Lovasz is not in your bed, from what I hear. Madeleine has forbidden it until after the wedding."

"She believes in the sanctity of marriage," Georgie lied. She kept her face carefully impassive, refusing to let her rival see how much she desired Silviu, and denying how difficult it had been for her to obey Madeleine's unreasonable command for abstinence.

Suzette tilted her chin. "You're really damned if you do and damned if you don't, aren't you? I heard that if you disobey the Mother's orders, Christiana will be blooded as the heir. But then, if you don't give in to your handsome betrothed, some other female will certainly offer to see to his needs."

"That was pitiful, sweetie." Georgie shook her head. "My betrothed isn't like you, desperately seeking an alternative to a less than adequate partner."

"Men are men—they're led by their cocks." Suzette smoothed her hands over her hips in a sensual threat that set Georgeanne's nerves to jangling. "I could offer to help him with that, darling. He might even get a twisted thrill out of having a woman who looks just like you, but with magic, in his bed."

"You clearly don't know Silviu very well." Fighting back intense anger at the thought of Suzette seducing Silviu, Georgie pressed a hand to her chest and opened her eyes wide. "But I completely understand the desire to have my betrothed rather than your husband. Mine is simply superior, in all ways."

Suzette trilled a laugh that sent shivers down Georgie's spine. "My husband is perfect compared to your betrothed, darling. Mine does as he's told, while you'll spend the rest of your life wrestling for control."

That didn't bother Georgie nearly as much as her cousin had hoped. Over the past two weeks, since their reunion at Silviu's sister's betrothal celebration, Georgeanne had developed a deep appreciation for her betrothed, and was working hard on building a comparable trust in him. Silviu was strong, intelligent and even compassionate when the situation warranted. He would be an asset to her, and she would never grow bored with him. She might even be in love with him, but she'd never say that out loud.

"You shame yourself by chasing after other women's husbands, Suzette. You'll fuck anyone *but* your own, won't you?"

"Such language." Suzette's dark eyes, so like Georgie's it was disconcerting, flashed with a dangerous light. "It's a miracle anyone can bear to speak with you in your diplomatic duties for this Family. Perhaps you should be removed from your post."

"I've single-handedly built our credibility to a level no other Family has experienced since before the Schism."

"Ah, the great divide." Suzette folded her arms over her chest, eyes running up and down Georgie's small frame as her lips curled. "Perhaps you think your marriage will benefit you in the wider witching world, but it will only hold you back in the Davenold Family."

"My marriage to Silviu will be an alliance between matriarchal and patriarchal traditions. Our union will reach across the divide between witches, and the Davenolds will have influence on the both sides of the Schism."

"It's a pipe dream. No two witches could ever be in such accord as to unite the witching world. Unification could only come through leadership of a single witch."

There was no point in arguing with Suzette. No matriarchal witch would ever follow a Father, and no patriarchal witch would ever follow a Mother. A single ruler would never be accepted by both sides of the divide—but therein lay the beauty of Georgie's alliance with Silviu. Her marriage to the youngest Lovasz son was a well-crafted plot set in motion the day of her birth. Each side of the Schism would feel represented when they took their rightful place at the helm.

"I pity you," Suzette continued. "Stuck with a patriarch for the rest of your life, and you know our Family will never tolerate such a witch in the High Male position of this coven."

"Jealousy is just eating you alive, isn't it?" Georgie asked with a shake of her head. "Just accept that you'll never be Mother."

"Madeleine is dying and she hasn't blooded an heir. I am her niece, my grandmother is her sister. And, since I have magic, I have a better chance at claiming the position than you."

Some emotion stronger and hotter than anger roared through Georgeanne. It wasn't just the threat to her goals. She didn't react the same way to the idea of her other cousin, Christiana, claiming Davenold Motherhood, and Chris was Madeleine's oldest granddaughter, groomed alongside Georgie to lead. Suzette's arrogant claim was an offense to the bedrock of Georgie's love of Family.

Suzette was too selfish and arrogant to lead. The thought of it was intolerable.

"You don't have any right," Georgie snapped. "You aren't worthy of the position. If you somehow managed to do the impossible and take this Family, you'll have a thousand challengers lined up in the first thirty minutes."

Suzette stiffened, but she also smiled, clearly anticipating. "No one would be able to take the power from me once it's mine."

"You wouldn't be blooded, and the power wouldn't have time to settle into you before you were challenged. Your connection to it would be weak, and very breakable."

Suzette's brows lifted. "They won't best me."

"Enough of this fantasy." Georgie waved her hand, her patience entirely too frayed over the events of the past few days to continue the conversation for much longer. "You won't be Mother. I would never allow it."

"Is that a physical threat? I know it's not a magical one."

Georgie had been relentlessly trained to take over the position of Davenold Mother. In spite of not having magic, she'd been treated as the front-running heir her entire life. Though her focus had been on politics rather than spells, she had no problem letting her rival see her strengths.

She slid forward, invading Suzette's personal space once again. "Let me make myself clear. I will kill you with my own bare hands before I let you rule this Family. Whether you feel threatened or not is your business."

"Don't underestimate me." Suzette's face folded into harsh lines, hatred radiating from her eyes.

"Don't underestimate *me*," Georgie returned. "I will do

everything in my power to keep my Family safe. Including taking you apart."

"It's so amusing that you really think you can best me when you have no magic. Your arrogance will be your downfall, darling."

"Anyone is free to try me." Georgie fought to regain control of herself. Clenching her fists at her sides, she took a deep breath. Silviu was always telling her that her mouth ran away with her when she was angry. This was one of those situations where the less was said, the better off Georgie would be.

"An open invitation?" Suzette pursed her lips and began sliding around Georgeanne as if cataloguing all her weaknesses. "I'll put out the word."

"No one in this Family would dream of challenging me, Suzette. They all know — "

"That they will suffer Madeleine's wrath if they lay hands on you. Yes, I'm aware. But Madeleine is so very ill, now."

"I don't need Grandmother's protection. The rest of this Family understands my leadership capabilities. I have been trained to wield the power, I have built relationships with other witching Families, and I am compassionate toward my own. You can make no such claims."

"When I am Mother — "

"You will *never* be Mother!" Georgie had had enough. Her back heated as if her muscles had caught fire, her jaw clenched. "You will die before I allow you to drag this Family down. We have worked far too hard, far too long, to let an arrogant bitch like you topple everything we've built."

Suzette threw back her head and laughed. The sound echoed through the entry hall, doubling back to Georgie from the old stone walls and massive columns. It grated on her nerves.

"What do you really think you could do? You have no notion of what you are dealing with." Suzette smiled and drifted toward the stairs, confidence making her seem to float. "But far be it from me to explain. I'd rather it be a surprise."

"Don't make the mistake of assuming you have support in this Family." Georgie lifted her gaze to watch Suzette ascend the steps.

"Being Bane, you are a weakness our coven cannot afford. Everyone knows it but you. Perhaps one day soon, I'll even prove it to you."

Georgeanne stood for a long moment in the entry hall, a chill invading her skin and exacerbating her newly acquired doubts. Suzette's words had carried a warning and Georgie frantically tried to decipher her cousin's meaning. She felt threatened in a way that went beyond the expected rivalry found in Families whose Mothers were in peril.

Suzette was dangerous, a natural troublemaker manipulative enough to plant seeds of doubt and known to dabble in dark magic. The last time Georgie had dealt with a dark magic witch, she had nearly lost her life. Her grandmother was still on bed rest and fading fast because of it.

Georgeanne was Bane-born, impervious to all uses of magic. Spells simply wouldn't harm her. Except one. One dark spell had found its way past the Bane shields, but Silviu's Reap power had conquered the magic. Georgie reminded herself that her betrothed's talents were beginning to unlock her own, and that together they were proving their strength.

And even if that one, single spell had shaken her confidence, Georgie could fake it until it shored itself up.

The massive double doors to the forecourt swung open, dragging Georgie from her thoughts. Shaking off her unease, she squinted into the early afternoon sunshine that poured through the doorway and saw a tall, familiar silhouette moving up the shallow steps beyond the portico.

Relief nearly took Georgie's legs out from under her as she rushed forward. If Suzette was intent on causing trouble during the bleak time the Davenolds found themselves in, it was just as well to have Milo Ivanov-Davenold on the estate, no matter that his brother-in-law, Adam, had a habit of sniping at him. Christiana's husband had a knack for soothing tempers and easing minds, a talent that came in handy with his business dealings and proved downright necessary for tense Family gatherings.

"Milo!" Georgie wrapped her arms around her cousin's husband with genuine affection. "I'm so glad you're here. We could really use a man with your gift, right about now."

"I caught the first flight out."

Though Georgie worried her cousin was too easily led by her husband, she'd never put the blame for that on Milo's shoulders. Christiana should be strong enough to stand firm against any man. While Adam disagreed with her, Georgie thought Milo was simply feeling his way forward in his new Family and his frequent suggestions weren't meant to challenge the status quo. Besides, she knew patience was always required when dealing with members of the volatile Ivanov coven.

Georgie gave Milo another squeeze. "Sorry I couldn't send the jet, it's picking up the aunts."

He pulled from her embrace, his emerald eyes—his only extraordinary feature—dulling in dismay. Georgie returned his stare, reflecting on his ordinary appearance and his habit of watching people too closely. He may rub certain Davenolds the wrong way, but Milo was always serene and tolerant, which, in Georgie's book, counted for a lot in stressful situations.

"The aunts are coming?" Milo's brows pulled together. "It must be bad then, Georgeanne."

"It is." She fought to keep her lips from trembling and blinked back her tears as she gave voice to a fear she'd desperately tried to ignore. "I think Madeleine might be dying."

Chapter Three

Milo

Milo would have preferred to be reunited with his wife in private first, but that was not to be. After sending his bags with a servant, Georgeanne led him up to a pretty parlor already occupied by a host of people he didn't know and, in one case, wished he didn't know. His gaze immediately found Christiana and he almost missed the ensuing introductions while he struggled to maintain his composure.

It was difficult to hide his emotions as his wife flinched and paled, a reaction that had Milo grinding his teeth every time she did it—which was much too frequently for his ego to handle calmly. Christiana rose slowly, smoothed her hands over her frilly skirt and moved toward him at a sedate pace. Reaching his side, she placed a hand on his elbow and squeezed. Milo's heart wrenched.

"Milo, this is Eliasz Levy and Ileana Lovasz." Georgie waved toward the beautiful couple.

Milo bowed over Ileana's knuckles. "Lovasz?"

"Silviu is with Grandmother now," Georgie explained. "He's trying to undo the magic harming her."

"Ah." Milo kept his shock to himself as best he was able. "And what magic is that? The only thing I understood when Christiana called was that Madeleine was ill."

"I was upset when I called." Just the sound of his wife's voice had Milo's body tightening after their prolonged absence. She'd been sent to Poland, then she'd attended the Ngozi–Levy wedding. To say he'd missed her would be an

22

understatement.

"First, meet your new sister-in-law, Tulah." Georgie nodded and gestured toward an exotic beauty. The woman stood behind Adam, a man so ridiculously identical to Christiana that Milo had to brace himself against the jealousy he felt at the twins' bond just to look at him.

Milo smiled at the woman and nodded toward his brother-in-law. Knowing it would please his wife, he kept his tone neutral. "Congratulations on your marriage."

Adam's response, however, was less than pleasant. "I'm surprised you found a moment to step away from your busy schedule, Ivanov."

Milo felt Christiana's spine snap straight under his palm. By continuing to use Milo's former surname, Adam was reminding the man he was an outsider. Not that he was likely to ever forget, considering the cool distance Christiana often created between them.

Milo's voice grew chilly as his ability to find his calm was compromised. "I do hope your marriage will make you happy enough that you no longer feel the need to insinuate yourself into mine."

Adam jerked forward a step, blue eyes narrowing. Tulah's brows shot up her forehead as she grabbed for her husband, her stick-thin arm enfolding his middle as if she could hold him back. Milo gritted his teeth and tried to tamp down his own emotions so that the situation didn't spiral out of control. He slowly regained a measure of peace through sheer willpower.

Georgeanne threw out her hands like a boxing referee sending the fighters to their respective corners. "This is not the time for pettiness."

"You're right," Milo agreed immediately. He looked around, his gaze moving steadily over the group before returning to ensnare Adam pointedly. "To be clear, however, I am never too busy for my wife or her Family. The Davenolds are my Family too, now."

Georgie gave him a smile. "Your presence is certainly

appreciated. Your talent will go a long way toward keeping the others calm. Silviu's been doing all he can to help Grandmother, but it doesn't seem to be enough. I can't break the effigy's hold on her, either."

"What are you talking about?" Milo asked.

"Adam found an effigy directed at Grandmother at the Ngozi residence." Georgie ran a hand through her chin-length curls. "It looked just like her, decorated with her own hair, and I managed to break its magic. I thought I stopped the spell."

Milo tried to focus through his shock. Georgie was Bane, so it was odd to hear that *she'd* broken such magic. "It wasn't Margaret, was it? She's talented with effigies and wants Suzette to inherit. Or perhaps even Suzette, as she prefers dark magic."

Georgie shook her head. "We thought it was Graves Ngozi, but nothing changed after he died. It's the opposite, actually. It just keeps getting worse."

"He died?"

"His Family Father killed him during the wedding ceremony. Muso refused to let Graves marry as punishment for killing Muso's son." Georgie's lips twisted, a rare showing of her true sentiments. "Muso had wanted his son killed and the magic transferred to him, but Graves stole it."

"Graves had strong personal magic," Christiana added. "Dark magic."

Milo clenched his jaw and tried not to dwell on the fact that his *pregnant* wife had been in the midst of a ceremony that had resulted in death. He searched for a sliver of serenity in the chaos of fear and frustration chewing on the deepest parts of him. Milo's gripes were too late, coming after the fact, and Christiana was an heir to the Davenold power. He couldn't publicly admonish her for the decision to attend the wedding, and even in private his censure would have to be restrained.

Georgie sighed. "Silviu's been trying to find out how the

dark magic is tied to Grandmother. She always looks better after he does whatever it is he's doing, but it's not enough."

"But the Davenold power—" Milo stuttered.

"Is losing the fight." Georgie blinked rapidly as if holding back tears, adding to the shock piling up inside Milo. The woman wasn't prone to crying jags. "Whatever's got a hold on her is stronger than our Family's magic."

Milo looked at his wife, an expert spell caster. "But, as the long-established Mother, Madeleine can draw on the combined strength of all who belonged to your bloodline, making her ridiculously powerful. I thought it would be nearly impossible for any spell to bring her down."

"It's a dark magic so insidious it can barely be felt," Christiana said. "Maybe black magic, which I sensed at the Ngozi residence. Adam and I have been combing the grimoires for more information because neither of us have ever seen anything like it."

"It's a strong witch who cast the spell," Adam added reluctantly. "I can only assume that there was either more than one effigy, or the destruction of the damned thing had unexpected consequences."

Georgie grimaced. "I burned it."

Milo flinched. "Why would you do that? Effigies are sympathetic magic, used to link witches over distance. Destruction of the doll can be dangerously unpredictable."

Adam glared at his cousin. "We tried to explain that."

"I was furious at Graves. I'd already broken the doll's spell and Margaret said it would rebound on its creator." Georgeanne shrugged. "But there was more magic we'd missed, already taken root inside Grandmother."

"Well, what's done is done." Milo took a deep breath flavored with his wife's subtle perfume. "All we can do is look forward and see what can be fixed from here."

"Damn, I wish we had thought of that," Adam drawled. "Thank God you're here, man."

Christiana narrowed her eyes. "Stop it."

"Hey"—Adam held up his hands—"I'm just pointing

out that Ivanov's presence here is pointless, useless and unwanted. Just like him."

Warmth spread through Milo as Christiana shivered and rose to his defense against her twin brother. "Like your wife's presence has been anything other than a burden for this Family? You married her without either her Father's permission or your Mother's, and almost started a war we can't currently afford with the Ngozis. And that was *after* you insinuated yourself into her Family's problems, which may have been the reason Grandmother was targeted in the first place!"

"My relationship with Tulah didn't cause any of this, and she's certainly not a burden. She's helping us however she can, even going so far as to search Suzette's room for more effigies!"

"It's a good thing she wasn't caught," Christiana sneered. "Suzette would have eaten your pretty kitty for a snack. Tulah's too weak to stand against the Davenold women."

Adam's lip lifted in a snarl. "She's put up with more bullshit than you'll ever—"

Christiana's hand tightened on Milo's arm as her brother's mouth snapped closed. Her voice was sickly sweet. "Than I'll ever *what*, Adam?"

He pressed his lips together until they were a white slash. Milo was amazed at the pain he heard in the man's next words. "Graves mistreated her, Chris. I won't let you do it too."

"Remember that the next time you want to pick a fight with my husband, then."

Tulah smiled nervously. "I know we took everyone by surprise. Adam married me to protect me from the Ngozi Father, but we do suit each other well."

"Oh, honey, this fight has nothing to do with you." Christiana relaxed so suddenly she nearly flowed against Milo's side. He gathered her closer, daring to put his arm around her, though he braced for her to pull away.

When she didn't, he jumped at the opportunity to soak

in the feel of her, her subtle perfume and the texture of her thick, silken hair under his lips as he tentatively brushed a kiss over her head. Milo wished Christiana fitted him perfectly, that he wasn't nearly a foot taller than her, that her hard angles could be smoothed by his softer ones, and vice versa. But she was a strong woman, a prickly woman, and sometimes that was better than his need for her to fit him. Sometimes, it was perfect.

So he would do whatever he could to make himself fit her, instead.

Milo slipped one hand between their bodies and cupped her still-flat belly. He knew she was strong enough to protect herself and their baby, but her safety was a fear he'd held deep and close since the moment she'd told him the happy news. It had taken all his willpower to remain calm when Madeleine had ordered her to travel to Europe without him.

"I'd like a moment with my wife," he announced, knowing the others probably heard the need in his tone. But, as Eliasz and Ileana were seemingly glued together and Adam appeared close to rabid over his new bride, Milo didn't care. He received a round of understanding glances, and a single hostile glare, but they all trooped out the door.

The moment they were alone, Milo captured his wife's lips. He was hungry, ravenous, on the verge of insanity with only his wife's kiss to anchor him—though he didn't dare show her that when he took her mouth in a soft press belying the need ravaging his gut. Christiana didn't respond well to male dominance.

So Milo didn't press, and was rewarded with a willing caress. He kept his hands motionless, one on her back, the other on her belly, and tried to be as non-threatening as possible. Christiana kissed him back with such sweetness that his hidden hopes rose.

He prayed for strength in his battle against a ghost, hoping that, one day, Chris would learn to love Milo as much as she'd loved her first husband. Her previous marriage had been a whirlwind romance and, though he knew how hurt Christiana had been by her first husband's infidelities, Milo feared she'd never get over the man's death.

He refused to consider the nasty rumors swirling through the witching world.

The kiss was over before Milo was ready, and Christiana moved away with agitated steps. He clenched his fists at his sides, trying not to reach for her, forcing himself not to grab her and crush her to him. Milo stared down into her tired, red-rimmed blue eyes and felt his heart punch up into his throat.

"How are you?"

"I'm not the one you should worry about." Christiana shrugged. "Grandmother is weak, pale and tired. She doesn't look good and sometimes I can barely hear her when she speaks."

Milo winced. "Did she give any indication of who she'll name as her heir?"

His wife's chin elevated sharply, but her tone was devoid of emotion. "No, but it definitely won't be Suzette."

"I never imagined it would be." Milo tried to hold her gaze, but Chris avoided him. "Has Georgeanne seemed any different to you?"

Christiana glanced at him quickly before looking away again. "No, why would she?"

"I wondered if Madeleine had secretly blooded your cousin as heir."

"We've always lived with the assumption that Georgie would inherit the Family power, Milo. It wouldn't come as a surprise to me if Madeleine blooded her."

"Madeleine has given you just as much attention," he pointed out, "and you have magic. Your cousin can't possibly be expected to lead a Family of witches being Bane. It's impossible."

Christiana drew herself up. "How do you know what's impossible? Look at the Levy Family. Daniel is very weak in magic, yet he's a strong, capable Father for them."

"Weak, but not Bane!" Milo ran a hand over his head. Frustration heated his veins but fear cooled them off again. "You really think you can follow a Mother without magic?"

"She's my cousin." Christiana blinked rapidly. "I would follow her anywhere, anytime."

"Such a lovely show of loyalty," Milo muttered past a twinge of bitter jealousy. "Too bad it's reserved for so few people."

"You have a complaint? I'm surprised you know where my loyalty lies, considering you are never in my company."

Not willing to stir that particular pot, Milo took a deep breath, fighting his resentment. "The magic won't choose either of your cousins. You are the strongest witch, the natural choice of the Davenold power if it must select its own host, which it will do if there's no heir."

"I don't want to talk about this, Milo."

He ignored her because he couldn't afford to listen. "You must be blooded so the magic has adequate time to settle in, Christiana. You need to plead your case to Madeleine while you still can."

"Instead, I choose to spend quality time with my grandmother, the woman who raised me. I'm closer to her than I am to the woman who gave birth to me, Milo. I want to talk to her about other things. Much more important things."

"There is nothing more important, Christiana." Again, Milo found himself taking deep breaths and searching for patience, tranquility. The long flight and two week separation from his stubborn, standoffish wife didn't help.

"I'm not going to campaign for my grandmother's position while she's on her deathbed."

True fear flashed through him. In his mind, Milo could see exactly what would happen. The magic would choose Christiana if Madeleine died without an heir, he had no doubts of that. Chris would accept, of course, but challengers would rise up to fight for the position of Mother.

Suzette would lead the charge.

Family leaders could be challenged at any time, but it was foolish to fight someone with the magical strength that flowed through the Mother. It was easier to fight for the position when a woman who had just acquired it wasn't blooded, without any real ties to the magic yet. Milo had seen it too often, witches throwing themselves into battle against their sisters and cousins when the Mother died without an heir.

He could not allow his pregnant wife to face such hostility. If Christiana wasn't properly blooded, Milo could lose everything.

Milo tried to keep his tone even. "Without Madeleine's sponsorship, you and our child will be vulnerable."

"I can handle myself. Thanks so much for your confidence, though."

He grabbed her shoulders, and though she flinched, Milo kept his hold extremely gentle. Christiana had a way of disappearing into herself if he didn't moderate his touch. "Chris, you must make her understand. She can't die without an heir, that would leave you open to challengers, and you can't meet those challengers while you're pregnant."

"I will not act as if Madeleine is dead when she's still fighting whatever is wrong with her."

"Everything you've wanted will be taken from you! From us." Milo was at a loss as his wife's face blanked, leaving no emotion visible to his scrutiny.

"Fine. I'll talk to her." Christiana jerked from his hold, spinning toward the window overlooking the sea beyond the gardens of the estate. Her fingers tangled in the heavy drapes and her back stiffened.

Milo eyed her tense body with a prickle of unease. "*Krasavitsa?*"

Her knuckles whitened on the drapes. "*Don't call me that!* I'm not Russian."

"But I am." Milo blinked at the poison in her words. She rarely spoke to him in such a way, almost zealously modulating her tones until very little emotion beyond gentle sarcasm could be detected. "And you are beautiful, so the endearment suits you."

"You're not the first man to pay me compliments while he schemes for more than he deserves." She turned to him, displaying delicate features tightening into a beauty that defied his ability to comprehend. Like her grandmother, Christiana only became prettier when she was angry, but Milo would have preferred not to have enhanced what he already thought was perfect.

"What schemes do you think I'm plotting?" he asked softly. "Why are you angry?"

"Is power all you can think about?" Her voice was cutting, her eyes locked on the wall behind him. "My grandmother is fighting for life and you want to know who the heir will be?"

"Chris, these are things that must be settled."

"Right this minute, Milo?" Her face flushed with anger, her eyes sparked blue flame. She was gorgeous and deadly. "I haven't seen you in two weeks and the first thing you say to me is that I should start a civil war in my Family?"

His stomach gave a warning jolt. "If your grandmother is that ill, then it is important to be prepared."

"Afraid you'll miss out on all the glorious power of being the Davenold High Male? You just *have* to be married to the Family Mother?"

Her accusations sparked his anger. After all Milo had gone through to get her—as his wife and in his bed—and everything he'd done to make her happy, to receive so little understanding from her was unacceptable. His heart and mind both rebelled until a hot wash of acid licked the interior of his skull.

Milo lived in a perpetual state of anxiety where his wife was concerned, always trying to moderate his behavior and keep her calm and content. Worry hounded him day and night. The eggshells he'd been walking on had cut deep. After the past six months of doing everything he could to earn her respect, all he'd managed to gain was her scorn.

But he took a moment to push his pain back, because she was the thing he wanted most in the world and he was determined to wear her down until she regarded him in the same way he regarded her. Marriage was for life among witches, and Milo constantly reminded himself that he had time to persuade her into giving him what he wanted.

"I'm looking out for you and me, yes," he said as evenly as he could manage. He worked his jaw, trying to loosen the knot that had taken hold. "For our child, our family."

"The Davenolds are my Family."

Her tone carried a dangerous current. Milo wrapped himself in patience and switched strategies. He moved toward his wife with false confidence until he caught her elbow and laid his other palm against her lower belly.

"And the family we created, *krasavitsa*? You, me and our child? Aren't we just as important?"

Chapter Four

Christiana

"Isn't our little family just as important as the wider Davenold coven, Christiana? Don't you value our child at least as much as you value your cousins, aunts and uncles?"

Milo's Russian accent flowed over Christiana, and, as usual, she had no idea how sounds that would be so rough from other mouths were so perfect from his. As he implored her to think of the life they'd created between them, she struggled to hide the swell of emotions he provoked. He stood close, heating her with his body and staring at her with such persuasion shining in his beautiful eyes that it was hard not to simply surrender.

The past few days—the past two weeks—surrounded by patriarchal Families had taken their toll. She felt as if the world had been turned on its head. With Madeleine ill and possibly dying, Georgie forming an inexplicable bond with Silviu, and Adam choosing a bride Christiana wasn't certain was good enough for him, fear, jealousy and exhaustion had begun to tear her apart.

Milo pressuring her to make a bid for Family leadership only added to her burdens. She took a deep breath and firmed her voice. "I will protect our baby with every talent at my disposal."

Milo's nostrils flared and she wondered what that meant when the gentleness in his gaze never flickered. Christiana had learned from past experience that a man's anger could almost always be judged by his eyes.

Milo released her elbow and backed off, leaving her colder

than she should have been. After six months of marriage, however, she was beginning to get used to the pulling sensation deep within her that both pushed her closer to her husband, and dragged her back from the danger he posed.

"We will speak of something else then," he said neutrally. "How do you like Tulah?"

"She appeals to my jaded brother, and the kitsune shape-changing abilities are something the Davenolds can make use of."

But that didn't stop the anger, resentment and betrayal from bubbling up in Christiana's stomach. As her veins burned and her muscles cramped, Chris sternly reminded herself that Adam was still *her* Magic Match, her twin, her brother. Tulah Ngozi-Davenold couldn't break that bond any more than Milo could.

Milo cocked his head, studying her with the perpetual hunger she always saw in his eyes. Christiana wondered what he was hungry for—her, her Family position or something else she hadn't thought of yet—but she was too much of a coward to ask. She had no idea what he saw or what he wanted when he stared at her that way, but his was a look that swamped her with vulnerability. It made her want to sit still until he figured it out, or jump up and find a place to hide so he never could. It imparted a misleading sense of safety and care that Chris rejected completely.

Christiana would never trust a husband again. Not after the last one.

But, *damn*, how she wished she could.

"So that is not a safe topic, either," he finally murmured, surprising her with his insight. He prowled a moment, restlessly moving through the little parlor before throwing himself onto a loveseat. To her enormous surprise, he patted his lap and smiled suggestively. "So perhaps it would be best if we limited our conversation to how much I missed you these past weeks?"

"You want me to sit on your lap?"

He nodded. "I have missed you, *krasavitsa*. Two weeks is

a very long time to go without my wife."

"We've been apart longer, when you're off on one of your oh so frequent business conferences."

"And every moment I spend away from your side is torture. Come here."

Uncertain of him and herself both, Chris gingerly perched on his knees. Milo's long arms wrapped around her and pulled her close, something he rarely did. He usually waited for her to make the first move, a habit wholly at odds with the way he'd tried to persuade her to make a bid for Motherhood.

But Chris liked the way he tucked her against his chest. She liked the deceptive strength in his arms and the heat of his body. She liked the way he felt, and admitted it had been a long two weeks without him, too. Slowly, she snaked her hands up his lean chest to his nape and wriggled closer, lifting her face toward his.

"My bed was empty and cold, Milo. And right in the middle of patriarchal Families, so I had to sleep with one eye open."

"It pleases me to hear how empty your bed has been, *krasavitsa*."

"As if I'd ever take a lover from that side of the Schism. Patriarchal witches believe matriarchs are worthless."

The corners of his eyes flinched the way they did when he was irritated, and she could have kicked herself for trying to make such a joke. Milo had been cheated on, and hadn't liked the experience any more than Chris had. She would never do that to him. She took her vows seriously and was about to tell him so, when Milo slid his long fingers under Christiana's chin gently enough to put her at ease.

"They're obviously wrong," he said. "You are valuable beyond measure."

A flash of suspicion stormed through her. "Because I'm one of the Davenold heirs?"

"No—" He brushed his lips over hers. "Because you are my beautiful wife. The answer to the prayers of my heart and the needs of my body."

"Prayers of your heart, Milo?" Chris rolled her eyes. "Really?"

"My heart wanted a child." He stroked down her back, caught the curves of her hips in his palms and shifted her until she straddled him, her skirt rising to her thighs and her knees pressing into the cushions of the loveseat. Surprising her again, Milo hauled Christiana over his lap until his growing cock nudged against her, with only the fabric of his trousers and her panties keeping them apart. "You say nothing of the needs of my body, *krasavitsa*."

Her eyes widened and her spine turned fluid, almost as if against her will. "It has been a long time, Milo. Maybe my body has needs, too."

"Then I will see to them."

"Here?" Her voice broke. His boldness thrilled her and surprised her in equal measure. Her husband wasn't an overly adventurous man—not that she complained. Chris' first husband had been exceedingly audacious and his behavior had worn thin to the point of pain. She'd been relieved when Milo had proven himself so different in that regard.

Milo was just Milo, and that was nearly perfect. Ordinary looks that would never garner too much attention on the street, with average, sandy blond hair cut conservatively, a lean face prone to laugh lines around his mouth and an easy-going charisma that won him friends in the boardroom but never seemed as threatening as Chris sensed he could be.

Only his gem-quality eyes set under a brow ridge that was slightly too masculine added a spark of interest to Milo's chameleon looks. Only the obvious strength in his long legs gave the impression of athleticism. Only his towering height and solid shoulders gave a hint that, just perhaps, the man wasn't as much of a pushover as people expected him to be.

He was a man Christiana wished she could love. But too much stood between them, not least of which was her fear that he saw her as nothing more than a woman who would lead him to greatness when her grandmother faltered.

Which looked to be soon.

"*Krasavitsa*? Where did you go?"

Chris blinked and pushed away her thoughts. With a quiet huff of self-censuring laughter, she let her spine relax until she rested against her husband's chest. "Nowhere. I'm right here, wondering if you're really planning on seducing me in a sitting room the whole Family has access to."

"Oh, yes, that is exactly my plan. I don't think I can make it to our room. Especially because I don't know where our room is yet, but I do know where my wife is."

Milo's big hand smoothed up her thigh, higher and higher until his fingertips edged against the cotton undies Christiana suddenly wished she'd never packed. At the very least, she wished she'd had the foresight to don a prettier pair before her husband arrived, but she'd had little use for pretty panties, so far away from the only man she'd let close enough to see them.

His fingers edged along the elastic and Milo's beautifully average face creased into a wicked smile. "You're wearing your granny panties."

"Don't make fun of me. They're comfortable. A pregnant woman wants to be comfortable."

His eyes flashed. "I like your underwear. When you wear them, I know they're for me, and not another man."

"Is that what you think of me? That I'm out looking for another man?" Reflex had Christiana jumping off his lap even as she fought the spark of outrage heating her blood. After all, it had been her own words that had cast suspicion. "It was just a bad joke—"

"No, Christiana." Milo closed his eyes. Then he raised his lashes and leveled her with a look hot enough to melt the un-sexy underwear right off her body. "I'm expressing my appreciation. Other women as beautiful as you would wear silk and lace, and make certain the men around her knew it."

Milo slid to the edge of the sofa in a move too fast for Christiana to process. He caught her before she could hop back and tossed her skirt up to her waist, anchoring the material in spite of her batting hands. Staring at what he'd revealed, his lips quirked. "But you wear cotton briefs with tiny unicorns on them."

"I know what it's like to be cheated on." She didn't know why her voice sounded so strangled. It wasn't as if the fact were a secret—half of witching society knew her first husband had had a string of mistresses, just as half of witching society knew Milo's first fiancée had run off with his cousin the day before their betrothal contract was to be sealed in blood and made permanent. "I wouldn't do that to you."

He nodded slowly and slid his fingers into the waistband of her unicorn panties. "War wounds, *krasavitsa*. I meant nothing by my remarks." Milo leaned forward and pressed a kiss to the lower curve of her belly before inching the cotton briefs down to breathe against the small patch of curls at the top of her mound. "Forgive me."

The heat of his mouth helped the heat of her lust make a resurgence. A slow tide of need crawled through her, beginning at the point of contact with her husband's lips and ending somewhere in the vicinity of her clenching heart. Christiana relaxed again, making no protest as her husband pulled her underpants down farther. She managed to use enough wit to cast a hastily constructed locking spell at the door.

In bed, Milo had earned her trust. Beginning with their first, awkward night together, he set a pattern of waiting for her to come to him—which admittedly frustrated Christiana, but also gave her a much needed sense of power over her own body. Milo was gentle to the point of exasperation, but Christiana would take that over the depravity and pain of her first husband any day. The two men were as dissimilar as lovers could get, the first man wild and silent, the current man tender and talkative.

Dirty talk was Milo's biggest kink, and Christiana had gained an appreciation for it over their six months together. So she was neither surprised, nor put off when he whispered, "I need to taste you, *krasavitsa*. I need to put my tongue to this little peak here and worship it."

He followed his statement with action, licking her clit in a hot, wet caress that warmed the nerves buried within it. Christiana took a breath and stared down at her husband's pale hair, sliding against her lower belly and adding to the soft sensations worming through her awareness. She felt, more than heard, his appreciative hum a moment before the flat of his tongue swiped out to coat her in fresh heat.

"The taste of you is divine, Christiana. Imprinted on my senses and capable of making me drunker than the finest vodka."

Her underpants slid lower, and so did Milo. Another lick had her gasping as his tongue reached farther, pushing between her folds with subtle, soft pressure.

"And the feel of your skin. Like silk, *krasavitsa*. I love to feel it slipping over my cock when I tease you."

Memories had her groaning. Milo smoothed his dick between her folds often, teasing her with his hard presence for long moments before finally capitulating to her impatience and sliding into her.

"I love the taste of your pleasure as your body floods for me." Milo pushed her panties to her ankles. "The only problem is, when I have my mouth on you, I can no longer tell you how much I enjoy it."

And with that last statement, he buried his face between her legs. Christiana grabbed his hair for balance as she instinctively widened her stance, but her unicorn panties hobbled her. She couldn't make enough room for him, so Milo made it for himself, his fingers pulling her folds until she felt spread wide, yet little more than her clit was on display for him.

He pressed closer, opening his lips to take the peak in and suckle — excruciatingly soft. Christiana gave a broken moan as the light pressure set fire to her nerves and she jerked, desperate for more. Milo chuckled and thrust his tongue deep between her swelling folds, until the very tip slipped against her entrance.

Christiana went to her tiptoes in an effort to keep her husband where he was. She wanted the velvet rasp of his tongue to ease the ache it had provoked. But he withdrew and sucked one lip, then the other into his hot mouth. Sensation washed through her sex, her clit perked up and pulsed in need. Her flesh tingled under the unyielding press of his imprisoning fingers as Milo's tongue surged forward again.

His nose was a hard pressure as he pushed deeper and lapped at her entrance. The ring of delicate muscle guarding her depths tingled and clenched. Her hips jerked and Chris gripped Milo's hair tighter, but he did not go any faster or harder. She tried to help him, to help herself, by writhing and riding his tongue as he pushed into her pussy.

"Milo, please, it's been too long." And never before him had Chris thought to say those words. After the first few months of her previous marriage, it took all the courage she had to climb into her husband's bed. She would have happily let any number of women take her place.

But Milo was different. Milo heated her straight through with a gentle dedication that left her wrecked and sinking in a sea of pleasure. She wanted his thick cock buried inside her and her pussy convulsing around him as he came, and so she demanded it in rough gasps.

"I know." But his acknowledgment of her need didn't prevent him from licking again, before pulling back to capture her clit. Hot lips, clever tongue and even the subtle pressure of teeth delicately wielded were brought to bear against the vulnerable peak.

Christiana couldn't help but tip her head back. Milo's gentleness had her reaching for more, utterly focused and lost in her own greed. She arched and cried, begging him to suck harder. His fingers, still holding her flesh spread wide, were another sensation that subtly manipulated her need. Milo had a way of making every nerve ending between her legs feel included, with not a single inch left neglected, yet not a single millimeter appeased.

The softness of Milo's mouth contrasted directly with the force of Christiana's climax. Before him, she'd never known that delicacy could gain such sharp results, but it was as if her own body made up for his moderation with a sensitivity beyond her comprehension. Everything within her pushed closer to the surface in a fierce surge, fighting to feel more, get more, demand more. Milo's gentleness made her eagerly attentive, so as not to miss a single thing.

Heat winged out, spiraled up her pussy and pulsed hard in her lower belly. She needed more. Inside, Christiana melted and knew she was dripping when Milo's tongue thrust back through her folds and he moaned.

"All that luscious cream, *krasavitsa*. Delicious. I could spend hours eating your pussy."

"I need you inside me," she wailed, denying his intentions.

Slowly, he released her and sat back on the loveseat. In a wild rush, Christiana stepped out of both her panties and her low heels and slid onto his lap. Yanking until his belt released, she raised her lips to his even as her fingers wrestled with the waistband of his trousers, the raw silk of the material rasping her thighs deliciously, but making the closure hard to hold on to.

While she worked, Milo tormented her further, denying her the kiss she so desperately wanted. "I love when you're impatient, Christiana. When everything you do and say lets me know how much you want my cock thrusting into your pussy. You want it so hard, but I will only give you soft. Soft rocking, pushing deeper, inch by inch, until you're about to go mad with the need for more."

"Don't tease me, Milo. I need you."

His hips jerked, driving his hard length against her knuckles and making Christiana ready to tear the damned material that kept him from her away with her nails and teeth. She growled in frustration as her pussy flexed deep within, mirroring her irritation, yet appreciating the anticipation.

Milo's hands slipped up her thighs, long fingers questing into the slick heat his mouth had called forth. Christiana stilled for a single heartbeat as her flesh flinched with raw need, then she attacked his waistband with renewed vigor, uncaring of whether or not she ripped the silk.

Milo was the sole proprietor of a multi-million dollar technology industry that had single-handedly saved the entire Ivanov Family from bankruptcy on at least one occasion. He could afford more business suits. Christiana pulled the button right off.

His hand shifted between her legs and Christiana's back arched as if Milo had stroked some hidden string that controlled the length of her nervous system. A ragged moan left her mouth as she pushed closer to his touch. Smooth fingertips pushed through her folds, slicking through her cream and rubbing it everywhere he could until she was completely slippery. The tip of his middle finger passed over her entrance with the lightest of pressures, causing Christiana's body to clench hard.

"You are so impatient, *krasavitsa*. I like knowing your pussy weeps for me to fill it. I like the feel of your silky honey sliding over my knuckles and I love that in just a little while, my cock will feel the same." His voice deepened dangerously. "As I fill your body, as I pleasure you until that very cream turns into a river that washes my—"

She stole the words from his mouth with a hungry kiss. Finally victorious against his pants, she surged forward to capture his lips in a harder caress than he'd ever given her. Her tongue thrust deep, gliding and licking, drawing the taste of her own climax from his mouth. She consumed him—lips fused, breath lost, tongues dancing.

And Milo kissed her back. It was the one intimacy they'd never fumbled. Only the emotions evoked were awkward, but not while lust raged and drowned out everything else.

Milo was a great kisser, leading her down heated paths with a confident tongue and soft lips. Every kiss was an indulgence, where he took her in and patiently taught her new things, where he gave of himself without reserve.

She felt a tug on her blouse buttons. One-handed, Milo worked them free with more finesse than she'd shown at his waistband. Barely touching her, he separated the halves and she arched into him, tempting him to put his hands on her. He did, but too gently, with a single fingertip tracing spiraling designs across the tops of the mounds.

"Are you still sensitive here, *krasavitsa*?"

"It's getting better." She could hardly answer, her need for his touch on her breasts was so great. "The doctor said it usually ends after the first trimester."

"Ah, then I will be gentle."

Milo was true to his word, carefully working the cups of her plain bra down to anchor them beneath her breasts. He dipped his head and seared her with his tongue—just his tongue. Hot and wet, it rasped over first one nipple, then the other, sparking life into nerves already vividly animated. Those nerves writhed as Christiana did, greedily pressing closer and yanking on some pathway through the center of her body that had her bucking on her husband's lap.

Hoping to inspire him, Chris ignored Milo's suit jacket and focused on his shirt, plucking the buttons in the same way she'd done to his trousers. She ripped them off and drove her hands against his chest, loving the fact that he wasn't bulky with muscle, but lean and fit. He could have been a dancer with his body type, but had been graced with enough intelligence to create his own business and lead it forward, gaining influence and acclaim throughout the world, beyond witching society.

When another gliding touch over her nipple brought a soft scream from her throat, Milo laughed softly. "Yes, still sensitive. I love your breasts, *krasavitsa*. So perfect, fitting my palms beautifully, but I won't hurt you."

His actions became interspersed with words. "So I will

lick this one." And he did. "Then I will lick that one. I will taste all this pretty pink flesh around and around each peak and blow" — he did — "until it is a hard little pebble my mouth waters to take in and suck."

He did not do the last. Instead, he looked up at her and grinned. "When you are past this awful too-sensitive time and I know I won't hurt you."

Frustration soared to new levels. She couldn't bear any more teasing, and refused to let Milo revert to a slow seduction when she was already dripping with urgency. She took all control, merging their mouths, sliding forward on his lap and gripping his dick.

Christiana moaned as she lodged Milo's tip against her heat. She arched, bore down, and he spread her open, stretching her entrance around the thick head as his ultra-fine skin impressed her attentive nerves. She bucked violently — once, twice, three times — and took him in completely, ignoring the hint of disquiet that trembled through her pussy at such a sudden, thick intrusion.

Milo reared back from their kiss and wrapped his arms around her hips, locking her to him and holding her immobile. His voice was strained and low. "Careful, Christiana. Go easy."

"No." She tossed her head and wriggled her hips. "I need you now."

"I don't want to hurt you or the baby. We will go slow."

Again she bucked. Her nails clawed at Milo's nape and her chest pressed to his, finally easing the frustration in her breasts. She gasped at the wondrous sensation of sliding her aching nipples against his body and alleviating at least a fraction of their agony. "Not slow, *now*."

His lids lowered over emerald eyes so hot they nearly glowed with his need. Milo's lips turned up at the corners and his chest swelled with breath. But his hands were granite at her hips, imprisoning her until her only movements were the clamping of her inner muscles around his cock.

Anticipation and eagerness, her need and urgency, the

heat of his rigid dick buried in her softest, wettest flesh combined with all the emotions she'd been struggling to contain over the past two weeks. Joy at being pregnant, fear at being pregnant in patriarchal strongholds, terror at losing her grandmother and the searing sense of relief Milo's presence in England seemed to encourage washed over her and pulled her inner walls tight. Convulsions shook her.

Christiana came with a sharp moan she muffled against Milo's throat, nails scratching his nape and hips jerking against his hold. Her nipples stabbed his chest and seemed to expand, pulse and erupt in their own miniature climaxes. Heat roared through her and she barely heard Milo's harsh gasp.

But she definitely heard his words. "Gods be damned, *krasavitsa*, I love the way you tighten on me like that."

His hands turned demanding, jerking her over his length. He pumped his hips twice, his cock thick and hard and dragging through her shuddering pussy. He pushed deep, surrendering to his own release with a growl Christiana felt rumble through his chest. A hint of his magic coasted over her skin and soothed her nerves. Panting, she slumped against her husband's heaving chest and let him hold her.

Chapter Five

Silviu

Mother Davenold's cryptic words rattled through Silviu's brain. Alone in his room, he could only come to a single conclusion — Madeleine's demands must be a manipulation Silviu hadn't planned for.

"Son of a bitch," he murmured. "Madeleine *never* intended to blood Georgie as her heir."

Silviu flicked his fingers and a silencing spell shot from their tips to spread around him in a translucent bubble that would prevent eavesdropping. He immediately dug out his phone and called his father. Vasile Lovasz was the only witch Silviu knew who was as manipulative as Madeleine. He may have already figured out Madeleine's secret goals, when Silviu had failed to even notice the wily old woman had any.

Vasile answered on the first ring, his monotone voice revealing none of the anticipation his question held. "Is Madeleine dead yet?"

"No." Silviu rubbed his forehead. "I called to ask you about the terms of my betrothal agreement."

"It was written twenty years ago, sealed in blood for the past decade. *Now* you need to know what it says?"

"I offered to change my name to Davenold if Madeleine blooded me as her heir."

A moment of silence had Silviu clutching the phone to his ear. Finally Vasile spoke in a glacial tone. "You'll be ineligible to take the High Seat. That would ruin my plans, Silviu."

When Madeleine left her position at the top of the witching hierarchy—for whatever reason—the Davenolds would not be allowed to regain the seat for a hundred years. It was the first law enacted after the opposing covens created their political system and had been strictly enforced through countless generations. But Silviu's mind had seized on a slim opportunity to achieve exactly what he wanted, and he had faith his influential talents would gain the advantage over any objections offered by the Council representatives.

"Georgeanne and I could hyphenate, become the Lovasz-Davenolds, which would still make me suitable to lead the Council."

"Madeleine would demand your power leave the Lovasz bloodline and merge into hers."

"Probably."

"I will not allow it." Vasile's voice snarled from the phone in a banked tide of fury. "What good would it do our Family to have the strongest Matched pair to ever exist combine their magic into another's bloodline?"

Hiding his newfound doubts concerning the details of Davenold inheritance, Silviu prodded his father carefully. "If Georgeanne becomes the Mother as we expected—"

"By the by," Vasile interrupted, "I'm pleased with the new paths your mind is traveling these days. I'm happy to see that you are overcoming the despicable weakness you tend to have for your betrothed."

Struggling to switch gears, Silviu shook his head. "What are you talking about?"

"I looked into the little matter you brought to my attention a few days ago." Vasile fell silent, but after a moment where Silviu failed to respond, he continued. "That archaic tradition of blood exchange?"

Silviu remembered the task he'd put before his father in a rush that left him dizzy. He hadn't dared ask the few Davenolds who knew the answer, so instead was forced to rely on his father's investigations. "Ah, marriage in the old way. What did you learn?"

During the Ngozi-Levy fiasco, Adam had been desperate to find a solution to gain Tulah's freedom. Madeleine's sister, Margaret, had suggested he bypass the resistance of the Ngozi Father by marrying Tulah in an ancient ritual of blood exchange—the very release of magic Madeleine had used to wed her Magic Match against her Family's wishes. Adam had done so, and his bond with his new wife could never be reversed.

Any betrothal sealed in blood paid homage to the long-ago traditions of witching society. Marriage was for life among their people, but Silviu wanted a deeper connection to Georgeanne, and the idea of a blood exchange appealed to him on a primal level.

She would be his, a part of the foundation of his magic, restructured into his DNA.

"I'm still considering all the ramifications," Vasile drawled, "but the prospect is favorable. I believe it may be to our advantage."

"How do I do it? Have you found a spell?"

"There is no set spell, according to every source I was able to find, which were few and far between. The concept has largely been dismissed in modern generations, or lost completely."

"If there is no spell, how can it work?" It was not a question Silviu could ask of Adam or Madeleine, both of whom had successfully performed the ritual, for fear of rousing their suspicions and harming his own cause.

"You must experience a deep connection to the person you are exchanging blood with. Every witch I've spoken to has also alluded to a sexual event, which isn't surprising, as sex and blood have been potent forces since the dawn of time. The magic does the rest, though there are drawbacks."

Silviu paced a tight circle at the foot of his bed. "Like what?"

"Connection at a soul-deep level, an interchange of magic that goes far beyond what's normal, even for a Matched pair. And Matches are especially vulnerable."

Silviu's pacing came to an immediate halt. As his Match, Georgeanne would naturally be able to draw on Silviu's strength, and their combined magic had already proven itself to be a compelling force. But Vasile hadn't been at the Ngozi wedding, hadn't witnessed the blinding connection Silviu and Georgie had forged when she'd been caught in a dark magic attack that had nearly stopped her heart forever.

Silviu's magic had pumped into her with all the power his fear and despair could call, filling her as if Georgie were an empty vessel. Everything he had, every ounce, had burst through the control he'd learned when he was a child. A control every witch found it necessary to learn. Georgeanne's own magic had struggled from under the dark spell, rising to meet Silviu's before turning into a life-giving force more frightening than even he had expected.

"On the other hand," Vasile continued, "such a connection would make my perfect plan even better."

Silviu dragged in a deep breath. "Which plan, Father? You have so many."

"My plan to pull all the Davenold magic into the Lovasz bloodline. With so much power at your control, you would rule the world, my boy."

Silviu went numb. He'd been raised with the expectation of ruling the witching world. He'd even heard his father's theories of how any children produced from his relationship with Georgie would wield enough talent to impose their authority over those outside their magical community. But Vasile had never before suggested that *Silviu* would achieve such significance.

It made him nervous. "What makes you think Georgeanne would passively allow such a thing to happen? She won't just hand over the Davenold power."

"What choice would she have? She's Bane! She's nothing more than a void to be filled with magic, which *you* will then have sole access to. She'll be filled with the Davenold power with no way to use it herself."

Silviu bit his tongue against a denial. Vasile had no way of knowing that Georgeanne could reach Silviu's magic better than she could her own—and he wasn't about to enlighten his scheming father of the possibility that she could do the same with the Davenold power. Vasile would figure it out soon enough, and Silviu prepared himself to fight for his wife.

Ice dripped down his spine. He'd been played from both ends, caught between Madeleine and Vasile, blind to nearly everything but having Georgie as his wife and rising to a position of power on the Council. His bride would never forgive such a betrayal, and neither would her Family.

He would lose her forever, no matter what kind of connection they may forge.

Silviu tried to keep his anger from infecting his voice. "Georgeanne might not be able to claim the power of her bloodlines."

"But you can," Vasile replied silkily. "I know you better than you think I do, my son. I know your strengths, your weaknesses and your compulsions. I bet you already tried to influence Madeleine to your way of thinking, haven't you?"

Silviu fought to speak past the burn in his throat. "She won't make me her heir."

"She doesn't need to. The old conspirator knows what you want, and Madeleine will rush to blood her heir before she dies. Georgeanne will take the Davenold power and hand it over to you before anyone is the wiser."

"And if she doesn't?"

"You ripped the Lovasz power from your grandfather in Poland. It will be no different with the Davenolds should Madeleine choose another, which is highly unlikely given all I've done to ensure your Magic Match inherited."

Silviu's thoughts raced. He'd been wrong about so many things. His father and Madeleine were steps ahead of him, and he felt like he was struggling to catch up to their machinations. His only advantage lay in the fact that a Bane witch and a Reap witch had never been Matched before, and he and Georgie were privately learning where their advantages lay.

If he was the Davenold leader, Georgie would have no problem reaching all that magic and if she was the Mother, it would be the same for Silviu. A constant flow between them, feeding into the Davenold bloodline.

But by holding onto the Lovasz surname, the magic would flow to the new Lovasz Family Father.

"Where does Costel fit into all this, Father? He holds the Lovasz power, and your plans would have me handing him the Davenold magic, as well."

A moment passed before Vasile responded. "I understand why you allowed your brother to claim Fatherhood, but familial loyalty will be tested when you take the Council. Don't expect your brother to be overjoyed when you eclipse him, especially after you threatened to kill him two weeks ago."

"I apologized for that." Silviu squeezed his eyes shut. "He's the Father—"

"As I said, anything you want is yours for the taking."

"Costel doesn't want power. It's exactly why he will make a good Father for our Family. There is no reason—"

"The Lovasz future rests on you, and you alone, Silviu. You will be the one to restore our Family to greatness."

"He's your son." Silviu's voice was a strangled scream as he tried to reason with Vasile. "He's your eldest child, the man everyone expected to lead—"

"He's been trained in your grandfather's image," Vasile snapped. "Alexandru has corrupted him and the only decent thing your brother will end up doing for our Family is handing the authority over to you."

"Only the Council seat." Reeling from his father's outpouring of bitterness, Silviu struggled to think and plan. "Now that he's the Lovasz Father, Costel doesn't have time to deal with relations between the covens. He never liked it, anyway."

"That was well done of you, Silviu." Satisfaction rang

in Vasile's voice. "I'll send Costel to the Council Palace to start the paperwork for your transition to the Family seat immediately. Then your name will already be present in the rolls when Madeleine dies. I would have sent him days ago, but your grandfather has been difficult."

"Can't you just wait until the meeting next month?"

"If the old bat dies before then, the coven representatives will have to gather to elect a new High Seat. We need you already in place when that happens."

Silviu leaned against a dresser as the weight of Vasile's expectations settled onto him. "I'll wait for word from Costel, then."

"In the meantime, seduce your betrothed and find a way to exchange your blood. Once you've formed that bond we can use it to limit her authority. You must use every weapon at your disposal to force her to walk your path." Vasile made a rough sound. "Remember what you're working toward, my boy."

Silviu gritted his teeth, but only said, "I'll do what I can, Father."

Chapter Six

Georgeanne

The view of the setting sun wasn't dramatic, but that suited Georgie's mood just fine. She was tired of drama, having had entirely too much of it lately. She might be used to dealing with multiple emergencies at one time, putting out numerous political fires all over the globe, but nothing that affected her, or her entire Family, so deeply as what she'd gone through the past few weeks.

So she ignored the curious stares of her distant cousins as she sat on the portico steps and watched the muted colors of the dying sun spread across the sky. Between her and the horizon were rolling green pastures, but behind the estate was the choppy North Sea. It was days like the ones she'd known lately that made Georgie wish the sun set in the east, because she far preferred the wild seascape to the bucolic beauty before her. It was hard to find peace with the scent of sheep and the sounds of a highway so near.

Georgie wasn't surprised when Christiana dropped to the step beside her — the pastureland view was much better suited to her cousin than her. Neither was she surprised by the faint frown marring Chris' beautiful forehead.

"The tension inside is too much for me, with everyone worried about Grandmother."

"Your husband will defuse the situation." Georgie sent her cousin a sideling glance. "How is Milo?"

Christiana shrugged. "Seemed to be doing well."

"Really?" Georgie inquired blandly. "There was an awful lot of screaming coming from that parlor for anyone to be

53

doing only *well*."

"Don't be ridiculous. Neither of us are screamers."

"Sounded like you missed him." Which surprised Georgie. No one who spent longer than five minutes in Chris and Milo's company could overlook the distance between them, though Georgie knew that was more her cousin's fault than Milo's.

"Of course, I missed him. He's my husband."

Georgie raised a brow at Chris' clipped tone but let it go. "It's good he came. We can use him to help settle the Family's feathers. This house is packed to the rafters, and you know the Davenolds gets along better when we're not all under the same roof."

"Milo might not be able to help with that." Chris snorted. "His magic works best when there is little to no resistance. The aunts don't like him."

"Your mother and mine do, so that's half of them."

"And the cousins are jealous."

"They don't count. They're just mad because he wields more influence than they do."

Christiana was prepared to be stubborn, however. "Adam doesn't like him."

"And you're not fond of Tulah." Georgie rolled her eyes. "You're both married now. Somehow, the two of you have to accept the other's spouse."

"The woman is a nonentity, a witch from the lowest rungs of a disreputable Family. I can't believe my brother would be so stupid as to let that kitsune cat get her claws into him." She whirled on Georgeanne. "I can't believe you allowed such a thing."

"I wasn't invited to the wedding, thank all that's sacred." Georgie grimaced. "I tried to stop them. I begged them not to do it and even ordered Adam not to dare without Madeleine's permission. He didn't listen and what's done is done."

"And he'll have to live with the consequences."

"We all will." Georgie sat up a bit straighter when

something vicious flashed through Christiana's eyes.

"If she hurts him, I'll kill her."

"I think our Family already has more than enough rumors concerning dead spouses, don't you?" Georgie forced ice into her tone and willed her cousin to agree. Chris' first marriage ended abruptly when her very healthy husband suddenly took ill and died, and even Madeleine's enormous influence couldn't stop rumors that Chris had a hand in it.

Christiana merely lifted a shoulder. "The man's heart was weaker than I knew. Milo is stronger. Grandmother gave us both strong men, didn't she?"

"And shouldn't that prove your grandmother has no confidence in your ability to lead this Family?"

Georgie and Chris both stiffened as the new voice rolled down the steps. The snide tone grated on Georgie's nerves and had Christiana growling. Clenching her fists in her lap, Georgie turned toward Suzette and wished she could find a way to get to her feet casually, but she couldn't without revealing how uncomfortable she was with the other woman looming over her.

Georgie had no choice but to brazen it out. She bared her teeth in what she hoped would be considered a smile by the other Davenolds in the yard. "Grandmother doesn't doubt our ability to lead. She simply made certain that we would both have good men backing us up. As she had with Grandfather."

Suzette ran her cold gaze over both her cousins. "A strong man overshadows a woman. Just look at your parents, Georgeanne."

Georgie's nails dug into her palms. "My mother isn't a leader and was never meant to be. Both Christiana and I have been thoroughly trained for the Motherhood position, however. You wouldn't know, sweetie, because you married a spineless slug, but a strong man is able to step back and let his woman command, all while using his strength to help her further her goals."

"My *spineless slug* wouldn't dream of challenging me in

the first place," Suzette said. "Can either of you two say the same thing?"

Christiana hummed low in her throat. "A challenge makes the marriage fun, darling. But then, you wouldn't know about that since you're neither fun, nor hardly married, no matter what papers you've signed. Has your marriage even been consummated?"

Outrage sparkled in the other woman's eyes. "My husband does what I tell him to do and he's my Magic Match. Meanwhile, everyone knows how much authority you hand over to your husband, Christiana. Tell me, is he still occupying your bed or has he found a better option yet? Like the first one did?"

Georgie could feel the waves of pain exploding off her cousin. She shifted, drawing Suzette's attention so Chris could have a minute to collect herself. "The first one was worthless. He's lucky Christiana agreed to marry him."

Suzette smirked. "Is that your story? I heard she hounded him like a lovesick puppy. Practically begged him to marry her, and he only did so to gain power in our Family."

"Ridiculous." Georgie spoke to cover Christiana's gasp. "We would never have given him power. He was relegated to the same position as your husband. Well below the lowest ranking female of the Family, and even beneath the other men."

Suzette transferred her gaze to Christiana, a malicious gleam entering her dark eyes. "Why don't you tell me the truth? You married the first one for his skill in bed, didn't you?" The woman winked. "I had him too, remember, so I know how very good he was. How very big his dick was."

Christiana's face lost all color. Anger buzzed in Georgie's skull, protective instincts rising fast as Chris rubbed her belly. It was a habit her cousin had taken on recently, an unconscious action performed whenever she felt in need of comfort, and it tore at Georgie's heart.

But Chris rallied quickly. "All this poison you spew. All because you will never be the Davenold Mother. That hits you hard doesn't it, Suzette? I bet that really burns. Here you are, heir to the secondary branch, and your people don't even want to follow you in that *insignificant* role."

"You don't know what you're talking about," the woman spat.

"No?" Chris lifted a brow. "Isn't it interesting that the entire Family would rather follow a Bane witch than let you lead? Really says something about your relations in this coven. It's not surprising — after all, you sleep with your cousins' cast-offs and are unable to have a child with your weak husband. What other deficiencies do you have that we don't know about?"

Suzette turned her red face back to Georgie, who didn't bother to hide her smirk. "You need to be Mother, don't you, Georgeanne? If you don't hold the position, whoever does is likely to exterminate the threat you pose to this Family before you can conceive the next generation of handicapped witches."

Georgie let her lips lift in a mocking smile. "It's best you accept your role in this Family, and not aspire to heights you will never reach."

"We will see, won't we?" The other woman swept past them dramatically.

Georgie watched her stride down to the drive as a car turned onto the paved path leading to the portico. Shielding her eyes from the sun with her hand, Georgeanne wondered who was coming and where they would sleep. The house was already packed.

Chris cupped her belly and leaned close. "Georgie, I think Suzette just threatened you. You'd better watch your back."

"I always do." Georgie didn't look away from the car as it came closer, slowing to a stop next to Suzette. "Who is that?"

The door opened and Suzette elevated her chin as if she were entertaining royalty. Or as if she were the royalty to be entertained. Shock resounded through Georgie as Daniel Levy emerged from the vehicle.

"What the hell is he doing here?"

The Levy Family Father was a weak witch but a powerful politician. Silviu had been doing everything he could to court the man's favor in his bid to rise through the Council ranks while Georgie added her years' worth of experience in working with Daniel to her betrothed's smooth sales pitch. They hoped the man would choose Silviu's brother-in-law, Eliasz, to fill his Family's newly vacated Council seat.

That was the only reason Georgie had accepted the invitation to the disastrous Ngozi wedding. Daniel's sister, Constance, had been the bride. Theirs was a relationship the Levy Father carefully hid from most, as un-Matched witches were limited to one child by the laws of nature, and dark magic was the only way to conceive more. Matches could give birth to dynasties, but Daniel's father had had to cast a complicated and dangerous spell in order to have his daughter.

Georgie held her breath, but Constance did not exit the vehicle. "Thank God."

Christiana snorted in understanding. "That's the last thing we need, for Constance to start lording it over Tulah and irritating Adam. We have enough to deal with."

"Yes, like the arrival of the Levy Father." Silviu's deep voice issued from directly behind Georgie's shoulder, startling her. "Who the hell invited him?"

Knowing she couldn't simply sit on the step like a lump while Suzette welcomed Daniel, Georgie stood and reached for Christiana's hand, hauling her up too. With her cousin to one side, Georgie wound her arm around her betrothed's and strove for a serene expression. She was determined to show no weakness.

"Don't let him know how ill Grandmother is," she whispered.

Silviu winced. "We may not be able to hide it."

"Suzette had to have known he was coming." Christiana knocked her elbow against Georgie's arm. "Her timing in joining us out here is otherwise uncanny, and there is nothing about that bitch I would describe in such a way."

Georgie agreed. "I wonder if Margaret knew, and if she did, why didn't she inform us of his arrival?"

Christiana raised a hand to block the last rays of sunlight from her eyes. "Probably because she knew you'd deny him entrance."

"We can't do that," Silviu murmured. "We need to stay on his good side, so while his presence here is the last thing I would prefer, he is a powerful Father and we must force ourselves to be hospitable."

Georgie grumbled under her breath but knew her betrothed spoke the truth. They couldn't afford to alienate such a potentially influential ally. She pasted a bright smile on her face and watched as Daniel greeted Suzette with an old-fashioned bow over her knuckles that sent sunlight glinting over his hair like spun gold. With the sunset behind him, it was difficult to make out his facial features, but Georgie assumed the man's cheerful countenance had to be compromised by the recent events at his sister's wedding.

But the expected stress was hardly visible on his face as Daniel turned Suzette toward the portico and climbed the long, shallow steps toward the waiting trio. His lips curled in a hesitant smile, and there were faint lines around his eyes and mouth, but the look he bent on Georgie wasn't as troubled as she'd imagined it would be. The man's blue eyes sparkled with humor in spite of everything that had happened.

He reached for Georgie's hand before greeting the others. "I do apologize for my intrusion, but I was still in England trying to clean up the mess Graves left behind, so I thought I'd stop in and see how your grandmother was faring."

Georgie held on to her smile as the man's driver began to haul numerous suitcases out of the car's trunk. "How kind, to be so concerned. Though I do wish I'd known you were coming so we could have procured a room suitable to your status."

"I've taken care of that," Suzette said. "After all, this is *my* home and I am perfectly capable of organizing matters."

"Nice to know you're capable of something." Christiana's insult came a scant moment before she addressed Daniel, with barely a pause. "Constance didn't travel with you?"

He smiled. "She and her mother are in Rome with my credit card. Retail therapy for their trauma."

"Well," Georgie stepped back and waved toward the house, "I do hope she's all right. Please, Daniel, come in and we'll see you settled. Are you hungry? Can we get you tea or coffee?"

"If it's possible, I'd like to see Madeleine."

"I'd have to check and see if her schedule allows visitors today."

Daniel nodded as he followed Georgie and Silviu inside. "Yes, of course. Has she recovered from her illness, then?"

"You know she's too stubborn to let a minor ailment keep her down." Georgie's confidence rang through the entry hall, bringing the entire little group to a halt. Silviu's hand came up to cover hers where it rested on his arm and he gave a brief squeeze, but otherwise held his peace.

She was grateful for his silence.

Then Suzette snorted. "She's hardly well."

"How would you know? You don't visit her." Christiana turned to Daniel and chirped, "With all the talent currently accumulated in this house, I have no doubt she'll be back to her usual whirlwind self in no time."

Daniel brows soared into his hairline. "Really? That's terrific. I'm so glad to hear it."

"Well, my grandmother is a remarkable woman, strong and well-loved, with a Family devoted to her recovery."

"But so old," Suzette interjected with patently false concern. "We do worry all our efforts to restore her health will fail dramatically, of course. Now then, Georgeanne, why don't you run along and see if Madeleine is well enough to receive visitors while I take care of Daniel."

Georgie fought to keep her expression from showing

the full extent of her anger and offense at being given a command by her arrogant cousin. She opened her mouth to reply but Silviu beat her to the punch.

"An excellent idea, if Daniel will excuse us?" The Levy Father nodded and Silviu continued. "Suzette can see to your comforts while Georgie and I inform Madeleine of your arrival."

Suzette gripped Daniel's arm and towed him toward a parlor. The moment the pair were out of sight, Georgie rounded on her betrothed. "What are you up to?"

"This is not about what I am up to, my love." He steered her up the staircase and glanced back to make certain Christiana followed. "Suzette knew he was coming. We should be wondering what *she* is up to."

"Then we should be down there with them, monitoring their interaction and putting a stop to whatever lies Suzette is filling Daniel's head with," Christiana spat. "Not all of us need to inform Madeleine—"

Silviu cut Christiana off with a rude noise. With a hostile glance over his shoulder as they reached the upstairs hallway, he informed her, "It doesn't matter what she says. Georgie and Daniel have an excellent working relationship. Suzette can play the welcoming hostess all day long, but our main concern should be showing the Levy Father Madeleine's strength."

"Yes," Georgie agreed, "her strength, *our* strength and no hint of weakness."

Silviu nodded. "We have already planted the seeds for his support in Council politics. Now we must show him that you, my love, have everything in hand while your grandmother is recovering. And we will also show him that it would be hasty for him to consider bold political moves, such as vying for the High Seat on the Council."

Georgie came to an abrupt stop, just outside Madeleine's bedroom door. "You think he's making a play for my grandmother's position?"

Silviu shrugged. "We must consider the possibility."

"Daniel has never given any hint that he wants the High Seat."

"But weakness can be exploited." Silviu rubbed his eyes. "Too much has happened recently and I am suspicious."

Chapter Seven

Milo

"I already have Silviu pushing me to blood an heir, Milo." The determination in the Davenold Mother's dark eyes was unwavering. "I simply don't have the patience for you to do the same."

He released a slow breath but not the tension in his muscles. Though her voice was thin and her body appeared more fragile than ever before, Madeleine's sharp eyes were still piercing. Milo was a little more than intimidated — not actually by the powerful old woman, but rather the real possibility that he may push too far and harm his own cause.

Milo knew he was one of the few witches who weren't living in fear of Madeleine Davenold. His own Family was much more vicious — the women more cutthroat and tyrannical, the men more prone to unjustified violence — and he'd survived very well, so the Davenolds, with their devotion to Family and a Mother who was eminently rational, was a cakewalk in comparison.

Besides, any fear Milo had of the elderly witch had dissipated nearly a year ago, when he'd presented her with a bold scheme of uniting his money with her political aspirations. And all he'd wanted in return was her eldest granddaughter's hand in marriage. He'd gotten what he wanted then, but was having a bit more difficulty getting what he wanted presently.

"It's not surprising that Silviu would petition for his betrothed," Milo conceded. "And while I am sorry you had to listen to a similar proposal from me, I do believe I have the right to make a case for my wife. Christiana is not Bane."

"Neither has she had much experience working with other covens in tense situations. Christiana has preferred to spend her time organizing the Davenolds and their charitable functions."

Milo blinked at the exasperation in Madeleine's voice. It wasn't like her to reveal her true feelings on topics concerning her heirs, and he figured her ailment must be forming cracks in her usual armor. "A good hostess is often the same thing as a wily diplomat. And, many of those functions were undertaken for the sole purpose of furthering your politics."

Madeleine's brows lowered. "I have no doubt that she would do well in the role of Mother, but let us not get ahead of ourselves."

"Madeleine, you are infected with a dark magic spell that neither Christiana nor Adam can unravel." Milo fought to unclench his teeth. "They are the best with spells I've ever known, so if they can't save you, it would be advantageous to put your affairs in order now."

Madeleine laughed, and Milo had no doubt her reaction would have been very different if some other witch had just said such a thing to her. But Milo wasn't just any other witch, and he had earned a rare respect from her. Most matriarchal men would never be allowed to be so candid with the Davenold Mother—or if they were, they would expect dire consequences.

Milo was a middle-of-the-hierarchy male from the magically mediocre Ivanov Family. His talent was a passive one, not especially useful outside his former Family or the life he'd built for himself. His gift for calm had been honed to razor-sharp efficacy among his own volatile coven, though his success rate dropped when his own emotions were compromised. While most witches had spent their formative years learning control to hold back their magic, Milo had spent his youth learning how to let it flow until it could slice through the taxing hostility his Family often belabored.

And he'd used that ability, the strength he'd fought so hard for, to build confidence in investors — both magical and non — until he'd gained enough capital to start his own business. Then he'd scratched and clawed his way into a position of influence, through the efforts of his own blood, sweat and tears, in spite of the Ivanov coven doing their best to drag him back down into the inglorious quagmire they'd become so accustomed to living in.

Madeleine had appreciated that.

"Milo, have I ever told you that you're my favorite grandson-in-law?"

"I'm currently your only grandson-in-law."

"Perhaps." Madeleine's mirth faded frighteningly quickly, leaving her with a sour expression on her mouth. With a shake of her head, she displaced her pucker. "I'm not ready to lose all hope just yet. I accept that, as thing are now, I'm dying. But I still have faith that my grandchildren can find the source of the spell, and if they do that, Georgeanne can break it."

"I don't understand how Georgie can break it. She doesn't have magic."

"We have discovered a talent unique to her, perhaps because she is Bane." Madeleine looked down at her fingers, pleating her blanket in a motion that came as close to revealing her nervousness as Milo had ever witnessed. "She can break dark magic, and I believe the more she works with her talent, the better she'll be able to access magic as a whole."

It was an odd turn of phrase Milo paused to consider. He watched the old woman for a long, silent moment, unwilling to rush into a conclusion that may be wrong, or never validated. There were limits to Madeleine's fondness for him after all, and he knew she'd never share a truth she believed would weaken her Family.

"Can Georgeanne even claim Motherhood without the

ability to access magic?"

Madeleine's eyes shot up to meet his. "We shall find out when I die, won't we? The girls will have to figure it out for themselves."

Milo went cold, in spite of the heat his anger produced. "Or you can avoid such a vulnerable experiment by simply announcing Christiana as your heir."

"Does she even want the position, Milo? I have no doubt she'd accept it, if there were no other choice except Suzette or some distant cousin, but against Georgie? They are closer than you appear to realize."

"I know exactly how close they are." And it irritated him sometimes, that his wife could be so loving toward a rival when he was left with nothing more than the scraps of her esteem.

"Georgeanne's temperament is better suited to the position of Mother. Christiana knows this. You know this." Madeleine's brows rose. "The girls have fostered the illusion of rivalry to entertain the wider witching world, but every Davenold knows that it would take a great deal to pit them against each other."

"A great deal," Milo held the old woman's stare, "like your death. I can't allow my wife to be targeted for challenges while she's pregnant. If you let the magic choose, I believe it will choose Chris, then Suzette will challenge, and perhaps Georgie will also challenge. Suzette will use magic, but you've made certain Georgie gained combat experience Christiana can't hope to compete against."

"You believe Suzette to be a lesser threat to your wife's safety?"

"No, she's too vengeful. Still, I have no choice but to place faith in my wife's talents."

Madeleine's voice firmed, as did her features, hammering home how angry she was growing. "Then why are you here, begging me to blood Christiana as my heir? Hold on to your faith and let me rest."

Milo jumped to his feet. "I'm here because both women

want Motherhood so badly I can't predict what they'll do to get it. Even Georgie—no matter how much she loves Christiana, she poses a threat, a non-magical threat, a weaponry expert kind of threat, and can't be brought down with a spell."

Madeleine snorted. "You are so pathetically in love with your wife you can't see straight. I must admit, I never expected that, when you asked for her hand in marriage."

"Mother Davenold," Milo clenched his fists, "my wife is pregnant with my only child. The only child I will ever bring into this world. The protection of my family is in your hands, and I wonder if you have any idea how difficult a thing that is for a man to trust to another."

"You are a matriarchal man. Surely it's not such a hardship for you to trust in your Mother?"

Illumination seared Milo's brain. He wasn't a political player, and only paid enough attention to protect his business interests, but Madeleine was a chess master, manipulative and intelligent, and wholly involved in intrigue deeper than Milo could fathom. "What is your game, Madeleine?"

Her eyes flashed with ire. "Even in death, I will protect my Family to the best of my ability. I have been graced with a gullible granddaughter, a Bane granddaughter and a spoiled, vindictive dark magic witch of a niece. These are to be my options for inheritance, a limited pool to choose from, I'm sure you will agree."

"You have better choices than most Families."

"*Because I have made it so!*" She levered herself up on the pillows with a jerky surge of action. "I have spent their entire lives readying my granddaughters for this very possibility, and I have yet to come to a decision about whom to blood. Twenty-three years, Milo, and I am still not certain who the best of the lot would be!"

"Perhaps you're uncertain because you don't want to face your own mortality. You've never wanted to ponder the matter, never wanted to believe you'd ever have to give up your power."

"You will watch your words with me, Milo."

The topic was too important for him to back down in the face of her hostility. He took courage from the lesson he'd learned a year ago, when he'd first begun his pursuit of Christiana—Madeleine would never respect a man who continuously kowtowed. There was a reason the Davenold Mother had grown so fond of him.

Milo held his own, though he forced a dollop more respect into his tone. "Have you ever seen a challenge, Madeleine?"

"I was a blooded heir."

He shook his head. "I'll take that as a no. You know the Ivanovs are famous for their challenges. Infamous, really. In my lifetime, we've had four Mothers. Four!"

Madeleine pursed her lips. "The Davenolds are very different."

"Not for much longer." Agitated, Milo paced at the side of her bed, willing her to understand. "Death brings out the worst in people. You're setting your Family up to go after one another with all the viciousness of starving dogs, yet hoping beyond reason that Family loyalty and sisterly affection will keep them to heel."

"This is nonsense, Milo. Georgeanne and Christiana will not battle."

He whirled on her. "And what of Suzette? What makes you think she won't bring every dirty trick she has to bear against Christiana?"

"What makes you think the magic will choose Christiana?"

"Georgie is Bane!" He threw out his hands. "I think the only way she can claim Motherhood is to literally wield a weapon against her challengers. Stab them, shoot them, strangle them, and keep threatening until the rest of the Family falls in line and surrenders to her leadership. Suzette has magic but it is—"

"Weaker than your wife's magic."

"Which is why Christiana will become Mother." Milo fought to keep from tearing his hair out. "But weak is a relative term for your Family and, without being blooded, my wife is vulnerable. Even more so while she's pregnant."

"You said you have faith in your wife's ability."

"Should I tell you to what lengths a witch will go when power is on the line?" Milo battled back bleak memories — emotions, sights, sounds and fears that had haunted him until he'd joined the Davenolds. "Should I tell you what measures desperate witches will take? How terrible fully released magic can be to the unfortunates who aren't able to get out the way of the challengers fast enough? Would you like to know what it looks like when one witch uses her talent to pry her opponent in halves? In halves, Madeleine!"

"Milo, stop this."

"Do you know the awful sound it makes when magic is used to rupture a woman's internal organs, all at once? Do you have any idea how much blood flows from the nose of a witch when her brain is hemorrhaging under the pressure of a spell?"

"*Milo.*"

"Have you ever seen a witch burst like a ripe melon after dark magic is lobbed her way? Suzette is a dark magic witch."

"Stop! *Stop this nonsense at once!*"

He didn't know if she was truly angry or simply unwilling to hear anymore. He didn't know, and didn't have time to figure it out as a dark corona exploded around her body. The percussion of magic sent him staggering back as it ripped through Madeleine' thin frame and shook her like a rag doll.

A pain sliced through his head but Milo ignored it and leaped for Madeleine. She convulsed on the bed, shaking the mattress as she arched and groaned. Trapped breath rattled in her chest and her fingers formed claws in the covers. Milo grabbed for her and immediately jerked his hands back as cold fire blistered his palms.

Panic nearly overwhelmed him, fear ripped into his gut. Blindly, he raced for the door, hauled it open and screamed into the hallway. "*Help!*"

His yell roared past his own wife, standing with Silviu and Georgie just outside Madeleine's bedroom. Christiana whirled on him with wide eyes. Her face tautened into immobility as she rushed toward him.

Milo slid to the side. "Madeleine needs help."

Silviu and Georgie followed in Christiana's wake, both of them pushing past Milo to enter Madeleine's room. He was on their heels, only pausing to slam the door shut in a vain attempt at hiding whatever had happened.

Silviu reached for Madeleine. Milo found himself yelling again. "No! Don't touch her!"

He lifted his hands to show them the raw blisters marking his palms. Silviu cursed, Christiana gasped. She came toward him with eyes held too wide. She lifted a hand and traced his top lip, drawing back with a smear of blood on her fingertip.

"What happened, Milo?"

He glanced over his wife's head toward the bed, where Silviu generated a dim silver light with a wave of his hands and a whispered chant. A complicated spell, requiring both motion and words, and strong enough to produce visible magic.

"We argued, and I upset her. I must have upset her more than I thought, because whatever dark magic is trapped inside her came barreling out. It blazed around her with a smoky aura and pushed me back with a pulse of violet light. I'm sorry, I didn't mean—"

"The spell attacking her has no ties to her emotional state." Christiana rushed to soothe him. "If it did, she wouldn't have gotten out of the Ngozi residence alive. It wasn't your fault, sweetie."

Milo wiped his nose with the back of his hand, vaguely surprised it was still bleeding. "Madeleine convulsed, the magic burned my hands."

"It's possible the magic could have come from Madeleine. Like a boiling pot, perhaps it can only be contained for so long." Silviu waved and a silver net settled over the Davenold Mother, holding her still. "Or it could have come from an outside source, a dark magic witch."

"Suzette," Christiana growled.

"But why now?" Georgie moved to sit on the bed and take her grandmother's limp hand. She showed no reaction to the soft pulse of purple light, no hint that her palm burned as Milo's had. "Suzette hasn't done anything like that so far, so why today? It seems too easy."

"Perhaps to weaken you in front of Daniel," Silviu murmured.

"I agree," Chris stated. "You know any other dark magic witches around here?"

Georgie shrugged. "Suzette's magic isn't as strong as Grandmother's."

"But Madeleine is weakened." Silviu took a deep breath. "I've lost the source of the magic, though I'm able to ease her muscles and some of the damage the magic has done inside her."

Christiana grabbed Milo's wrist and pulled him toward the chair. Her fingers shook against his skin, clenching and releasing spasmodically while her pulse fluttered in her throat. His chest tightened at the expression in her eyes, at the deep concern he'd never expected to see. She might occasionally defend him against her twin, but Milo had always assumed it was because she was a matriarch and he was her property to protect. However, with Christiana's pretty eyes showing her distress, hope filled him and sent a soothing warmth through Milo's veins at the thought that, just perhaps, she cared for him at least as much as for her grandmother and cousin.

Milo relaxed into the chair as his wife dropped to her knees before him and began muttering a spell. Her cool palms cupped his jaw and ice slammed into his burning skull with all the relief of a cold drink on a hot day. His muscles lost more of their tension as Christiana set about stemming the blood flowing from his nose and healing whatever damage had been caused in his head.

Beyond her, Georgie and Silviu worked over Madeleine. Silviu's silver magic blazed gold the moment the pair touched, but, though Milo blinked in surprise, he said nothing. He'd only just met Silviu in the hallway on his way to visit Madeleine, and so had no way of knowing what the connection between Georgie and her betrothed could be.

But now Milo knew they were Magic Matches, a gift he wouldn't have thought a Bane witch would have. Their Match was either a blessing that may save his wife from being chosen as the next Mother, or a curse that would only result in her death immediately upon accepting the position. His blood ran cold.

Chris distracted Milo from his dark thoughts by taking his hand and sending a comforting blast of magic deep into his palm. He stared at her as she healed the blisters, leaving only a dull throb behind as she moved on to his next hand.

"Better?" she whispered.

"Thank you, *krasavitsa*."

"Madeleine is calm now," Georgie announced. "Sleeping and no longer in pain."

"This grows more frustrating by the day." Silviu backed away from Madeleine and strode toward the window, looking down on the view of rolling farmland as if it held all the answers he sought. "And with Daniel Levy here, it grows more complicated."

"When did the Levy Father arrive?" Milo glanced between the other three witches.

Chris grimaced. "Just now. Suzette is entertaining him."

"We need to strategize," Silviu announced as he turned from the window. "I want Eliasz's input as to what Daniel hopes to accomplish by coming here."

"Eliasz Levy?" Milo couldn't hide his doubt. "What makes you think he'll tell you anything about his own Family Father?"

"Bad blood and ancient history," Georgie muttered. "Fatherhood should have come down Eliasz's line, but

Daniel's grandfather manipulated events to his own advantage. Eliasz and Daniel are barely on speaking terms."

Silviu nodded. "I trust Eliasz. I'm going to ward Madeleine's door for protection, and to hide her from Daniel for a while, then go talk to my brother-in-law."

"We'll all go," Georgie stated. "There are a lot of different perspectives to be gained from the people we trust, and we might need them all to figure this dark magic out."

Chapter Eight

Christiana

"As far as I know, Daniel's never even hinted that he would want the High Seat."

Chris hefted a brow in Eliasz's direction. "Maybe because it wasn't an immediate possibility until now."

"Daniel's too weak in magic." Eliasz settled onto the arm of the chair his betrothed was curled into and shook his head. "He also wouldn't have time to perform those duties on top of his familial obligations."

"Maybe the Council would prefer someone that weak," Silviu suggested with an odd glance at Georgeanne, "rather than a powerful witch who could commandeer the combined magic of all the covens."

"My grandmother is powerful and they gave the position to her." Chris blew out a breath and glared at the group occupying the library.

Besides Eliasz and Ileana, Adam and Tulah huddled together on a leather couch, and Georgie and Silviu sat at a small table illuminated by a miniature green lamp. Milo leaned against a wall of bookshelves, a small splotch of dried blood still under his nose. Just a few feet from her husband, Chris paced in front of the fireplace, periodically glancing up at the portrait of her great-grandmother hanging above the marble mantle.

Georgie looked like their ancestor. The Davenold women tended to share the same face, except for Christiana, who took after her father's Family. The only thing Chris had inherited from her great-grandmother was a talent for spell casting, which was not helping Christiana find a solution to Madeleine's ailment as much as she'd hoped.

She scowled at the table, where a pile of grimoires were spread between Georgie, Silviu and the chair Chris had recently vacated. After spending the last few days squinting at very small, handwritten text detailing countless spells, her head had begun to throb at the thought of rereading the old, bound tomes. She'd been unable to keep her seat as the group pondered their situation.

Christiana narrowed her eyes. "As Eliasz pointed out, the Levys are a big Family and Daniel wields tremendous influence. The one advantage the other councilmen have over him is his magical deficiencies."

Georgie hummed low in her throat. "Tulah, did you overhear anything during your stay with the Ngozi Family that could help us? Did you or your mother hear Daniel and Graves, or Daniel and any of his Family members discussing anything of relevance?"

"Not really," the woman answered. "But Graves was always...submissive to Daniel."

Christiana looked at her sister-in-law and tried not to let her irritation derail her train of thought. Adam had rushed into marriage—and quick marriages weren't known for working out well, a fact Chris had learned the hard way—but Adam was currently staring at his new bride with the softest expression Christiana had ever seen on his face, so there was little she could protest. Forcing herself to be honest, Chris admitted the problem originated from within her. Jealousy was a bitch. She wanted Adam's focus to be on her until she was more settled in her own new marriage.

Six months wasn't enough to feel comfortable with a man like Milo Ivanov.

"Daniel needed the alliance with Graves to balance the Ngozi-Njele match," Eliasz said. "Muso married his wife to make a stand against the witch hunts in Africa, but there were political ramifications that made Daniel nervous."

"Which is why we believe he'll support your bid for the

Council seat." Silviu tipped his head toward his brother-in-law. "Our alliance offers a much better foundation than anything Constance's marriage to Graves would have provided."

Georgie drummed her fingers on the tabletop. "Tulah, do you have any idea why Graves would have wanted an alliance with Daniel?"

When Tulah merely shook her head, Eliasz answered. "Most patriarchal witches would kill for an alliance with the Levy Family, and to be so connected to the Father could only benefit Graves."

"True." Georgie grimaced. "To be honest, I can't really see Daniel being involved in whatever plot we're dealing with. He simply doesn't have the magical ability, and while Graves did, he's dead, so we need to broaden our imagination a bit and figure out what's really going on."

"He could be taking advantage of the opportunity though," Milo said. "I've had business dealings with Daniel before, so I know a little of how his mind works."

Christiana's stomach hollowed out and it took effort not to stumble as she came to sudden halt in front of her husband. Old suspicions heated her veins, pulled at her spine and drowned her in pain. She spoke through clenched teeth. "If you know Daniel, you know Constance."

Anger stormed through her as Milo's ears flushed pink. "Yes, they're frequently together," he admitted.

"She's shameless. Did she try to seduce you, Milo?"

His eyes darkened, became hunted. His ears flared red and Christiana thought she would be ill. Lips pressed tight, she spun away from her husband, pretending his answer didn't matter. He caught her arm before she managed a single step. Out of habit, Christiana flinched, though his hold caused no pain.

Adam was on his feet and across the room in a heartbeat. He ripped Milo's fingers from Christiana's arm. "Get your fucking hands off her!"

Time stilled as Christiana stared at her brother in shock.

Old memories reared their ugly heads until she had to fight her tears, and she knew her brother shared some of the pain moving through her chest. They both remembered, which was part of the problem. And it was her fault that her brother was so burdened by her past mistakes.

Chris was hardly able to speak past the guilt threatening to choke her. "He didn't hurt me, Adam."

But her words were hardly out of her mouth before Milo leaned close and snarled in her brother's face. "She's my wife. I'll touch her however I want to, whenever I want to, and I am more than fed up at your interference!"

Adam's finger stabbed the air just beneath Milo's nose. "You don't put your hands on her in anger."

"Do not think I will allow you to involve yourself in my marriage for much longer." Milo straightened to his full height, several inches over Adam and even more over Christiana. "I have struggled to keep my patience because the two of you are close enough that jealousy was to be expected."

"You're way off base," Adam growled. "This has nothing to do with jealousy and everything to do with your treatment of my sister."

"Adam," Chris tried again, "he didn't hurt me. It's fine."

"It's not fine! He puts his hands on you again, I'll kill him."

Georgie leaped into the fray with hands outstretched, pushing between the men. "That's enough, all of you. Grandmother is growing weaker while you bicker like petty children."

Milo focused his emerald gaze on Christiana with all the heat of a laser. His thinned lips and lowered brows belied his silky tone as he said, "I have never touched Constance Gage-Levy, not even to shake her hand, let alone fuck her. Which, knowing him and his role in this Family, is more than your brother can say to his wife."

With a growl, Adam launched himself at Milo. But Silviu was on his feet and moving in quick, grabbing Adam a moment before the angry Davenold crushed Christiana and Georgie between him and his opponent. Milo pulled Christiana out of the way fast enough to make her lose her balance, forcing him to hold her with only her toes touching the floor.

Silviu pushed Adam away. "Have you lost your mind?"

"Stop this now!" The commanding dominance in Georgie's voice was equal to that of a Mother who'd long held the position. "We do not have time for this."

Tulah, mocha skin reddened with a wash of humiliation, slowly rose from the couch to take hold of Adam's hand. He immediately stepped back from Silviu's outstretched arm, the only thing that held him back from attacking Milo, and wrapped his wife in a tight embrace.

Tulah lifted her chin. "I know what was between Adam and Constance. But the past is the past, and we need to focus on the future, now."

"Yes," Ileana slowly rose to her feet and lifted her hands slightly, "let's focus on what's truly important. We'll all *calm down* and brainstorm."

Her words brought a cooling sensation along Christiana's skin. It was exceedingly pleasant, as if someone had just spoken such a rational truth that fear, panic, doubt and irritability couldn't hope to survive. Christiana found herself relaxing into her husband's arms, just as everyone else in the room lost much of their tension.

Milo brushed a kiss over Chris' hair and stroked his hands down her back. "My apologies, *krasavitsa*, for upsetting you."

With a sidelong glance at Ileana, Georgie smoothed her chin-length curls. "We are here to discuss dark magic, its influence over our grandmother and where the source could be located. We are not here to referee a fight between two valuable members of our Family."

"Generally, magic needs to be close to work." Ileana met her brother's indecipherable stare with a small shrug "However, things like effigies can extend the distance of a spell, provided they have some piece of the targeted witch woven into the fabric of their construction. Like Madeleine's hair on the doll found at Graves' residence. Something similar could be at play here."

Silviu turned to Christiana. "Could a spell go farther if there was already the taint of dark magic clinging to a witch? Could we be dealing with multiple attacks and just not know it?"

Chris shrugged. "I don't deal with dark magic, so I have no way of knowing its properties. I still say we start with a thorough investigation of Suzette."

"I don't necessarily doubt her involvement, but she would need help. Even when combined with her husband's talents — they're Matches — " Georgie added for Eliasz and Ileana's benefit, "her magic would still be too weak to bring Grandmother down."

"Like I said at the Ngozi residence," Chris told them, "it's a strong witch who cast that spell. Not many are able to hide their tracks that effectively, but I think I found something."

Adam drove his fingers through his hair. "It's a long shot, though."

"I'll take it," Silviu said.

Christiana moved toward the table. "I've read these damned tomes until I felt like my eyes would fall out of my skull. Most of this deals with everyday stuff. Silencing spells, some herbal remedies, truth serums. Stupid crap we all learned as kids."

Silviu stared at Christiana long enough to make her fidget as she shuffled through the books. She could see the distrust in his eyes, but also the willingness to hear her out. She assumed that meant he'd finally realized Christiana wasn't trying to kill her Family members, as he'd accused her of doing so many times before.

Finally, Christiana uncovered the book she sought, with frayed edges and dog-eared pages. She flipped through it quickly before laying the grimoire flat on the table and pointing to the tiny, handwritten spell. "This is our best shot and that's pretty sad."

Silviu came over to squint at the page. "Those are nonsense words."

"It's Gaelic. My paternal grandmother insisted Adam and I learn four different dialects." Chris rolled her eyes. "Georgie got to learn romance languages and I got to learn how to spit while I speak."

Silviu's lips twitched. "What does it do?"

"This is a simple locator spell," Adam said.

"That's why it's sad." Chris winced. "Because there's nothing fancy about this spell, yet it's so simplistic it might have a better chance of cutting through the block. It's little known and hardly been used in centuries, so the dark magic witch might be vulnerable to it."

"I don't know about that," Eliasz called out. "Remember, the last time we tried looking for the witch, we ran into a big brick wall. It seems like our villain has every seam sewed tight."

"Try it anyway," Georgie said. "What's the harm in trying?"

Adam shrugged. "Just a little bloodletting."

"*What*? No." Milo stomped toward the table and grabbed Christiana by the shoulders. He bent a hostile glare on Silviu that didn't appear all that effective.

"I can sympathize with your need to keep your wife safe," Silviu murmured. "But a few drops of blood are nothing to get excited about. The possible rewards far outweigh the cost."

"She's pregnant!"

"It won't hurt the baby, Milo." Chris twisted her lips and narrowed her eyes at Silviu. "And while I hate to agree, if there is a chance this spell could help us stop the one hurting Grandmother, I'm all for giving it a try."

He crooked his finger at his sister. "Ileana, come lend us your strength."

Christiana prepared herself for the force of the magic that would shortly bolster her own. Only a few days ago, she'd worked with the Lovaszes in a previous attempt to locate the dark magic witch and she'd learned how strong they were. They had tired her out, but this time, her Match would be with her, and Christiana hoped that meant their magical strength would be easier to handle.

Adam took her right hand in a tight grip. Visible to everyone in the room, golden magic formed a ball in the twins' cupped palms as they mumbled a quick spell every witch knew by heart. Heat blazed out from the ball they held and swiped a line over their palms. Skin split and blood flowed, pooling into the creases between their hands. The golden Matched Magic Christiana and Adam generated absorbed the blood and flared brightly.

The easy spell they'd spoken turned into a garbled mess of sounds between one word and the next. With years of practice, Christiana led her brother into the new spell, chanting in unison even as they made the switch. The magical ball in their palms pulsed with power as their other, still-linked, hands began to dance in a complicated pattern of dips, twists and rotations. And their magic grew.

"I knew they were strong," Chris dimly heard Silviu whisper, "but their Matched Magic is even more powerful than I expected."

Christiana tuned out the murmurs of the others and raised her voice. The words of the spell grew weighted and stretched out, seeming to reach to the far corners of the room and bringing an intense wave of pressure. Everything slowed down—Chris' heartbeat, her thoughts, time, maybe even the rotation of the Earth.

Squinting against the glare of magic, Chris saw Tulah standing stock still, Eliasz's hair ruffling in a phantom wind and Ileana breathing deeply. Silviu's face hardened into granite and Milo gritted his teeth. Georgie alone seemed unaffected, but her Bane shields were in full force, creating an illusion much like a wind-tunnel, with the twins' magic parting to flow past her in streaks of gold light.

Then Ileana's magic rose to full life. Her strength poured

into the twins' spell, swelling their magic past their natural limitations. With a surge of fear, Chris realized Ileana had held back in their previous attempt. She suddenly found herself on dangerous ground, off-balance and struggling to keep her feet under her as the floor seemed to pitch.

Then she felt Silviu's magic streaming into the chaos. For a moment, the world steadied, but the powerful force whipped along the seams of the twin's spell and elevated it beyond Christiana's ability to hold. Invisible flames licked over her body until she clenched her teeth against a scream. The power only escalated, flying beyond the walls of the library, and Chris wondered if they would all be torn apart by the magic they'd called to their command.

"I will keep you steady. I won't let us fall." Silviu's jaw bulged. Sweat popped out on his brow and, staggering, he gripped the edge of the table.

Christiana could feel the sheer amount of raw magic moving through him, through them all. He was a conduit for the spell, and it intimidated her. No witch should wield so much magic. Pain sparked, pinpricks along her skin, as if she were slowly being flayed alive. Still, Silviu pushed them all past their limits.

Christiana was on the verge of letting go, stopping the spell before they all died from it, but, before she could surrender to her pain and fear, her cousin gripped Silviu's bicep. The moment Georgie touched her betrothed, the world exploded in a haze of gold much stronger than the radiance Chris and Adam had produced. She watched the waver on the air as Georgie's Bane shields snapped and flickered and almost lost focus when the imperviousness settled down.

Georgie glowed. The room stopped spinning. The pain disappeared, the pressure eased and a stabilizing force rippled through Christiana, easing the sharp edges of her terror at Silviu's strength. The magic stuffing the room evened out with the new void to fill—and Chris could literally *see* Georgie being filled with magic.

Then she saw nothing but darkness with golden threads snaking out in all directions. The cords drew closer to some magnetic force, the shadows began to clear. Just as the haze lifted, a snarling black cloud shifted the entire scene rolling out in Christiana's mind, surging forward and chomping down on her spell with a terrible pain. A yellow starburst seared her retinas. The magic shut off abruptly.

"Suzette," Christiana croaked. She cleared her throat and wobbled on her feet, leaning back against her husband as Milo rushed to brace her weight.

Adam staggered toward the couch, Tulah in his wake. She petted him as he dropped to the cushions. His voice was as strained as his sister's when he said, "We found her magic, and Graves' leftover spell. And another's. Don't know who, because it was all dark."

"He or she is hiding." Without thought, Christiana turned into her husband's embrace. "But Suzette holds the answer, if you can get her to talk."

"Not likely," Georgie snorted. "We'll need more evidence before we confront her."

Silviu reached out and cupped her cheek. "Are you all right, my love?"

"Yeah." Her eyes sparkled. Georgie was the only one in the room not showing signs of strain, exhaustion or fear. "Are you, Silver? It looked pretty bad there, for a minute."

Chris watched curiously as Silviu ran his thumb over her cousin's lower lip. "You fixed it."

"In spite of getting a step closer to confirming our cousin has a hand in all this, there's little more we can do about the situation tonight." Adam got off the couch and moved toward the door in a drunken stumble as Tulah pretended to support his weight with her slight body. "I need to lay down."

Though she gave a murmur of agreement for her brother's sentiment, Christiana made no protest when Milo swept her into his arms and carried her from the room. She laid her cheek against his chest and relaxed, too exhausted to do anything but trust her husband to take care of her.

Chapter Nine

Silviu

A plan solidified in Silviu's head while Georgie effortlessly dealt with ten different issues at the breakfast table. He was surprised by how needy the Davenold witches seemed – Suzette's husband in particular, and Silviu gained some insight as to why so many held such a low opinion of the man. Though he was honest enough to admit he'd never paid much attention to such things in his own coven. There had been no need – Silviu wasn't the heir – yet he found his regard for many of Georgie's Family members dropping swiftly.

His betrothed handled herself with poise and patience. Silviu's groin tightened with the desire to fully claim her. Seeing her solve minor problems and settle major disputes with ease was a surprising turn-on. All that grace, confidence and dominance packed into such a tiny woman. His woman.

Silviu, midway down the breakfast table, sipped his coffee and pushed aside a cold whisper of guilt. Instead, he pictured Georgie spread out beneath him, intimate flesh shining with the need of her passion, and remembered her taste on his lips. He thought of the way she looked as she bent down and took his cock in her mouth, the beautiful way she responded to his instructions.

He saw again the silken pillows of her breasts mounded around his length as he slid between them. He remembered the combined taste of their blood after they shared a too-rough kiss. He thought of the suspicions sliding through his dreams all night long.

Before then their magic was separate, swirling together like stripes on a candy cane, two distinct parts. After Georgie had tasted his blood, Silviu began to notice her presence within him more and more. Even when they were hundreds of miles apart, a deep awareness of her heartbeat had settled into his chest.

Silviu shifted on his chair as his dick hardened into full life with one heavy surge of desire. He needed to complete what they'd started in Poland and combine their distinct essences into one united whole. Georgie's body, her pleasure, magic and power were his for the taking. And Silviu planned to take.

Finally breakfast was over and Davenold witches drifted off. Silviu hurried to claim Georgie's attention before any more problems could arise and take her from him. "I'd like a moment of your time, my love."

In spite of her tranquility, she seemed vaguely frazzled, as if there was too much to do and not enough time in the day to do it. Heaving a sigh, she let him take her hand. "Your moment will have to be in my grandmother's office, then. There's some paperwork I need to look over."

"I thought your father handled many of these things you are taking on."

Liking the way her skirt swished around her legs, he made no protest when Georgie led the way from the dining room. "There is only so much he has the authority to do. Solving Family dilemmas isn't his job."

Frustration heated the back of Silviu's neck. "I'd hoped for a little more than a small moment, love."

"Make an appointment," she snapped. "Silviu, I have a lot going on right now. I appreciate you doing what you can to help my grandmother, but while she's ill the Family problems come to me. I have a job to do and I can't let everybody down."

"They could solve most of these problems themselves." He shook his head, irritation tightening his muscles. "They bring you silly things for no other reason than to occupy your time."

She steered him to the right and opened an inconspicuous door. Inside wasn't what he'd expected, until he reminded himself that the estate belonged to the secondary branch and wasn't Madeleine's primary residence. In New Hampshire, the Davenold Mother had a bright, opulent office, but the space he followed his betrothed into was dimly lit with a single, narrow window and filled with an overly large desk.

It was perfect.

"You have to understand how nervous they are." Georgie's tone turned mildly scolding, "Our Mother is ill with no cure we can find and the Family is frightened. I must provide them with the leader they need."

Put that way, the Davenolds' dependence on her made more sense. "You are the natural choice," he conceded.

"Yes, and if I'm not available, the witches here are more likely to go to Suzette than Christiana. Most of the people running around here belong to the secondary branch. What did you need to talk to me about?"

There was no way he could tell her the truth. He knew she would reject him outright if she had even a hint of his plans. He would scare her off and offend her at the same time.

A flick of his fingers locked the door before he leaped on her. Silviu trapped Georgie against the desk and hauled her to his chest, his mouth coming down on hers before she could protest. He crushed her close, pressing his rigid dick to her belly and smoothing his hands down her back in a single, hard stroke.

He wondered if she could taste his desperation as he twisted his lips against hers and thrust his tongue into her mouth. If she could feel the thrum of his magic sliding over her, sinking into her, and if she would understand what it meant, if she understood what he was doing. He wondered if he cared what she thought as she went to her toes and moaned. Silviu pressed his advantage.

Her lack of magical knowledge was his saving grace and he fully intended to use it to the best of his ability while he still had the advantage. Before her suspicions became engaged. He gripped her hips and dragged her against his cock until Georgie was clinging to him for balance. He kneaded her ass and bit her lip.

She broke the kiss with a gasp. "Silver, I don't have time—"

"Make time," he growled, attacking her mouth again. He licked and rubbed, used the hard edge of his teeth against her soft curves and sucked her lower lip. "I need you, Georgie."

She pulled her mouth out of his reach and let her head fall back with a groan. But her hands slid over his chest and her hips swayed against his. "Tonight—"

"Right now." He licked the pulse in her neck. "I've barely even spoken to you since the Ngozi fiasco. I need to touch you, Georgie."

He slid his hands beneath her skirt, closing his eyes at the warmth of her thighs, the quiver in the lean muscles he followed. He pressed and rubbed, stroked and smoothed, and felt a slice of heat deep in his chest. Her desire mingling with his.

He wondered if she felt him as he felt her.

Silviu found the edge of her panties and pushed his fingers beneath, filling his palms with the smooth globes of her ass. Georgie made a broken noise deep in her throat when he squeezed. He suddenly needed so much more. His plans remained sharp in his mind but raw lust for her took over all thought and motivation.

Silviu swung her up on the edge of the desk and threw her skirt over her thighs. His knees nearly buckled at the glimpse of the tiny scrap of black lace covering her mound. He spread her legs wide and smoothed his hands higher with a force he'd never used with her before.

Georgie gripped the edge of the desk and shimmied in a way that had his scalp burning. Magic pulsed between them, golden flickers erupting to light the dim office with the power of a small sun. Silviu swore the force came straight from his cock.

He grabbed the fabric riding the crease of her thigh and sent his power shooting from his fingertips to slice through the material. Her panties fell away, anchored only by the hold they maintained around her other leg. He repeated the process and ripped them off.

Georgie gasped, moaned, spread her legs wider. Silviu rushed to fill the void. He couldn't afford to slow down, couldn't afford to give her a moment to think, to doubt—or protest. His dick ached, his heart hurt and his conscience whimpered.

But it wouldn't stop him.

He slid his fingertips through her creamy folds and found her clit. He wrapped all five fingers around the little bud and sent his magic spinning over her flesh while he pulled and tugged as if their future depended on her pleasure.

Because it did.

"Oh my God," she breathed. "Wait, let me—"

He stepped closer and caught her lips with his. Silviu couldn't wait. Waiting would destroy everything they'd both worked for their entire lives. All the pain of the past would be meaningless if he waited.

Without hesitation, he set out to conquer his dominant bride through his kiss. With no concessions to her authority, he possessed her mouth and owned it. His tongue slid against hers, wet velvet and slick silk. He forced her mouth wider and surged deeper, taking in the flavors of sweet breakfast tea and minty toothpaste along with the addictive taste of Georgeanne.

He released her clit and reached lower. Giving her no time to process his actions, he slammed two fingers deep into her pussy and nearly lost his mind as her wet heat closed around his knuckles. He pushed, he shoved, then he curled his fingers and dragged them back from her scalding grip. She wriggled and he dove in again. Her left knee jerked up to his waist.

He worked his other hand between them to fight the closure straining over his heavy cock. With a groan of relief, he freed himself. Silviu pulled his fingers from Georgie's body and positioned the head of his dick against her saturated opening in the same breathless moment.

He thought he'd take her by surprise, or even that she would remain passive, since he'd crested her entrance before without pushing farther. But perhaps she felt the difference in his intentions this time, because her hand caught his shaft. Her fingers tightened, halting his forward progress and Silviu thought he'd be felled by the heat of her soft palm. Gold light blazed between their groins, stroking over them both with maddening sensation.

Georgie wrenched her mouth from his, eyes wide, chest heaving, breath panting over his lips. "Silver?"

Against the prodding of his brain, his body paused. His heart twisted, his belly folded over itself. Silviu nudged against her, dampening his crest in her honey, but he couldn't force himself any farther. His brain urged him on — plots and plans and manipulations requiring his entry to her hot depths — but his heart required her permission.

Georgie's fingers tightened around him. Her dark eyes met and held his, searching as he struggled to show her only the lust coursing through him. Only the love, as he tried to hide the rest. She broke the stare as her entrance flexed around him, looking down as a small gasp broke from her lips.

"We can't," she whispered. "Madeleine said…"

He followed her gaze and nearly lost all control. His cock butted up to her entrance, her body stretching around the tip, a slow slide of cream oozing between their flesh. The heat of her licked over him and small muscles flickered against him, begging for his entry. Georgie's desire swelled until it beat against his skin and filled his spinal cord from within.

His hips jerked, sinking his cock a half inch inside her

pussy before he could stop. Silviu thought he might die at the pleasure — and the searing need for full penetration, a long slide into hot, wet depths that would close around him so tight, so beautifully, that their magics would have no other choice but to permanently reside in each other's souls.

Georgie made another noise. "Silver."

He didn't know if she was asking him to stop or begging him to continue. His voice was mere sound, vibrating with lust. "I need you, Georgeanne. I need to sink into you and make you mine."

"Grandmother said —"

"She's sick, Georgie." He shifted, slid a fraction deeper. His cock throbbed brutally. "She won't be able to protect you, but I can. Let me in, my love. Say yes and I'll fill you with my body and my magic. Forever can start right now."

Temptation swept across Georgeanne's face. She wanted it, wanted him. Silviu already knew that, felt her need as he felt his own, but it was a powerful thing to have her expression validate it. Georgie was always so closed off, with only a polite countenance on her face.

She wasn't polite now. Her lips were swollen, her cheeks flushed. Her dark eyes shone with lust and she was splayed before him, legs held wide, his cock stretching her, flesh shining with her need. She was the most beautiful thing he'd ever seen.

Her fingers clasped his dick in a ruthless grip and Silviu let her hold on to the pretense that she could stop him from driving into her, prevent him from filling her with one hard stroke. Contrarily, to give her doubt and to ease his ache, Silviu nudged — a gentle pressure, both a warning and a promise. It felt too good not to do it again, so he did — over and over until she shifted with him in a mindless dance and her body grew slick and slippery.

He knew the very moment she stopped thinking. He saw her gaze blank, her lips fall open. Georgie's head tipped back and her fingers relaxed around his cock. Silviu rocked, hips tightening with the preparation of surging forward and claiming his bride. Cementing their relationship and connecting their magic in a way that could never be undone.

Someone hammered on the door.

"Georgeanne?" A high, feminine voice pushed through the barrier. "There's an issue that needs your immediate attention. Are you in there? Is the door is locked? I can't seem to get it open."

Georgie's logic snapped back into her brain with a suddenness Silviu could feel in his own. Her entire body stiffened, her pussy clamping down on his crest with her surprise. He groaned at the hot grip, and nearly cried at the instant banishment of desire from her gaze.

"That's my mother." She pushed at his chest as another, more impatient, banging came at the door.

"Georgeanne!" A deep voice immediately recognizable as her father came to them. "At least fifteen people saw you come in here with Silviu Lovasz. Open this door at once!"

The situation was regrettably similar to what had happened ten years ago. Georgie's father had found them naked and entangled when they were teenagers, and had helped keep the betrothed pair apart for a decade. Gritting his teeth against the agony searing his mind and body, Silviu reluctantly stepped back, knowing the moment had passed and he'd lost his chance.

He fought to keep from sending his magic winging through the door to kill Georgie's parents where they stood.

Georgie slid off the desk to stand on shaky legs and smoothed her hair. Silviu stuffed his stiff cock back into his pants with a grimace. Awkwardly, he forced his throbbing body to bend and snatch her panties from the floor.

"That was too close," she hissed. "That can't happen again."

"It will," he promised her. "I want you, I need you, and you are mine. The next time I get my hands on you, and that will be no later than the end of this day, I will fuck you breathless. To the point you won't even be able to scream your pleasure."

"Georgeanne!" her father yelled.

"*One minute*," she called back. She spun on Silviu with a heated look that had nothing to do with lust. "I will say when, do you understand me? When I have permission, I will share my body completely, but until my grandmother approves, I won't risk everything I've worked for just because you make me come."

He didn't have the heart to tell her how wrong she was. He didn't have the words to explain how they'd both been used and betrayed by the people who'd sworn to love them and protect them at all costs. Silviu couldn't bear to tell her that neither of them would find any help in achieving the goals their Families had given them. It was up to them to forge a new path through a dangerous minefield of intrigue and manipulation.

So he stepped close and shoved his hand under her skirt. With unerring accuracy, he found her entrance and pushed two fingers deep inside. Hot, scalding, a promise of heaven and everything Silviu had ever hoped to achieve in life. Ignoring the insistent pounding on the door, he filled her with his fingers as she went to her toes and clutched his shoulders.

"I will have you, Georgeanne. This is between us and no longer involves anyone else. They can't keep me from you ever again. I won't let them."

He pulled his fingers from her body without regard for the way she staggered back on trembling legs. He didn't dare hold on to her any longer. He licked the taste of her from his knuckles even as he opened the door and caught her father's gaze.

"She's mine," Silviu snarled in the other man's face. "This time, there's nothing you can do to stop me from claiming her." Then he stormed down the hall and away from the woman who was both the greatest pleasure and the sharpest pain of his life.

Chapter Ten

Georgeanne

"I don't appreciate your hovering, children."

Georgie jerked at the breathless, dry sound of Madeleine's whisper, and jumped to her feet. Leaning forward, her hand shot out to grip the old woman's wrist but Georgie forced her fingers to close more gently than the fear running through her demanded. Her grandmother's pulse was weak, but steady.

"We just wanted to check on you. How do you feel?"

The old woman's fingers curled as Christiana approached from the other side of the bed and carefully perched on the edge. Both women had felt the need to look in on the elderly woman who'd raised them, and Georgie was more than grateful for her cousin's company during the bedside vigil.

Madeleine held both her granddaughters' hands. "I am as hale as can be expected under the circumstances."

"You nearly gave Milo a heart attack," Chris said. "He's terrified that he upset you to the point of harm. He thinks that's why the magic reacted the way it did."

"It was a strange feeling." Madeleine's eyes glazed with memory. "But I doubt it was caused by him. Put his mind at rest."

Georgie gave a soft, unamused laugh. "We wish we could, but as none of us have restful minds, we're having trouble helping each other through it."

Madeleine turned a troubled gaze on her youngest granddaughter. "I'm worried for you, child."

"For me? Why?"

Georgie looked her grandmother over. The lines in her face had deepened, the black pools of her eyes had grown darker. She was too pale and her chest rose laboriously. Georgie's stomach twisted into knots, made only more agonizing by the fear mirrored in Christiana's gaze as they exchanged glances.

"Many reasons." Madeleine weakly squeezed her fingers. "I worry that when you marry Silviu and become a Lovasz, you'll have no one to protect you from their men. I worry they will not treat you well, Georgeanne."

An image of her betrothed flashed through Georgie's mind. The unexpected vulnerability he wore only when they were alone, the possessive way he touched her. His promise to care for her, her Family and her heart. His defense of her against his own grandfather and the way he'd filled her with his magic to fight off Graves' dark and destructive spell.

Georgie was learning there were more than just friendly feelings behind his care for her. She was beginning to trust that he might actually love her.

"Silviu will protect me."

Grief swept over Madeleine's features. "You are Bane and I needed to find you a strong husband." Obsidian eyes hardened in her aged face. "I am many things, but never let it be said I do not love my Family. That I do not care for them and use everything at my disposal to see them well settled in the world."

Georgie tamped down the coldness rising in her spine. "You taught me to take care of myself. I am a matriarchal witch and don't need a man to defend me."

"But you do need a strong witch to unlock the potential for your children. And that is another fear I have, a fear of your failure."

Georgie released her grandmother's hand and rose to her feet. Barely aware of what she was doing, she crossed her arms over the sharp pain stabbing her in the chest. "It had been my understanding that any child I bore would inherit all this supposed magic I have locked inside me."

Madeleine's eyes fluttered closed, only to reopen and pin her granddaughter with a predatory glare. "I want my Family to be strong."

"Of course." Acid roiled in Georgie's stomach. "And I'm not strong enough?"

"You are fierce, cunning and diplomatic when your anger doesn't get away from you. You have a generous spirit that calls to other witches and gains their trust. You have many strengths, child, but magic is not on that list."

Georgie pulled a frozen, polite mask over her features. She'd heard all this before—from too many witches to count—and tried to be reasonable about the whole thing, but inadequacy still choked her.

"Silviu is your Magic Match." Madeleine watched Georgie closely. "The bond between two such witches is unpredictable. Hate, love, indifference. The magic plays no part in the development of emotions. Quite the opposite."

Georgie said nothing as she tightened her arms over her chest. She had no idea where her grandmother's thoughts were leading. A glance at her cousin showed a similar confusion on Chris' face.

"What has happened between you and Silviu?" Madeleine asked.

"Nothing." Georgie swallowed against the sudden dryness in her throat. "We're learning how to work together. We haven't even argued in a few days."

Madeleine didn't blink. Ice crawled up Georgie's spine at the change in the woman's tone. "I ordered you to stay out of his bed."

"And I obeyed." Georgie ignored the heat threatening to melt her cheekbones, though she wondered how her face could feel so hot when the rest of her felt close to frostbitten with anxiety.

They'd come close—so close Georgeanne's body held an empty ache deep inside, where she needed to feel her betrothed lodged, hard and hot and heavy. They'd gotten creative, they'd shared pleasure in a variety of ways, but she'd obeyed her grandmother even at the cost of her own sanity, to say nothing of Silviu's. Georgie lifted her chin and met her grandmother's gaze directly, determined to hide her discomfort.

The Christians' Hell would freeze before Georgie admitted how far she'd gone with Silviu. The sun would implode before she admitted to her grandmother how his touch made her burn and yearn for more. She would let her own tongue be ripped from her mouth before she gave voice to the riot in her heart and soul—wanting to trust Silviu completely, but terrified he played a deeper game than she imagined.

"Perhaps you did not obey as strictly as I had expected." Madeleine shuffled on her pillows, struggling to sit up straighter. Georgie did not rush to help her. "What do you think, Christiana?"

Her cousin reared back, mouth working as her eyes went wide. "I don't know. But judging by the way they both act, I believe she's telling the truth. Neither one acts as if they've just been laid."

"Don't be vulgar!" Madeleine' snarled.

"I didn't have sex with him," Georgie told her grandmother bluntly.

"Do stop playing these ridiculous games with me, Georgeanne!" Madeleine's voice snapped with anger, in spite of its fragility. "At the Ngozi wedding, you died. I *felt* you die! Yet Silviu's magic was able to call you back to life."

Georgie's spine would certainly snap if it grew any stiffer. "It was my understanding that a Reap witch would have extra abilities."

"There is a connection between you that should not exist. Matched Magic enhanced by emotions and forged into a bond I only know one way to create. Did you share blood and sex, Georgeanne?"

"We did not." She shook her head. "That was Adam and

Tulah, remember?"

"I don't give a damn about Adam and Tulah." Madeleine waved sharply. "They are not Reap and Bane! Adam cannot bring Tulah back from the brink of death and no amount of blood sharing will ever link those two the way you and Silviu seem to have done."

Gritting her teeth, Georgie sank down onto the chair beside the bed and forced her arms to uncross. "I don't know what to tell you, Grandmother. As you've said, he's a Reap Witch and I am Bane. You and he both claim he is my Magic Match. Perhaps the rules don't apply to us as they do to others because of these things."

Madeleine collapsed back to the pillows, gasping though her glare remained sharp on Georgie's face. "There has never been a Reap witch alive at the same time as a Bane witch. Perhaps you are correct, Georgeanne, but we must figure out this connection quickly."

"Why?"

The old woman was silent long enough to make Georgie fidget. Regret stamped itself on Madeleine's face, smoothing the sagging flesh over her cheekbones. "Where do your loyalties lie, child?"

Offense sliced through Georgeanne and would have brought her to her knees if she hadn't already been seated. As it was, her grandmother's question was like a physical blow, sending a gasp out of Georgie before she could stop it. "After all the things I have done for my Family, *for you*, you would ask that?"

"Who will you choose? Silviu, or the Davenolds?"

Pain trembled along the pathways of Georgie's nerves, making it difficult to think or focus. Nausea closed her throat around a lump of fear. Though unwilling to admit to her feelings for him, Georgie could not imagine life with any man other than Silviu. Would not imagine it.

But neither would she survive without her Family.

She cleared her throat. "Are you suggesting I might have to make that choice?"

The old woman's cheeks lost another ten years of age — a sure sign of her anger. "Would that I had a third granddaughter. One that did not surrender all to a man."

"I have surrendered nothing," Georgie protested.

Madeleine transferred her gaze to Christiana without responding. The ticking of the clock on the wall underscored the tense moments until she said, "You both give too much away. Christiana is too eager to please her husband for fear he'll transfer his attentions to a mistress, and Georgeanne is willing to turn herself inside out to be loved."

"That is unfair." The words brought another wave of physical pain as they gritted through Georgie's teeth.

Chris nodded in agreement. "We are both only striving to find a measure of peace within the relationships *you* have locked us into. You picked our men, and we can't be held responsible for that."

"But you are responsible for the way you deal with them." Madeleine's lips thinned. "Neither of you have shown strength of will against them."

"Silviu and I are constantly engaged in a battle of wills!" Georgie looked over at Chris, recognizing the insulted confusion on her cousin's face as an exact match for her own.

"And Milo is away on business more than he's home with me."

"But neither of you have set your men firmly in their place. You give them too much, you allow them too much."

"Surely you compromised with Grandfather upon occasion." Georgie got back to her feet, looming over her grandmother with her fists pressed to her hips.

"He knew his place! Never would he have spoken to a Family Mother the way your two husbands have spoken to me."

Christiana flinched. "What are you talking about?"

"Each demands you be blooded as heir." Madeleine glared at Georgeanne. "Silviu went so far as to suggest I blood him as my heir."

Georgie rubbed her eyes. "What can you expect from a patriarchal—"

"I am still the Davenold Mother!" Madeleine's magic rose in a rush, strong in spite of the darkness dragging her down. As she'd said, she was still their Mother with all the power of the bloodline at her command. It was just too bad the Davenold magic wasn't enough to win the battle against the spell invading her.

"And I will talk to him," Georgie tried to speak over the old woman's wrath, but she failed.

"I am not yet in my grave and I will choose my heir as I see fit or I will let the magic choose its own! No man will rule my Family so long as I have a say in it. Definitely not a patriarchal son from a Family known for its strain of madness." Madeleine's head swung toward Christiana. "And certainly not a matriarchal man who should know better, and yet came of age in a Family more prone to thug tactics than any other. He knows he has you wrapped around his little finger, that you are vulnerable to his wishes and desires."

Christiana went pale. "I don't want to be Mother. I told him that."

Madeleine's brows flew over her thin, quivering nose. "But he still asked me to make you my heir."

"But we did not." Georgie threw her hands out. "We are content to let you choose, so for you to suggest neither of us is good enough to take the position—"

"Then that's your fault!" Christiana interrupted with a sudden eruption of courage and boldness. Georgie was impressed in spite of herself, unwilling to go so far as her cousin, who was now also on her feet and gesturing wildly.

"You're the one that signed the betrothal agreements," Chris yelled. "You think I wanted another husband? Absolutely not! But I did as I was told so that I would have a child. Did Georgeanne ask to be betrothed to a patriarchal man that scares the daylights out everyone that sees even an ounce of his true power? She was an infant, so I hardly think so."

Georgie cast a nervous glance at her grandmother, and almost fell over at the amused smile curling her lips. A spark of pride glowed in her tired eyes, and remained there no matter which granddaughter she looked at. Georgeanne forcibly pushed through the fog of her confusion, fear and offense to try to discern what her grandmother was really doing.

Madeleine answered the unspoken question. "Suzette wants to be Mother. She should be kept from the position at all costs, no matter what you two have to do. One of you will be chosen by the Davenold magic, I have no doubt of that. What I doubt, is your ability to rule alone, without your spouse unduly influencing you. You must support each other, girls."

Christiana swung on Georgie with a red face and a heaving chest. Her lips were pressed too tight to say a word, but Georgie understood. Still, she had no answer, so she could only shake her head as Madeleine began to speak again.

"Georgie, I do question your loyalty. There is too much between you and Silviu that can't be explained through any other reasoning but that have you fallen in love with him, and perhaps are more loyal to him than to your Family. And such a sentiment has added to the connection you already shared as Matches."

"No..." But the protest died in Georgie's throat because she didn't know if she lied or not. And the look her grandmother sent her way made it clear that a falsehood would not be tolerated.

"It has happened before," Madeleine snapped. "You chose Silviu over your Family and gave yourself into his keeping. I should have broken the betrothal then, knowing you'd been so compromised. I only pray our Family doesn't suffer from your reckless mistake."

Georgie looked away. Everyone believed her surrender to her betrothed so many years ago had been a crime — perhaps of transferred loyalty and disobedience. A crime of a young girl's potential to destroy her Family's hopes and dreams. Georgie had thought so too, until reuniting with Silviu in Poland had caused her to doubt her Family's motives in sending her away.

"And Christiana," Madeleine continued, "you are no politician. I know you would be a loving Mother, organized and fierce. But you can't hope to stand against the leaders of the other covens. So I am at a loss. Perhaps the Davenold magic will have clearer sight than I."

Georgie slowly turned back to her grandmother. "You won't choose an heir?"

"No, I will not blood either of you." Madeleine took a deep breath and rearranged herself on the pillows. "The magic will choose between you or it will find a better host. Either way, the Family will be served."

"You can't be serious." Georgie dropped back onto the chair as her knees gave way.

Her heart seemed to rip into pieces. Georgie wasn't stupid—she understood the improbability of the magic naturally choosing her as its host. She understood the near impossibility of being able to take the Davenold power through the Bane shields. She'd lived with her imperviousness all her life, after all.

But Georgie had also lived with the implied promise of being blooded as the heir. Though she'd never admitted to it, she'd pinned every goal and dream she'd ever held on the expectation that her grandmother would force the Davenold magic to come to Georgie's command.

Something fractured in the deepest parts of her soul, letting pain leak out and infect every muscle in her body.

Madeleine's lips pinched. "With my own mortality pressing down on me, I feel the only decision I can make, is no decision at all."

Chapter Eleven

Milo

Milo walked into the tucked-away sitting room and immediately wished he'd chosen any other spot in the house to make a few private business calls. He tried to force his legs to carry him back out, as well as compel his brain to erase the horrid scene that would, no doubt, be permanently etched onto his retinas. But shock and cold suspicion held him immobile on the threshold.

He was just in time to watch Daniel Levy pull his pale penis from Suzette's mouth and spurt on the woman's lips. Milo's stomach tried to revolt. White streams dripped off Suzette's chin while she writhed on her knees on the floor, her formerly filled mouth pouting now, and whining.

"Daniel! You said when everything was in place you'd give me your child. Aren't we there yet?"

Milo blinked and pressed a hand to his stomach. The couple before him were the farthest thing from sexy he could imagine, with Daniel's softening cock hanging out of his fly and Suzette's neckline pulled below her breasts.

Daniel huffed and rolled his shoulders before tucking his penis behind his zipper. "Not yet, darling. Soon."

Suzette pouted harder. Then her head whipped around, her gaze pinning Milo to the spot. Tremendous heat filled his face until he felt as if the tips of his ears would catch fire. Daniel also whirled, a terrible, inflexible stillness settling over his features.

Nausea crowded his throat, strangling Milo's words. "My apologies, I didn't realize this room was occupied."

He gave a slightly hysterical laugh. "But I suppose I should have, with the crowd that's gathered. There are few places a man can find privacy."

"Might I suggest your bedroom?" Daniel snapped.

The other man's irritation, though perfectly understandable, still rankled. Milo lifted his brow. "Might I suggest the same to you?"

Suzette made an odd purring noise that gained the attention of both men. She smiled as she wiped her face and licked her fingers suggestively. Then she trailed those fingers down her throat, over her collarbone, and circled one naked nipple. "Maybe Milo would like to join the fun?"

Of all the women in the world, Suzette would be last on his list of sexual prospects. Maybe a few places beyond last. Milo knew full well that Christiana's first husband had made use of Suzette's body — the woman had never been shy about throwing that fact into Chris' face. Christiana had even told Milo how she'd caught them together on more than one occasion.

His wife's voice had been filled with such pain during the telling that Suzette had forever been relegated to a repulsive category in Milo's mind that defied description. He'd spent too long working to gain Christiana's trust. Adultery wasn't something Milo tolerated well after his own experiences at being cast in the role of cuckold, but his resistance was even more fortified by his unwillingness to hurt his wife and cause irreparable damage to their fragile relationship.

He couldn't keep the disgust from his face. "There is nothing to enjoy here. Please forgive my intrusion."

Finally Milo's feet unglued themselves from the floor, but Daniel's cold words stopped his retreat. "I do hope you know the advantages of discretion."

Milo cleared his throat. "I have no intention of giving anyone a play-by-play of what I've seen here, if that's what you mean."

Daniel crossed his arms over his chest. "I think you saw

nothing."

Milo dearly wished the other man's statement was true, but it mostly sounded like a threat. He took a deep breath. Considering the behavior of his former Family, Milo had long ago learned not to back down in the face of threats. He certainly wouldn't fold before a patriarchal witch he'd just caught in a compromising situation with a married woman few others tolerated.

Milo gathered his calm and sent it out into the room, hoping the others' emotions would be simple enough to soothe. "As I've said, I have no intentions of discussing the nature of your relationship with Suzette. Beyond that, I'm afraid I can give no promises."

"I suppose that will have to do, considering you're matriarchal." Daniel's impassive mask cracked, allowing a glimmer of rage to show through before he corrected his expression. He was obviously not in the mood to be calmed, but suddenly, neither was Milo.

He took exception to the way the Levy Father spat the word *matriarchal* as if it were something that soiled his mouth. "Yes, I follow the old ways, the traditional ways set forth in a time when our ancestors were strong and united. A time before too many arrogant bastards decided women only held value as a receptacle for their seed and went to war for the right to subjugate them."

"Do you have concerns for your business dealings?" Daniel asked silkily. "I can make your investors very nervous, should rumors of my involvement with Suzette start circulating."

Milo drew himself up as anger heated his blood and pulled his muscles taut. "Be careful of who you're threatening, Daniel. I am a Davenold now, but I come from a Family that would happily murder you in public for an extra helping of butter on their bread. If my association with my own cousins hasn't managed to tar my reputation, what do you think *you* can do? Perhaps you should ask yourself why I've been so successful in business, and take that into account the next time you feel the need to try wielding your false authority over me."

"False authority? I am the Levy Father!"

"And I am matriarchal. You have no influence over me, *Father*." Milo clenched his fists in an effort to keep his voice moderate. His nerves were jangling and his adrenaline pumped steady streams of fire into his blood, but he couldn't back down without losing face. "You want to feel important? Leave this matriarchal household and find hospitality with one of your own covens."

"How dare you speak so rudely?" Suzette got to her feet less than gracefully from her kneeling position. Her words were cold and her features were drawn into immobile lines, but she made no move to cover her breasts as she stomped closer and practically pressed them to Milo's shirt front. "You are just a man in a matriarchal Family. It's not your right to even have an opinion."

In many ways, she was correct and Milo was constantly bringing censure down on his head by sharing thoughts better left unvoiced. He couldn't help himself — if he saw an area to be improved, he offered his opinion. But a deep part of him rebelled at her attempts to put him in his place — mostly because his place was still above her, and always would be unless she became the Davenold Mother.

"I am married to the eldest granddaughter of the primary branch, Suzette. I am currently the second-highest ranking male in the entire coven. You are a daughter of the secondary branch, and until you come into your inheritance, are beneath more women than I can count on my fingers. I have more rights in this Family than you."

Suzette's eyes flashed with rage, Daniel's face reddened and Milo knew things were going too far. He didn't want to fight and he didn't want to delay his departure any longer. He was sick of looking at Suzette's bare breasts, but he couldn't afford to simply leave because their anger might be redirected toward his wife, and Milo couldn't tolerate that.

So he called his magic again. Generally having little need for its full power since becoming a Davenold, he kept it banked, simmering just under his skin with a gentle dispersion that helped everyone find a natural peace. Because of its subtlety, Milo's talent was stronger than most could credit, though occasionally, and specifically in Adam's company, hostile emotions caused Milo to have a great deal of difficulty in controlling his ability, if he didn't lose it altogether.

But now magic flowed through him in a warm rush, rising to his skin and wafting out in a colorless cloud of tranquility. Because of the Levy Father's resilient rage, Milo let his calm grow as he used to do so often amongst his own Family, and willed it to trap Daniel and Suzette in a happy miasma. Using the full force of his talent, Milo knew the exact moment when the couple before him lost their anger. Both of them sagged slightly, their faces losing tension, their spines losing military stiffness.

"What the hell is going on here?" Christiana's sudden entrance to the room startled Milo into losing focus. His magic evaporated enough to wipe the growing smiles off Daniel and Suzette's faces. Milo's heart dropped to his toes as his wife's eyes widened, swept the room, and gained a harsh glimmer of distrust.

Milo jumped back with the cold realization of just how close Suzette stood with her bared breasts. His mouth worked while his brain tried to form a logical retelling of events, but the Davenold bitch beat him to the explanations.

And hers was a bold lie, designed to hurt, as it poured from her pouting lips.

"I'm so sorry, sweetie," Suzette said in a sugared tone. She readjusted her neckline with vulgar shimmy that had her breasts bouncing. "I did try for discretion, *this time*, but Milo is just so scrumptious I guess I forgot to ward the door. Daniel caught us in the act, I'm afraid, so, once again, everyone will know how you were cheated on by your husband."

"No!" Milo shouted. "Not at all!"

His sunken heart nearly shattered at the look on Christiana's face. Milo was sucked into some dark vortex, bouncing between complete shock at Suzette's audacity and utter rage at his wife's willingness to believe her. He clenched his fists and shook his head, trembling under an icy wave of panic as his magic dissipated completely.

"It wasn't me," Milo told his unnaturally still wife.

"Come now," Daniel urged, "you've been caught. There's nothing for it but to own your mistakes and move forward from there. Perhaps you and your wife should discuss this penchant for other women you seem to have."

Milo stabbed a finger toward the Levy Father. "My wife will not believe you. You can threaten all you want, do your damnedest to ruin my business and my marriage, but you will not succeed. Your lies will catch up to you."

In response, Daniel turned to Christiana with a deeply regretful expression Milo would have believed himself, if he hadn't seen the man fucking Suzette's mouth with his own eyes. The Levy Father took Christiana's elbow and steered her out of the room. "I'm so sorry your current husband proved to be as unfaithful as the last, my dear. Please, as I'm sure you're very upset by all of this, let me assist you to your room."

Milo saw red.

Though he'd been frequently irritated and often angry in his life, he was far from the most volatile member of his former Family. He suddenly understood just why so many of his cousins were unreasonably violent. The sight of Daniel's hand on his wife, the false concern on the lying bastard's face and the way he led Christiana away from her husband only served to send Milo's rage into the stratosphere.

He lurched forward, his long legs outpacing Daniel and Christiana in only three steps. With a push against the Levy Father's chest, Milo ripped the man's hand from Chris' elbow and sent him staggering back. Christiana gasped and stiffened, but Milo didn't bother to moderate his emotions for her comfort.

He clamped a hand on her wrist and hauled her away without a word. He stormed down the hall with a pace that barely let his wife keep to her feet, but she never protested. He dragged her past innumerable Davenolds, all too shocked to stop him, all too surprised to help a woman that might possibly be their next Mother. Some distant cousin tore off through the hallway, no doubt searching for stauncher help than any they passed.

Once inside their bedroom, Milo slammed the door and released his wife. She stumbled away, one hand rising to rub her softly rounded belly, the other wiping at her mouth as if she were about to be ill. Panting, she moved around the bed and collapsed into the chair before the window, only to pop back up and pace.

"You will listen to me, Christiana. I was not with that woman. I have never been with her, and never will be with her. I walked in to find *Daniel* with her."

"I can't believe this," she whispered. "I can't fucking believe this."

"Good! Don't believe it. *Believe me.*"

Christiana suddenly stopped pacing and sank back into the chair. Her hands rose to cover her eyes and her shoulders shook, but Milo didn't believe she was crying, in spite of the breath breaking from her lips and the low keening rising in her throat.

He crossed the room in four strides, dropping down in front of her chair and tearing her hands from her eyes. Beneath his fingers, her pulse raced but her wrists and hands were icy cold. He tried to warm them with his own palms and breathed over them as he kissed her knuckles.

"*Krasavitsa*, you will listen to me." He fought through his own pain to find the gentle river of his magic and forced it to rise faster than ever. He willed it toward his wife with little hope that it could cut through the agony shining in her eyes. "We have been married for six months. I have tried to be the very best husband I can, and have done everything in my power to make you happy. I have never lied to you."

Christiana's face crumpled. "She was naked."

"I walked into that room while she on her knees sucking Daniel's dick. It had nothing to do with me."

"Why were you there?"

"I wanted to make a few phone calls."

"No." Chris shook her head hard enough to send her thick hair flying over shoulders. "Why were you *still* there? Why didn't you leave when you saw them?"

The smallest measure of ease infiltrated Milo's spine. If she was asking him a question like that, she was at least willing to entertain the possibility that he was telling the truth. He rubbed her knuckles and pushed more magic at her without the slightest bit of remorse at his manipulation. His marriage was on the line, after all.

"Daniel threatened me. He wanted me to keep his affair with Suzette secret, and he threatened to harm my company if I didn't do as he wanted."

His wife's perfectly arched brows lifted toward her hairline. "You can't be serious."

"I didn't want his anger to spill over to you so I was trying to soothe his fears and his anger."

Christiana pulled her hands from his hold to push against Milo's chest. Reluctantly, he let her escape and she bounded to her feet. She gestured wildly. "Why the hell would Daniel Levy give a damn who knows? For that matter, why would Daniel want to screw Suzette?"

"She said something about having his child."

But as soon as he said those words, Milo knew he'd stepped into the realm of total disbelief. Christiana's eyes widened, her nostrils flared and her porcelain skin flushed scarlet. She clenched her fists against her hips and scoffed.

"Oh, please, Milo, I'm sure. I'm absolutely sure that Daniel Levy, Father of his Family with the obligation of having a Levy child would have that child with Suzette Davenold, potential heir to a matriarchal household."

Milo's head snapped back. "Oh, hell. Maybe that's their plan."

"There is no plan," Chris sneered. "Witches get one child. One. Daniel's not going to waste it on Suzette."

"Maybe he would." Milo slowly rose to his feet. "Unite the Davenolds with the Levys under one leader."

"No witch can hold two houses, and certainly not when those houses are on opposite sides of the Schism." Christiana crossed her arms over her chest. "Why don't you tell me the truth now?"

"I am telling you the truth, *krasavitsa*."

"Come on, Milo, at least tell me why. Why Suzette? Of all the skanks in the world, why pick her? Convenience? Curiosity? Does that fucking bitch have a golden cunt, or something? Why do all my men go after her, huh?"

Milo cranked his magic higher. "I know what your first husband did. You know what my first fiancée did. We talked about this months ago, *krasavitsa*, and swore we'd never seek another. We'd never have affairs, we'd always be faithful."

"Sure, faithful. I don't know what you do on all your damn business trips. I don't know."

"Then you will have to trust me." Milo forced the words through clenched teeth, but tried hard to maintain his calm. His emotions were approaching a flashpoint, and if he didn't get them under control, he'd lose all magical ability. He and his wife would never work this misunderstanding out if that happened. "For six months, Christiana, I have been open to you. Honest and faithful. I beg you now, *trust* me."

Chapter Twelve

Christiana

Why Suzette?

Christiana's brain felt as if it had been set on fire. She was much too hot, there was a ringing in her ears and she could hardly catch her breath. Her stomach knotted and bounced like a yo-yo. And in the face of her anger, her betrayal, her husband stared at her with eyes glittering with rage, yet his voice was calm.

So fucking calm.

He'd courted her for months, slowly and gently until she felt less like a feral animal in his presence and more like a woman. He'd made her feel beautiful and desirable again, and hadn't shown himself in possession of a dark side in the entire six months of their marriage. Every time Milo kept his voice calm in spite of the anger flashing in his beautiful eyes, every time he clenched his fists at his sides rather than let his palm fly out to meet her cheek, she fell under his unique spell a little bit more.

So different from the first one. She struggled to remember that.

But her heart hurt. Staring at him, watching his posture and listening to his voice, no woman would believe he wasn't telling the truth. Christiana couldn't rid herself of the doubt, though. The one thing she clung to was the rage heating his eyes. She wanted to believe with every fiber of her being that a man as angry as she knew her husband to be just then was truly slandered. She just didn't know if she could.

With steps quickened by her determination, she flew back to her husband. But whatever he saw in her face must have filled him with more surprise or fear or suspicion than she could have imagined, because he stumbled back. His calves slammed into the chair in front of the window and he lost his balance, falling down to the cushions.

Perfect. She dropped to her knees between his spread thighs.

Christiana tore at his waistband but Milo grabbed her wrists. "*Krasavitsa?*"

"Open your pants, Milo."

"This means you believe me?"

Clenching her jaw hard enough to rival the pain in her chest, Chris shook her head and worked his fly open. "I want to see you."

She wondered what special charm Suzette wielded to make her desirable to men. Christiana couldn't understand it, but a fierce need to prove herself *more* desirable rose inside her with a burn she couldn't ignore. She needed validation, she needed to force Milo into comparisons and deem Chris the winner of the contest. She needed him to know that she was the better choice so he would never turn to Suzette again.

Christiana peeled the fabric back and worked her husband's underwear down until his dick was on display. She stared at his flesh—his clean flesh, smelling of just Milo and not a rotten whore's pussy. The sight, smell and feel of a used cock was burned into Chris' memories and resurfaced in her nightmares, along with everything her husband had made her do to him after he'd been with another woman, but before he'd bothered to bathe.

Milo's cock was soft and smooth. There was no whiff of realized pleasure—neither his nor a woman's—no sticky residue, no lingering dampness. Chris grasped him in her hand and explored, just to make sure. Milo gripped her wrist and tried to tug her away from his uncooperative penis.

"What are you doing, Christiana?"

She glared at him, her need to be better than Suzette eating her from the inside out. "Why aren't you getting hard for me, Milo? Am I not the one you want?"

He grimaced. "*Krasavitsa*, I just walked in on Daniel pushing his dick into your cousin's mouth. Then he threatened me to keep my silence, and accused me of taking the woman myself. I have no idea what you are doing, or what you want, but I do not think I'm in the mood to have your hands on me, just now."

"No?" Christiana didn't know if she was angry or offended, miserable or sick of being bested by her devious cousin. She only knew she wanted her husband to respond to her touch. "You don't want my hand, but how about my mouth?"

She dove down on him with no preliminaries or finesse. With his body's resistance to her manual stimulation, Christiana was able to take nearly his whole cock in her mouth. Fierce satisfaction roared through her at her husband's yelp of surprise. And the flinch of interest in his length.

Christiana didn't suck dick. She hated it—had hated it since the first time her previous husband had come home with another woman's pleasure still coating his shaft and held Christiana to him as he'd forced himself into her mouth and made her lick him clean. Milo had caught the backlash of that disgust, but he'd never pushed her to pleasure him orally.

But now Christiana dusted off her rusty skills and put them to work. She sucked and stroked and licked in a wild and wanton rush that had always pleased her first husband. She burrowed closer and increased her speed as Milo gasped and his cock began to stiffen. His hands dropped to her hair and she prepared herself for hard fingers holding her too tight, too close, without enough room to catch a breath.

Instead, Milo pulled her away. His wide-eyed gaze crashed into hers. "What the hell are you doing?"

"I'm sucking you off." Chris twisted against his hold but he didn't release her. Neither did he hurt her, though, and she began to calm. But that only brought a deep fear that she'd never measure up, that she couldn't be what a man needed or give him what he wanted. She blinked rapidly to push back the tears that burned her ducts.

"Like that, *krasavitsa*? Where is the pleasure for you?" Milo finally released her hair, and used one finger to stroke her cheek. "You don't have to —"

"I want to!"

Milo sighed and sat back. For a long moment he stared at her while Chris sat still, fear of inadequacy holding her immobile, doubts keeping her back on her heels. She swallowed and blinked, the only movement she dared under her husband's watchful, perpetually hungry gaze.

"If you want to take me in your mouth, Christiana, then do as you will with me. But don't do what you think *I* want because, in this, you are wrong. Do only what *you* want."

"But... But how will you like it?"

Milo's brow lifted. "I will have the mouth of the most beautiful woman I've ever met on my dick. I will like it just fine, *krasavitsa*."

The look in his eyes suggested he meant it. Somewhere deep inside her, Milo's words formed wings and freed her. All thoughts of Suzette fled. All memories of her first husband were temporarily buried. Christiana's doubts and fears paled to insignificance in that moment, and her sole focus narrowed down to Milo and what she wanted to do to him.

Chris reached for Milo slowly, stroking her palms up his expensively clad thighs as she shuffled forward. She let her fingers play over his shaft lightly, glancing up in concern at his clenched teeth, but Milo only smiled. A grim smile, but a smile nonetheless. He didn't grab for her again, but clamped his hands around the arms of the chair and spread his legs wider.

She wrapped her fingers around him and learned his

shape in a way she'd never done before. She learned the texture of his skin, the heat of him as he grew to full life, the places where he was most sensitive. She stroked over the wide crest and watched it darken in need. She looked up to measure her husband's response and watched his eyes darken in hunger.

He overflowed her palm. Her fingers weren't long enough to fully enclose him, but she made up for that lack by smoothing the full length of his cock between both her palms. Milo caught his breath as she slid from base to tip and circled the head. She looked up and he nodded.

"What you want, *krasavitsa*. Fast or slow, so long as it's for you."

She glanced down, looked back up and drowned in Milo's emerald gaze. Holding it, she lowered her head and opened her mouth, licking across the top of his cock. Long, slow licks, letting herself get used to him, to her actions, to her own desires. Trusting him to let her do what she wanted and what she needed, making her own decisions.

She took the first inch into her mouth. Her lips stretched, her tongue ached in the very back of her throat and a surge of raw lust overtook her senses. His taste infiltrated her head — clean, lusty male, Milo's unique essence. Still holding her husband's eyes, Chris sucked and bobbed lower, taking another half inch before pulling back to lick the tip again.

"So pretty, Christiana," Milo groaned raggedly. "Your mouth is so hot, so wet."

She sucked him back in and used her hands over the inches she left behind. Stroking and pulling, rubbing and licking, she worked as much as she was able as her throat tingled and flexed under a force that could only be magic. Before she realized she could, she'd taken another few inches, bending so low that she had to break eye contact.

"So good," Milo said in a rough voice sounding of frayed control. "You feel so good, *krasavitsa*, words can't describe. I love feeling your lips around me, closing tight. And when — *yes* — when you suck me like that."

116

With Milo's encouragement leading her on and making her bolder, Christiana took more, sucked harder, licked longer. Up and down, she worked his cock until a sense of her own sexual power filled her, obliterating half of the memories she'd carried and erasing all of her former distaste. She found new excitement in pleasuring Milo, pulling back to meet his brilliant gaze, letting his words sink into her soul, and allowing his magic to coast over her skin in a way she'd always rejected before.

She wriggled on her knees as heat flooded her system. The lust coursing through her pulsed in her lower belly and tingled through her thighs. She pressed them together, hoping to alleviate the need building between her legs, but it only made the ache in her pussy worse.

She drove down on her husband's cock, sucking him deep, the tip hitting close to the back of her throat. Except for the burning stretch at the corners of her mouth, there was no discomfort. Christiana loved that Milo didn't choke her, loved that he didn't hold her down until she couldn't breathe and take away all her control.

Milo's dirty words swirled around her — encouragements, instructions, pleas — and his hips lifted, though his thighs tensed around her rib cage as if he fought to rise. She sucked him harder, gripped him tighter and moved one hand into his pants to find and fondle his balls. Milo groaned and surged up, filling her mouth in a hard lunge that made Christiana groan in turn.

"Enough, enough, *krasavitsa*." Milo banged his hands against the chair arms, but he didn't pull her away. "Please, Christiana, I want to be buried inside you. I want to feel your silken flesh close around me as you find your pleasure."

She pulled back and licked, squeezed his balls. "In my mouth."

"No," he gasped. "It can't be good for the baby. Please, Chris."

Whether it was good for their baby or not, a fierce pulse in her clit was the only reason Christiana backed off and gave in to her husband's demands. She wanted him to fill her, wanted to feel him thrusting into her, stretching her so wide and making her come around his thick shaft until she was utterly spent. But not before she gave him one last flick with her tongue and teased him with her hands, fingers crawling over every crevice of his flesh from his balls to the very tip of his flushed cock.

"Back up, *krasavitsa*."

Christiana obeyed, even when Milo made a weak gesture for her to lie down on the floor. He practically oozed off the chair to join her on the carpet, his chest heaving and his eyes brighter than she'd ever seen. With shaking fingers, he unbuttoned her pants and pulled them down, giving a quiet huff of laughter as she lifted her hips and he revealed her sheep-covered underwear.

He took them off too, and lowered his mouth to her mound. "Your turn, *krasavitsa*."

His tongue painted a bold stripe through her slit. Chris' legs fell open and she raised her hips, arching into the heat of her husband's caress. He prodded her entrance with the tip of his tongue and slid in with a hot, subtle pressure that broke Christiana completely.

"No, now, Milo. I can't wait any longer. I need to feel you inside me."

But Milo would not be rushed, and with every stroke she felt his care of her. Using lips, tongue and fingers, her husband prepared her thoroughly, playing with her pussy until she writhed beneath him, sucking her clit until she creamed around his thrusting knuckles. Taking her higher until she begged.

Then he scooped her up, held her close to his chest and rolled until his back hit the floor. Christiana was draped over him and he rearranged her legs so that his thick cock pulsed between her folds. As his hold relaxed, she pushed up to look down at him.

He answered her unspoken question. "I won't pound you into the floor."

It was another element to his care of her and made Chris want to open her heart and let him in. Instead, she focused on the feel of him lodged between her legs as she slowly shifted over him. She swiveled her hips and painted his cock with her cream, sliding her sensitized flesh over him.

Christiana planted her knees on the floor and lifted enough to fit her hand between their bodies. She grasped his dick, stroked and squeezed and guided it toward her wet entrance. His tip lodged against the flickering muscle of her opening and Chris paused, letting anticipation build as Milo stared at the place his body met hers.

"Beautiful, *krasavitsa*. Now sink down on my cock so I can feel how tight your pussy is Let me feel how much you need me to fill you."

She did. Denying her urgency, she rolled her spine and took him into her body without hurry. Sliding down her husband's cock in a ruthlessly controlled descent, she tensed her thighs and braced her knees against the floor. In spite of how much she wanted him, Chris kept her pace easy as she rode him, taking a little more of his flesh with every fluid twist of her hips until he was fully lodged within her.

The whole time, Milo watched his dick disappear into her pussy. When he was fully buried, he shuddered and gripped her hips, holding her to him for one long moment that sent Christiana's need past the realms of bearable. Her spine arched and her inner muscles constricted. Then Milo looked up, words tumbling from his mouth.

"So wet for me. So hot. I could drown in you, Christiana. Your pussy is like spun silk, enfolding me in pure fire. You make me lose my mind, you feel so good. Come down here and kiss me."

His hands on her back urged her toward his chest until Christiana complied. She flexed her spine and stretched, reaching for his mouth even as she slid over his cock. And Milo was waiting for her, directing her with a big hand cupping her ass, bucking his hips, lifting his head to find her mouth.

Milo was a great kisser. From the first time their lips had met, Christiana had liked kissing her husband. Deep and sure, his tongue thrust in and took control, leading and guiding as he ravaged her mouth with the greatest of confidence. She fell into his kiss as she always did, and fell in love with him a little bit more.

She rocked on his body, rode his cock and sucked his tongue. An awareness of wielding her own power added to the sensations tingling through her. Chris' clit rubbed Milo's lower abdomen with every shift as she lay on his chest and his hand on her ass pushed her harder into every thrust. They moved together, gaining speed and pleasure as the heat rose in Christiana's veins and set her spine on fire, melting it until she was a supple creature of lust, driving her man into bliss.

Her pussy pulsed and rippled. The muscles at her entrance quivered as Milo's cock scorched her flesh and her inner walls clamped around his shaft, making movement difficult, increasing the pressure and the friction until Christiana felt as if she were about to lose her mind.

Milo grunted and groaned, finally releasing her mouth to snatch a breath and fill her ears with more dirty words. Christiana let them flow through her as her lower body went taut and needy, grasping and sucking, doing its best to drag Milo deeper. Heat blossomed and exploded, surging the full length of Christiana's spine in a toe-curling bolt of electricity.

She arched and screamed, levering herself up with her hands against Milo's chest. She threw her head back as she arched and pumped her hips, grinding against him, bouncing on his dick as her pussy tightened and imploded. For the first time, Christiana screamed her pleasure to the ceiling, and heard Milo grunt in response as he pulled her closer, stiffened and stilled. Heat and magic blasted her senses.

Finally she melted onto his chest and focused on breathing. Milo's hands ran over her back, clumsy but generous. Slowly, his cock softened and slipped from her body, releasing a warm, sticky flood, Christiana couldn't help but be smug about. His cock was coated with her residue now, not Suzette's.

As she came back to herself, she became aware of a furious pounding on the door. The kind of banging that came only after long minutes of more polite knocks. Muffled words came to her, then Adam's voice rose enough to slip past the barrier intent on holding them back.

"Chris! God damn it, Christiana, open this door or I'll break it down!"

Christiana groaned and wriggled, unwilling to move. But Milo poked her and sat up, displacing her from her comfortable position. "You better answer before Adam blows that door to hell."

With another groan, Chris hauled herself to her feet and staggered across the room. She was dripping with Milo's pleasure and refused to put her pants back on, so she crossed her legs and stood behind the door as she cracked it open. Peering around the edge, with only her head and shoulders visible, she blinked at her brother and Tulah.

"Are you okay?" Tulah immediately demanded.

"Yes. Why?'

"Why?" Adam took a threatening step forward. "Thirty different people tracked me down to tell me how Milo dragged you through the halls. What did he do to you?"

Chris lifted her chin and tightened her hold on the doorknob. "He didn't hurt me."

"Are you sure?" Tulah leaned to the side, trying to see farther into the room. Chris inched the door back toward the jamb to prevent her from spying Milo, getting to his feet but not yet adjusting his pants.

Adam narrowed his eyes. "Open the door."

"I'm fine!"

But her brother didn't care. He smashed his palm against the door, tearing the knob from Christiana's grip and throwing it open. Chris stumbled and tried to wrench her shirt's hem down to her knees, though it was only long enough to cover the bare essentials. Milo froze in the act of rebuttoning his pants, eyes narrowing on Adam's face until Chris thought for sure he must be casting a death spell.

Tulah's mouth dropped and her cheeks took on a deep tint of red. "Well, that explains the screaming. Sorry to bother you. Adam just had to check."

"Yeah." Chris closed the door in their faces.

Chapter Thirteen

Silviu

"Good luck, my love."

Georgie rolled her eyes. "This is an informal meeting, Silviu. There are things that need to be organized and planned in the larger Family. I figure, since we're all here, I might as well get some them out of the way."

"While you still have a chance and a fairly clear mind." Silviu snaked his arm around his betrothed's waist and hauled her close. He dipped his head, catching her lips with his own. Soft and gentle, unlike the majority of kisses they'd shared, he took his time tasting her without asking for more. He hoped his caress heated her as much as it did him, and hoped it suggested how much hotter things could get the next time they managed to find a moment alone in the crowded house.

Drawing back, Silviu glanced over Georgie's shoulder. Through the dining room doorway, he saw the Family gathering around the massive table for the meeting he'd been expressly uninvited to. He had to put up the appearance of wanting to join the group so as not to arouse Georgie's suspicions, but Silviu planned to use the opportunity to further his own goals.

"Don't let Suzette get to you. Show strength in front of your Family, not pettiness."

"I've got this covered, thanks." Georgie wriggled from his embrace.

"You're sure you won't need me?"

"We've been over this, Silviu. You're not a Davenold."

With the suspicions he held, her words rankled, and he suddenly wasn't quite ready to let her go. Again Silviu caught Georgie close, surprised when she came without protest or hesitation.

Teasing them both, he pressed a much tamer kiss on her than he would have liked — but what he would have liked required disrobing, and her Family was watching. So he kept his caress shallow and smooth, and didn't demand too much more. Silviu stroked his hands up her torso, stopping just shy of her breasts, his lips quirking against hers as Georgie arched into his touch. He licked the seam of her mouth but pulled back before she could open for him.

It was Georgie who started the next kiss and nearly blew his discretion to hell. She lifted to her toes, her arms sliding up his chest to clutch at his nape. Silviu's control cracked. He pulled her into his arms and spun, putting her back to the wall. He leaned in until he knew his body heated her entire front and he could swear he felt her nipples harden between them. The handful of Davenolds edging past on their way to the meeting faded from his awareness.

Silviu couldn't help but slide his hands down Georgie's back and catch her bottom. And once he'd done that, he couldn't stop himself from rocking her against him, her lower belly brushing his fast-growing cock through their combined layers of clothing.

Lips parted, tongues met and their kiss became a battle for dominance, both determined to win the sensual war raging between them. He met Georgie's thrust with a bold stroke and a fresh surge of need. His magic dangerously close to the surface, Silviu had a hell of a time controlling its force with Georgie pressed against him and sharing such pleasure.

A harsh clearing of a throat saved him from his maddening lust. Just one more lick away from ripping Georgie's blouse off with his teeth, Silviu pulled back from the kiss with mixed feelings. On one hand, he was on fire for his woman, but on the other, she wouldn't thank him for fucking her in the hall.

"We are waiting for you, Georgeanne." Mason Davenold's voice held cold censure.

Silviu opened his eyes to see a torrent of gold illuminating the hallway. Through the glow, he saw Georgie's father standing at his daughter's elbow. Silviu glared at the man, and couldn't help but remember when the Davenold male had caught Silviu in his daughter's bed so many years ago. He wore the same inflexible expression, though the past decade had added lines around his eyes and most of his hair had turned gray. Mason was the highest ranking male in the Family, and made certain to remind Silviu of that fact every time they bumped into each other.

Since he blamed the man for every ounce of pain caused at Georgie's ten-year absence from his life, Silviu tried to avoid her father.

Georgie blushed and stepped out of Silviu's arms. "Sure, Dad."

"Have a good meeting, my love. I will be in my bedroom, if you should feel the need to find me when your gathering is complete." With an admittedly antagonistic smile at her father, Silviu turned on his heel.

A hard hand caught his elbow, stopping him before he could take a step. Georgie's father waited a moment more, ignoring Silviu's raised eyebrow, as Georgie slipped into the dining room. Her voice drifted back to the men, calling the Davenolds to order.

"You watch yourself, Lovasz."

Silviu pulled his arm from the other man's grip. "Or what? She's twenty-three, Mason, and no longer under your control. She's an adult. I've warned you, you can't take her from me again."

Mason did his best to intimidate, but Silviu wasn't a teenager anymore. When his glower didn't work, Georgie's father tried using words. "Madeleine was very clear. You are not to have her until you're married, and if you disobey that command she will blood another as her heir. Georgie can't afford that, Silviu."

"Neither of us can." Silviu held up his hands as he stepped away, then immediately destroyed the illusion of surrender. "But make no mistake, I *will* have her. I will have everything I've set my mind on getting, Mason. That includes Georgie, naked and in my bed."

The other man's face twisted with impotence. "You wait until you have a daughter, and you find her in bed with a boy on the verge of manhood when she's only thirteen. Tell me you'd react differently."

"She's my Magic Match."

Mason pushed his nose into Silviu's face. "She was a child. *My child*. And for your crimes and her naiveté I had to send her away, into a fucking war zone. I put the blame for that at your feet."

"And here I've been putting the blame at Madeleine's. And yours."

Mason drew back and ran a hand through his gray hair. Suddenly, he looked twenty years older, not at all like the enraged papa who'd dragged his daughter out of bed on a long-ago Beltane night. "I think you love her," he said in a much quieter voice.

"I do." Even saying the words sent a shaft of pain through Silviu's chest. Georgeanne was the one thing that was his alone — strong, confident and graceful, everything a man like him could hope for. But beyond that, she was his Match, and he knew her in a way he didn't even know himself, in spite of their decade apart.

"That's the only reason I've been keeping my peace." Mason glared at him. "But you need to toe Madeleine's line or you'll throw away everything my daughter has worked for."

"We both need to be in positions of power to protect ourselves, and the children we'll have. I'm well aware of what's at stake."

"I don't like it."

Silviu blew out a harsh breath, just shy of a frustrated

groan. "Neither do I, but Georgie and I have been nothing more than pawns on a chessboard our entire lives, and fate is stacked against us so that we can't hope to live a normal life. I would love nothing more than to take her away and live by ourselves forever. But there are too many counting on us."

Mason's scowl grew darker. "Liar. You love the politics and intrigues. You were born to manipulate and this is exactly what you want, what you've been bred to do. I worry for my daughter, Silviu."

"Georgie was raised the same way I was."

"That's what worries me. Where does the truth between you begin, where do the manipulations start to cut? I hope, for your sake and for my daughter's, your relationship has a better foundation than any agreement between Madeleine and your father can provide. I truly hope you're not lying about your feelings for her, because you'll break her in a way Madeleine was never able to do."

Mason Davenold didn't give Silviu a chance to answer. He spun toward the dining room and disappeared inside, closing the door firmly. Leaving Silviu with a cold knot in his stomach and a heart full of doubt.

* * * *

"You're late," Ileana accused as he entered his bedroom.

Silviu was hosting his own Family meeting while the Davenolds gathered downstairs. Ileana and Eliasz were seated on his bed, a platter piled high with food between them. They'd been given fair warning that they would be on their own for dinner, though the kitchen had compiled some leftovers for them. Silviu had no idea what, or where, Daniel Levy was eating that night, but he hadn't been invited to either meeting.

He cast a silencing spell over the room. "I was having a discussion with Mason Davenold."

Ileana stopped stuffing chocolate cake in her mouth and

stared at him with round eyes. "You okay?"

"Yes, for once it was a fairly…moderate conversation." Silviu waved a hand and glanced at the computer they'd commandeered from Margaret's office. They'd have to put it back before the Davenolds' meeting concluded or they'd end up answering questions better left unasked.

"We were waiting for you," Eliasz told him, reading Silviu's expression correctly. "You probably still have a few minutes, if you want to grab something to eat."

"I'd rather hear what my brother has to say."

The computer rested on a low table someone had dragged to the foot of the bed. Silviu bent over the keyboard, adjusted the webcam and waited for his brother to appear on screen. A minute's pause brought the three Lovasz offspring together for the first time in nearly two weeks. It was the longest separation between them Silviu could remember in years.

Costel was the oldest brother, the heir and now the new Family Father. Though the Lovasz children were often at odds, the three had found safety in numbers against their grandfather's tyranny and their father's ruthless manipulation. For all Costel's faults—arrogance, haughtiness, pride and pomposity—he was devoted to Family, which proved to be his saving grace.

That, and he'd willingly thrown himself into a fight their grandfather, Alexandru, had provoked, risking his own life to protect Georgeanne's. Since then, Silviu found a greater measure of patience and tolerance for his older brother. Ileana, too, was pleased with Costel, after he'd swiftly approved her betrothal to Eliasz and even sealed the agreement in blood.

Silviu gazed on the face that, even with the pixilation of the old computer, was remarkably similar to his own. Though Costel's features were a little broader and less refined, he shared the same silver eyes as his brother and sister, the same dark hair, the same sharp cheekbones. But where Silviu and Ileana had gained a touch of their departed mother's refinement, Costel looked exactly like what he was — a hardworking farmer.

A rather terrified farmer, at the moment. Silviu frowned. "What's wrong?"

His brother sighed and pulled an impassive mask over his features. Though Silviu knew he'd perfected that look in the face of Alexandru's insanity, it didn't do enough to hide Costel's unease. "I'm at the Council headquarters and I've started on the hundred reams of documents it will take to transfer my seat to you."

"A lot of paperwork hasn't put that look in your eyes." Silviu leaned forward. "What happened?"

Costel pursed his lips. "Bijoux Laurent is here."

"Ah," Eliasz groaned. "I forgot about her."

Ileana put a hand on Silviu's shoulder and pulled him back so she could look at her older brother too. "Who is Bijoux Laurent?"

Costel's eyes rolled skyward. "A pampered princess. Her father is Emeric Laurent, first and favorite cousin to the Family Father, Cyril. Emeric is the Council Administrator."

"He's my mother's cousin too," Eliasz stated.

"Surely you knew Bijoux would be there, Costel," Silviu said as evenly as possible. Not even a minute into their conversation and already his brother was irritating him. "It's her house, after all."

Ileana shot him a sideways glance. "What?"

Costel explained. "The Council used to be hosted by Families, each primary branch given their turn, rotating between patriarchal and matriarchal covens. Needless to say, that caused a few problems, so in the late Middle Ages a permanent palace was built to house the Council."

"No one noticed a palace built and occupied by witches during a time of witch hunts?" Ileana glared between Silviu and the computer screen.

Eliasz stretched over their dinner platter to stroke her shoulder. His Family, in particular, had been hit hard by the European witch hunts, and terrible tales were still told by the grandparents of his branch. "Magic was our best defense against those who would hurt us."

"That was the time of large landholders ruling over their demesne from newly renovated castles." Silviu shrugged. "The Council palace isn't anywhere near as grand as a royal residence, but the architecture is quite nice in the photos I've seen."

"The Families now take turns providing the person who runs it all," Costel added. "Every generation, a new Administrator is chosen from among the covens, rotating between Matriarchal and Patriarchal houses. Laurent's held the position for decades."

"I thought the High Seat ran it all." Ileana ran a hand through her hair. "I don't like not knowing this. How did I not know this?"

Again, Silviu shrugged. "There was no reason for you to be taught the ins and outs of how the Council works."

"You're just a female," Costel told her.

Ileana narrowed her eyes, but didn't lose her temper. "What does the Administrator do?"

"Everything," Costel groaned. "The Administrator lives at Council headquarters full-time, taking care of all the paperwork, filing all the necessary documents concerning Council issues as well as Family issues, like births, deaths, betrothals and marriages."

She reared back and reached for Eliasz. "Since when does the Council have to approve marriages?"

"They don't, they just file the paperwork." Costel pinched the bridge of his nose. "This is all beside the point."

Silviu leaned forward and glared into the webcam. "What *is* the point?"

Costel's chin jerked higher. "Have you ever met Bijoux Laurent?"

"No, but I know that she has such a complete dislike for politics that she refuses to even remain at the palace while the Council meets. Why concern yourself with her?"

"Madeleine banishes her from the palace when the Council

is in session, or whenever Madeleine is in residence." Costel closed his eyes. "Bijoux stays in a cottage at the edge of the property, but she's here now and I don't know what to do."

"Oh, hell," Eliasz whispered.

"What are you talking about?" Ileana demanded.

Silviu almost flinched as Costel's eyes snapped open. The emotion churning in the silver depths seemed to pierce straight through the computer screen. "Bijoux is telepathic, Silviu."

"Telepathy is a deceptive talent," Silviu said, slowly enough that Costel's face took on an expression of grave offense. "Unpredictable at best, considering the witches who wield it can't distinguish fact from fiction in another's thoughts. This is nothing to be alarmed at."

"She's uncannily accurate, not like other intrusive talents," Costel snapped. "I'm only a little ashamed to admit she scares the hell out of me. I'm terrified of what she'll see in my head, of what she'll learn."

Silviu took a deep breath and risked a glance at Eliasz. Hearing rumors on the breeze, as his future brother-in-law did, was considered mildly intrusive. Any word spoken was — theoretically — accessible to Eliasz's knowing, but his talent was unreliable. Silviu would even describe it as downright faulty, at times.

He turned back to the computer. "You have proof of her accuracy?"

"Unfortunately." Costel ran a hand through his hair. "I don't even know what I know of importance, but I am sick unto death of this Family tearing itself apart and would do a great deal to keep the peace between us, Silviu. I don't know if I can hold your secrets safe from her."

Silviu cursed. In Poland, he'd had to show his hand and use his enormous strength to dethrone Alexandru. Costel had been there and had received the Lovasz magic Silviu had forced from their grandfather. The dilemma was clear — Costel was afraid Bijoux would learn information that could cause the Lovasz Family a great deal of trouble.

Silviu grimaced. "Can you avoid her?"

"I've been here for three hours and already ran into her four times." Costel released a long-held breath. "As usual, she's searching me out."

"As usual?"

Costel's brows lowered. "It's the same every time I come here. She's a thorn in my side."

"Maybe she's interested in you," Ileana suggested. "You're handsome, young and a new Father. That combination doesn't come along every day."

Sheer horror stole over Costel's face. "I know what she wants, Ileana, but her father would mount my balls to the gate if I so much as smiled at Bijoux. He's extremely protective, doesn't even let her leave the property. Unfortunately, I am often the only male she gets to see."

"Why?" Ileana asked.

"I have a habit of coming early to the meetings to… prepare."

Silviu watched his brother fidget. Costel wasn't as politically astute as either Silviu or even Ileana, so it was no hardship to imagine him poring over an upcoming agenda in advance. As the Lovasz coven representative, he would need ample time to study an issue before he could make a suitable decision.

"I'm surprised you've even been allowed to meet her," Eliasz snorted. "Bijoux's father is convinced some man will take one look at his daughter, fall madly in lust and ravish her."

Ileana's mouth dropped. "Is she pretty then?"

"She's beautiful," Costel breathed.

Surprised at the vehemence his brother voiced, Silviu stared into the webcam for a long moment as the wheels in his mind started turning faster. "Costel, perhaps you *should* seduce Bijoux Laurent. The best way to keep our secrets to ourselves in the company of a telepathic witch, is to think of something else. So think of Bijoux, undressed and waiting for your pleasure."

Costel's mouth worked for a minute. His entire body shuddered. "You have no idea what you ask of me."

"It may not be much longer before the Council is called to session." Silviu looked away as he swallowed against the lump in his throat that made those words surprisingly hard to say. In spite of his current anger with Madeleine, she occupied a special place in his heart. The tutors she'd sent had done more to brighten his grim childhood than anything his own Family had done, and he knew they'd done it at her request.

"Father told me. I'll complete the paperwork as quickly as I'm able." The new Lovasz Father then transferred his gaze to Eliasz. "And congratulations."

"For what?"

"Isn't Daniel giving you the Levy seat?"

Eliasz's brows flew upward. "Not to my knowledge. Why?"

"Bijoux said he filed a lot of paperwork here at the Council. I just assumed he'd nominated you to the newly vacant seat."

"He was strongly considering it, but hasn't yet said anything to me." Eliasz frowned.

Silviu's suspicions of Daniel wanting the High Seat in conjunction with filed documents at the Council Palace had him sitting straighter. Suddenly, his farfetched theory seemed eminently plausible. And not only that, but it provided a decent reason why Graves would have thrown his lot in with Daniel enough to marry Constance, though he was in love with her father. He wondered how, or even if, Suzette fit into the picture his imagination was creating.

"Perhaps," Silviu finally drawled, "you should find out, Eliasz. Why don't you and Ileana join Costel at the Council Palace?"

Chapter Fourteen

Georgeanne

Beyond Georgie's bedroom door, the house had grown quiet for the night, though the hour was earlier than it usually was when everyone settled down. Most nights, distant conversations could still be heard past midnight, and even after a hush spread over the estate, Georgie occasionally heard her father's footsteps patrolling the hall outside her room. She tried not to let his distrust upset her.

He had good reason to doubt her, after all. A fact which was hammered home with a soft whisper of her door opening just enough to let Silviu slip through.

"No guard tonight, my love?"

She shook her head. "What are you doing here?"

Silviu's grin widened into a predatory expression. Full of sharp edges and lustful intent, it was a look guaranteed to make any woman weak in the knees. Georgie snatched a discreet breath and tried to find the words to send him on his way.

But then Silviu stepped toward her, wrapped his arms around her waist and hauled her to his chest so fast her feet came out of her shoes. And he felt good against her. Solid and stable, safe in a time of too much fear and change.

Holding her in his arms, he stepped toward Georgie's bed, put his lips to hers and whispered, "Let me love you."

She had a hundred reasons to refuse, but Georgie didn't feel like fighting him. It was all too much — her grandmother, Suzette, dark magic. And that was on top of the longest two weeks of her life and the sensual promise left unfulfilled when she and Silviu had been interrupted by her parents in the estate office.

She needed him and she wanted him, so she kissed him.

Soft and decadent, unlike almost every other kiss they'd shared. Tender in its way, as Georgie slid her tongue past Silviu's lips. He met her with more serenity than he ever showed before as all dominance games were put aside, and they took the opportunity to be two normal people eager to stoke the passion igniting between them.

Silviu groaned and met her thrusts, gently taking the lead in a sensuous waltz that danced them both deeper into their desire. Yet he remained unhurried, and Georgie knew it was because he'd gotten everything he'd wanted just then — her surrender and all night to enjoy it.

His tongue was bold against hers, but teased her into sharing in her downfall, his lips soft against hers, encouraging her to nip and brush and press close. She fell into him and took Silviu into her when he followed her down.

He laid her on the bed and climbed up next to her. She rested on her back, her head on the lower edge of her pillows as he bent over her and kissed her again. Slow and brief, it still conveyed enough promise that both knew how they would end this night.

Silviu pulled back and brushed his lips over her nose. "I love you, Georgie. I will take very good care of you."

A promise she hadn't expected, but filled her chest with warmth nonetheless. He stared down at her with the vulnerable expression he only wore with her, with heat in his eyes and a curious softness. As if she were precious, as if she were something he would die for because he couldn't live without her.

A deep sentiment, an unasked question. The potentially catastrophic ramifications couldn't compete with the look in Silviu's eyes. Georgie nodded her answer, unable to speak past the sudden tightness of her throat. Knowing her eyes were too wide, she met his gaze and nodded again. He smiled and sat back on his heels.

He brushed her curls off her face before he let his hands drift lower. He traced the curve of her jaw, her neck and her shoulders. His hands wrapped around her arms and followed them down, linking his fingers with hers and giving them a brief squeeze before letting them go. Then he reached for her shirt buttons.

One by one, he released them and Georgie's shirt slid open. Silviu pushed his hand under her back, urging her to sit up so he could pull the material from her body. His hammered-steel gaze focused on the swell of her breasts as they rose from the pink lace cups of her bra and he licked his lips. Then he licked her.

She arched back until his bracing palm burning into her spine was all that kept her from collapsing to the mattress. Silviu placed a kiss on each mound before tucking his face into the curve of her throat.

"You're so beautiful, Georgie, and I need you so much."

She wasn't the only one left unfulfilled over the past few days of constant monitoring. All the Davenolds had seemed delighted to occupy her time so that she hardly had a minute alone with Silviu except in the office that morning. With his magic bubbling up inside her soul, Georgie could feel Silviu fighting to hold on to his control and make this moment special for them.

His magic rose and infiltrated her defenses from within. A Trojan horse Georgie couldn't find enough wits to examine in that moment. She could feel Silviu's urgency catapulting through her veins, his adrenaline heating her blood and his lust pouring into her belly. She was on fire, nervous but eager, and ready to take the next step.

She unhooked her bra and tossed it away, uncaring of where it landed. Then she curled her fingers in Silviu's hair and dragged his face back to her chest, urging his lips closer to her peaked nipple and arching so he couldn't miss her unspoken command. With a groan, he sucked her into his mouth.

Hot, wet *perfect* suction and the zing of fast-rising magic pulled her spine taut. Silver light flared and almost immediately morphed into gold. Ribbons of sensation twined through her body, wrapped her muscles and pulled tight. Silviu's lips worked her nipple, licking and lapping, dragging the edge of his teeth over her, swiping her flesh with his tongue until Georgie was sure she'd lose her mind. Then he turned his attention to its twin.

"Oh, God, Silver, please." Georgie lifted against him using her handhold in his hair. "Please give me more. Give me magic."

"Reach for it, Georgie. My magic is yours, available any time you want it."

She reached as he sucked her nipple. She followed her senses down into a cool darkness, pushing past the familiar Bane blocks to find the golden thread linking her to Silviu. She grabbed for it as he licked her breasts, mounded them and fondled, squeezing, kneading and building her passion ever higher. Heat exploded inside her as her lust was magnified by his.

She squirmed under the onslaught, melting and wanting more. Every time he filled her with magic she understood why he was so adamant about their connection, and with his Reap strength loading her up like a vessel created specifically to house his overflow, she didn't know if she'd ever be able to deny him again. This was what she'd been born for and trained for—to be his Match in every way, to let him fill her.

She'd been born for him to love.

Silviu trailed light kisses down her ribs, following his rough hands as they created formless patterns and swirled across her skin. His touch was hard and almost impatient, yet his fight to remain slow was easily observed and shot a hot lick of lust through Georgie's core. Her abdominal muscles rippled and flexed, following his touch attentively as golden streaks lit the room around them. Silviu moved over her and Georgie's legs became restless as a new wave of anticipation lifted her hips off the mattress.

He met her eyes as he unfastened her trousers, but looked down to watch as he revealed her delicate pink panties. A flush spread across his cheekbones and his breath hitched. "You're mine tonight, love. Forever mine."

"Get your clothes off," she whispered. Begged. She braced her weight against her elbow as she rose off the mattress and reached for his shirt. Silviu unbuttoned the top three buttons before impatiently hauling the fabric off over his head.

Georgie put her hand to his chest and soaked in the feel of hot, hard muscles dusted with dark hair angling down into his pants in wicked temptation. She followed the lines of his body and appreciated the fact that he was hers.

"Lift your hips, love."

She did as she was told and Silviu pulled her pants off, flinging them over his shoulder. He bent to press a kiss to the center of the pink lace still covering her before curving his fingers under the material and pulling them down too. Slowly, like its own caress, he dragged the lace down her thighs and over her calves, finally whipping them over her toes.

A gentle kiss just above her curls was immediately followed by a blazing lick over her clit. Georgie gasped and fell back to the mattress, pressing her shoulders hard to the bed as she lifted toward Silviu's mouth. His hands caught her hips and pushed her back down, his fingers making tiny circles that sent sensation sliding through nerves she never considered important before Silviu taught her how wrong she was.

Again he pulled back, but his eyes were locked on her sex. He licked his lips and tore at the button of his trousers. "You taste so good, love."

"Taste some more," she panted. "I want your mouth on me."

The heat in his eyes burned her, but he turned away — only long enough to toe off his shoes and shed the rest of his clothes. Then he returned, smoothing his hands up her thighs with a gentle pressure that had her spreading them farther, letting him make room for himself.

He knelt between her legs and Georgie tried to memorize everything about the way he looked. His hungry gaze, the muscle jumping in his jaw, the rigidity of his broad shoulders and the flinching of his abdominal muscles. Her eyes tracked lower and her belly jolted at the sight of his flushed cock, hard and long and ready for her.

Her attention was redirected as Silviu dropped down and licked through her folds. Warm and wet, his talented tongue had learned enough about her to know exactly where she needed his touch the most. Slicking up her slit, he circled her clit with a hard stroke, flicking it until the little peak felt twice its normal size and hot enough to burn his mouth. Georgie drove her fingers into his hair to hold him there, but he pulled against her grip until his tongue slipped down low, sliding against nerves humming in need.

She writhed and arched, spreading her legs until the tendons within them ached. Georgie planted one foot on the mattress and lifted, riding Silviu's tongue as he stroked over her entrance and pushed inside.

Soft pressure and unbearable heat invaded her body, magic tingled over her skin. She felt Silviu's groan against her flesh. Three thrusts of his tongue brought her close to the edge, her breathing broken, moans exploding from her mouth as she wriggled and fought to get closer.

Silviu trailed nipping kisses up her folds until he returned to her clit. He opened his mouth on her and sucked her in. His fingers teased her entrance and slid deep, stroking slowly, curling gently until the sensory memory of his tongue pushing inside her was replaced with the delicious rasping of his knuckles against her inner walls. His magic roared in her ears.

Mouth, fingers and magic — Silviu brought every sensual weapon at his disposal to bear against her vulnerable, aching flesh. He stretched her, working her pussy with dazzling finesse without ever breaking the concentration directed toward her clit. Heat grew and spread between her legs until Georgie felt her own cream sliding down her folds, adding to the sensations Silviu's mouth poured over her.

She was perched on the edge of climax when he released her from the exquisite torture. Lifting back to his knees, Silviu stared between her legs as he panted and licked his damp lips. His fingers, wet with her honey, left her body to curl around his cock and stroke, his expression tightening as if he could already feel her pussy enclosing him.

"I want to remember you just like this, Georgie. Spread out for me, needing, wanting. Creamy with the pleasure I give you."

His rasping words tugged on her spine. Watching him touch himself, watching his big hand slide up and down his shaft and spreading her honey over his flesh, Georgie almost came. A fierce shudder went through her, all her nerves sparking and jangling, the magic coasting over her brightening until golden flares seared the inside of her eyelids when she closed them.

Then she raised her lashes and pushed up, mouth watering to taste him as he'd tasted her. She sat up awkwardly and ran her hands over his chest, trailing her fingers through the dusting of hair, tracing the sensual line at his hip directing her toward his hard cock. Silviu's hand fell away as Georgie took hold of his heavy shaft.

His whole body jerked and she gripped him tighter, sliding to his tip, just the way he'd taught her to do. She ran her thumb over the weeping crest and said, "I want to play too. I'm tired of being passive tonight."

A broken laugh shot from Silviu's mouth. "I don't know if I can handle you being active right now, love. Not being so close to what I need, with you giving me what I want."

With one hand on his cock and the other on his chest, Georgie pushed him, giving him no other choice but to roll over and lie down on his back. She swung a knee over his legs and straddled his calves, still squeezing and stroking his dick. Her excitement heightened, slicing through her spine until it was all she could do to remain even partially upright.

"That's too bad," she breathed over the tip of his cock as she lowered toward him, "because I will be an active participant, or no participant at all. Don't you want me to participate, Silver?"

She licked his cock, base to tip with a single stroke of her tongue. Flattening it on his flesh, dragging it up, flicking just the tip over the little slit gracing the center of his crest. She rolled her eyes up to meet his and watched his silver gaze turned to molten mercury.

His fingers caught the curls bobbing around her jaw. "*Yes*. Yes, I want you with me."

"Grit your teeth and stay strong, Silviu." She licked the flushed head. "Just for a little while longer."

She opened her mouth and swallowed his length in a slow slide that didn't stop until he bumped her throat. He'd taught her that, too. Georgie relaxed her jaw and tightened her lips, pulling up as slowly as she could while his groans filled her ears. As soon as the depth was more comfortable, she sucked—hard then soft, working her tongue over as much of him as she could while her hand wrapped his base and squeezed.

Then she went wild as Silviu's need, desire and imagination infiltrated her own on a hot tide of gold magic. As if they were her thoughts, wicked images filled her mind and she acted on them without hesitation. She drove down on him, taking more than she had before and holding still—though her hands were busy on his shaft and balls, kneading and fondling, gently tugging and roughly stroking. Only her need for air forced her head back. She bobbed over him, sucking and licking, treating his wide crest like her favorite candy, savoring him.

Silviu's fingers turned to granite around her scalp. Georgie kept her eyes on his face as she pleasured him, loving the way his nostrils flared and his eyes widened and narrowed in a repeating pattern of vulnerability. His chest heaved and his muscles knotted as a flush spread over his skin. She loved the power he handed to her when she took his cock in her mouth, loved that she could reduce such a reserved, controlled man to such a helpless mass of writhing pleasure. He gave it to her — she knew — and she took advantage for as long as he let her.

But he was at the edge and pulled her mouth away all too soon. She felt his hunger growl in her own body. Needing him, needing so much more, Georgie shuffled forward until his cock was a hot presence just an inch away from where she needed him most. She could hardly catch her breath as excitement and nervousness swept through her.

Everything was about to change.

Silviu grabbed her hips. His thumbs skimmed the inner crease of her thighs as they descended to pull her folds back and reveal her to his sight. She stilled and let him look, watching the lust in his eyes increase to impossible degrees. She swore she felt his heart kicking against her ribs.

"All my life," he said in a dark, deep voice, "you've been the only thing that was mine. The only thing I ever really wanted. The moment I met you, Georgie, my whole world changed."

His thumbs shifted and pulled her folds farther apart. She felt exposed in a new way, a thrilling way. The sensation snuck into the deepest parts of her, making her feel daring and wicked, but also emphasizing the level of her sharing. She was giving him her body, and they both knew it.

Georgie levered her full weight up to her knees and directed Silviu's cock to her entrance. She smoothed the wide tip between her spread folds and fought to keep her eyes open, so she could watch Silviu's face as he watched her take him in. She snatched a shaky breath as he lodged against her wet opening and her muscles flickered around him.

Nervousness held her still regardless of her body's

clamoring for his entry. Her pussy flexed deep inside, needing him to fill her, demanding it. Her cream slid down his shaft, coating her own fingers as she held him to her and tried to gather herself mentally. He didn't rush her, in spite of the tension infusing his features, the muscles bulging in his arms or the tightness of his hands at her hips. He fought for breath and bit his lip, watching and waiting, giving her the power in this, too.

Georgie pressed down and stopped just as his crest stretched the ring of muscle guarding her depths. There was the briefest flare of discomfort—not pain, but unexpected enough to make her pause.

"Readjust the angle, love," he reassured her in a strangled voice. "Shift a little."

The fit felt too tight as he was, but she trusted him. Georgie shuffled forward and the discomfort disappeared. Her fingers tightened on his shaft and she pressed down again.

Though she stretched and burned, her descent was easy. Still, she only took a fraction of an inch, not even the whole crest, before she paused for another breath. Her pussy protested her delay with a violent pang that jolted her whole body and drove another half inch of his cock into her.

"Slide down on me, Georgie." Silviu's voice sounded like rocks being crushed into gravel. "Take me in. You were born to take me, Georgie, my love."

"I want to appreciate this, to *feel* it."

A frantic knock rattled the door in its frame. "*Georgeanne*! We have an emergency."

Her head whipped around. Silviu cursed vilely. "Don't fucking answer that."

"It's Aunt Lydia, Madeleine's eldest daughter."

"Georgeanne, please! Madeleine—" The voice on the other side of the door broke. "Mother is dying, Georgeanne. You have to come immediately. We need your help!"

Chapter Fifteen

Milo

"Call me as soon as you learn anything, no matter the time."

It was late enough that Milo's eyes were gritty with lack of sleep when he ended his call. Suspicions snarled through his mind, so he'd outlined his questions to his lawyer and put him on the case. Milo didn't care that his contacts lived in different time zones. He wanted answers and his conscience wasn't bothered by the thought that many would be woken up, and others would be prevented from getting any sleep at all.

Chris had warded their bedroom after her brother had interrupted their afterglow, making their space one of the most private in the house. Milo hadn't left the room in over an hour. Christiana hadn't come in

He went in search of his wife and found her in the library with her twin. Adam's voice was a soft hush coming from the far end of the room, where they huddled together at a small table piled with books. Their dark heads were nearly pressed together, both of them standing with their backs to Milo, who paused on the threshold.

"There is no guarantee this spell will work, Chris."

Milo thought Adam was referring to another spell to find the source of the magic harming Madeleine. His tongue burned with a denial, the vision of so much raw magic racing past his wife in metallic-hued streamers fresh in his memory and permanently etched into his growing list of fears. With the Lovaszes adding their strength to the twins,

Milo had been terrified his pregnant wife would be injured, and refused to allow her to cast another.

But Adam's next words poured into Milo's worries and channeled them into new territories. "You're trying to repel magic and this thing is all garbled. It would be safer to let the Davenold power choose, and if it chooses you, maybe we can find a spell to pass it on, instead."

Chris shook her head firmly. "I don't want it at all! I don't want the power to come to me. I don't want to pass it on. Let Georgie and Suzette fight over it."

"I'd rather you not give Suzette the opportunity, considering she might have had a hand in Grandmother's illness."

"As much as I would love to lay that crime at her feet, we've been investigating her involvement all day and have found nothing. But, if Suzette *is* responsible, I don't want to be the next target."

"I'm just afraid this particular spell could hurt you," Adam said. "You're pregnant, and you know as well as I do that makes these results a little less predictable."

"The baby won't be hurt. Less predictable doesn't mean harmful."

"The spell could rebound—"

"It's not going to rebound, Adam." Chris propped her fists on her hips. "This may be the best time to do such a complicated spell, anyway. While I'm pregnant, whatever magic the baby has is added to mine."

"But this spell could weaken the baby's magic, too. You are trying to repel the Davenold power, which means weakening your own to the point that you have no hope of inheriting."

"It's not like it's permanent," Christiana scoffed.

Adam drove his fingers through his hair. "But you don't know what the results could be! That's the meaning of unpredictable."

"It's a chance I have to take. Madeleine isn't blooding an heir, Adam." Even from across the room, Milo saw his wife's jaw clench as she spoke. "I can't risk the magic coming to me."

Milo had heard enough. "What the hell are you two talking about?"

Christiana flinched as if he'd slapped her. Her face lost all hint of color and her eyes widened. She moved her lips and Milo could *see* a lie rising to them, but her brother spoke before she could.

"None of your business, Ivanov." Adam turned and pinned him with a death stare.

Milo was offended and angered on too many levels to count. Between his exhaustion and the hostility Adam had already provoked between them, Milo couldn't hold on to his calm.

"Anything concerning my wife, and especially my child, is my business." He crossed the library in a furious rush, his long legs eating the distance. "What spell are you trying to cast, Christiana?"

"It's nothing." Her shoulder rose, and she made an obvious effort to paste a nonchalant expression on her face, but she failed to hide her sudden tension.

"Don't lie to me when our child's health might be compromised."

"Don't be dramatic." Chris crossed her arms over her chest. "Either of you. This is a simple temporary binding spell and won't affect the baby at all."

Milo was surprised his heart didn't stop. He didn't know as much about spell casting as his wife, but every witch knew the dangers of binding. It weakened a witch, limited their magic and left them vulnerable to attack.

His wife had blatantly lied to him, as if she thought Milo were stupid. As Adam had pointed out, a binding spell could affect a babe in utero. The baby would be weakened as its mother was, but more than that, Christiana would be vulnerable to attack and unable to protect the life she sheltered.

"I won't let you do that," Milo told her in a strangled

voice.

"It's not your call," Adam replied.

Milo turned on him with all of the fear-filled wrath he couldn't expend on his wife. "*Stay the fuck out of it, Davenold.* She's *my* wife, she carries *my* child. Madeleine is dying and if Christiana is weakened she'll fall under Suzette's magic."

"That's the point, Milo!" Christiana threw her hands up. "I don't want to be Mother. A temporary binding will decrease my magic so that the Davenold power won't even consider me to be an option."

"Have you lost your mind?" Milo stared at his wife in horror. "What if temporary for you means permanent for our child? Have you thought of how you would handle having a Bane-made offspring?"

Christiana's chin jerked up. "The Davenolds are well versed in dealing with Bane witches."

"Can you live with yourself if that comes to pass?" Milo made a sharp gesture with his hand. "Won't the guilt of your crime eat you alive?"

"No." Chris' throat worked. "I won't feel guilty because I would have done what I had to do. Sometimes, hard decisions must be made for the best—"

"Whose best? Suzette is certainly not the best choice for this Family, and Georgeanne doesn't stand a chance of inheriting naturally."

"You're wrong, Milo. She will be Mother."

He gritted his teeth and gripped his hair. "This isn't going to work."

"How would you know?" Adam challenged. "You don't know a damned thing about spells. Your talent's as useless as—"

"It *could* work," Christiana spoke over her brother. "I agree that I can't fight a challenge pregnant. We only get one shot at being parents and I won't risk losing our child, Milo. But I can avoid even the possibility of inheriting by casting a spell to put me out of the running altogether."

"Chris, I can't let you—" Milo shook his head, but it didn't dislodge the ringing in his ears or the hazy shock filling his skull.

"If I don't inherit, Suzette has no reason to challenge me."

"What the hell do you know about transferring power anyway, Ivanov?" Adam demanded.

"More than you'll ever understand." Milo put his hands to his head. "Just talk to your grandmother, Christiana. If she bloods you as her heir then the Davenold magic will have more to hold on to. You'll be safe from challenges."

"I don't want to be her heir!" Christiana gestured wildly. "I don't want to be Mother."

Milo's temper snapped. "But you will be! Georgeanne cannot take the power as a Bane witch and no matter how many binding spells you cast, you will still be stronger than Suzette."

"But there are others! Cousins—"

"Christiana! You are the eldest granddaughter of the primary branch and have known your Magic Match since before you were born. Inheritance is weighted in your favor. The Davenold power will come to you whether you want it or not!"

"You're not listening to me, Milo!"

"*You're not making any fucking sense!*"

Milo's heart beat too fast to let him catch his breath. Horrible visions rolled through his mind, taunting him with images of Christiana falling under Suzette's attack. While he knew his wife could win a magical battle even at half strength, he worried for their baby. And if Chris lost their child, he had no way of predicting what would happen to them, as a couple.

She was almost four months pregnant and anything could go wrong. Since she'd discovered she was with child, her attitude toward him had softened the smallest amount. Milo held hope that their child would build a bridge between them and help usher them into a bright, loving future.

If she miscarried, it would break them both in ways Milo couldn't bear to contemplate.

"I am doing this, Milo. This is my choice."

His throat became a desert it was nearly impossible to push words through. "And I don't get a say? I don't get to help you decide things that could impact our lives to such a degree?"

Her brows lowered and her eyes glittered. "You have no say. I've heard it all before, Milo. You want to be High Male, you want to wield your power over everyone else, you—"

"*Don't* put words in my mouth!" he screamed.

Adam got in his face before he could continue. "Don't fucking take that tone with my sister."

He ignored his brother-in-law, pushing him to the side so Milo could see his wife. "Don't pin false ambitions on me just because every other man you've ever known would give their left eye for such a thing. You really think I want that? After all this time, after all I've done, you really think I just want more power?"

"I don't know what you want." Her tone matched his in strength and volume. "All I know is that the minute you got here and saw how sick Grandmother is, you've pushed me to be blooded as her heir. I don't want it. You're the one who wants it."

"I want you *safe*, Christiana. The only way to make you safe is to get Madeleine to—"

"Stop!" she commanded. "My mind is made up. It doesn't matter if you like it or not, because your vote doesn't count."

Without thought, Milo made to grab his wife. He didn't intend on hurting her, he just wanted to touch her, as if a physical connection could help her see reason. Or maybe help him figure out what her reasoning was. He was confused, terrified and desperate.

But Christiana flinched back with a gasp, arms rising defensively as if preparing to block a blow. Adam slid in front of his twin faster than Milo's sluggish mind could process. A cold wave of magic penetrated Milo's fearful haze, leaving him even more confused and beyond offended at the response of the twins he faced.

"Touch her and we'll kill you." Adam spoke as if he meant it. Anticipated it.

Milo tried to see past him, but every time Milo shifted, Adam slid sideways, blocking his view of his wife. Still fighting to understand what was going on, Milo didn't bother to modulate his tone to soothe his brother-in-law. "You actually think Christiana will help you kill her own husband?"

"What do you think happened to the first one?" Adam's smile sent ice sliding down Milo's spine.

Ice on top of the cold. Hurt and offense and a sudden onslaught of suspicion. Milo wanted to hurl insults at his meddling brother-in-law, wanted to question his wife until he understood why she was letting her brother challenge her husband in such a way. But he said nothing as pain snarled in the deepest parts of his soul and sent a bleak hopelessness spiraling through his chest.

Milo simply turned his back on his silent wife and her twin, and walked away, too many doubts and fears fogging his brain to respond.

Chapter Sixteen

Christiana

Too many emotions rioted within Christiana for her to find enough calm to concentrate on the tricky and archaic binding spell. She was angry with her brother, irritated at her husband and livid with herself, and all of those emotions were amplified when the dark sky beyond the window split with a flash of light and a crash of thunder.

Listening to the rain, she let her rage infect her voice when she said, "You acted like an ass, Adam."

"Me?" His eyes widened. "Milo—"

She cut her twin off. "What right do you have, saying things better left unsaid?"

"Milo treats you as if you can't make your own decisions."

"So do you, sometimes!" Christiana felt as if she had acted like a victim, and her weakness ripped through her, but at that moment, she was more worried about her husband's future treatment of her than his conduct just moments ago. "You shouldn't have said what you said. That was over the line."

"He moved to grab you, Chris!"

"He's never hurt me."

After all she and her twin had gone through, the hard times they'd faced together, Christiana almost lost her nerve. She didn't want to push him too far, didn't want to risk the loss of his support or his presence from her life. Again. But she took a deep breath, clenched her fists and reminded herself that Adam was her brother, her twin and her Magic Match. She told herself that he was closer to her than any other person in the world.

Then she told herself that maybe he shouldn't be.

She lifted her chin. "I am a Davenold heir, and while I don't want the damned job, I'm still strong enough to be in the running, so you will give me the respect that position deserves. You will give my husband the respect he garners from my position in this Family."

Adam's lips thinned and he pressed his fists to his hips. "Don't count on it."

"You will be polite, Adam! I will not give Milo any reason to keep me from you."

Her brother opened his mouth, but before he could speak, Georgie's voice coursed through the library. "What the hell is going on? I could hear you yelling from down the hall."

Chris rubbed her forehead as weariness stole over her. "I wanted to cast a spell to decrease my magic so that I wouldn't inherit the Davenold power and Milo caught us. We fought." She turned a glare on her brother. "Adam didn't help."

Georgie stumbled to a stop halfway across the room. "A spell? You can't inherit?"

"She didn't cast it," Adam grumbled. "She —"

"Is about to become the Davenold Mother," Georgie interrupted in a strangled tone. "Madeleine's dying. You should come soon, if you want to say goodbye."

Christiana swayed on her feet. Her body grew numb in insidious degrees, cold fear slowly working its way down to her toes. She pressed her hand to her belly.

"Fix her!" Adam demanded. "Where the hell is Silviu? Get him to help her like he did before."

"We've tried. She won't make it till morning." Georgie bit her trembling lip and shook her head. Then she set her sights on Christiana. "We need you to keep it together, now. You're going to take the power —"

"No! I don't want it!" Chris forced her legs to take her toward the door. "You'll be the heir, like everyone has always planned."

"I haven't been blooded, Chris. I might not be able to—"
Georgie released a shaky breath. "Just come on, and prepare
yourself. I have to get back so I can help Silviu keep her
stable."

Georgie spun on her heel and raced from the room. In
a matter of seconds, Christiana followed as fast as her
shakiness would allow. Adam veered off down the hallway
that led to his bedroom, and Chris knew he went to find his
wife.

Rain pelted the windows and thunder shook the panes
until Christiana jumped every time lightning flashed. The
timing of the storm seemed like an omen. She wished she
knew where Milo was, but she didn't have time to look for
him, or soothe his anger, and she feared he wouldn't be
supportive in her hour of need.

Chest throbbing from both her near-run through the
hallways and her emotional upheaval, she came to a stop
in front of Madeleine's bedroom door. Chris faltered.
Madeleine was more a mother to her than the woman
who'd given birth to her. Madeleine was also the woman
who'd commanded her to marry Milo. She was probably
the only person who could answer any of the thousand
questions suddenly burning Christiana's brain.

If there was time to ask them.

The door was open and a crowd had gathered. Fear roiled
like acid in her belly and temporarily shoved everything
else out her mind as Chris pushed into the bedroom. Her
aunts were to one side of the bed, Georgie joined Silviu on
the opposite. As Georgie took Silviu's free hand while the
other waved over Madeleine's still body, a soft golden glow
spread through the room.

Chris joined her aunts. "What happened, Lydia?"

The woman, who looked just like Georgie but fifty years
older, and just like Madeleine but twenty years younger,
sniffled into a handkerchief. Lydia looked unsteady on her
feet, but answered with only a small waver in her voice. "I
was sitting with Mother a while ago and there was some

explosion of dark light around her. She started convulsing. She's failing fast and I can't stop it. I needed help, so..."

"You got Silviu and Georgie," Chris finished for her.

"It's progressed too far," Georgie whispered. Her gaze, when she met Chris' eyes, was bleak and beyond miserable.

Christiana could hear her grandmother breathing evenly in a dry, rasping wheeze. Displacing her aunts, Chris edged onto the mattress. Madeleine was a tiny lump under the covers, small in a way Christiana had never known her to be, as if she were fading. Her cheeks were jaundiced and lined with age, stress and fatigue. Her eyelids drooped and her mouth hung open. Biting her lip until the sting cleared the tears threatening to fall, Christiana fought to hide her reaction from her grandmother.

She should have known that Madeleine would see too much however, in spite of the glaze of pain dulling her eyes. "I must look terrible," the old woman whispered. "But you don't look well yourself, Christiana."

"I don't want to be Mother." Chris' voice was hardly audible, but she knew her grandmother heard.

"I know. Though you've always done your part to put our Family in an advantageous position, you've never liked to make important decisions. You're too afraid of making a mistake."

"Can you blame me? I have a terrible track record."

"The one truly important decision you made..." Madeleine's eyes closed, her breath rattled in her chest. "Self-fulfilling prophesy, child."

"What do you mean?"

Madeleine's left eye opened, then slid closed. "You were afraid to do things on your own, so you found a man who would do it for you. But a pretty face and too much arrogance do not make a strong man."

Christiana found herself breathing as harshly as her grandmother. They'd never discussed her first marriage before. She certainly never expected to discuss it in front of witnesses. "I made a mistake, yes."

"Had I known the extent of that mistake, the bastard would have died sooner."

Christiana froze. Had it come from anyone else, she could have dismissed the tone of that snarled statement, but she'd learned long ago to never underestimate her grandmother's intelligence. Chris' throat tried to lock around her words, but they ripped out in a whisper that was nearly soundless. "How did you know?"

"Adam told me." Madeleine's soft words were punctuated by hard gasps. "I, too, made a mistake. Many. I shouldn't have let you marry him. I shouldn't have let him isolate you from the Family. I shouldn't have let him keep you in hell for five years. Forgive me, Christiana."

"There is nothing to forgive. The fault was mine."

Madeleine's face twisted with pain. "I tried to do better for you, with Milo."

Comparisons rolled through Christiana's mind, between her first marriage and her second. How much she wanted to love her second husband, and how much she'd thought she'd loved the first. How unspeakably grateful she'd been that Milo wanted a child, and how pleased he'd been when she'd told him of her pregnancy. The first had also wanted a child, had demanded it to cement his position among her Family, but within months Christiana had known she couldn't risk bringing another into their pain-filled union.

Six months into her second marriage, and she wondered if the comparisons were growing closer than she could survive. Doubt and mistrust created a thick haze she couldn't quite displace long enough to judge Milo's intentions.

"Why did you make me marry again, Grandmother?"

Madeleine's eyes opened. "I didn't make you. Milo asked and you said yes."

"I thought I had no choice." Christiana pressed a hand to her chest. "You told me you wanted the match, that I should strongly consider it. I thought that meant..."

"I told him he had to court you. I wasn't about to force you into another marriage when you were just regaining confidence after the first. Milo is a good man and I thought you knew that too."

"I don't know if he's a good man. I don't know what he does when I'm not with him. I don't know what he wants from me."

"Yes, you do." Madeleine dragged in a huge breath that shook the covers and had her choking on the intake. Eyes watering, she coughed and shuddered. Christiana grabbed for the water glass on the bedside table and positioned the straw so her grandmother could drink.

"Easy," Silviu warned.

When Madeleine regained the ability, she said in a voice grown soft with fatigue rather than contemplation, "Strength comes in many forms. Milo is worthy of trust. Just because he is quiet and unassuming doesn't mean he's weak."

"I'm supposed to be strong."

"Every strong woman needs the support of a strong man, Christiana."

"He's argumentative and opinionated."

Madeleine caught her gaze. "You patronize him with agreement and let your resentment grow. Then you allow others to suspect Milo holds too much sway over you. Work *with* him, rather than against him."

Christiana looked away from her grandmother, but she couldn't bear looking at the bedside witnesses to her confusion, so she gave all her concentration to carefully repositioning the water glass on the table. "The last time I let a man make the decisions, I got hurt."

"Milo is a charmer. A businessman who knows he'll gain more through cooperation than domination. I thought he'd be perfect for you." Madeleine's gaze flicked toward Georgie and Silviu. "I made sure both my granddaughters were well-settled with men who could give them what they needed."

Chris transferred her watery gaze to the covers and watched as she worked the fabric between her fingers.

"Milo fights with Adam."

"Adam oversteps his bounds. He feels he failed you, and so he worries. He couldn't save you, so he saved Tulah and eventually he'll realize his attention should be focused on her."

"Adam's not really the problem," Chris confessed.

"I know, but you've only been married six months. It needs time."

"How much time?"

"That depends on you, child. Start speaking your mind. Be the hostess you were born to be, a woman who keeps everyone organized and in their place. Expect the people around you to be gracious and conciliatory, and they will rise to your expectations. They are matriarchal men—they've been trained since birth to do this."

A strange quiver went through Christiana's stomach. Not quite fear, and nothing close to the anger she'd felt earlier, she couldn't describe its source. Perhaps hope, but that emotion had cut her deep and left her bleeding. Perhaps strength, but that one had left her a shrew vacillating between defending her brother and defending her husband.

Maybe it was daring. Chris didn't think she'd been very daring in her life, but she felt ready to embrace the concept. For her husband, their child and her marriage, she would try.

She lifted her eyes to Madeleine, but the old woman was nearing sleep. "Grandmother? Milo is pushing me to be blooded as your heir. He's worried about a challenge while I'm pregnant."

"His Family grew volatile and aggressive after they lost a Mother too soon," Madeleine panted brokenly. "He's protective and he's seen more death than most witches, and that is saying something, child."

Christiana thought her sentiments bore repeating—every hour on the hour, if necessary. She leaned closer and lowered her voice until she was positive no one else could hear her. "I don't want to be Mother, but I don't want

157

Suzette to be Mother either."

Madeleine answered just as softly. "It won't matter, Christiana. Georgeanne will take the High Seat when I'm gone, and the position of Davenold Mother will be obsolete until the end of her lifetime. Our Family won't follow a different Mother when the High Seat is one of us."

Chris blinked in surprise. A new round of questions rose to her lips, but she bit them back because Madeleine's rough breathing had softened. Her small body stilled, with barely a rise in the covers.

Chapter Seventeen

Silviu

Silviu's eyes burned, but he didn't close them. His throat was dry, but he didn't dare leave to get a drink of water. There were dark circles under Georgeanne's eyes, and Silviu knew he'd see the same under his, if he looked in a mirror.

He stood next to Madeleine's bed, level with her pillows. He was one of the few standing close enough to the old woman to hear the rattling of her breath and see the faint yellowness of her skin. She looked more fragile than he'd ever seen her, and he feared there was no hope left.

His chest ached and a restless need to *do* something, to fix the problem heated his muscles. Madeleine had access to every bit of Davenold magic yet hadn't been able to fight the dark spell consuming her, but Silviu still hoped to find an answer. He wondered if he was as arrogant as his betrothed had so often accused, but he couldn't stop his thoughts.

"I want Christiana and Adam to lend me their assistance," he whispered to Georgie, nodding to indicate the space behind him, where Christiana perched on a low dresser. The woman had maintained a stony silence for nearly an hour. "I want to ask for all their magic, a last ditch effort to save your grandmother."

"Do you really think it will help?" Georgie asked.

Silviu hesitated. He glanced at Adam, leaning against the dresser by Chris' knee, but the Davenold male shook his head and hugged Tulah closer.

For hours, Silviu and Georgie had worked over Madeleine. For hours he'd pumped every bit of magic he could into the woman's body, trying in vain to fight the dark spell invading her at the deepest levels. Madeleine's daughter, Lydia, was strong, but whatever healing she'd attempted had only delayed the inevitable.

Not even the power that could build between them helped Silviu and Georgie find the source of the dark magic and eradicate it completely. There was nothing they could do except ease the old woman's pain and gather the Family so they had a chance to say goodbye.

"Leave Chris alone," Georgie ordered as Silviu let his silence lengthen. "She has a lot on her mind, right now."

Surreptitiously shifting his weight, he glanced around at the multitudes of nearly identical women and the men they'd married. Silviu had underestimated how beloved Madeleine was, and hadn't expected the entire household to participate in the bedside vigil. With so many Davenolds packed into Madeleine's room, the space was growing hot and stuffy.

Madeleine's three daughters were opposite the bed from him and Georgie, with Mason Davenold standing behind his wife and speaking softly into his cell phone — a quiet update on Madeleine's decline to her only son, who lived in Kuwait and was unable to join his former Family in England. At the foot of the bed, Margaret stared at her sister with damp eyes but her small family unit was lost in the crowd gathered in the hall just outside the door. Not everyone could fit into Madeleine's bedroom.

A murmur went through the group in the hallway and bodies began to shift. A moment later, Suzette pushed through and made a space for herself next to her grandmother. Margaret swung on her with a cold glare. Silviu barely acknowledged the new arrival when she smiled at him but angled his back toward the wall to better observe the large group.

Christiana hopped off the dresser and came to stand next

to Georgie. She kept her voice to a low whisper suitable to such an atmosphere, yet it emphasized the direness of the situation to an alarming degree. "You don't have to answer for me, Georgie. If there's anything I can do to help stop this, I will give it my all."

"No, I doubt our combined magic will have any effect. The darkness is too entrenched." Silviu put a hand on Georgie's back and rubbed a slow circle. "We don't know what else to do. Unless you learned of a new spell?"

Adam leaned forward to answer. "What we did before was our best hope. It didn't help then, and it won't help now. If you can't find the witch who cast the original spell and make him or her undo it, everything else is just a shot in the dark."

"Graves cast the spell," Georgie murmured. "He's dead, so that's not an option."

"And yet, the spell continues to work very effectively." Adam shook his head. "That's not normal."

"He was strong," Tulah reminded them. "Bloated on other people's power."

Silviu clenched his jaw. "I can't help but wonder if we'd have had more success against it if we had been here with Lydia, if the results of our endeavors would have been different."

"Maybe not," Christiana said. "Maybe the original caster isn't dead. Or maybe someone else picked up where Graves left off."

Silviu met her gaze. "You think it was two separate attacks?"

"It could be." Christiana shrugged. "I can't think of a single witch who'd have enough power that their spell would last beyond death."

"Except, perhaps, the black magic witch we traced before," he mused. "Who is most likely still living."

"According to Milo," Chris said softly, "the first attack was awful. Aunt Lydia described the same thing. If Grandmother was any weaker, she wouldn't have held out this long."

Adam took an audible breath as he ran his gaze over his grandmother. Then he closed his eyes, shook his head and pulled his wife close. "She won't make it this time."

Silviu's heart was surprisingly heavy. This was his first death vigil, the first person he'd cared about that stood on the precipice. He'd never known his grandmother and his mother had died only weeks after his birth. Losing Madeleine hurt more than he'd ever expected, but he also admitted that he never *had* expected it. Looking at Georgie, he knew she'd held impossible hope too. No matter that he'd understood how ill Madeleine was, no matter that he'd pushed her to name an heir, somewhere inside him was the stubborn belief that the tough old woman would pull through.

Even now.

But the covers rose less frequently and Madeleine remained still. A sudden glow lit her chest and Silviu winced as a sharp pang of grief tore through him. She only had moments, and with the magic beginning to seep out of her in silver swirls, he had to face the undeniable truth.

Next to him, Georgie lost her breath on a nearly inaudible moan. Like him, she had the ability to see magic in use, but he doubted the others around them saw what they did. Davenolds continued to cry softly and turn their faces into the chests of their husbands. No one else's eyes widened the way his did, no one else's gaze was captured by the silver mist emanating from the fragile body like Georgie's was.

"No," she whispered. She took a step forward, away from his hand at her back, as if she could physically stop Madeleine's life from leaving her.

But the magic continued to rise. The air wavered and spit silver sparks. A questing tendril reached out, searching for its next host. Like a snake dancing to a charmer's tune, it slowly made its way toward Christiana and soft magical light coasted over her as if petting her hair, stirring it on a phantom breeze. Silviu watched helplessly, holding his breath until the magic backed off and left Christiana completely.

The silver tendril twisted toward Georgie and Silviu released his breath so fast his head spun. Georgie stiffened and braced herself, and Silviu's memory flashed back to the night they stood in the gardens at the Levy estate as he'd pried his grandfather's magic away. Georgie had been at his side, lending her strength to his magic, watching as the Lovasz power left Alexandru and filled Costel in a blaze of silver light. Costel had acted like it hurt. As the magic reached Georgeanne, Silviu found himself wondering, and knew his betrothed wondered the same.

The magic licked over her and shone brighter. Georgie closed her eyes as the light sank into her skin and her curls danced in a soft wind. Silviu could have fallen to his knees and thanked every deity mankind had ever known as it seemed his betrothed was able to take the Davenold power.

Then the Bane shields snapped into place with a rush of jewel-toned lights. Georgie's skin lit up in a magical rainbow and the silver tendril reared back, snapping and hissing with a flurry of sparks. Georgie jerked and her eyes opened. Her gasp was lost to the soft sobs of the crowd.

A silver ball rose from Madeleine's chest, the bulk of the Davenold power. The covers lifted and fell, then remained silent. Silviu's stomach clenched, fear overrode his nervous system. A cold sweat made his skin clammy, sticking his shirt to his shoulders.

His attention was divided between Madeleine's still chest and the massive ball of energy hovering just above her body. The magic dipped and swayed, but only his eyes and Georgie's tracked its movements. Then the Davenold power veered toward the one woman Silviu would do anything to prevent taking it. Suzette tilted her head back and opened her arms as the Davenold magic entered her.

Without thought, yet completely cognizant of what he was doing, Silviu reached for his betrothed. His Magic

Match. The woman's whose heartbeat was felt in his chest.

And he prayed she would forgive him.

He pulled Georgie to him and sent the full power of his Reap magic blasting through her, breaking through the Bane shields as if they never existed. Waves of energy, raw magic gifted to them by fate when they were born under the most magical moons their community knew, brightened the room.

A matter of moments changed everything. Seconds. Not even enough time for anyone to realize what was happening, or what he'd done to manipulate the situation. Mere moments threatened everything he'd ever worked for, everything he'd ever prayed for, bled for and cried for.

Silviu shoved everything he had into Georgie, filling her up completely until she overflowed and magic leaked out of every pore. Gold light erupted and grew until every Davenold in the bedroom stopped crying and squinted in their direction. Rivaling a small sun, he and Georgie turned brilliant with their combined power.

The Davenold magic paused a moment before it was wholly absorbed into Suzette.

Silviu ripped it away.

The silver was sucked into the river of gold and dragged back to Georgie. Visible to everyone now, the Davenold magic flared and covered the expected heir. Her hair danced, jewel-toned light sparking over her skin in rippling waves. Silviu sent his talent out to catch the Davenold magic and pulled as hard as he could.

The energy was a writhing mass of power. Warm and cool in turns, it was similar to what he'd taken from his grandfather, but tempered with an overriding love that could only have come from Madeleine. As ruthless as she'd been, as manipulative and tyrannical, no one could deny her love of Family. And that love was infused in every fiber of strength the Davenold magic possessed.

Georgie's Bane resistance tried to rear up, but Silviu forced it down and away. He dragged her bloodline's power into her, and when her Bane shields threatened to send it back out, he pulled it into himself.

His chest burned for an eon before it turned to ice. He could hardly catch his breath as a great pressure tried to crack his ribs. He held tighter to his bride, hiding his grimace against her shoulder blades as he doubled over. Pain shivered through him, then it was done.

A matter of moments, and everything had changed.

Madeleine's daughters fell over the bed, sobbing hard as they realized their mother was truly gone. Margaret stared at her sister's body and Mason stared at his daughter. Suzette glared at Georgeanne. The rest of the Family nodded to the woman they thought was their new Mother, a gesture of acceptance as well as relief and respect.

Georgie shuddered and pulled from Silviu's hold. The golden light died out as she turned — too slowly, too controlled. Silviu swallowed against the sickness rising in his throat. Anger was communicated in every line of Georgeanne's body, though her face was brutally impassive.

Until she met his gaze, and showed him the extent of her rage. Her pain, her betrayal at what he'd done.

Silviu Lovasz had become the Davenold Mother.

Chapter Eighteen

Georgeanne

Georgie's anger burned brighter as Silviu threw her bedroom door open with a blast of silver magic that melted the lock she'd engaged.

"Get. Out." She pushed the words through gritted teeth.

Silviu had infiltrated her defenses. Georgie had recognized it and the dangers of it, and had tried for so long to maintain distance between him and her heart. She knew she should have trusted her Family when, for ten years, they'd screamed that Silviu had seduced her for the sole purpose of compromising her loyalty.

Then they'd been reunited and he'd worn that damned vulnerable expression that made her think that *just maybe* he'd held deeper feelings for her than Madeleine had supposed all those years ago. He'd fought for her, had pleasured her.

Had betrayed her.

The Davenold magic had left Suzette and returned to her, filled her and was just as quickly shoved back out by her Bane imperviousness. And Silviu's Reap magic had caught it and dragged it back in. In and in some more — so far *in* it went out again, and came to rest in him.

She'd almost showed her weakness to the gathered Davenolds. The numbing shock that had infiltrated Georgie had been the only thing that had kept her on her feet when something in her chest froze, then shattered. She feared it was her heart.

Silviu took a step forward, lifting his hand. "Georgie,

love, please listen to me."

Agony streaked through her, emotional chaos took hold and swept her away. "Get the fuck out."

"Let me explain, love."

Georgie swung on him with a balled fist and a heart bleeding anger. Her knuckles connected with his jaw and his head snapped to the right. Fire blazed through her hand and wrist, but she didn't care if she'd broken them, didn't care if she broke her entire arm, because it simply couldn't compare to the pain the rest of her was busy trying not to feel.

"Save your lies for someone who gives a shit!"

"Georgie—"

She tried to hit him again, but he leaped back. Just the tips of her knuckles rapped his chest, not nearly hard enough to appease the rage burning her alive. Her face felt too tight as she stared at him, her body shook so hard her bones hurt.

"Georgie, I had to. The magic was going to Suzette."

"She's a fucking Davenold, at least!" Georgie backed off but kept her fists clenched. "She could be challenged!"

"She cannot be Mother."

"So instead, a Lovasz male is?" Georgie bared her teeth and fought for breath. "Did you get want you wanted, you bastard? All this fucking time, telling me how much you loved me, and all to be the Davenold Mother?"

Just saying the words brought a new wave of pain. Georgie swayed on her feet. She struggled to shove all the chaos back, to lock it away in some dark place where it wouldn't burn her so badly. Where it wouldn't make her feel like she was dying.

Silviu's brows lifted. "Of course not."

"Why didn't you just keep your grandfather's power, you fucking magic thief? Or isn't Lovasz Fatherhood enough for you? You're tired of being connected to such a miserable excuse for a Family—you thought you'd take the largest matriarchal house, instead?"

"It's not like that, Georgeanne. I did it for you."

"*Stop* fucking lying!" She gripped her hair in a vain attempt at keeping her skull from exploding. "You did it for you. Everything is for you. Every fucking thing in my life has all been for you."

"How can you say that?" He moved toward her again, but she backed up quickly. "Your grandmother has worked on *your* behalf, not mine."

"*And for what*?" she screamed. "To get you into the High Seat. Manipulating the world to get *you* where *you* want to be."

"That's hardly true."

"*And I got sent to the gods-damned witch hunts*." Georgie tugged her hair harder. "And you'd think I would have learned my fucking lesson, but no, you come back into my life and I just jump right into your bed again."

Grief passed over his face. "I never meant for you to be sent away."

"All these things you never meant, Silviu," she sneered. "But it's awful damn convenient *for you* that they happened."

"Hardly, I—"

"You never meant to get me banished, but you sure as hell meant to eat my pussy that Beltane night, didn't you? Hoping to gain my loyalty before I grew up enough to understand how despicable you are!"

"No! And it's not like I planned—"

"You never meant for me to get hurt, but you *'proved'*"—Georgie's fingers jerked to quote the air—"your loyalty to me, your concern, your *love*, by defeating your grandfather, by defending me against Graves and Muso, by pretending to take care of my grandmother."

"I will protect you with every drop of my magic. I will take care of—"

"Your magic? Did you even use it to help my grandmother, or was that another fucking lie?"

"You know better, Georgeanne."

"What I know, is that you kept me alive at the Ngozi wedding so I could hand you all the power and influence

I worked *my ass* off for, didn't you? So much easier than ripping the Davenold power out of a new Mother like you did to your grandfather. This way, you get to safely hide behind *me*. And I'm the one who will take the fall when I can't use my Family's power!"

"At the Ngozi residence, I filled you with my magic because I couldn't handle even the *thought* of you dying." Silviu's voice lost its cajoling tone and took on a sharp edge. "I filled you with my magic because you *were* dying, and I love you."

She didn't believe him. She didn't know if she'd ever believe him again. His betrayal hurt on such a deep level, she didn't know what to think or feel, or how to recover. What had come before was awful—constantly reminded how different she was, never being like anyone else, banished as a teenager, made to learn politics and work on behalf of her Family while in a constant state of terror that she'd screw up.

But she did it for the people she loved, for Madeleine and her parents, her cousins. She did it for the hope of leading her Family and earning the right to take care of them.

Instead, she'd handed them into the keeping of a patriarchal Reap witch willing to do *anything* to get his way.

"You don't fucking love me." Bitterness sliced through Georgie, adding to the cacophony inside her. "You don't love me at all—you love the *concept* of me."

"No—"

"You love that I am the one thing in the whole damned world your miserable grandfather can't take away. You love that I am the single witch that can make your magic stronger. You love that I can get you to the top of the fucking dog pile and make your life into the glorious thing you've stolen, cheated and lied for."

Silviu shot forward, but Georgie was faster. She slid around him and dropped into a ready half-crouch that had him stilling in his tracks. Georgie was on her toes, right fist lifted and left hand raised in fair warning—more than he deserved.

He took a deep breath. "I do love you, Georgeanne. I have always loved you."

"*Bullshit*. You used me."

"I know you are hurt, and I'm sorry." Silviu's voice remained hard, as if his patience was being sorely tried. "I know you need to lead your Family and —"

"You *know*?" Georgie felt like screaming again. "You don't know a fucking thing, apparently."

"I know you —"

"*You don't know me!*" Georgie threw her fists out. Her voice bounced off the walls and she didn't give a damn who might be out in the hall, eavesdropping. "We haven't seen each other in ten fucking years. Two weeks doesn't change anything. You don't know me at all!"

"I have always known you." Silviu made his own fist and thumped it against his chest. "I have always felt you here, from the moment I met you. The moment I touched you and our magic converged. Your power and your strength —"

"Is that all you care about, Silviu? Power and strength, and just maybe magic, too?"

He picked up the gauntlet Georgie hadn't realized she was throwing down. "I know you're desperate to be loved. I never meant for you to be sent away because of my crimes, but you were and I know that tore you apart. Your whole life, you were told that you were different, and made to feel lesser because of it. I know you worked hard to overcome what everyone else saw as weakness, and that made you into a woman who's too damn afraid to take a chance on the man who loves her!"

"And I was right to be distrustful, wasn't I?" She made a sweeping, mocking gesture. "Because the man who professes undying love for me, the one who swears he did everything *for me* just stole my Family's fucking magic!"

"*It was going to Suzette!*"

"Who I could have challenged!" Georgie met Silviu's roar with one of her own. "I might have been able to take the

Davenold magic from her legally, and the power would remain with a *Davenold*. A matriarchal witch, *not* you."

Silviu's tone turned low, dark and ugly. "You can't take the magic, Georgeanne. You are Bane."

His words, though she'd heard them from countless others before, had her flinching. She stared at him stonily, trying to breathe, trying to think and pull her anger back inside her. Desperately trying to hold herself together.

Too many times both he and Madeleine had told Georgie that her anger let her mouth get her in trouble. So she closed it. She fought to find logic, to regain some sense of self beyond the bloody mess his betrayal had left inside her. She would need all the skill she'd been forced to acquire to make things right for her Family.

"The magic tried," he continued when she said nothing. "You know it as well as I do. The magic couldn't push past your shields, and even with me helping, *your* magic rejected the magic of your Family. I did the only thing I could to protect you."

"You mean you did the only thing you could to protect your goals. I bet you fucking planned this. Your father probably gave you an itemized agenda to achieve your ends."

Her whisper ripped from her, and apparently did more damage than all her previous screaming. Silviu jerked. His skin paled, his silver eyes turned luminescent with distress. He shook his head and Georgie saw his throat bob as he swallowed.

"For you, Georgie. Everything has always been for you."

"You're a liar, Silviu."

Suddenly Georgie was beyond tired. Her eyes burned in warning and only her stubbornness held back her tears. Her legs were shaking too badly to hold her for much longer, but she refused to sit down while Silviu was still in her room.

She needed to get away from him.

But Silviu didn't seem to be done with her yet. "I worry

for you. The only reason someone hasn't tried to kill you, my love, is because they feared your grandmother. Look at what my grandfather did. Do you think he's alone in thinking of you as defective?"

"No, he's got you for company."

"*No.*" Again Silviu stepped toward her, only to pull up short. "I don't think there is anything wrong with you, but others do, and others are afraid. I need us to be strong, and hold a position of strength, to keep you safe, Georgie."

"To keep yourself safe." She shook her head, but she couldn't seem to make her voice stronger. "You know what will happen when more people find out you're a Reap witch. Muso is probably already gathering an army to come after you, and you need me to unlock your magic to meet the threat they pose."

"I'm hard to kill."

"So am I," she argued.

"But now we know you can break magic, and that means everything just got more dangerous."

"Go tell your bullshit to someone who hasn't lived with Bane shields their whole life. They might believe you. I don't." She wished she were as numb as she sounded. "Never again."

"Georgie, you're my Magic Match. We have to work through this, you have to listen and believe me, or our magic will destabilize."

"Your magic, I don't have any. And I don't give a fuck what happens to you."

"*Ours!*" Silviu snapped. "And destabilization will make it too dangerous for everyone to tolerate, and they will come after us faster."

She had no idea what he meant, and she didn't care. She only knew she was done—utterly and completely finished with the conversation and with him. If he wouldn't leave her room, she would. She turned on her heel and strode toward the door.

Silviu reached her just as she was opening it. "Georgie,

wait—"

"No. No more." In spite of the clenching deep in her belly, it was surprisingly easy to keep her tone level as conviction filled her. "No more lies, no more manipulations. If it's the last thing I do, I will find a way to break our betrothal. Sealed in blood or not, I refuse to marry you."

"You can't," Silviu gasped.

"I can break magic now," she reminded him. "I'm sure I can cancel a contract."

His hand shook as he tried to press the door closed even as Georgie fought to pull it open. Then another hand curved around the wooden edge and helped Georgie gain freedom. Adam's stormy gaze touched on Georgie first, then shot over her shoulder to pin Silviu in place.

"You okay, honey?" Adam asked. Georgie didn't answer as she slipped under her cousin's arm with a giant wave of relief that threatened to bring her to her knees.

"Georgeanne!" Silviu tried to get past Adam, but the Davenold male blocked his way. Silviu drew himself up and passively remained in her room as a terrible expression crossed his face—a mixture of rage, grief and unbearable pain.

Georgie knew just how the emotional combination felt. She repeated herself in front of her new witness. "I will find a way to break our betrothal. I won't marry you."

"It's too late, Georgie," Silviu said quietly. "I think we've already married in the old way. Blood, sex and magic."

The extent of his lies knew no bounds. Georgie ground her teeth. "We both know that's impossible. I haven't fucked you."

"In Poland, I tasted your blood and you tasted mine. We were bound together, and I think that's how we defeated the dark magic spell that hit you at the Ngozi wedding."

Adam gathered his jaw off his chest. "That's how you were able to save her life."

Silviu shrugged and a hint of apology darkened his eyes. "Our magic got away from us and created a bond that can't be undone."

"What fucking spell did you cast, Silviu?" With some emotion that went miles past wrath, Georgie looked at Adam, the only person she had access to who'd married in the ancient ritual so powerful that the witches who knew of it kept it as secret as possible. "What spell did he use that could trap a Bane witch in marriage?"

Adam lifted his hands and shook his head. "There is no real spell, honey. If you two were together, if blood flowed and if your magic was released with your pleasure and there was intent… You could have married by accident. But you need full consummation."

Silviu winced. "The bond has been forged."

Georgie ground her teeth harder and ignored her so-called husband. "What intent?"

Adam shrugged. "Intent to marry. Intent to share a life. Love. It's all a promise the magic can make good. But…but you're Bane, so I don't understand how…"

"My magic can reach hers." Silviu never took his eyes off her. "I'm certain we're married, Georgie, and it can't be undone."

She lifted her chin. "We'll see about that."

Chapter Nineteen

Milo

It took the better part of the night to receive the phone call Milo had been waiting for. Waiting on pins and needles, his intuition screaming at him, making him edgy enough to pace the quiet sitting room he'd found deserted on the ground floor.

When the phone rang, his hand clenched around it. It had practically been glued to his palm for hours, as he occupied himself with a torturous observation of the clock, slowly ticking toward dawn. He answered the call on the first ring.

"Cunningham, tell me you found something."

"I'm not sure."

Milo had immigrated to New York just before his marriage to Christiana. Milo's previous lawyer had reached the age of retirement, and with the uprooting of Tundra Tech to the United States of America, had completed his service to Milo by vetting several American corporate lawyers to replace him. Joseph Cunningham was sharp-minded, ruthless and stubborn, and his brilliance had been an asset to Milo's company.

As an added bonus, Cunningham was also Family of sorts, having married one of Milo's distant cousins and made aware of the witching world, though he wasn't a witch himself. It was a rarity for non-witches to be brought into the fold, but Milo felt that made the man capable of evaluating any situation from multiple perspectives. For Cunningham to be unsure of what he'd discovered in the course of an investigation was unusual, and set Milo's mental alarms to clanging.

"Tell me," he demanded.

Cunningham cleared his throat. "It's damn hard to dig up any dirt on the Levy Father."

For hours, Milo had gotten the same response from his battalion of sources. Daniel Levy was an upstanding citizen. Daniel Levy was a dedicated Father, a political powerhouse who always seemed to be on the right side of any issue. He was a fair man, a good man, a minor investor in several profitable businesses, but he didn't own controlling shares of anything.

Milo knew the businesses in question—average returns on investments, more than adequate for a small household, but nothing that would amount to what the Levy Father would need to keep his large primary residence running. Not with all the hangers-on in his entourage, to say nothing of the expense of keeping a private jet and traveling whenever the whim took him—which was often, judging by the reports coming in. Milo's suspicions only grew, with the evidence of such a paragon's mediocre finances.

His business sense told him something was off, and it was a little voice Milo had learned not to ignore. It was the same voice that had kept him from several bad investments, the same whisper that had kept him from brokering deals with men who later proved to be criminal in their business practices.

He gritted his teeth. "There has to be something."

"Oh, there is," Cunningham assured him. "It took a while, but I kept trying because no man is a saint. Those who appear to be are usually just better at hiding things. And the things they're hiding are usually worse than most could imagine, but—"

"So you did find something?" Milo had to forcibly relax his hand around the phone.

"Nothing illegal yet, just unusual." Cunningham's frustration rang through the phone. "Milo, I've been doing backflips all day, trying to figure out what that man is up to, and all I've found is questionable sources of income, odd political donations and massive balance transfers to various offshore accounts."

"He's got his fingers in a lot of pies. Much of his income should come from his investments, but there's a discrepancy between his earnings and expenditures. I take it that's the questionable income sources you're referring to?"

"No," Cunningham said. "He owns shares of a company called Green Witch Mining Industries, and that's where the bulk of his money is earned. But the—"

Milo cut the man off. "My sources told me Daniel doesn't own controlling shares of any company."

"He doesn't. But he does own a hefty minor stake, about thirty percent, and I found a statement of intent detailing an exchange of another thirty percent into his control. The transfer of stock options was supposed to happen a few days ago, but there must be a holdup somewhere because it hasn't gone through."

"How did you find this information, Cunningham? I had no idea—"

"Daniel's involvement is hidden behind several dummy corporations. I had to pull some very valuable strings to find his connection to Green Witch Mining. The company operates throughout Asia, Africa and South America, and Daniel inherited his shares upon the death of his grandfather, who bought them nearly fifteen years ago."

"I've never heard of Green Witch Mining."

Cunningham made a noise of agreement. "Like I said, several dummy corporations were set up for purposes of concealment. And you know as well as I do that when fake companies are created to hide the activities of a real one, there's usually something illegal going on."

"But you haven't found evidence of illegality." Milo exhaled roughly. "What *have* you found?"

"The former Levy Father bought his shares from an African startup, G.N. Gozi Enterprises, another dummy corporation from what I can tell, which immediately went defunct after the sale. The records were poorly kept, and on the surface it looks as if the company went out of business, but when I dug deep I found an extensive operation still in existence."

"G. N. Gozi." Milo's thoughts raced. "Graves Ngozi? Could that be the basis for the alliance between the two covens? Is that why the former Levy Father was so determined to marry Constance to Graves, and why Daniel honored the contract?"

"I don't know," Cunningham answered slowly. "But I can tell you the shares of Green Witch were bought for a song. There is one other major shareholder, who owns controlling interest, but I haven't figured out who that is, yet."

"If it's Graves Ngozi, he died last week. Maybe that's why the transfer hasn't gone through. Keep searching."

"Of course," Cunningham sniffed. "Beyond the mining company, the majority of Daniel's portfolio is real estate, both in America and internationally."

Milo didn't see anything suspicious in that. "The Levys are a large Family."

"Is it typical for a Family Father to charge rent to other Family members?"

"Yes, each residence must pay for itself, so the people who live there contribute to the bills."

"But to the Family account," Cunningham said, "to cover various Family needs, right? The rent Daniel charges goes into his personal bank account, and the offshore accounts, if my informant is correct about the sums."

Milo stilled. "He can only collect payment at the residences he controls. Not the residences owned by the larger Family."

"Isn't it the same thing?"

"The Family owns the overall residential network, but not every witch lives in a Family home." Milo turned in his chair to stare at the night-darkened window. The slowing patter of rain against the glass underscored his thoughts.

"The network breaks down into primary, secondary, tertiary, etcetera, with each paying into the larger till."

"So the branch leader controls only the houses belonging to that particular branch? And they can only collect rent for those properties?"

"Yes," Milo confirmed. "The properties are passed down through inheritance when the new leader takes over. Each branch is responsible for collecting enough money to maintain their network of homes, as well as contribute to the larger Family accounts, in accordance with their status."

"I see. The secondary branch would pay much more than a minor branch ten times removed from the primary. But is it common for a primary branch to own so much land outside their main locale?"

"The Davenolds are headquartered in the United States, so the primary branch owns all their residences in that country. But Madeleine also owns a great deal of land in Peru and Australia. Maybe ten houses in the primary network altogether, but hundreds of thousands of acres."

"Daniel owns three times that," Cunningham murmured. "And I noticed you didn't say your Mother owned any property where secondary or tertiary branches were located."

"For a higher branch to have a residence too near another with decent status is considered aggressive and rude in the extreme."

"Well, I'm glad that's settled, because Daniel owns property in Israel, near the secondary branch, and in Argentina, near the fourth."

Milo thought back to Georgeanne's comment on Eliasz's relationship with Daniel. "Nothing in Poland? That's where the tertiary branch is."

"No, but he does have a small house in Luxembourg and a lot of European interests. Which brings me to my next point—his political donations. He gives a whopping amount to various political campaigns in New England and the Midwest as well as several special interest groups. He, or his Family, is getting around campaign laws by donating as individuals."

Milo wasn't interested in politics beyond how it affected his company. He couldn't see how Daniel's campaign contributions would matter. "What does that have to do with Europe?"

"He's throwing money at all kinds of things over there, my friend." Cunningham cleared his throat. "Don't ask me what I had to do to get this information, but suffice it to say, Daniel's spending more money than he should rightfully have in Britain, Portugal, the Baltics and Norway."

"Why? What policies could he be trying to influence?"

"I don't know yet. That's just Europe. He's got some things going on in South America too, but most of his money is going into India, Iran and Hong Kong."

In a flash of insight that blinded him to all else, Milo finally understood. "They're all matriarchal strongholds."

"Iran is a matriarchal stronghold?"

"The Gholami Family is ancient and extensive," Milo explained absently, "Before the Ottoman Empire dominated, they extended over the entire Middle East and into Northern Africa. They're the next biggest Family on this side of the schism after the Davenolds, but they tend to be quiet about themselves. My wife's uncle is married to the Gholami Daughter, and his daughter is heir. They live in Kuwait, but the primary network is headquartered just outside Tehran."

"Huh, go figure." Cunningham spoke in such a way Milo could almost see the man cock his head. "But I thought a patriarchal Family ruled Far East Asia?"

"Japan, but the Marsh Family relocated to Hong Kong from Scotland nearly a hundred years ago." Milo gripped the phone tighter. "What the hell is Daniel doing giving money to political endeavors in matriarchal strongholds?"

"Again," Cunningham told him, "I don't know. Just like I don't know where he got the money to throw around. His Green Witch interests bring in a lot, but even combined with the rents he collects on his properties, it isn't enough."

"The money just appears out of thin air?" Milo knew Daniel didn't have enough magic for such a conjuring.

"It's hard to say, considering the confusion associated with the activity of his offshore accounts. Millions of dollars every quarter are transferred, but God only knows where it originally came from." Again, Cunningham's frustration was easily detectable. "I've got my nephew working on that."

"What?" Milo's chin jerked down in surprise. "I can't have word of this—"

"Never fear, my friend, he'll keep his mouth shut. He owes me. He got caught hacking into the Department of Defense database three years ago and I argued him out of major jail time and into a sweet job. He works for the Pentagon now."

Milo closed his eyes. He'd have to tell his wife and Georgie, and see what they made of this new information. "What do you think Daniel's doing, Cunningham?"

"I've got no clue. It's all over the board, different political movements, some of which run counter to what he's funding in other places."

"Keep digging, and let me know if you find anything else." Milo took a deep breath to fortify himself as he switched gears. Putting thoughts of Daniel Levy away for the moment, he focused on the issue burning in the back of his mind. "What about the other matter I asked you to look into?"

"Ah, um, I've received the medical reports," Cunningham said hesitantly, the soft shuffle of papers sounding through the phone. "He'd gotten a check-up not too long before his death from his primary doctor. Clean bill of health."

"What did he die of?"

"Massive coronary. He died instantly, Milo. The autopsy showed massive damage to his heart."

"So his doctor missed something?"

A long pause had Milo's nerves pulling tight. Finally,

Cunningham said, "You've heard the rumors, right?"

He had, but he'd never believed them until Adam's threat. Doubts iced Milo's heart, but he had to know what he was dealing with in order to find a way forward. "They say Christiana killed her first husband because he couldn't get her pregnant."

"Yeah." The word sighed through the phone. "That's what they say. Is it possible for a witch to kill someone and make it look like a natural death?"

"Anything's possible." Milo looked up as movement flashed in his peripheral vision. Georgie hesitated on the threshold of the sitting room, looking pale and exhausted, and close to tears. "I have to go, Cunningham. If you learn anything more, call me."

Milo slipped his phone into his pocket. Georgie smiled weakly and inched into the room. "Sorry," she said. "I didn't mean to interrupt."

He debated with himself for roughly two seconds, but Milo had spent his whole life looking to females to lead him in familial matters. "I need to ask you something, Georgie."

"I don't know how much help I can be right now." She walked toward the sofa and snagged the blanket off the back.

Milo was determined. "What if someone you loved might have done something that you're not sure you can forgive? But you know the only way forward is to rebuild the trust you might have lost?"

Georgie went still. Her expression blanked and she hugged the afghan to her chest. She opened her mouth, but Milo was unprepared for the harshness of the words that ripped free. "Is this about Silviu?"

"No." Milo blinked. "Someone might have done something bad. Or maybe not. But I don't know the whole story."

He stopped his jumbled explanation with a groan and rubbed his hands over his face. "I don't know what I'm trying to ask. My thoughts are scattered and I'm having trouble thinking past what I want to be true."

"Well, I can commiserate." Georgie rounded the sofa and collapsed onto the cushions. "I guess it depends on what this 'bad thing' is." Georgie tipped her head back and gave him a look that left Milo feeling evaluated in a way he'd only felt in Madeleine's company. "Let me ask you a question."

"All right."

"I know you don't like to talk about what happened when Mother Ivanova died, but I need to know about the challenges the next Mother faced."

Milo exhaled roughly as he swung to stare at the rain-streaked window. His eyes saw the reflection of the sitting room, but his mind saw the destruction of his Family home, the war between his cousins, the loss of peace. "It was terrible. The challenges tore my Family apart."

"Would it have been better to let the inheriting Mother continue on in that role?"

"Greed overcomes too many, Georgeanne. Who can say whether or not a woman the magic chooses would be better to lead than one who fights for the right to? I only wish she'd have been given a chance to prove herself unworthy before my cousin challenged. Once that door was opened, it couldn't be closed, and my Family suffered for it."

"The challenges proved to be a weakness for the Family as a whole," Georgie mused.

Milo turned to her and drew himself up. Clenching his fists, he told her, "I won't let you challenge my wife."

Georgie blinked, then her face softened into one of terrible sadness. "Oh, Milo. I forgot you weren't there." She shook her head and exhaled loudly. "I suggest you go find your wife. There is something she needs to tell you."

Chapter Twenty

Christiana

Christiana would have stayed with her aunts at her grandmother's bedside, but there was nothing left for her to do. The aunts had everything in hand, the preparations they discussed being the last obligation they could fulfill for their mother. Chris didn't want to take that from them, or interject herself in their solemn task. She'd wept when Family members filed past to pay their final respects, but after a half hour, she couldn't bear to watch any longer.

For a while, she wandered the quiet hallways. With so many people in the house, there was usually a great deal of noise, especially so close to dawn when the house staff began their day and the jet-lagged visitors couldn't sleep. That morning, with Madeleine's passing breaking so many Davenold hearts, the storm blowing outside was the only significant sound penetrating Christiana's awareness.

Madeleine's words haunted Christiana. Her own words to Adam haunted her, too — she'd accused him of letting her past mistakes influence his behavior toward her. Christiana knew she did the same and with her grandmother's wisdom still ringing in her ears, while that strange quiver of daring still ran through her, she was ready to try to change that.

It was bad timing, but Christiana needed to do exactly what Madeleine said. It was the last obligation *she* could fulfill for her grandmother. She went to Adam's room. He answered her knock quickly.

Without preamble, she blurted, "Stop antagonizing my husband, and stop treating me like a victim."

Adam's brows lifted. "Where *is* your husband, Chris?"

The expression Milo had worn when he'd left the library nourished her fears, but she lifted a shoulder as nonchalantly as she could. "I don't know. Probably asleep."

"He wasn't at Madeleine's bedside," Adam pointed out. "And you didn't go get him."

"Can you blame me, after you insinuated that we would murder him?"

Christiana clenched her fists and fought to ignore the anxiety tearing holes in her stomach. She knew she'd have to face Milo at some point in time, but she hadn't been able to bring herself to find him with Madeleine at the edge of death. She couldn't bear to have his hungry gaze watching her as she dealt with such a loss, and she certainly couldn't bear it if the look he perpetually bestowed on her had changed to one of permanent suspicion.

"You caught him with Suzette already, a woman who will do anything to hurt you. And now, when you need him most, you don't where he is? Where is Suzette?"

Chris regretted telling Adam anything about her husband. She was doing her best to hold on to hope, to give Milo the benefit of the doubt, but her brother's words cut deep. "Suzette was with the rest of us."

"She came in late, and left right after Georgie. I find that suspicious."

Chris shook her head and swallowed against the growing lump in her throat. "Milo said she was having an affair with Daniel."

"And *what*, is that just a sudden thing?" Adam's brows descended and a black look overtook his features. "Or is Daniel a convenient scapegoat? Milo's known Suzette for months. How long has she known the busy Levy Father?"

"*Stop.*" Christiana raised her hand and glanced around the eerily empty hallway. She'd feel better having this discussion behind closed and warded doors, with a strong silencing spell for added protection, but Adam hadn't invite her into his room. "What is wrong with you? You can't keep doing this."

"And you can't keep—"

"*Adam.*" Tulah appeared behind her husband and pulled the door open farther. Her eyes wide and scandalized, she scolded him. "Stop casting aspersions. Your sister is smart enough to know if her husband is lying to her."

"She didn't before," Adam shot back.

"Oh, yes, I did," Chris protested. "I knew he lied, and I chose to ignore it. I chose to live with it because I didn't know how to get out of the situation I found myself in and I was embarrassed. Everything is different this time."

Adam stared at her for a long minute before speaking. "I don't like Milo."

"Because he challenges what you say." Chris nodded at Tulah. "You've managed to marry in such a way that you get to stay a Davenold rather than go to another woman's Family. Milo threatens your position here, and he questions you, your ideas and your authority. But he outranks you, Adam, and you need to step back for him, as well as for me."

"He needs to treat you better."

Tulah folded her arms over her chest. "That's for your sister to decide."

Adam reached out to wrap his wife in a one-armed embrace. "You don't understand, Tulah."

"I understand you're arguing with your sister about how she should act in *her* marriage."

"I'm sorry I dragged you into the mess I made before," Chris rushed to say. "I really am, Adam, but I need to move past that and you remember too much. I should have taken some time with Milo and learned how to settle into this new marriage, but I've been leaning on you and letting you fight my battles for me."

"You're my sister. I will protect you until the day I die."

"Thank you, but I need to handle things on my own." Chris wiped her palms on her pants but forced her gaze to meet her brother's so he could see her determination. "You need to stay out of my marriage."

Her brother's eyes held a stubborn denial. Chris watched as his expression hardened, and his mouth opened. She prepared herself for almost anything, knowing Adam's persistent dislike of her husband.

But Tulah spoke before Adam could find the words. "Just last week you told me I had to stand up for myself, make some changes if I wanted my life to improve. I did. I told the truth about Muso and Graves, and I said yes to your marriage proposal. You encouraged me, but you let me make my own decisions. Christiana is asking for the same thing."

"It's not the same thing!"

"Of course it is." Tulah proved herself as stubborn as her husband, gaining a new measure of respect from Christiana.

Adam shook his head. "Don't defend her. After everything she's said about you—"

"Now you're just sowing discord." Tulah's lips thinned.

"It certainly seems like it," Chris muttered. She reached out to give her new sister-in-law's shoulder a soft squeeze. "I haven't always been fair to you, Tulah, and for that, I apologize. The circumstances of your marriage to my brother were upsetting to me, but I also accept that what's done is done."

"Wow, so enthusiastic," Adam sneered.

"At least I'm willing to try!" Chris rounded on her brother. "I'm not picking fights with Tulah every time we pass in the hallways. I'm not actively working to make you distrust her."

Tulah stared at Christiana with a meaningful gleam in her eyes. "Sometimes a woman has to fight for herself, so she knows she can."

"She knows," Adam snarled. "Still, I—"

Tulah curled her fingers over his waistband and gave a little shake. "You believed in me, Adam, so I believed in myself, and I did what I had to, no matter the consequences."

"I need you to believe in me too, Adam." Chris jumped

on Tulah's words. "Madeleine did, so there's no reason you can't."

"Shit." He rubbed a hand over his face. "Between you and Georgie, I swear to God—"

"I need you to take a step back and let me handle things. Milo is my husband, chosen for me by Madeleine, and you need to respect that."

"Let's try to give each other the space needed to settle into our new lives," Tulah suggested. "So much is happening so quickly that I think we all need a little time to adjust."

Christiana nodded. "That's what Madeleine said."

Adam leaned against the door jamb and rolled his eyes up to stare at the ceiling. "You're my sister, Chris. I believe you can do almost anything you put your mind to, but that doesn't mean I won't be right there. I've got your back."

"And I have yours." She sighed, then lifted her chin. "But until an hour ago, I was a Davenold heir, fully capable of taking our Family's magic and fully capable of seeing to all our Family's needs. I won't let you treat me like a victim ever again."

He ran his tongue over his teeth. "Well, look who put her balls on today."

"That's right." Chris felt strength fill her, remake her and set her on a new path. "And I won't be taking them off again. If I need your help, I'll ask. I promise. Until then, focus on your marriage, not mine."

She walked away with her head held high, but called herself a liar the moment she reached her bedroom. Milo wasn't there, and it didn't look like he'd stopped in while she'd been gone. The bed was perfectly made, there were no neckties tossed haphazardly over the foot, as her husband was wont to do.

Christiana paced as her newly found strength deserted her, vile images running through her imagination. Adam's words speared into her resolve. She'd caught her first husband with other women too many times. She'd caught him with Suzette too many times.

She argued with herself. She held firm to her belief that her current husband was innocent of adultery. She fought back the rising tide of nausea at the thought he hadn't come to bed, and remembered her brother's needless antagonism in the library. Milo was upset, perhaps he needed space, just as Christiana had needed her dying grandmother's last words of wisdom.

Chris leaned against a dresser and struggled to hold back her tears – though she couldn't say if they were born of grief over losing her grandmother, or fear of losing her husband. Too many emotions battered her, and with the rain pelting the windows, the dawn held no hope of a bright, new day.

But sometime after the storm blew itself out and the wind died down, Christiana remembered what she'd told her brother. As the sun finally managed to heft itself over the horizon, she remembered who she was, what she was, and even found a way to dig down into the core of what she'd been before her first marriage. Strength, daring, fear or courage – the motivation didn't matter, she would fight for herself this time.

Because, as the hours ticked by and Milo still hadn't come to bed, all the grief inside Christiana wrapped itself up in a brittle shell of pure fucking rage.

Chapter Twenty-One

Silviu

"Have you seen Georgeanne?" Silviu asked the same question, over and over, of every Family member he came across.

The unfamiliar cousin shook her head. "No."

He was sick of hearing that reply, with no further helpful information on where his wife had gone next. Time and time again, Silviu had rubbed his aching chest and moved on to the next cousin, with the same result.

Sheer willpower had Silviu holding on to his patience as his panic grew and a dull throb resounded through him. He was thrown back to the days when he'd searched for Georgeanne on foreign soil, on three different continents, with Motherhouses around the world defying his quest and throwing up bureaucratic obstacles. In spite of his determination, he couldn't find his reluctant bride.

All the while, his cell phone was a near constant buzz in his pocket. Costel was close to the last person he wanted to talk to just then, no matter what crisis had roused the man from his bed at that ungodly hour. His brother could wait. Costel was Father, more than capable of handling his own crises so, each time the phone vibrated, Silviu ground his teeth and refocused his attention on whatever Davenold he was interrogating.

Fruitless hours later, Silviu's frayed impatience had completely unraveled. His phone vibrated yet again, and Silviu was ready to wage war on his brother. His tension and frustration transmitted to his answering of the call, with a jab of his finger and a clenching of his jaw, as he stomped through the dark gardens some distant cousin *thought* Georgie had found refuge in.

"*What*, Costel?"

"Oh, thank God," came the breathless reply. "Where are you?"

"I'm busy." Silviu eyed the horizon, which was just lightening with the rising of a cloud-covered sun. "And don't you think it's a little early for a phone call?"

"No." Then his brother's voice firmed and rose to a decibel that had Silviu pulling the phone from his ear. "*Why haven't you been answering your phone?*"

"Excuse me?" Silviu went rigid on the garden path as he took exception to his brother's tone. "The sun isn't even up yet. I have been busy. Leave a message, and I will call you back when I'm *not* busy."

"Listen, Silviu—"

"I'm serious, Costel. Whatever is wrong, I'm sorry, but I've got my hands full here—"

"And where is *here*?"

Silviu blinked at a row of bushes that had been flattened by the night's storm. Costel was typically rude and arrogant, but always in a way that strangely implied a simple character flaw, rather than a purposeful insult. But something in the way his brother was questioning Silviu put him on high alert. Once again, he forced himself to grope for patience.

"I'm still in England. What's wrong, Costel? What happened that has you so upset?"

"I was worried about you. I can't feel you anymore." The voice that came through the phone was shaky and low. Not at all like Costel, who, in fact, excelled at handling crises, as he'd gotten a lot of practice through the years.

Costel sounded terrified.

Silviu lifted his eyes to the sky and rubbed his chest. "What do you mean, you can't *feel* me? How do you feel me from another country?"

"Well..." His brother hesitated, making Silviu want to reach through the phone and shake the words from his mouth. "I could feel your magic," he finally said. "And then I couldn't. It woke me up."

"Costel, I know it's early. But please attempt to be logical and explain what you mean, in the most straightforward terms you can find."

A great sigh filled Silviu's ear. A few irritating moments passed before Costel spoke. "I was sleeping and I felt your sudden absence. When I realized I couldn't feel you, no matter how hard I focused, I grew worried and tried to call you. You didn't answer, and I grew *more* worried."

"I see." Silviu unclenched his jaw. "Now please explain this *feeling me* business. I don't understand, and I'm not sure I like knowing you can feel me, Costel. I didn't know of this talent of yours, and I must say, I find it extremely intrusive."

"It's not a talent." Silviu could hear Costel's low curse, quite a bit of rustling, then another sigh. He knew what was happening without having to see his brother—Costel was debating what to tell him and how. His brother had never been a successful poker player. Or politician.

Silviu's hard-won patience was rewarded when Costel finally stopped cursing. "I'm the Father now, with all the Lovasz power hosted within me. When I concentrate, I can feel any member of the Family and know if they are safe. I feel—well, *felt*—you and Ileana very easily, and almost constantly, without the need to focus. So when your... thread was cut off so abruptly a few hours ago, I was worried for you."

Silviu had no idea a Family leader could do such a thing, though it made sense. His mind boggled, but to cover his shock, he asked, "You were worried for me?"

"Of course I was. You're in the middle of a matriarchal Family. God only knows what they'll try to do to you."

"And you just...stopped feeling me?" Silviu arranged the timeline of events in his mind. It had to have happened when he became the Davenold Mother. The absorption of his new Family's magic must have acted in a similar manner to a Bestowal ritual, where a witch's power was transferred to their new bloodline upon marriage. Silviu ceased to be a Lovasz, and so Costel was no longer able to detect his magic.

"Yes. The absence was quite sudden, Silviu." Costel cleared his throat. "What happened a few hours ago?"

"Madeleine died." Silviu stepped into a walled section of the garden, saw that it was empty and stepped back out.

"Good God, please extend my condolences. Did Georgeanne become the Mother?"

There was no way in the Christian's Hell that Silviu would reveal what truly happened. Not to Costel, who was still on speaking terms with their grandfather, and far too easily influenced by their father. There was no reason why he should know Silviu was the new Davenold Mother, and no way could he keep a secret of that magnitude.

"She leads her Family," Silviu replied evasively.

"But Georgeanne *is* the Mother?"

Silviu took a slow breath at Costel's doggedness. "It was expected."

"Did something...happen between you two?"

Again Silviu came to a stand-still. He shivered as a cold blast of air sliced through his shirt and quickly evaluated his brother's question. He didn't dare give a straightforward answer, so instead he countered Costel's query with one of his own. "Like what?"

"Like marriage. Did Madeleine marry the two of you?"

"No, she didn't. But we are married."

"Maybe it's the Bane influence, then, coming after the Bestowal. Part of your ceremony combined your blood right?"

"It did." Mild alarm shot through Silviu, beating back a measure of the chill in the air rushing past him. He had never attended any wedding but the Ngozi affair, which had stopped short of actually being a wedding. He knew how important blood was to a great number of witching ceremonies, but he had no idea what his brother was talking about.

Silviu asked as cagily as he could, "Exactly what were you thinking, though? Which blood ceremony?"

"The one for Magic Matches." Costel spoke as if Silviu were an idiot. "The bride and groom each prick their fingers and combine the drops of blood on a piece of linen blessed by the Family or branch leader. Then the linen is burned over the Wedding Candle."

Silviu pinched the bridge of his nose. "Ah. Yes."

"It's symbolic of the merging of their magic. Was something done differently? Who performed the ceremony?"

"Mmm." Silviu gripped the phone tighter. "It was a private affair between the two of us."

"What does that mean?" Costel made a rough noise. "Were you married before Madeleine died?"

"Yes." Silviu rubbed his eyes and wished he trusted his brother enough to be honest with him. He would love to spill every secret he was fighting to hide to someone who may actually know the answers to some of the thousand questions sticking in his throat. But Costel was too easily manipulated by their paternal parents.

"Did she perform the Bestowal ritual?"

"Costel…" Ignoring his brother's question, Silviu tried hard not to sound as if he were fishing for information more important than it may seem to be on the surface. "Have you ever felt Georgie within the Lovasz magic?"

"Why would I?"

Silviu squinted at a marble angel pouring water into an overflowing fountain as he tried to puzzle his suspicions out. "She's my wife, a Lovasz, according to the treaty Father signed with Madeleine all those years ago."

"That makes no sense," Costel snapped. "The Davenold Mother can't be a Lovasz."

"So I gather."

"Our father knew that, Silviu. Why would he write such a

thing into your betrothal contract?"

"Who knows why our father does half the things he does?" Silviu couldn't tell his brother about Vasile's plans of revenge against the chosen Lovasz heir. He couldn't voice the bitterness their father had succumbed to, or the ruthless manipulations he undertook to get Silviu into the top leadership position of their society.

Everything Vasile had done was to undermine Costel's authority, with the sole purpose of striking out at the former Lovasz father, Alexandru. But Silviu couldn't tell his brother such a hurtful truth.

Instead, Silviu told his brother, "Georgie and I married before Madeleine died, and blood was exchanged. Did you feel her, Costel? You never answered."

"No. Who performed the Bestowal?"

"I don't know if we did that. But we've been married long enough that you should have felt her too, if you were able."

"It doesn't work like that, Silviu. The ritual of Bestowal is what transfers magic—"

"I know what it is."

Costel snorted. "Well, without it, an individual's magic stays with the Family they were born into, no matter their last name."

"Then, perhaps that's why our father wrote the betrothal contract the way he did."

"Mmm, so the Bane wouldn't weaken our bloodline. Perhaps."

Silviu gritted his teeth. "Do not call my wife a weakness."

"Trust me," Costel sighed, "I don't think she's weak. I watched her stand against our grandfather and I saw those shields of hers in action. I also saw the two of you combine your magic, and... Maybe that's what's at work here."

Grimacing at the remembrance of their time Poland, Silviu asked, "What do you mean?"

"The wedding ceremony for Magic Matches that combines your blood. Georgie's Bane shields probably extend to you now and that's probably why I couldn't feel you anymore."

"I can't use her shields. Why would you think that?"

"Didn't our father ever explain this to you? He knew you would marry your Match, he really should have prepared you." Costel made a disgusted noise. "Matches who marry try to strengthen their bond so their magic can be more stable. There is some exploitation of talent between successful witches."

Silviu rubbed his chest as a particularly strong pang ripped through his ribs. Once again, he had been played for a fool. None of his tutors had explained the concept in detail, Madeleine had never hinted at such a thing and his father had only barely glossed over the possibility. Silviu closed his eyes as the realization hit him—his father's manipulations knew no bounds. "How does that work?"

"Magic Matches favor the stronger witch."

"Yes, I know." Silviu's eyes snapped open as sudden realization lit his brain on fire. His surprise was enough to make him laugh out loud as he swayed on his feet. "Our father thought I could use her shields, but he's wrong, Costel. She can access my magic, but I can't access hers."

"Then," his brother spoke slowly, "that means she's the stronger witch."

"She's the key to me reaching all of my strength. *All* of it, Costel. More than I could ever wield on my own."

For a long moment, both men were silent, each digesting the possibilities. Finally, Costel said, "I suggest you take the Matriarchal ways to heart, then. I've seen the extent of your power, and I wouldn't want it destabilized from any ill-will between you and your new wife. I don't envy you, Silviu. You'll have to learn to be her doormat."

Silviu's stomach cramped. "We'll figure everything out between us. In the meantime, I need to know more about how you *feel* the Lovasz Family members. Madeleine died before we could learn this information."

"Perhaps I should talk to Georgeanne directly."

"She's busy." Silviu refused to admit he couldn't locate her. "I'll relay the information. How does a Family leader find a witch's... Thread, you called it? How do you do it, Costel?"

"There are no special tricks. The ability just comes with the new position. I concentrate. I think about the witch and the Lovasz magic, and it doesn't take much time before that Family member's thread stands out."

Silviu pressed a hand to his chest, wondering about the ache he'd been dealing with. He'd put the mild discomfort down to his own troubles with Georgie, the need to do something to regain her trust, his empathy and maybe even guilt. But perhaps he was feeling the effects of the Davenolds' combined sadness.

"Can you trace the Family members? Find out where they are?" Silviu could use such a trick — but he was disappointed.

"No," Costel answered, "the bloodline's power only lets me feel how they're doing. Whether they are alive, or wounded, and whatnot. Sometimes the magic works without my participation, especially if the emotion is strong. But Grandfather said that happens only rarely."

Silviu didn't trust his grandfather's observations. The man had spent a lifetime ignoring everything that didn't concern him directly. Still, Silviu filed the information away to examine and test at a later date. "But, as the Father, Costel, you draw on the strength of each Lovasz."

"Yes, but I can't use their talent. Keeping tabs on my Family's wellbeing is the extent of it."

Silviu cleared his throat. "I may have more questions about that, later."

"I'll be seeing you shortly," Costel reminded him. "The High Seat is dead, so the Council will be calling a meeting soon."

"Yeah." More responsibilities piled their weight onto Silviu's shoulders. "I'm sending Ileana and Eliasz down today, as soon the morning progresses a little. Tell me how things are going with the paperwork."

"Your paperwork is complete and being fast-tracked,

thanks to Bijoux Laurent."

Silviu cocked his head as a new and unfamiliar tone entered his brother's voice at the moment he said the woman's name. "And how is *that* going?"

"She scares me, Silviu. More than I can tell."

Chapter Twenty-Two

Georgeanne

Lying on the couch in her favorite sitting room, Georgie heard approaching footsteps. She knew who it was and didn't particularly care to see him just then, but Milo's question on the merits of forgiveness had caused havoc in her chest.

And in her mind, where a small voice had been attempting to force her to consider what she would have done, if the situation had been reversed.

Silviu looked as exhausted as she felt. Georgie sat up as he came to a stop on the threshold. His eyes lit with the peculiar vulnerability he only shared with her as his gaze raked her face like a physical caress, one she practically felt against her skin, dragging goosebumps in its wake. He came toward her, but took a seat in the chair to the left of the couch. Her stomach knotted.

"When I was young," Silviu's fingers clenched around the arms of his chair, "Madeleine's tutors used to read me stories about princesses locked in ivory towers by evil witches. I knew exactly how those girls felt."

Georgie lifted her brows, but held her silence.

He took a deep breath and continued. "And before I met you, I'll admit, I was in love with the concept of you. The one thing in my life that was mine. Not Costel's, not something Alexandru could take away. Just mine. My reward for all those fucking hours I spent alone, learning about Reap witches, Bane witches and politics. My reward for all the pressure my father put on me."

"I'm not just an extension of you—"

His cold stare stopped her words. "When I met you, Georgie, when I looked into your eyes, I saw the same thing I saw in my own. Loneliness like mine, as different as me, put under the same amount of pressure as me. I knew you like I knew myself. Like a piece of me had been returned and I hadn't even known it was missing until it came back."

"Really?" She shook her head and struggled to speak evenly. "Then you should have known how I would feel—"

"I couldn't let Suzette take your Family's power!" Silviu closed his eyes, only to open them quickly and pin her with a steely glare. "But you couldn't take it either. Your bloodline's magic couldn't push past the Bane shields, even with me helping."

"You knew." Her voice emerged scratchy and hoarse. Bitterness burned her tongue. Georgie cleared her throat. "You knew, all this time, that the magic wouldn't come to me."

"I suspected, and Madeleine told me her doubts."

"It would have been nice for one of the two of you to share with me, huh? Maybe I had similar doubts, Silviu. Maybe we could have talked about it and come up with a plan both of us could live with."

"You can access the magic through me. I don't want to lead your Family, Georgeanne, but I swear to you, so long as your Family's power dwells inside me, I will die before I let them come to harm. I will take care of you all."

Disbelief seared her skull. "And I should just trust you, right?"

"I have been very careful with you, Georgie." He met her gaze with a possessive look too raw for her to feel comfortable with. "I have been trying to moderate myself for your benefit. You're not good at handling strong sentiments beyond loyalty, courage and protectiveness. You were ostracized and abandoned at too young an age to simply accept the kind of love I have for you."

"I've never been fond of your dramatic streak."

He sat forward with a quick jerk of his spine, his intensity beating against her. "Mine is an all-consuming love. Fiery, ready to burn us both to ash and remake us into one being in two bodies."

Wariness and hope waged war in her chest. A part of her liked his possessiveness. A part of her reveled in his dominance and wanted to pit hers against it, and take bets on who would win. But to give in meant breaking down the meager protection she'd managed to keep between him and her heart, and with his betrayal still reconstructing the landscape of their relationship, as well as her Family, she couldn't lower her guard.

Silviu reached for her but she jerked her hand up to stop him. "Don't touch me!"

Georgie had to get out of the room. Restlessness infected her like a terminal disease, stealing her breath and making her itch. Her muscles tensed in preparation for her departure, but a dark corona exploded around her and pushed her back to the couch cushions.

She gasped, but there was no pain. Just enormous pressure bearing down on her with a weight that should have cracked her bones. Surprise held her immobile as a thick fog spread over her legs. Beneath the mist, a faint silver sheen ranged the length of her thighs — her Bane imperviousness rising to form a protective barrier.

And Georgie was grateful. The presence of the dark magic meant she didn't have to think about Silviu. She didn't have to consider his words, or decipher how much truth was in them. Dealing with a dark magic attack was infinitely easier than seeing her way through the tangle of lies and hurt she felt lost within.

She moved her hands over the mist. Sticky tendrils reached for her, persistent black cords that writhed in a mass that sent thin shoots out to brush her fingers. Her shields flared and sent the magic rearing back every time the spell touched her. "It's testing its boundaries, can you see?"

Silviu exhaled slowly. "It's testing *you*, love. Looking for weakness. This spell is being directed as we speak."

"Maybe we can find the source."

"I already know who it is," Silviu snarled as he studied the fog. "There is one woman in this house who both works with dark magic and has shown hostility to you. This is the first challenge."

"But I'm not the Mother."

"Your Family doesn't know that. And I'll make certain they never learn."

Georgie let the sensation of the sticky spell sink into her fingertips. It was similar to whatever had caught hold of her grandmother. Though she could see it, the magic held the flavor of secrecy, all traces of the casting witch buried so deep Georgie couldn't get a handle on who could be so bold. Her cousin's magic had never felt like that.

"Do you know for sure that Suzette is doing this, Silviu? You know, with certainty, that this is her magic? Because it doesn't feel like it to me."

"No, I can't get a sense of this magic," he snapped. "But I can make an educated guess, Georgeanne."

She dropped her gaze and began to move her fingers over the dark fog. "I don't know that much about magic, Silviu. You know I was taught different things because Madeleine didn't see the point of a Bane witch learning spells and whatnot. But I can feel the difference between witches."

"You said the same thing about Graves and the germ within the effigy that targeted your grandmother, and you were wrong." Silviu sighed. "Do you remember when you reached inside yourself and let your magic rise? I want you to reach even farther, and find mine."

"Fine. Give me your hand." Though reluctant, Georgie lifted her own.

He refused her. "At Graves' wedding, my magic found you across the room. We weren't touching, yet it filled you and brought you back to me."

"You sent it my way, Silviu. What did you do to fill me

up like that?"

"I don't think I did anything." He shook his head and pursed his lips. "Quite the opposite, in fact. Just try, love. It's important."

With a doubtful glance up at his face, Georgie obeyed. She'd had some practice, and found the process to be easier every time. She dug down into the cool depths of her Bane void, following the pull of Silviu's magic until she located a golden thread in the very center of her soul. She caught it and became aware of the enormous power he wielded. She pulled, and his strength geysered up into her body, heating her veins and filling her heart.

Georgie felt a jerk in the vicinity of her navel. She knew the instant Silviu lowered every block he had in place, sending his magic to her in a torrent that rushed through her. The sensation was just as exhilarating as when he'd shoved his magic into her while the twins had performed their spell—but better, because it was just between the two of them.

She'd been getting used to the odd occasions when she felt Silviu's heartbeat within her own chest. She'd been getting used to the simple, inexplicable knowledge that he was all right, doing well wherever he was in the house. She'd been getting used to the flashes of his emotions her intuition picked up even when she couldn't see or touch him.

But nothing had prepared her for the moment Silviu gifted her with every ounce of his magic. Crossing the space between them and twining them together seamlessly, his power filled her and anchored her until she almost felt as if his magic were hers—as if she was a normal witch with normal talents. Georgie became a part of him, and Silviu became a part of her. Merged and Matched.

For a moment, the pain of his betrayal was forgotten in the flood of their magical connection.

The dark mist covering Georgie's lap took on new dimensions. Like fog separating, the insubstantial mass peeled back in layers, allowing her to see the webbing of the spell hidden within. When faced with the harmful effigy of her grandmother, Georgie had broken the spell at the repeating intersections of two magical strains. One strain manifested as red light, the other as black. But the spell currently misting over her lap had no such connections. Violet strands of magic were wrapped in narrow cords of black, with no juncture where Georgie could separate the two.

She took a deep breath. "This magic feels like something fragile wrapped in something very, very strong. See how the black wraps the violet?"

Georgie ran her fingers over a thread of magic and it snapped. She was only vaguely surprised that it reacted the same way the effigy's spell had, but still she grew more confident in her ability to destroy it. One by one, the threads frayed and gave way, diminishing the power that covered her. Shockingly easy.

Silviu's eyes jolted from her to the final thread she was destroying "As if a weaker spell anchors a dangerous spell. Yes, I think you're right."

"So what does that mean?"

She released Silviu's magic and had the distinct impression that it slithered down into her Bane void and coiled tight, ready to be used again at a moment's notice. The Reap strength suddenly felt intolerably intrusive. Georgie tried to ignore the sensation.

"It had to be an enhancement," Silviu mused.

"Graves." Georgie clearly remembered several occasions where the Ngozi man had claimed such assistance.

"Maybe we're both right, love, and it's Suzette's dark magic aided by another. The strong witch no one seems to be able to find, perhaps?"

Beyond exhausted, Georgie slumped into the couch cushions. "Don't Magic Matches do that?"

"This is different. Matches have magic that merges and flows together like ours does. Seamless to the point no one would be able to tell where the strength of my magic starts and yours begins. The magic works on the same frequency, so it's impossible to distinguish."

"Suzette and her husband are Matches so I thought—" Georgie rubbed her eyes. "Never mind. Even combining their talents, my cousin and her husband couldn't reach the strength in that dark magic."

Georgie's thoughts tumbled and slid, jumping from one subject to another too quickly for her to figure anything out. Dark witches, strong witches and dangerous witches were beyond her ability to contemplate just then, as she fidgeted under Silviu's watchful, hungry gaze. He was too intense, and his magic was too abrasive inside her. She was too aware of it, too wary of it.

She wondered what his magic, hiding within her, meant for her independence. She wondered if he could track her through it, or feel her through it as she'd started to feel him. She wondered if it would grow stronger the more she used it, and if it would eventually take over and make her into an extension of him—the very thing she couldn't afford to be, and never *wanted* to be.

Georgie fought against the sensation of being trapped. She'd worked too hard for the respect of the witching world, had sacrificed too much to simply be an afterthought hooked to Silviu's rising star. Her sense of self had been compromised, but she refused to let him strip it from her altogether.

"I'm going to go, now." Georgie hauled herself off the couch through willpower and the driving need to find a quiet place away from Silviu to think about what had just happened. Not the challenge—the spell had been easy enough to break and was only remarkable in that it had enough weight to push her down—but what came before. She needed to digest Silviu's words, his tone as he'd said them and the way his magic so easily came to her call.

"Wait!" For a moment, Silviu wore a hunted expression and his eyes cast around the sitting room. Georgie knew he was only stalling her departure when he walked to the bookcase against the far wall and told her, "I was reading your great-grandmother's journal earlier. It's a history of the Davenold Magic Matches. I've never seen a Family so dedicated to building a dynasty."

"Ah, Matches." As if their previous ponderings had conjured her, Suzette swept into the sitting room. "They're overrated, you know. One little argument can upset the fragile balance between them and destabilize the magic they share."

Georgie gritted her teeth. "Did you come to evaluate the outcome of your laughable attempt at a challenge, sweetie?"

"I don't need to challenge you now, darling." The other woman's eyes widened. "When the time is right, I will challenge for the Davenold power and it will come to me easily, as it should have done before *you* came along."

Georgie worked her jaw to see if that would alleviate some of the angry pressure building in her ears. "You delude yourself."

"I was the only heir for years," Suzette spat. "You and Christiana stole what would have been mine."

Georgie could only shake her head. "Your magic can't harm me. I suggest you abandon whatever plans you've concocted before you hurt yourself."

Suzette leaned close to Georgie and whispered, "Who says I'll challenge you with magic? Perhaps I'll simply wait for your Match to destabilize. After all, everyone could hear the two of you arguing earlier."

Then the woman sauntered over to Silviu. She leaned against his chest and sent her finger skating up his shirt front. "When you're ready to have a *real* witch in your bed," she purred, "you know where to find me."

"What the fuck?" Silviu pushed Suzette back as the woman reached for his waistband.

Georgie saw red. Her veins caught fire. She was positive her anger flowed off her shoulders in thick waves. No matter what he'd done, no matter how badly he'd hurt her, Silviu was still *hers*, and Georgie would be damned if she ever let Suzette corrupt what she'd claimed.

Georgie clenched her fists. "Can you be any more pathetic? You continuously throw yourself at your cousins' men."

"He needs a real woman, not a defective tease like you." Suzette winked. Then she pressed herself to Silviu's chest again, her hands busy as he attempted to twist away.

His eyes met Georgie's and she understood his hesitation. He'd once promised to let her handle the conflicts they would face on the Matriarchal side of the Schism. He'd promised to let her lead when it came to her Family's affairs.

Maybe — just maybe — he was trying to avoid undermining her authority.

"If you don't get your fucking hands off my husband," Georgie's brows lowered, along with her voice, "I'll break every finger on them."

A sly smile curved Suzette's lips. "Such diplomacy, sweetie."

"Sometimes diplomacy requires fighting for what's yours." Georgie's hand flashed out to grab a fistful of Suzette's hair. She used her anchor to rip the woman away from Silviu's body. "And he's *mine*."

Suzette grabbed a vase off a table as she staggered by it and hurled it at Georgie's head. It missed her by a fraction of an inch. She couldn't have cared less, but Silviu lost his temper.

"*Stop it!*"

Magic exploded from him. Silver light filled the room in a blinding display, sinking into Suzette and stilling her until she appeared paralyzed. Silver ropes also coiled around Georgie, and she felt the unchecked compulsion in his words a bare moment before her Bane imperviousness rose up and gobbled Silviu's magic whole.

Shocked and incensed, Georgie spun on him. "You just used your magic against me? To *influence* me?"

"I didn't mean to." He raised hands in a gesture of apologetic surrender.

She wasn't appeased. "That's the second time you've

done that. You tried the same thing at the Ngozi residence, Silviu."

"It's been a long day, and with you using my —"

"Your magic?" Georgie sneered. Just as she was starting to think that there *was* a way forward for them, that Silviu would help her regain the trust she'd lost in him, he once again proved how unscrupulous he could be. "Well, *my* magic feels that particular talent you seem to depend so heavily on is an attack. And I agree."

"I'm sorry, my love." Silviu reached for her, but she stepped away. Regret pulled at his features. "I just lost control for a minute."

"Listen to your fucking lies. Do you even know when to stop telling them?" Georgie threaded her fingers through her hair and tugged, hoping the sharp pain would offset the deep ache inside her. "You didn't *lose* control. You tried to take it."

"I didn't mean to use my magic against you, Georgeanne. I didn't —"

Georgie held up her hand to stop his pitiful explanations. She glanced at Suzette, who stood swaying, eyes blank, perfectly passive as a thin stream of drool tracked down her chin.

Silviu would have done that to her, if Georgie's imperviousness hadn't fought back. It was too much. *He* was too much, and she knew he would only keep going now that he felt secure in their relationship and thought she couldn't find a way free of it.

Even Georgie's throat ached, as she pushed her words through it. "I was a fool to ever trust you, Silviu."

Chapter Twenty-Three

Milo

His wife was in the chair before the window, glaring at him as Milo entered their bedroom. The bed was still made, unslept in, and her clothes were the ones she'd worn the night before. She looked exhausted, miserable and angrier than he'd ever seen her.

Georgie had told him to find his wife. She'd refused to explain why, but the expression on Christiana's face was harsh enough Milo wished he'd followed the command sooner. He'd needed a few more moments to think, however, and had delayed.

"What is wrong, *krasavitsa*?"

Christiana's voice held enough cold energy to cut. "Where were you last night?"

"First I made some phone calls. Then I was thinking things over, trying to gain a new perspective." Milo shrugged out of his rumpled business jacket and yanked at his wilted tie. "Then I walked along the beach for a while. Then—"

"*Sure you did.* Lots of people spend all night outdoors watching the tides on such a cold, rainy autumn evening. Lots of people walk the beach in the middle of a thunderstorm." She hurled her bitter laugh at him like a weapon. "And lots of people also fuck Suzette, a woman I've already caught you with once."

It had taken hours for him to find his sense of calm. And within minutes of walking through his bedroom door, his wife threatened to blow it all to hell. Milo struggled to keep his voice even. "You didn't catch me doing anything,

Christiana, because I have done nothing. I told you, your cousin was with Daniel, not me. I don't want her."

"Of course," she drawled. "But tell me, Milo, why don't I believe you?"

Irritation pulled his scalp tight. "Perhaps because you are so adept at lying yourself, *krasavitsa*, that you simply expect others to lie, as well."

"Or *maybe*," she scoffed, "it's because you don't look like a man who spent the night in the rain. You look like a man who found himself a warm, dry bed in this crowded house. Whose bed, Milo?"

"I didn't say I spent all night outside." His chest seemed to cave in as he stared at her. So beautiful, so powerful, so angry at him with a dark glint of betrayal in her pretty eyes. "But neither did I find a bed. If I wanted to share a bed with someone, I would have shared it with my wife."

One look at Christiana told him she was beyond belief. Her chin jerked and her mouth fell open on a smug, sour smile. A sharp breath huffed through her curled lips as if she would laugh in derision. Then her eyes narrowed and Milo was trapped in her hostility.

"Who did you fuck last night? Because it sure as hell wasn't me."

He'd truly thought he would have enough patience to wear her down, little by little, even if it took years. He'd been wrong. He'd thought that he only needed to prove himself worthy of her respect and she'd give it, as her grandmother had done. As almost everyone else he'd ever met had done. He'd taken the time to court her, woo her, seduce her — and not just her body, but her mind and loyalty, too.

All for naught.

Hanging onto his patience by his fingernails, he shook his head. "You know how I feel about adultery, Christiana."

"Yeah, when you're the victim. Men don't give a shit about *being* the adulterer though, so long as they get to come."

He gritted his teeth. "Since the day your grandmother

gave me permission to court you, I have been with no one else, Christiana. Your accusation is both unfair and offensive."

"And yet, you didn't come back last night, and I have no proof you were where you say you were."

"And you can't simply trust me?" Milo's gut clenched.

"No."

"Well, that seems to be your problem. Not mine." Balling his expensive jacket together with his tie, he flung it toward the dresser, the muscles in his arm knotting and flexing with a need for violence. "I'm not the liar here."

"How dare you take that tone of voice with me, Milo?" Christiana sprang from the chair and planted her hands on her hips. "I'm not the one who was caught with a half-naked woman pressed to my body! I'm not the one that left my spouse to sit and wonder all night long."

"No, you may have done something much worse." He turned to confront her directly. "What happened to your first husband?"

"He died."

"How did he die, Christiana?"

"Heart attack." She smirked. "No doubt taking on too many mistresses at one time. A person's heart can surely only handle so much stimulation before it gives out. You should keep that in mind."

His stomach rolled, but he had to ask. "Did you kill him? Adam as good as confessed to being in league with you for murder, and I want to know the truth!"

Her cheeks burned red, her fists pressed harder to her hips. "Think you can distract me from your infidelities? Think you can accuse me of murder and I'll forget you spent the night fucking someone else?"

"*There is no one else!*" Milo sliced the air with a stiffened hand. "Now who's trying to turn the conversation?"

"We're not having a conversation. You're getting the hell out of this room. You can spend the rest of *all* your nights with your whore."

"Did you kill your first husband, Christiana?"

She tossed her head and stormed around the bed, clearly intending on making her exit. Fear and anger spiked into Milo's heart with the force of a blunt object.

He exploded. He shot across the room and jumped in front of her, blocking the path to the door. Her eyes widened and she jerked back violently, but for once Milo didn't care about her reaction. He took no measures to gentle his movements or put her at ease. She wasn't leaving until she told him what he wanted to know.

"Did you kill your first husband?"

"Get out of my way."

Milo raised his voice. "Did you kill him?"

"*Move.*"

"Did you kill him, Christiana?" Milo grabbed her by the shoulders and barely restrained himself from shaking her. "Did you kill him in a jealous fit because he had a string of mistresses?"

"Jealous?" Her word rose sharply at the end. "Hardly jealous! I would have preferred not to have been a laughingstock throughout the wider witching world, as every-fucking-body knew just how many lovers he'd taken before I did, but I was most certainly not jealous!"

"Scores!" Milo nearly screamed. "He fucked anybody in a skirt. And I know that pissed you off."

"He could have screwed a platoon of women and I couldn't have cared less, so long as it kept him out of my bed!" She pushed at Milo's chest, but he refused to budge.

"Then how did he die?" Milo's roar bounced around the room like a beast intent on doing damage. He did shake her then, unable to hold back, unable to listen to another word that didn't explain what Adam had insinuated. "*Did you fucking kill your husband?*"

"*Yes*! I killed that bastard!" Eyes of blue flame scorched him alive. Chris struggled in his grip, thrashing and beating his chest. "I killed him with a dark magic spell that would have ripped me apart, had my Magic Match not been there to help me cast it."

Milo released her and staggered back, heart thumping, knees turning to water. His lungs tightened, a band of shock squeezed around his chest until it was a battle to breathe at all. Pain ricocheted inside him until all his nerves shut down to protect themselves.

"And you know what?" Christiana advanced on him with all the deadly intent of an avenging Valkyrie. "I'd do it again, I'd have let that fucking spell kill me too, if Adam hadn't helped minimize the damage. It was better than letting him beat me until I died! It was better than him using his dick as weapon against me. It was better than all the pain he heaped on me since the minute we'd married."

Numbed shock morphed into icy rage between one pained heartbeat and the next. Everything inside Milo stilled. "What?"

"He beat me." The words were pushed between Chris' teeth, rasping into their freedom with a sound that conveyed her pain more than anything else ever could. "He hurt me and forced me into his bed when I didn't want to be there anymore. He used my body in ways I can't even think about without vomiting."

Milo's legs did collapse then. He fell onto the edge of the bed and gripped his skull, unable to take his eyes off his wife. "Why didn't you separate? Why didn't you leave him and go back to your Family? Your grandmother would have taken you in and protected you."

"He made me doubt, Milo." The confession gritted out as if Christiana could hardly speak the words. Tears gathered and fell, but she didn't bother to wipe them away. "He made me think that it was all my fault and that if I could just change, it would get better. He tore me down until I believed I was unworthy of anyone coming to my rescue. Until I was ashamed to admit I needed rescuing. I was a Davenold heir, Madeleine's eldest granddaughter, and I wasn't strong enough to help myself out of a situation *everyone* begged me not to get myself into!"

"Christiana—"

"They warned me that we wouldn't suit. My mother, my grandmother, even Georgie. They told me I was rushing, that I wasn't looking deeper than his pretty face. But I wouldn't listen. I was so damned *stupid*."

"I doubt they understood it would be so bad."

"I didn't know what to do." Her arms came up to wrap around herself, painting a picture of such misery Milo's heart stopped. She looked so alone, so fragile, so broken. "Adam figured out what was happening and we…"

"You did save yourself." Calm finally wormed through Milo, distant and alien, as if it belonged to someone else, but present and lending him much-needed strength. He had to be strong for her, in spite of the trembling inside his body that he couldn't seem to stem.

He forced his legs to function and stood up. He crossed the space between them, for the first time understanding why Christiana always flinched and backed away. The whole time they'd been married that action had irritated him until it left him raw, but now he had the reason.

And it left him a bloody mess.

He stalked her as she backed away until she trapped herself against the door. With nowhere else to go, she had no choice but to step into Milo's body as he caught her and pulled her close. For a long minute he simply breathed her in, nose buried in her hair, his shaking hands stroking her stiff back, his arms enfolding her in a place where he knew he could keep her safe.

"I'm so sorry, *krasavitsa*." Cold rage burned through him. "If I could, I would dig up his fucking corpse and kill him again."

"I had to do it," she whispered. "I *had* to."

Milo's arms tightened around her. "Everyone knew how you'd fallen in love with him, and the whirlwind your romance had been. Everyone knew how much you wanted him."

"And everyone knew how many mistresses he had before

and after our wedding. I was pitied, made a fool of."

"I thought you still loved him." Milo fought for oxygen. "There were rumors that you killed him because he couldn't give you a child, but I couldn't imagine such a thing. And you were so resistant when I first began courting you... I just thought you still loved him."

"I cast every spell I could think of to keep from getting pregnant." Christiana jerked in his arms and Milo wondered what memories were haunting her. "I didn't want his baby and I hadn't loved him in a very long time."

Milo didn't know if he could handle the telling of the tale, but he knew he needed to hear it, if only because she needed to say it. But not standing up on trembling legs, holding his wife too tight yet wishing he could hold her tighter. He needed to pull her directly into his body, but as that was impossible, he picked her up and carried her to their bed. He left her long enough to remove both their shoes then climbed up with her, dragging her back into his embrace.

And miracle of miracles, Christiana cuddled closer, tucking her face into his neck until her tears ran down into his collar. Milo made soothing noises that neither stopped her crying nor made him feel calmer. He stroked her back as she wept, and she finally quieted enough to tell him about her first marriage.

"It was really hard, growing up with Georgie," she began. "She always got so much attention, but I was Madeleine's oldest granddaughter. I was supposed to be special, but Georgie is Bane. I didn't understand what that meant, or what was expected of her because of it, until after I married."

"You wanted attention?"

She jerked in his hold, but didn't pull away. "When Thomas Marsh looked at me like I was *everything*, I was totally sucked in."

Milo tried not to tense at the mention of her first husband's name. It rarely passed her lips, and even her Family refused to refer to him as anything other than her 'first husband' or 'that cheating bastard'. Milo dragged a slow breath in through his nostrils as Christiana sniffled and continued.

"I was twenty-one. I fought to marry Thomas, argued and pleaded until there was really no other option but for Madeleine to give in, because I would have run off with him, otherwise. She knew before I did, I think, that he would take me away from them. From my Family."

Milo closed his eyes. "What happened?"

"Little things at first. He told me I was too fat or too skinny. He didn't like my makeup or my clothes. He hated my underwear. He wanted me to cut my hair. Then it got worse, like I couldn't do anything right."

"He undermined your confidence."

"I started pulling away from everyone and I let his words, and then his actions, make me choose isolation, rather than show my shame to my Family." Christiana muffled a bitter sob against his shoulder. "Georgie told me I shouldn't marry him, but she had Silviu, and she was traveling to all these adventurous places and living what I'd imagined to be some grand, glamorous life."

"You married your first husband because you were jealous of Georgie?"

Her next words were so low Milo strained his ears to hear them. "It sounds stupid, right? It took five years of living in my own personal nightmare to understand that she'd been sent away for rushing into things with Silviu. To finally understand that a region where witches are still hunted and executed is neither fun nor luxurious. And I started wondering if she'd felt as alone as I had."

It was a convoluted explanation, but Milo knew that the most important decisions often weren't based on logic. His own Family was proof of how emotions could tangle and knot around rational thought until the consequences turned deadly. What mattered was that Christiana had rushed into marriage for what she'd thought were the right reasons, only to realize it had been a knee-jerk reaction to the oddity of her circumstances growing up.

Right or wrong, the need to be someone's priority was a

hard emotion to deny.

So Milo didn't ask any more questions or make any more comments. He refused to make Christiana feel inadequate just because she had made poor decisions in her youth – after all, who hadn't? Milo himself was guilty of trusting the wrong woman, only to have her elope with his cousin, saving him from making the biggest mistake of his life. Christiana hadn't been as lucky.

Her tale continued and Milo gritted his teeth as she told him of her first husband's mockery, insults and slander, all carefully designed to shake, then break her confidence. When she started pulling away from her Family, the abuse began. Hiding bruises and feeling both ashamed and stupid all while still trying to protect and defend her first husband, Christiana pulled away even more, until she hardly spoke to her Family at all.

The women her first husband had been with were legion. The few times she visited her Family, Christiana had caught her husband actively trying to seduce her cousins, to say nothing of the torrid and very public affair the man had carried on with Suzette. But by then, Christiana only felt foolish rather than jealous or hurt, because she was terrified of being the woman in her husband's bed.

"I don't want to tell you everything he did to me," Chris told Milo.

Milo pressed his lips to his wife's forehead and thanked everything he held sacred that she didn't. Hearing the rest was hard enough – he really couldn't stomach a listing of the sexual abuse his wife had been forced to endure for five years. Cupping her jaw, he tipped her face up to his. "Tell me how you saved yourself, then."

"Adam came to visit, unexpectedly." She blinked fast and drew a shaky breath as her cheeks paled and her eyes dimmed. "He thought he'd be funny and let himself into the house to scare me. I didn't have time to hide the bruises."

"Was Thomas there?"

She shook her head. "I was already starting to look for

217

ways to get away without Thomas following me and bringing me back. He used to tell me that he wouldn't let me go, because one day I would be the Davenold Mother and he would be the High Male, and he refused to let me fuck that up for him."

Milo held his silence as his wife trembled and breathed. She pressed close and he pulled her closer, until her bones were hard ridges digging into his muscles, but he could hardly feel the discomfort. Now that he knew where Adam's protectiveness toward Christiana came from, Milo wondered if he could find more patience when dealing with the man. When Christiana's story continued, he knew he could.

"I had a spell book out," she whispered. "It was a comprehensive tome, and some spells were dark magic. I'd just read one spell and rejected it, because it's not a talent of mine. Dark spells have always gone badly for me, so I don't cast them. Then Adam found me and flipped out because of what I looked like. We were still arguing, I was begging him to leave, when Thomas came home."

"But Adam confronted him." Milo could envision the scene very well.

Chris lowered her voice to an impossible degree. "Thomas and Adam fought and Adam was winning. Adam hit him and Thomas fell back into his closet. Where he kept a gun."

"A witch with a gun?" Magic was always the primary weapon in any fight between witches, as a point of pride. But Milo knew that Adam was strong, and Christiana had just detailed how immoral Thomas was.

"I just reacted," she said slowly. "I saw the gun pointed at my twin and was more afraid than I had been at any other point in my marriage. The last spell in my mind was dark. I'm not good with dark magic, it doesn't feel right, but I cast that spell, and it ripped through me, tearing me apart. Thomas staggered back and Adam ran for me, grabbed me. He helped me balance the strength of the spell and direct it all at Thomas."

Christiana shifted and Milo forced his arms to unlock enough to allow her to draw back. She pulled up to her knees, wrapping her arms around her body and staring at him with pain-filled, defiant eyes. Her chin notched up, but her expression was perfectly blank.

"I killed my first husband, Milo. And I'm not sorry."

Chapter Twenty-Four

Christiana

Her stomach was in knots. Burning, dripping with acid that roiled and rose to tear the flesh from her esophagus. Her heart thumped against her ribs, but in that moment Christiana would have sworn it had stopped completely.

Milo knew she was a murderer now. Her reserved, composed, powerful husband, a man with extensive business dealings, a man who had far too much to lose to throw it all away for a relationship with a murderess, knew his wife had committed a heartless crime. And knew she'd have done it again, in the same situation.

Milo slowly sat up, crossing his legs. Very slowly, he reached for her. So slow, and Christiana finally realized why, as he cupped her jaw and tilted her damp face up to his so she could see the truth in his eyes. He didn't want to hurt her, didn't want to scare her. And just maybe he even loved her.

Relief almost had her collapsing to the bed.

"How," he asked her with amazement in his tone, "did you ever find enough courage to agree to marry me?"

She gave him a weak smile even as her breath broke on a sob of hysterical laughter. "Madeleine asked me to date you and then she told me she wanted me to marry you, so I hadn't thought I had a choice, really. And you were so nice to me… I figured she couldn't do worse than I did."

"We met at a children's charity, remember?" She nodded and he continued. "You were beautiful, the most beautiful woman I'd ever seen, in a blue dress I wanted to peel off you. There was a small child who reached out for you and grabbed your dress. It was wrinkled the rest of the night."

She remembered the event vividly. It wasn't primarily for witches, though there were many in attendance. The charity was for victims of domestic violence, hosted by Davenold Family Enterprises a bare two months after the death of her husband. Madeleine had put her foot down and ordered Christiana to not only attend, but also to organize the gathering she hadn't wanted to be any part of. Madeleine had sworn it would be cathartic, and had introduced her to Milo only an hour into the event.

"That dress was ruined forever," she said on a shaky laugh. "There was something sticky on his hands and it ruined the silk."

"The women in my Family would have yelled at the child for that. Pushed him away, punished him." Milo grimaced. "I'm sure some would have beaten him. But you smiled and picked him up, and I saw your generosity shining out of you. In that moment, I knew you would be mine. I wouldn't settle for anyone else."

"I don't know why."

Milo leaned forward and brushed his lips over hers. "I wanted to get out of my Family," he admitted quietly. "I wanted a nice, peaceful Family where I wouldn't have to constantly guard my back. But even if you were from a *terrible* Family, I would have wanted you. Even if you were the lowest ranking member of your Family, I would have wanted you. And my wanting you has nothing to do with who your grandmother is, or your potential to be Mother."

"I'm not the Mother, Milo. Georgie is."

His eyes widened, then closed. Pain spread over his face, and for a moment Christiana thought he was disappointed at her lack of inheritance.

Then he said, "I'm so sorry, *krasavitsa*. I'll miss your grandmother very much." His eyes opened, and they blazed with relief. "But I am very happy that you will be safe from challenges."

221

"You don't mind that I'm not the Mother?"

"I've never cared about your position in your Family. Your safety is my primary concern, and I didn't know how I would keep you safe, if you inherited."

A warm tendril of hope curled through her. "You told me that *krasavitsa* means beautiful. You make me feel beautiful, maybe even valuable, and though you scare the hell out of me sometimes with the way you look at me, I need you to know that I do trust you to not physically hurt me."

"You flinch when I reach for you, or even when I enter a room."

She dropped her eyes, her lips twisting without her permission, her fingers curling against her ribs as she held herself a little tighter. "War wounds, like you once said to me."

He stilled. "Christiana, I will do my best to never hurt you in any way, but in return, I need your full trust in all aspects of our relationship. I need you to know there are no other women. I want you, all of you, and I need you to believe in me, because these walls you keep between us need to come down."

"I'm trying."

"*Krasavitsa*, I swear to you, you have final say over anything that happens between us. Only what you want, when you want it. I will never force you to do anything."

"What if I don't trust myself to make good decisions?" She risked a glance at his face and pushed the words from her throat. "What if I just want you to...to...take care of me?"

Milo's emerald eyes took on a glint that made them glow like the rarest of jewels. He shuffled forward and caught her hips, rising to his knees as he pulled her toward him. "I will give you whatever you need."

She hesitated, then blurted, "A matriarchal witch isn't supposed to need a man to take care of her."

"Everyone needs someone, Christiana. I know your strength, and now I know the full scope of it, but that doesn't mean I would ever leave you to face hardships on your own. From the first, it has always been my intention to take care of you. What you need to learn, is that it is possible for me to do so without taking over completely."

His face held open honesty, his eyes glimmered with truth and concern. Something that had been coiled tight deep inside Christiana's chest loosened. "What did you need to think about, last night?"

A sad smile came and went on Milo's mouth. He urged her ever closer, but then surprised her by making her spin around on her knees until her back was to him. The mattress shook a moment before his heat lit her spine on fire and his thighs slid under hers. He pulled her down to sit on his lap and wrapped his arms around her.

His lips coasted over the shell of her ear and his whispered words infiltrated her head on a soft ribbon of pain. His pain. "I wanted your respect. I've worked for it, and thought, with time, you would come to realize that I am worthy of it. I was afraid that perhaps you never would, that your twin would always hold more influence with you, and that you would always keep yourself separate from me."

"I'm…" Christiana took a huge breath, releasing it slowly. "I'm afraid."

"I know that now." His lips found the pulse just under her ear, his hands loosened enough to let one drop down and tug at the button of her trousers. "And I will have patience. I am a very patient man, *krasavitsa*."

Fear, the remnants of her anger and a mix of other emotions too volatile to name coalesced into a new beast. One that had Christiana's body heating and melting, muscles flinching with a sudden desire to be connected to her husband as intimately as possible.

"What did," her voice broke as his fingers slipped under her panties and stroked — too lightly — over her clit, "you decide?"

"That I would try harder to gain your trust. That I would simply ask you what I wanted to know, and hope you told me the truth."

"And if I didn't?" Christiana's head tipped back against his shoulder. She couldn't see him, but she felt a slight tension infuse him, then dissipate.

"But you did tell me the truth, *krasavitsa*." His fingers pushed lower, sliding through her folds in a slow glide that left her wriggling on his lap. "So it no longer matters. That is what we need between us. Truth will bring trust. Can you trust me, Christiana?"

It getting difficult to think, with Milo's hand playing between her legs and his chest brushing her spine with every breath he took. She couldn't see him, and she didn't particularly like that he was behind her, but she realized that was his intention. Almost always before, he put her on top of him, letting her lead in all ways, giving her full control.

He wanted to prove she could trust him, he wanted prove he could take care of her and not hurt her. And she needed to prove to herself that Milo was deserving of the trust she so desperately wanted to give him.

"I trust you, Milo." She hoped that was true.

"Good," he breathed into her ear. "Because I'm going to fuck you just like this, behind you and leaving you no control. You simply have to trust that I will not hurt you, that you can tell me to stop whenever you want, but you will have no way to stop me beyond your words, *krasavitsa*."

He didn't give her time to respond. Instead, he tipped her off his lap. Christiana just managed to release her arms from where they'd been hugging her own ribcage in time to catch herself against the mattress. Milo shifted his legs to the outside of hers and wrestled her pants over her hips, leaving them around her knees.

Chris tried to move her legs, but her pants and Milo's embrace wouldn't let her shift more than an inch. Excitement rose within her, along with a twist of fear. The last time she'd been in that particular position hadn't gone well for her.

But then Milo huffed and planted a hand on her butt cheek, still covered by her underwear. "I like the little stars and comets, *krasavitsa*. It reminds me of what I'm aiming for."

Her first husband had made fun of her underwear until she'd switched over to lace and silk, which he hadn't liked any better. When she was free again, she'd gotten rid of almost every pair of uncomfortable panties she owned, and reverted back to the cotton briefs. Even knowing her current husband didn't mind her underwear, Milo's words soothed some part of her that still waited for terrible things to begin. She relaxed, even as he pulled her starred briefs down and restrained her further.

His hands fully enclosed her cheeks, gripped and spread them. "Do you have any idea how beautiful you are?" he groaned. "The sight of you spread for me, your pussy opened and waiting for my cock to fill you?"

She could imagine. His fingers had made her eager, her clit was still humming from his fondling, and she could feel his gaze burning her intimate flesh so that her folds seemed to swell under his stare. She wriggled, and the sensation of being spread magnified until her spine caught fire and her arms lost tension.

She collapsed to the bed with a moan. "Please, Milo."

"Please what?"

"Fill me."

A dark chuckle came from behind her and he removed one hand from her bottom. The light touch of his fingers drifted over her, between her legs, reaching without any kind of pressure. A phantom touch, one she could have just imagined. He moved away, his legs releasing hers from their cage as his big hand slid up her back and pushed her more firmly to the mattress.

Then his breath. A warm gust flowed over her folds and had her arching, lifting her ass and searching for more. Another dark chuckle was quickly followed by a long swipe of his tongue, a gentle probing of her entrance. Christiana stilled in appreciation, but then her body's demands sent her hips soaring upward.

Milo pulled away again. His hands dove under her shirt and pushed it up, his clever fingers unhooked her bra. Both articles of clothing were discarded without any help from her. He manipulated her arms, lifting her to release the material, then he laid her back down on her belly. And ripped her pants off.

Heat flared in her core. She'd always had the sense that Milo was more dangerous than he let on, and the restrained violence in his removal of her pants only hammered that thought home. Again, her desire was tempered by the flavor of alarm, but Chris took a deep breath and clung to her husband's promise.

She was still in control and a word from her would stop it all. Her body didn't want to stop, and somewhere inside her lust-slowed brain, she knew she had to ride this experiment out if she was to have any hope of getting what she really wanted. A true marriage, free of fear but filled with trust.

So she bit her lip to stifle her unwarranted protests as Milo pulled her up to her knees again. She expected him to remove his own clothing, and was surprised when he pressed against her still fully dressed. He curled his long frame around hers and captured her legs between his. The fabric of his shirt and pants rasped every nerve between her shoulders and her toes.

"Feel how I am still clothed, *krasavitsa*?" He licked a hot trail up her nape. "You are the vulnerable one, naked and exposed, while I am in control, yes?"

His clothing rubbed against her skin deliciously, the texture and friction of it totally absorbing Christiana's awareness until she struggled to pull her thoughts from considering where her husband could possibly be taking her so she could answer him. "No, I'm in control. If I want to stop, you'll stop."

"You hope I stop," he said in a dark voice. "You'll trust me to stop."

"Yes."

He rewarded her with a gentle kiss on her shoulder and a hand sliding between her legs. Her senses slewed to that hand and the heat radiating from it, encompassing her folds as he pushed forward and captured her clit. He simply held it for a long moment, imprinting his heat on her nerves, building her need to such a height she fidgeted, and pulled against him when he didn't let go.

Sensation speared into her and she writhed again. If Milo wouldn't pet and stroke her, she'd tug against him and achieve nearly the same results. She shimmied and shifted, arched and bucked, and all the while his fingers remained clamped around her clit as he patiently let her pleasure herself against him.

Urgency sparked in her blood and coiled in her pussy as her frustration elevated to impossible degrees. "Milo!"

A wicked laugh sounded against her shoulder and his fingers unclamped, sliding to slip around her entrance. He circled and pressed, but didn't enter. Christiana wriggled some more as she melted inside and his fingers grew ever more slippery against her flesh.

"Is this what you wanted, *krasavitsa*?" His fingers stilled, but every nerve in the delicate muscle guarding her entrance quivered as if urging him on.

She groaned and dropped her forehead to the mattress, lifting her ass and stretching her spine to slide her body over his fingers. "Don't stop, Milo."

"This is enough to satisfy your hungry pussy?" One single finger slid into her.

She caught her breath. Her hands fisted in the covers as she pushed back and moved in a series of short jerks that had her bouncing on his finger. Milo's cock was thick—his long, elegant fingers couldn't compare, especially when only one had penetrated the wet depths of her body. "No, it's not enough. I want more."

"Hmm, you are growing very wet for this one finger, *krasavitsa*. Are you certain it's not enough?" His hot breath wafted over her nape. "Even if I do this?"

His finger curled and crooked, as if beckoning her climax closer from within. His fingertip pressed against her inner walls firmly, a bliss-filled impression that still wasn't enough, in spite of the shudder that jolted through her.

"No. More, Milo." Speech was truly growing difficult, and Christiana began to wonder how her husband always managed to keep up a steady stream of erotic words until the moment his own climax hit him. Just those three words stuck in her throat.

A second finger worked into her and she lifted higher, making his entry easier. She was contorted between him and the mattress, her cheek pressing hard to the covers, her spine aching from its severe arch. His thighs, trapping her and holding her up, were the only reason her knees hadn't given way.

Milo moved his fingers inside her. Apart and together, curling them, stroking and thrusting, pushing and stretching. Christiana moaned and fought for breath, knowing he would soon give her more, wanting them all, wanting his thick dick slamming into her. Her fear was an emotion long gone and forgotten as Milo pushed her deeper into heated ecstasy.

Three fingers filled her and she felt the intrusion in the lower depths of her belly. Her urgency took on a life of its own as Milo slowed down, pushing deep in unhurried thrusts, pulling out with controlled force. Every time he filled her, he added an extra push of his palm against her flesh that seemed to reverberate in her lonely clit. His wrist spread her ass cheeks and added to the sensation of total fullness. As she lost her breath completely, she couldn't imagine anything better.

Until Milo pulled his hand away and pushed his dick into her. One heavy, hard slide, a steady push into her depths with no stopping, no pulling out, no theatrics. Just thick, hot cock stuffing her more than his fingers ever could. With him behind her, she felt him in new ways, as if he was bigger than she knew him to be as he slid through soft, silken tissues and tunneled into places she was convinced he'd never been before.

He pushed all the way in and stopped. "Your greedy pussy is sucking my dick, *krasavitsa*. You're so wet around me. So hot I swear you're burning me alive."

Her inner walls rippled around him, and his words combined with the deep need her body's hidden movements produced to make her extra aware of his presence inside her. She gasped and panted, dug her nails into the covers and twisted the fabric until her fingers ached. But Milo did not move. Long minutes ticked by as she listened to his rough breathing and waited for him to ride her hard.

"Milo?"

"You cannot imagine what you look like." His guttural voice conveyed his strain. "Bent over before me, your ass cheeks framing my dick and your satin pussy flexing all around me. You are at my mercy, *krasavitsa*. What are you going to do about it?"

She had no idea, but the fact that he was waiting for her to do *something* managed to penetrate the lust hazing her thought processes. She didn't know what and couldn't guess, so she decided to please herself, as she'd done when he'd held her clit without moving.

It took every ounce of strength she possessed to push up on her trembling arms. Her head swam, her pussy pulsed and a shudder worked the full length of her spine. She almost collapsed, but she gritted her teeth and braced herself as best she could.

Then she lurched forward and drove back hard. She slammed her body onto Milo's thick cock—and he hadn't moved a muscle. That one movement cost Christiana's sanity a great deal. Urgency snarled and turned rabid, her muscles clenched on her bones and forced her to repeat the action before she could process what she'd done. But she let go completely, and let her body do what it wanted, praying for the strength to get the job done.

She rocked, forward and back. Her hips circled and dipped, her legs trembled. She drove her body over her husband's dick until he lost his words completely, broken grunts echoing around them as Christiana moaned and gasped. Her spine hurt and her arms knotted with the effort, but still she rode her husband, the needs of her body urging her on and quickening her pace.

She was unhinged and out of control, taking Milo in spite of his warning that he was in charge. He'd put her in the vulnerable position, but with her pussy flowing over his cock, and with the rest of his body completely covered in clothes, it felt like she held all the power. She took from her husband as he remained still, slipping over his flesh, sucking his length into her depths and reducing him to a wordless, grunting state.

Then her rhythm faltered. Rather than thrusting, she ended up trembling beyond control, lurching against him as her inner muscles tightened. It wasn't enough. Chris sobbed and dropped back to the mattress, her hips jerking, shaking with an orgasm hovering just beyond her reach, taunting her maliciously.

"Help me, Milo!"

He scooped her up and hauled her back as he quickly rearranged his legs. Her ass met his thighs and he thrust up, powerful and dominant, his arms wrapped around her. She'd thought she'd been stuffed before, but this new position provided even greater depth. Her folds were stretched as his entire length drove into her, and she felt every inch in places both front and back, high and low. She was so full, she was afraid to move, and resigned herself to grinding against him.

Milo had other ideas. His one arm wrapped her waist, his other hand stroked her clit. Christiana melted into sheer sensation as he took over, driving into her and allowing her body to flow around his, relaxing and tensing as pleasure sprinted forward and ripped her apart.

He slammed into her over and over. His lips found her

ear, his voice was barely his own. "Anything for you. What you want. Your pleasure is my pleasure."

Christiana arched against him, her nails dug bloody crescents into his thighs. Still Milo hammered into her until they rose and fell in mutual bliss, their bodies merged and writhing. Her breasts bounced with the force, their sensitivity adding to the experience of being truly taken by her husband. After she'd taken him.

Christiana exploded, liquefied into a Milo-molded puddle of ecstasy. She clamped around his thick cock and felt her inner walls massaging him even as they pleasured themselves, rippling, flexing and dissolving as fear was permanently eradicated and only pleasure was left behind. Heat spiraled up her spine with a hint of magic until it spread over her shoulders and infected her husband.

He rammed deep and stilled, a harsh groan ripping past her ear. His arm tightened around her, his fingers jerked on her clit and he tucked his face into her shoulder. He shuddered and his heat swept her away, finally releasing her body from the brutal arch she'd been locked into.

Soothing magic stole over her as Milo's heartbeat returned to normal against her back. Locked tight in his embrace, she knew when he'd recovered enough to think again. She felt his knotted muscles relax completely, even as he wielded enough strength to pull out, pick her up and lay her back down. He collapsed next to her and hauled her to his chest.

Christiana snuggled into his body and let his soothing, peaceful magic infiltrate the deepest parts of her soul. She kissed his chest and fought to find the right words. "You give me my courage back."

"You never lost your courage, *krasavitsa*. But know that my entire world is built around you and our child. Even if you want me to take care of every aspect of our lives, the control will always rest with you because of how I feel about you."

It was on the tip of her tongue to ask exactly *how* he felt about her. The look in his eyes, the care he'd shown with her and his forgiveness of her crimes all added up to one emotion. But she was sleepy and wrapped in her husband's arms, and everything else could wait.

Chapter Twenty-Five

Silviu

Silviu figured it was impossible to feel any worse than he already did. His sister proved him wrong.

The clock had just struck noon when Ileana and Eliasz descended the steps, fully prepared to leave the house and England altogether on their way to the Council headquarters. Silviu was waiting for them, watching them approach with gritty eyes and a face he knew was frozen into a blank expression.

"Where is everyone?" Eliasz called out. "Even mourners need to eat, but there was hardly anyone at the brunch buffet laid out in the dining room. It was pretty much us, Suzette and Daniel."

Silviu managed to mutter, "Most of the Davenolds are still sleeping."

Staring at him, Eliasz stumbled off the bottom stop before pulling an impenetrable mask over his features, showing no expression whatsoever after his initial surprise. Ileana donned compassion like a cloak. Silviu knew he must look terrible to gain such reactions.

"Are you all right, Silver?" His sister rushed over to him. "I know you were fond of Mother Davenold, but you need—"

"It's not that, Iley."

Silviu had made an effort to hide his weakness from the few Davenolds who were awake after their long night and even longer morning. He'd tried to walk smoothly, with his shoulders back and his head held high. Otherwise, Silviu feared he'd shuffle through the Davenold estate hunched over and clutching his stomach.

Guilt pressed him to the floor, his belly developed a hollow pit and his eyes puckered with his lack of sleep. And the panic that had slipped its leash when, once again, he lost his wife after betraying her, had developed weight in his gut.

He couldn't hide his sorrow from his sister. She gave him a tentative, confused smile and tried to make light of his bleakness. "Surely you can't be worried about me leaving you alone in a house of grieving matriarchs?"

"I'll fit right in. I'm grieving too. Just not what you think."

Ileana turned and suggested her betrothed take the bags and load the car. Obviously eager to escape his tormented brother-in-law, Eliasz hurried to obey. When they were alone in the entry hall, she asked, "What's wrong then, Silver?"

"Georgie's angry with me."

His sister lifted her brows. "She's frequently angry with you. You've never looked like this before."

"I did something intolerable." His whisper was a strangled stream of sound going no farther than Ileana's ears. "I don't know if she'll forgive me."

"She'll forgive you, Silver. She always does."

He shook his head and looked away, staring at a marble column as an image of his bride flashed before his eyes. He saw the pain in her gaze, the betrayal that had pulled her skin tight over her cheekbones. The slight quiver in her bottom lip, her pale face. He heard the anguish in her voice, the rage, confusion and heartache.

He also heard Mason's words as they rose up from the depths of his memory. *You'll break her in a way Madeleine was never able to do.* He feared his father-in-law was correct, that Silviu had somehow managed to kick down every last wall between him and Georgie, and that without those protections she would founder under the grief of his decision. She'd been hurt too deeply in the past, by too many who were supposed to love her.

And he'd done it on purpose. Silviu had been determined to dig down into her wounds, to rip off the festered scabs of Georgie's isolation and banishment. He'd promised he'd always take care of her, love her, support her. He knew he'd been making progress. He could feel it every time they merged their magic, he could see it in her eyes every time Georgie looked at him in her unguarded moments. He'd gloried in it the last time they were together, just hours ago, when she'd been willing to surrender her body in spite of her grandmother's edict.

"I hurt her, Iley. I can't even find her right now, let alone form the words to make her forgive me."

"How did you hurt her?"

He didn't hesitate. Ileana was the one person in the world he could trust his secrets with. Though she'd shared too much with Eliasz concerning their Family talents, Silviu knew she'd keep her mouth shut about the situation he was currently in. It was far too important. A hot current burned his veins from the inside out with the need to share with his sister.

But he still gave her a warning. "Say nothing to *anyone*, and guard your thoughts fiercely while you're at the Council Headquarters."

Her eyes flew wide. "Good God, Silver. What did you do?"

"I became the new Davenold Mother."

"Oh, my God." Ileana staggered back. Her faced paled and she groped for the staircase's banister, using it as a guide when she collapsed onto the steps.

Wearily, Silviu took a seat next to her and dropped his head into his hands. "Georgie's Bane. She couldn't take the Davenold power when Madeleine died. So I did."

"But... But you're a Lovasz. You're a patriarchal man. How could you think a matriarchal Family would accept you? How could you think Georgeanne would be so tolerant—"

"I didn't have much choice!" Silviu sat up straight in an explosive motion. "I couldn't let Suzette take it, and it was halfway sunk inside her when I tore it away."

Ileana went completely still. "Like you did with Grandfather?"

"Not quite, but essentially the same concept."

After a long, tense moment, his sister drew a deep breath. "Georgie couldn't take the power at all?"

"No. Her Bane shields rejected it twice." He rubbed a hand over his too-dry eyes.

"Well, you need to explain it to her." Ileana grimaced. "I don't know if your reasons were right or wrong, I don't know what you expected to get out of this and I don't want to know. If you have sunk to our father's level, I'd rather be blissfully unaware. *But*," she said before he could protest, "tell Georgie the truth. No matter how painful, no matter how wrong, no matter how manipulative."

He doubted his sister's strategy, but didn't argue. "I don't know if she'll listen to me."

"Make her listen."

"It's not that easy." Silviu hunched over again, bracing his elbows on his knees. He stared at the floor as he made his next confession. "I had a chance, and she was calm enough to hear me out. But then she was challenged with a dark magic spell, and Suzette came in and picked a fight."

"Why would Georgie be challenged if —"

"Nobody knows what I've done, except her. The Davenolds have all accepted that she inherited her bloodline's power."

"But not Suzette?"

"She believed enough to challenge, and I know it had to be her." Silviu closed his eyes and sighed. "She's the only one here who works with dark magic. Anyway, they fought and I yelled for them to stop, but I lost control and used my magic."

Again, his sister held her silence. The moment drew out until even Silviu's racing heartbeat seemed too sluggish as he waited for her to respond.

"You used your magic?" Ileana finally asked, each word slow enough to shame Silviu anew. "Georgie told me that she can see magic."

"Yeah. She knew what I did."

"Oh, boy," Ileana whispered. "You've never shown her your patriarchal dominance before."

"She's seen more than you think."

With an inhalation that echoed through the entry, Ileana pushed to her feet. Then she tugged Silviu to his and prodded him toward the door. "Maybe this is a good time to show her more. Put it on full display."

"What are you talking about?" Shame and irritation roughened Silviu's words, but he accepted the pain as his due. "I hurt her, Iley. I can't turn around now and browbeat her into surrendering all she's ever worked for into my keeping. I need to figure out how to make her forgive me and work with me."

"Georgie's more like you than you might realize." Ileana opened the heavy doors leading out to the portico and led him through. "She's a manipulative witch too, so she might understand your reasons. Just explain. Tell her the whole sordid, dirty truth. Don't dare lie, Silver."

Eliasz stood at the bottom of the shallow steps loading the last of his bags into the trunk. Above him, the sky was still heavy with clouds but the ground was drying beneath a strengthening sun. Around him, all else was silent but for the gentle crying of unseen sheep and the soft roar of the North Sea's tide in the distance.

Eliasz looked up as they came down the steps. "Everything all right? I don't mean to rush you, but we'll miss our flight if we don't leave soon."

Silviu held out his hand for Eliasz to shake. "Just a mess I've got to clean up."

"You seem pretty good at cleaning up messes."

"Let's hope so," Silviu murmured. "Remember, when you reach Council headquarters, shield your thoughts from Bijoux Laurent."

Ileana quickly wrapped her arms around him. "Deal with your mess, Silver. We'll see you soon."

He hugged his sister and she got into the car with Eliasz when the Davenold driver started the engine. As Silviu watched the car take Ileana farther and farther away, leaving him without his most trusted ally, a cold tendril of loneliness filled him with doubt, fear and panic. Once again, impatience found him and set him into motion.

He swung on his heel, ready to storm back inside and search for his bride. Though it seemed he was destined to always be a few steps behind her, Georgie was *somewhere* and he was determined. He would find her, as he'd done before, then he would take his sister's advice.

Silviu didn't get far. The moment he turned, he stumbled to a quick stop, startled by Suzette's presence, a mere foot away. She smiled at him, striking a provocative pose with her hand on her cocked hip and her cleavage on display.

"What's wrong, Silviu?"

Just the sight of that particular woman had Silviu's patience evaporating without a trace. Anger blazed through him, incinerating his exhaustion, fear and panic. The idea that she'd almost stolen everything he and Georgie had worked for—everything they'd been promised—cut him deep and rubbed over his wounds like grains of salt. If it hadn't been for her, Silviu wouldn't have used his magic to stop a physical attack on his wife that left Georgie feeling more betrayed than she'd already been.

"What do you want, Suzette?"

She trailed a finger over her low neckline. "I thought you might be regretting your alliance with a Bane witch. I can make you feel better, if you need a...helping hand."

"Do you think I'm stupid?" Silviu bared his teeth. "You think I don't know when a jealous whore is attempting to destabilize the magic I share with my Match?"

Suzette's jaw clenched, but her hand stroked over the curve of her hip in clear invitation. "I thought you'd like to know what an experienced woman was like in bed, rather than a novice who couldn't possibly understand what it takes to pleasure a strong, patriarchal man."

"But you do, don't you?" Silviu remembered a rumor Eliasz had learned from the breeze and passed on—Suzette had been caught in a compromising position with the Levy Father. "Would your experience have come from Daniel Levy? Or the dark witch who killed your grandmother?"

"I've heard the Lovasz line was plagued with madness," she sneered. "But I had no idea the extent of it. It's a shame you've proven to be such a weakness, because Georgie will need all the advantages she can get in her new role."

"Are you fucking the mysterious villain, hoping to breed his stronger magic into any child you might bear?" Silviu watched the woman's facial expressions closely, but she gave little away. "Or did he order you to service Daniel as a reward for his loyalty? You've been married for a long time, with nothing to show for it. Is that because you had your greedy sights set on something more than your weak husband could give you?"

Suzette's face blanched, but Silviu didn't know if it was because he'd stumbled over the truth, or if she was vulnerable to the attacks her own Family had lobbed her way so often. Perhaps it hurt more, hearing the same words from a man she hardly knew.

"No man orders me to do anything." Suzette slid back into her seductress persona, though it seemed forced. She tossed her curls and lifted a brow. "I choose the men in my bed, and if you're not careful, you'll be uninvited. Cut off from all the...possibilities of our association, and I promise you wouldn't want that."

Silviu's anger blazed higher. His disgust for the Davenold woman left a sour taste in his mouth. "You are a shining example of all I find distasteful on the matriarchal side of the Schism. You're a bitch in heat, using your body to gain power instead of employing what few brain cells you have."

Her eyes went wide and her sultry pose snapped into a

rigid stance. "How dare you?"

"Oh, I dare. I'm the Davenold High Male now." He slid forward, letting all pretense at being a domesticated man drop completely. "I outrank you. There are no *possibilities* to be gained from *any* association between us."

"You're not married to Georgeanne yet!"

"Georgeanne is most definitely my wife, and she is your Family Mother. I'd be careful, if I were you."

Suzette scoffed. "I'm not the one who should be careful."

Even in the midst of his anger, Silviu cataloged the woman's strengths and weaknesses. He'd taken her measure days ago, and had seen nothing to make him change his opinion since. The Davenolds were a magically strong Family, but Suzette was far from the most gifted member of the coven.

Georgie not only had her Bane shields to protect her from spells, but access to all the magic inside Silviu. And she was specifically trained in combat. Suzette didn't stand a chance.

His lip curled. "Georgeanne will take you apart."

"Unlikely," Suzette spat. "I have strengths and allies of my own. And one day, you will sincerely regret not taking me up on my offer while it was still on the table."

Silviu's mind locked down and focused completely. He stepped forward with predatory intent, his emotional chaos stilled in the hunt as he scented blood. "What allies, Suzette? The dark magic witch who wields the talent to make your spells stronger?"

"You believe I need enhancement?" Her chin lifted. "I have a Magic Match. You should know how a Match can boost a witch's natural talents."

She was backpedaling. Silviu took another step forward, not even blinking as he watched her. "Bullshit. We both know you have little talent. Who are you working with, Suzette? Who is strong enough to make you think you can stand against me and Georgeanne?"

The woman's chin launched even higher and she started sliding back toward the portico steps. "I am a high ranking

Davenold. I am a matriarchal female, with countless generations behind me, following in the true path of Motherhood. I have no need of enhancement."

"Your rank is an accident of your birth. Even your grandmother's support of you has been silenced." Silviu stalked Suzette step for step and threw accusations at her, watching closely for any signs he'd hit his mark. "Are you working with Daniel? Does *he* know who the dark magic witch is? Was Daniel promised the Council High Seat?"

"You watch yourself, Silviu Lovasz." Her voice was low and strained, her legs shook as she leaped backward toward the portico. Spinning on her heel, she raced up the steps and disappeared inside the house.

Silviu suddenly felt depleted. His prey had escaped and other concerns hovered on the edges of his awareness, waiting to fill the void her absence had left. As tired as he was, multitasking wasn't an option, so he shoved all thoughts of Suzette to the back of his mind. Madeleine was beyond the dark witch's schemes now, he had no evidence Daniel Levy was making a play for the Council High Seat and Georgie could stand firm against any magical challenge her cousin could conjure. Silviu had other priorities.

He needed to find his bride and beg her forgiveness.

Chapter Twenty-Six

Georgeanne

Georgie tensed as the soft crunch of footsteps grew louder. With the sound of the waves filling her ears, her visitor had gotten closer than Georgie knew. She started to turn, more than aware of how vulnerable she currently was, sitting on the rocky part of the beach well above the place where the sea washed the finer sand, but then an afghan was thrown over her shoulders and Christiana's voice broke through the low roar of the surf and the soft cawing of sea birds.

"Georgie, what are you doing out here without even a jacket? I could see you shivering from my bedroom window."

The wildness had called to Georgeanne. "I like the turbulence of the water, the rocky beach, the cold wind."

"Why?"

The beach was a piece of freedom hidden behind the ruthlessly maintained gardens of the estate, which in turn was hidden behind a rolling pastureland as tame as anything man could create. Sitting on the beach gave Georgie the illusion she was wholly insignificant and free to live as she pleased, like what she pleased, love as she pleased.

But the well-planned gardens above the shingle beach were a physical reminder that she couldn't lie to herself any longer. Her whole life was anything but insignificant. Being Bane, it was a miracle she'd been allowed to reach adulthood, let alone been treated well by the former Davenold Mother and honored as an heir to the Family power.

"It reminds me that life is filled with things beyond politics, Chris."

Georgie had been set up to inherit power — well-trained, manipulated, abandoned to the Asian witch hunts, and betrothed to a patriarchal male who just so happened to be a Reap witch. But she had gained nothing for her troubles.

"What's going on, Georgie? Are you okay?"

Never before had Georgie felt so hemmed in, yet she had been her whole life. All her choices and decisions were nothing more than trickery, a devious slight-of-hand perpetuated by the one person she'd always trusted wholeheartedly. She'd thought Madeleine had her best interests at heart.

But Georgie couldn't say all that to Christiana, and didn't dare admit how angry she was, how betrayed she felt, or how lost and confused, foundering in the deep end of her own emotions. A Mother had to be strong at all times, so Georgie *was* strong, or gave a great pretense, at least.

Just as she would try her best to pretend to be the Davenold Mother. As soon as she figured out how to pretend her heart wasn't broken.

Instead of giving voice to the chaos in her mind, Georgie asked, "What are you doing out here? Did you get any sleep?"

"Well, the baby has taken up residence on my bladder and when I got up, I looked out the window and saw you sitting down here. Are you hungry?" Chris dropped down next to Georgie. "Everyone's schedule is so messed up the servants have resorted to putting out an all-day buffet. I brought you a sandwich."

Georgie shook her head as her cousin offered her a napkin-wrapped bundle. "Did Milo find you?"

"Yeah. We worked some things out." Chris leaned her shoulder against Georgie's. "What's going on with you? Thinking about Grandmother?"

"Thinking about a lot of things." Georgie wondered why

the cold air had failed to numb her emotions as she scooped up a handful of the small pebbles digging into her legs. She fought for calm, and tried to project nothing more than gentle contemplation in front of her cousin.

"Like what?"

"I wanted to be Mother. Just not like this." Georgie tossed a pebble. Then another, as she tried to center herself.

"I wasn't ready to let Grandmother go yet, either."

Not quite what Georgie meant, but that sentiment was in the emotional mix, too. "Did you want to be Mother, Chris?"

"You know I didn't." A harsh laugh broke from Christiana's throat, quickly cut off. "I can hardly deal with my own drama, let alone an entire coven's."

"But you *had* wanted to be, not so long ago."

"Well, Madeleine made it a competition, you know? I wanted to win, until I realized what first place entailed. I'm happy to let you do all the heavy lifting."

Georgie tilted her face into the wind and breathed in the salty air. The sunshine did little to warm her, and she was grateful for the afghan her cousin had brought. "I want to take care of my Family. I want to lead them into the future."

"I think you'll be a great Mother. Is that what's bothering you? It's normal to be scared, Georgie."

She was scared, but not for the reasons Christiana supposed. Still, she only said, "Suzette might have challenged me."

"What? Goddess, that was fast."

Georgie quickly told her cousin about the dark magic spell, but nothing else. She couldn't bear to tell Chris about Suzette's threat, how jealous Georgie had gotten or how Silviu had used his magic against her. "She'll challenge me again."

"So what? What could she do to you?" Chris shifted against Georgie's side. "You'll win and the Family will be relieved they aren't under Suzette's rule."

Georgie stifled a hysterical laugh as she thought of

what her Family would think about the true Mother. Relief wouldn't even be in the top hundred reactions the Davenolds would have.

"You know I used to be jealous of you, Georgie?" Chris scraped her hand over the small pebbles making their seaside vigil faintly uncomfortable. "Even though you were Bane, Grandmother always gave you so much attention, and your parents lived with us. My mom didn't visit as often as I would have liked. It fueled my need to be better than you."

"Not everything was a competition."

"Yes it was, it was just a friendly competition. Me, you and Adam," Chris snorted. "We were our own little family, and only Madeleine understood why. But you still had other family, right there in our house. Parents that read to you and tucked you in at night."

"They did that for you too, Chris." Georgie remembered plenty of times when she and her cousins had snuggled into the same bed, listening to Georgie's mother read their bedtime story.

"But they weren't *mine*." Chris gave a soft moan of unspeakable sorrow. "Confessions are apparently my thing today, so... You're why I fought so hard to marry the first time."

"Me?" Georgie glanced at her cousin in time to see her nod.

"You had Silviu. Granted, you weren't allowed on the same continent after your little Beltane stunt, but we all knew he was your Magic Match. I would never have a relationship like that with my husband."

Her words brought new pain to Georgie's fractured heart. She tried to ignore it and focus on her cousin's confession. "That's what you and Madeleine were talking about before she passed?"

"Mmm. I fought too hard to get what I thought I wanted, but all I could think, at the time, was how you had *everything*. And I just wanted a *little* something of my own."

Chris made a noise filled with bitterness. "Be careful what you wish for."

"Yeah, tell me about it."

It was on the tip of Georgie's tongue to tell her cousin that she'd been jealous too—of Chris' magic, her acceptance by the rest of the Family, the bond she shared with Adam. The three of them had always been close, no matter what others chose to believe, but Georgie had still felt like the third wheel, shut out from the twins' inside jokes and shared knowledge of spells Georgie would never learn.

But she didn't say any of that. Georgie knew she had little right to complain—after all, she'd been given a great deal more than most witches. A family, parents and grandparents and a closeness with her cousins that made them more like siblings. She'd been given a stable upbringing, until she'd ruined it. She been given a fiancé—a husband—who wielded enough strength to steal a witch's birthright and take it for himself.

And Georgie had been given a tiny, dark voice in the back of her mind that whispered how she'd *also* been given the ability to reach her husband's magic and use it as if it were her own. She silenced that voice.

Suddenly Chris laughed, but it was a harsh sound and not at all amused. "Looking back, I'd take my childhood over yours, but at the time I didn't really see it that way. Please forgive me."

Georgie shook her head. "What am I supposed to be forgiving?"

"I'm sorry it took so long to start thinking about what was going on with you, what was expected of you, the pressure we put on you. I didn't even think of what it would be like for you to be Bane, though I was as mean about it as everyone else."

"No," Georgie told her fiercely, "you weren't."

"Adam and I were always casting harmful spells at you, just because we knew you couldn't be hurt. We were awful to you," Chris groaned. "I guess it wasn't easy living with us."

Georgie shrugged. "It made me strong. Just not strong enough for Grandmother to blood as her heir."

"But you're Mother now, so it all worked out."

Georgie breathed deep, fighting the pressure behind her eyes. She couldn't lose control of herself or her perceptive cousin might guess the true source of her need to be alone. She felt too raw to be around others, and would have preferred Christiana go away too, but she couldn't say so without revealing too much. Georgie quickly changed the subject.

"What happened, Chris? You got married and drifted away. We hardly ever saw you. When you came back, you were different."

Chris' answer took a long time. "I trusted the wrong man, and that changes a woman, I guess."

Georgie gathered the afghan closer as her cousin's words sank in. She could relate. Ten years ago she'd convinced herself that Silviu was manipulating her naiveté in order to win her to his side, against her own Family's advantage. She fought to bury all traces of warm feelings for him, only to have them crash back down on both her head and her heart when they'd reunited for his sister's betrothal.

The past two weeks had changed the way she saw him. Silviu had fought for her on several occasions and promised to keep her safe, as well as her Family. She'd believed him, she'd wanted to give him what she thought they both needed—trust and love—and had struggled to get rid of her doubts. Especially after feeling him just inside her body, their magic reacting to each other and her need for him rising too fast to contain.

"How do you know who to trust?" Georgie finally asked, keeping her voice low so as not to reveal its tremble.

When she was young, it had been so simple. Silviu wanted her and she wanted him. She hadn't taken into account how that would affect their Families or their future. It was just them, with no political motivations casting everything he said and did into the shadows of her suspicion.

Suspicions he'd proven true.

Chris shook her head. "You're asking the wrong woman."

"Do you trust Milo?"

"I want to. I'm learning to. I..." Her cousin stared out at the sea for a never-ending minute. Finally, Chris said, "I found him with Suzette."

Georgie whipped around to face her cousin. "You what?"

"Him and her. And Daniel Levy. They were together in that little blue parlor that juts out into the rose garden." Chris gave a single nod. "Suzette's boobs were on display."

"I wouldn't have thought Milo..." Georgie rubbed her forehead. "What were they doing?"

Chris shrugged. "Only the gods know. Suzette said she and Milo were interrupted by Daniel."

"Suzette said? What did Milo say?"

"He denied it, of course." Chris shot Georgie a strange look. "Daniel said the same thing Suzette did. I don't think they were telling the truth, though."

"She's a liar, Chris." Georgie took a deep breath and glared at the horizon. "I wouldn't trust Suzette if she told me her eyes were brown, and I can see that for myself."

"Georgie... My first husband..."

"Was a lying, cheating ass. Milo isn't."

"I know and I believe him." Chris folded over her own drawn-up knees, resting her chin on them as her arms curled around her calves. "We talked about it. He was mad, but we worked through it."

"Suzette made a play for Silviu." Georgie closed her mouth abruptly, unwilling to give voice to the upheaval such a small moment in time had caused her.

Another quiet moment passed. Then Georgie tossed the rest of the pebbles in her hand all at once and bunched a corner of the afghan in her fists. "I don't know if I can trust him. I don't know how..."

Christiana leaned against Georgie's shoulder. "That's our fault. All our fault—the whole Family. We screwed your head up."

"He did something I don't know how to forgive."

Chris jolted. "Not Suzette?"

"No. He…"

"Did he hit you, Georgie?"

"No, of course not." Georgie sighed. She simply couldn't tell her cousin what had happened. "He broke my trust."

"After what we all did to you, trust is probably a sore point." Chris studied Georgie's face intently. Then she sighed. "I can't imagine what it was like, growing up being you."

"Now you're sounding as dramatic as Silviu."

"Growing up in a Family that constantly told you how different you were couldn't have been easy. It's no wonder you let Silviu in your bed when you were so young. You two have a lot in common."

Momentarily sidetracked from the pain gnawing on her heart, Georgie stared at Chris, and really listened to her words. "Everyone thinks I let him take advantage of me. Now my loyalty is questioned, no matter what I've done to prove myself."

Christiana's voice turned wistful. "You were young and lonely. He was a cute boy that paid you an awful lot of attention."

"He's four years older than me." Georgie had to force her next statement. "Maybe he did take advantage."

"Maybe not. Hell, that was probably the first time in his life he'd been released from the dungeon Grandmother always said the Lovaszes kept him in, let alone seen a girl that wasn't his sister. And to know he would get to have you one day, well, that was probably too much to ask him to have patience with."

Georgie focused her gaze on the sea. "You don't think what we did was wrong?"

"Oh, I absolutely think it was wrong and it chills me to wonder if, one day, my child might be so reckless." Chris reached out to cup Georgie's chin and smoothed her windblown curls from her eyes in a gesture Georgie remembered from their childhood. "But he loves you. Even I can see that."

Once, a distant cousin had tortured her. For days at a Family gathering, the girl had taunted Georgie, even throwing rocks at her when magic proved to be a useless weapon. Georgeanne had drawn into herself, hiding away and hoping she could simply fade from existence until Christiana had found her, held her chin the way she was doing then, and wiped away her tears as Georgie told her what happened. And Christiana had found that cousin and lit her up with a spell that had left her bald for the next year.

When Madeleine had found out, Georgie had begun combat training with the men. She was different, Bane, with no magic to protect herself. The training had come in handy the next year, when she'd been sent away to deal with the witch hunts.

Christiana sighed. "You were too young, sweetie, but that doesn't mean they get to roast you over the coals for the rest of your life."

To her horror, Georgie's eyes welled up. She tried to pull away from her cousin, but Christiana tightened her grip on Georgie's chin and used the tips of her fingers to wipe away the tears as they trickled free.

"You love him," Chris said quietly. "I can see how much you love him, and maybe I haven't given Silviu enough credit. I think he's earned a measure of my faith, for what it's worth."

"He hurt me. I don't know how to trust him again, how to move forward." Georgie was amazed her cousin could understand the uneven words that ripped from her mouth.

But Christiana did and her lips twisted. "You'd be amazed at what a woman can forgive, when she's in love."

Chapter Twenty-Seven

Milo

When Christiana didn't come back to bed, Milo heaved a sigh and got up. Showered and shaved, he felt a little more human, but didn't have the energy to drag on anything more complicated than sweatpants and a cotton shirt. Coffee was his first priority.

He headed downstairs, surprised when he found the dining room to be fairly crowded at such an odd hour of the afternoon. Davenolds were lined up in front of large coffee urns and pots of tea. The lower ranking members, acting in their capacity of servants, were laying out fresh trays of fruits, eggs, sausages and sandwiches on the sideboard.

Milo joined Silviu in the line. The Lovasz man looked like he needed sleep even more than Milo. "Haven't been to bed yet, have you?"

Silviu turned with raised brows. Seeing Milo, his shoulders relaxed and his eyes dropped to his mug, stained with the dregs of at least one previous cup of coffee. "No. Have you seen Georgie?"

"I haven't, but I'd like to find her and fall to my knees before her in gratitude."

"Why?"

"She's Mother." Milo shrugged. "That means my wife isn't, and therefore Christiana is safe from all challenges."

"I guess that is a relief for you."

Milo heard the hollowness in Silviu's voice. Wincing, he considered that perhaps he'd put his foot in his mouth, as Georgie was still a target for power-hungry witches. "I meant no offense."

"No," Silviu dismissed Milo's apology with a wave of his hand, "I understand completely. I take heart in the fact that Georgie is Bane, and any challengers will have a difficult time gaining an advantage against her."

"I'm sure she's prepared," Milo offered. "Suzette's been quite vocal in her intentions, even before we understood how bad off Madeleine was."

"Mmm, Suzette is a problem. Maybe I'll keep you close, Milo. Your magic is strong, and I could use a man like you."

There were worse things in life than to be thought useful to the Family High Male. Milo debated with himself for a single heartbeat, but after the threats the Levy Father had tried to throw his way, he was more than willing to air the man's dirty laundry. He leaned closer to Silviu. "Suzette's sleeping with Daniel Levy. Apparently, he's promised to impregnate her."

Silviu stiffened. His face remained unchanged, a blank expression pasted over his features, but his eyes gleamed with satisfaction. "Did he? I'd heard they were having an affair, but I didn't know about their pregnancy plans."

"I think he's trying to gain influence on this side of the Schism."

Silviu's predatory gaze shifted and focused on a spot over Milo's shoulders. "I think we should ask him."

With his back to the door, Milo couldn't see who entered. But Silviu was ahead of him in the coffee line and, turned the way he was, obviously had an excellent view. Wanting to share the view, Milo spun around.

Daniel Levy stepped into the dining room. His eyes immediately landed on Milo and Silviu, and he froze. Shock briefly passed over his face — there and gone before Milo could figure out why it was present at all. The Levy Father's eyes wandered over Silviu. His brows lifted for a fraction of a moment before he settled into his charismatic, political persona. His expression smoothed into one of soft regret, as he leaned toward a small group of people and offered his condolences.

"Interesting," Silviu breathed. "I wonder how long he's known Suzette? I wonder how disappointed he is that she's not the Mother, if he's looking for more influence on this side of the Schism."

"You think Suzette would be able to help him reach his political goals?" Milo shook his head, wishing, yet again, that he'd paid more attention to issues beyond what directly affected his business. "I don't see how."

"The Davenolds are very influential, the largest Motherhouse. It would be very nerve-wracking to the rest of the witching world if this Family created an alliance with the enormous Levy Family."

"Suzette's already married. How can there be an alliance?"

"If Suzette bore Daniel a child…" Silviu's voice drifted off as he watched Daniel promenade around the circumference of the room. "There's no telling what the ramifications would be."

"Well," Milo pointed out, "Georgie is Mother and she—"

"And she's upset with you, Silviu." Christiana's voice cut through their quiet conversation, and though her words didn't reach farther than them, they carried force.

Both men whirled to face her. Wholly occupied with watching Daniel as he pushed farther into the crowd, neither man had seen her enter the dining room. Milo ran a critical eye over his wife. Her cheeks were red, her hair was windblown and her soft black pants were dusty. Her blue eyes narrowed on Silviu, but gentled when she transferred her gaze to Milo.

"Where is she?" Silviu demanded.

Christiana's eyes narrowed again. "I don't know what you did to her, but she said you broke her trust."

Silviu's glare took on a maniacal gleam. "*Where* is she?"

"On the beach, but she needs a minute to herself. So help me, by all that's sacred, I—"

Silviu wasn't listening. He pushed past Christiana fast enough to make her wobble. Milo put a hand on his wife's back to steady her, but she was already following on Silviu's heels.

"Damn it, Silviu! She—" Christiana reached for Silviu's shoulder.

Magic exploded in a dark corona. Davenold witches in the immediate vicinity were repulsed, slamming into walls and falling to the floor. Christiana arched violently, her mouth opening on a silent shriek as a blaze of silver magic lit her skin on fire. The silver was almost immediately sucked into her body. Her eyes rolled back in her head and she crumpled.

Milo screamed. He jumped for his wife in sheer panic, unknowing of what was happening. Even as his brain shut down, his body launched into action. He grabbed his wife just before she hit the floor.

His palms burned with cold, his skin blistered until tears pricked his eyes. But he didn't let go. He hauled Christiana to his chest and gritted his teeth against the pain, dimly wondering what his pregnant wife felt with the dark magic racing through her. She convulsed hard enough to shake Milo on his knees when he dropped to the hardwood.

He shook her some more, though his arms clutched her tighter. "*Christiana!* Chris!"

All around him chaos reigned, though he hardly paid attention to anything beyond his shuddering wife. Like snapshots, pictures frozen in time, he was only aware of a few things—Adam and Tulah frozen on the threshold, the weariness on their faces instantly replaced by horrified shock. Silviu flinching and spinning back, his lips thinning into a grim line. Milo only cared enough to know help was there with him.

Adam shoved a distant cousin to the wall as he raced past and knelt next to Milo. Eyes wide, face without color, he reached for his sister with trembling hands. It was everything Milo could do to relax his hold so Christiana's Magic Match could help her.

"Do something, Adam," Milo demanded in a hoarse

voice. "*Save her!*"

Adam laid a hand on her shoulder, only to draw it back with a sharp gasp. A blister sprung up on his palm.

Anger ripped a path through Milo's senses. He took one hand off his wife and reached for her twin, twisting his fingers in Adam's collar until the man choked. He hauled him close, nose to nose, and snarled. "Do something to save her or I swear by all I hold sacred, I will fucking kill you!"

Silviu braced his weight with a knee on the floor and grabbed Milo's hand. Peeling the fingers away from Adam's shirt, he told them, "Help her, don't fight each other."

With a grim look promising retribution for their disobedience, Silviu caught Christiana's flopping wrist. A muscle along his jaw jumped, but he didn't let go. Following suit, Adam grabbed her shoulders and grunted. His nostrils flared and pain etched lines around his drawn mouth, but he, too, held on.

"She's already saving herself," Silviu muttered. "Gods, she's powerful."

Silviu closed his eyes and Milo felt magic stir and rise. Coasting over his skin in ceaseless waves, the weight of the Lovasz man's strength impinged on Milo's awareness. Too much to take, too much to imagine, but Milo didn't give a damn. He was beyond fear, ready to use everything Silviu could give his wife, ready to demand even more.

The pressure of Silviu's magic increased, pressing and pulling until Milo felt he was leagues underwater and ready to implode. His bones creaked, his ears jolted with a sharp pain, but he gritted his teeth and bore it. Anything for Christiana, even if it meant letting the powerful Lovasz's magic tear him apart.

But somewhere in the pressurized bubble Silviu created, Milo felt a teasing glide along his magical pathways. Like an unseen summons, Silviu's magic drew Milo's out and directed it to where it would be most useful. The Lovasz man's power seemed to influence and enhance the well of calm Milo barely remembered he possessed in that moment, and Milo would have sworn his magic was taking new shapes, gaining new life, becoming something so much more than just an agent of peace.

Slowly, Christiana stilled. The convulsing stopped, but she was barely breathing and her face was slack. Milo's lungs folded in on themselves, his veins ran with lava as true terror set in. He forced his gaze away from her to glare at her twin.

Adam was utterly focused. Whatever spell Silviu had cast was also working on him, evident in the faint gold light surrounding his palm where it rested against Chris' shoulder. Adam's face surged with color then paled again, the lines around his mouth and eyes deepening and his lips tightening until they nearly disappeared.

"She's remarkable," Silviu whispered. "She managed to block the worst of it. Christiana's reflexes must be frighteningly fast."

"She had a lot of practice," Adam gasped. "Five years' worth."

Milo wrapped his body around his wife's as he knelt on the floor. Shoulders bent, his face buried in her hair, he supported her weight and held on tight, refusing to entertain the possibility that he would lose her as she'd just lost Madeleine. The only place he'd left for Adam and Silviu was Chris' one shoulder and wrist.

Milo didn't dare tear her away, no matter how much he wanted to.

"We need to get her to her room," Adam said shakily.

"Yes," Silviu immediately agreed. "You need to get her stable. Don't let go of her, Adam, your magic is helping to strengthen hers." Silviu tipped his head and narrowed his eyes at Christiana. "Your individual strengths are quite amazing. She saved the baby, too. Now you just need to help her recall herself."

"What do you mean?" Milo asked in a rush. In the fear and chaos, he'd almost forgotten about his baby. Christiana's health stole his sole focus, but Silviu's words reminded Milo that he had more to lose than he could bear to contemplate.

Everything that held meaning in his life was on the verge of slipping away forever.

"Did you see the flash of silver light?" Silviu glanced at Milo.

He struggled to remember, as everything had happened so fast. "Yes. Dark light, and a silver flash—"

"That was Christiana," Silviu interrupted. "I don't quite know what she did, but she threw every ounce of her strength into a barrier protecting the baby. It's been resting calmly this whole time, no matter what else was happening within her."

Milo's spine lost tension he didn't know he had. With the way he was draped over his wife, he wouldn't have thought he could get any lower to the floor, but he did. He felt like he was dissolving, but the baby's health was only one worry soothed amidst more volatile fears.

Silviu stood up, moving his hand from Christiana's wrist to Milo's shoulder. He squeezed in comfort and support. "Get her to her room, get her comfortable and let Adam help her."

"You're not coming?"

Silviu shook his head and gestured to the witches surrounding them, still lying on the floor, leaning against the walls, or staggering in circles. "They all need some help, and I've got to find Georgie."

"Why would someone attack Christiana now that Georgie is the Mother?"

"I saw the magic. Dark magic." Adam looked up, confusion welling in his eyes. "Silviu was the target. She just got in the way. Why target you, though? Who?"

Silviu's lips thinned. "I have to help the others."

Silviu moved toward the closest group of affected Davenolds. Milo willed strength into his rubbery legs and hoisted Christiana against his chest as he stood. Adam rose too, maintaining his hold on his sister. Awkwardly, the two men moved through the house, both unwilling to release their hold on the woman they loved.

* * * *

"Why isn't she waking up?"

The longer Christiana remained still, the more terrified Milo grew. All he could see was Madeleine wasting away until she was nothing more than a tiny lump under her heavy blankets. All he could remember was the way the old woman had convulsed, just as Christiana had. Milo feared his wife would never recover, no matter that Silviu had said she was strong—Madeleine had been strong too, with all the Davenold power at her fingertips, and neither she, nor Silviu had found a way to fight the dark spell.

"It's only been a half hour," Adam reminded him. "And she probably needs to sleep, after last night. I promise you, the spell has dissipated and she's out of danger."

Milo buried his face in the sheets and prayed harder than he ever had, to any deity that cared to listen. He knelt next to the bed while he held his wife's hand, forcing himself not to crawl under the covers with her and stretch out along her side until after Adam achieved whatever miracle he was working on. The Davenold man perched at the edge of the bed, holding Chris' other hand as well as maintaining his hold on her shoulder. By now, Milo was certain Adam's hand had cramped into place, just as he was certain Tulah's legs must be numb from being curled under her body as she waited in the chair by the window.

She was a soothing presence for the two men, a wall standing between their distrust of each and their fear. When one of them tossed out an irritated word, Tulah reminded them what they were there for, showing a surprising patience and strength of mind that easily hauled both men back to the direness of the situation and the need for cooperation. Her willingness to stay and lend her quiet support was enough to make Milo fond of her.

Christiana's family grouping seemed fond of Tulah, as

well. They were ranged along the wall by the wardrobe, with her mother, Melody, slouched in a chair the eldest of her three children, Terrence, had procured for her. Roger rubbed his wife's shoulders as he leaned against a low dresser. Milo was hardly aware of their presence but for the magic they all sent out in a near constant stream of softly whispered spells. Spoken for maximum effect.

"You're in love with her, aren't you?"

Adam's toneless question had Milo's head snapping up. Their gazes clashed, but for the first time, there was no hint of hostility in Adam's. On the chair, Tulah shifted. Melody, Roger and Terrence stopped chanting.

Milo's eyes teared up as he pushed his response through a throat so dry it was raw. "I can't lose her. I don't what I'll do if…"

"We're not going to lose her." Melody's strident tone was completely at odds with her weary appearance.

Milo's heart hurt, sunk in his toes as it was, leaden with fear and a strain of despair he fought to deny. Melody's confident voice lent Milo faith. He'd been trained from birth to follow a woman's lead and if a strong woman said everything would be fine, Milo could hold on to hope.

He looked at his mother-in-law, trying to regain some composure. "I think she'd be surprised to see you here, watching over her. She doesn't think you love her as much as you love Terrence." He jerked his chin in Adam's direction. "Neither of them do."

"What do you know about it?" Adam challenged.

"I know you two were raised in Madeleine's house. I know when Chris is upset she has a habit of calling her grandmother and Georgie's mom before she calls her own mother." Milo raised his brows. "She's my wife. Did you really think I wouldn't learn anything about her, or you by default, in the time we've been together?"

"I did what I thought was best," Melody said softly. "She's the first granddaughter, and there were things my mother needed to teach her that she never taught us. I knew she'd be better protected in Madeleine's house, and Adam couldn't be without her, so I had to send him, too."

Tulah rearranged her legs until her knees were tucked under chin and she faced her in-laws. "Terrence is your favorite, though."

"He was the only one Madeleine left with me." Melody reached out to pat her eldest son's leg. "Adam hardly ever visits and during Chris' first marriage, I had to go out of my way to track her down, just to hear her voice on the phone."

"We almost lost her then, as she pulled away and stopped calling," Roger stated. "I refuse to allow her to slip away now."

"You have no idea." Milo's voice was low and he wondered if his in-laws even heard him.

But Adam did. "And you do? She doesn't trust you."

"She's learning to." Milo met the other man's gaze with a steely glare of his own. "I'm not like the other, and she's starting to realize it."

"She told you about her first husband?"

"She told me *everything*. Like I said, she's my wife."

Adam deflated. Tulah got off the chair and stood next to him, stroking his back as he wrapped one arm around her hips and dragged her close. He turned his face into her ribcage but the flexing of his back showed how big a breath he took.

Milo's laugh was rusty and filled with pain, but genuine as he watched his brother-in-law embrace his new wife. "Chris was worried about your relationship," Milo said. "She shouldn't have been."

Adam's words were muffled in Tulah's shirt, but easily heard. "Maybe I shouldn't be as worried about her marriage. If she told you what happened in the first, and *I* don't even know the extent of it, then she must trust you more than I realized."

After that, no one said anything for a long time. Milo lifted Christiana's hand and kissed her knuckles as he let the silence grow. Melody took a seat at the foot of the bed and rubbed her hand over Christiana's calf and, though she wasn't saying a word, Milo could feel her magic rising and trembling over Christiana's skin.

His mind caught on that fact, and he began to wonder just how magically powerful the Davenolds were. Milo had been a part of his new coven for six months, and he'd met a number of his new Family, but he'd never had a reason to question before. They were stronger than the Ivanovs and that had been enough to bring him relief. But with the memory of Silviu's unbelievable strength still fresh in his mind, he started to turn the matter over with serious thought.

"I know how strong my wife is. Strong enough that I truly thought she'd inherit." He glanced at Melody. "I've been told, on several occasions by several different people, that Suzette is weak in magic."

The woman grimaced. "Weak is a relative term, around here, but Suzette's magic is still stronger than the Mother of your former Family."

Milo nodded. "Yes, but that's not surprising. Dafna Ivanova became Mother through a mixture of trickery, magic and several literal knives in the backs of her potential rivals. Her husband is a man prone to violence, and I believe he takes great joy in snapping necks with his bare hands. After she became Mother, no one was willing to challenge."

"And you became a Davenold," Melody mused. "I heard there was an exodus of men from the Ivanov Family after she took the throne."

"Her husband is an unreasonably jealous man." Milo turned to Adam and asked, "Were you able to see where the dark magic spell came from?"

He shook his head. "I'm surprised I saw it at all. I've only seen magic once before. But when the blast brought nearly everyone else down, Suzette was still on her feet."

Melody looked between them. "Is that why you suspect her, Milo?"

"No, I found Suzette and Daniel together, in a

compromising position. Daniel threatened my business, so I looked into him. He's been trying to gain influence in matriarchal strongholds. He must have an alliance with Suzette, because they've discussed having a baby."

"You can't be serious," Melody gasped.

"That would be tricky, in terms of how every other coven would react." Adam cocked his head. "And the dark magic spell didn't come from either of those two witches. It was way too strong."

"Yet still, everything points back to Suzette." Milo fisted his hands in the blankets. "Witches have been known to go to great lengths to challenge in such a way as to catch the one they're challenging off-guard."

Melody exhaled loudly through her nose. "Then why bother with Christiana? She's not the Mother. Your theory—"

"Still works," Milo interrupted, "since the spell was meant for Silviu. Christiana simply got in the way."

Adam's brows lowered. "A distraction strategy, especially since magic doesn't work on Georgie. The offending witch should have figured that out by now, and switched tactics."

"Are we certain Georgie is still impervious to magic?" Milo glanced around the group. "Perhaps things are different, now that she holds the Davenold power."

"We should find some answers to these questions." Adam closed his eyes. The golden glow of visible Matched Magic flared brightly, then dwindled down. After a brief moment, he let go of his sister, flexed his hand and got to his feet. "Chris is stable. There isn't much more I can do for her, but I can nose around and see if I find any more clues."

Roger, Terrence and Tulah voiced their intentions of helping him. With a sigh, Melody also reluctantly rose to her feet. She leaned past Milo to press a kiss to her daughter's forehead. "There are many things I must see to. One of them will be a thorough questioning of Margaret, to find out exactly what Suzette's talents are, and exactly how long she's known Daniel Levy."

Milo nodded. "I'm going to stay here."

Adam pulled open the door and waved the others through. "Come find us immediately if anything changes."

Milo sat utterly still for a full thirty seconds after they'd gone, appreciating his new Family. The Ivanovs had become a divided lot, but the Davenolds loved each other, and they were strong and determined. Milo clutched at the hope Christiana's family group had brought him.

Then he got into his bed and did what he'd wanted to do from the first. He pulled his wife close and held her tight. To his surprise, her arms stole around his neck.

"Thank Goddess they're gone," she whispered. "They're all so damned loud."

Losing his breath, his arms clamped around his wife. "How long have you been awake?"

"Long to enough to know you love me."

Milo's heart dug its way out of his toes and climbed back into its proper position as warmth unfurled and rocketed through his muscles so fast he felt deboned. He closed his eyes to hold back his tears and kissed his wife's hair.

"Yes, *krasavitsa*. I love you very much."

Chapter Twenty-Eight

Christiana

Emerging from the connecting bathroom, Christiana paused to consider her sleeping husband. In spite of her nap, exhaustion pulled at her, but her mind spun with too many thoughts to let her truly rest. Dark magic and magical attacks, her husband and the life she sheltered within her created a never-ending stream of confusion.

She didn't remember all that much from the dark magic attack, only a terrible cold followed by a scorching heat along her spine. And the instantaneous panic that had her pushing every molecule of magic at her disposal toward her womb. Protecting the baby she so fiercely wanted. She'd known she would leave herself vulnerable, but she'd have made the same choice again in a heartbeat.

Five years of hell had left her uncertain of whether she'd ever have a child, but after marrying Milo, Christiana had wanted to get pregnant as soon as possible. He was her last chance to conceive, and she figured she might as well hurry up before he turned mean.

But six months in, and he still wasn't mean. He swore he was faithful and had cooperated with Adam. And he loved her.

She needed him to love her.

Stretching, she evaluated her body. She felt good. Nothing hurt, she didn't sense any lingering ill effects from the dark magic. The spell that had caught her had been formless, and its lack of direction had helped her get a handle on it. It had been powerful, but indiscriminate in its intent to harm. The added boost she got from her Magic Match had accelerated both the battle against the dark magic and her healing.

She worked the last of the knots out of her muscles before walking toward the bed. Milo lay on his side — he hadn't moved when she'd gotten up. The blankets were kicked down, Milo's bare toes resting on top of them, though a corner of the sheet lay across his knees. His breathing was even, his mouth parted in sleep.

Chris tugged off her shirt and shimmied out of her pants, leaving them on the floor as she climbed up next to her husband, then onto his body. He shifted enough that her hand at his shoulder put him on his back. His breathing hitched but evened out again as he settled. Christiana straddled his lower abdomen and sent her fingers gliding under his shirt, pushing it up as she followed the lean lines of his stomach. She leaned over him until her naked breasts tingled from his heat, and stretched a little to reach his mouth.

She kissed him awake. Soft brushes and light nips, following the curves of his lips from corner to corner. She returned to the very center and focused on his bottom lip, where there was a hint of plumpness to tease her senses. She sucked that part into her mouth and ran her tongue over it, nibbled a little.

Milo stirred. He kissed her back, just as gently as she kissed him, just as much of a tease as she was, before he came into full consciousness. Then he jolted and his big hands caught her hips, lighting her nerves and making her yearn, even as he shifted her back.

"Are you all right, *krasavitsa*?"

She smiled. Any other man would have asked that question in a tone that implied he already knew the answer, given the fact that she was straddling her husband and a glance down would tell him just how 'all right' she was. But Milo spoke in a tone just shy of panic, as if the attack had just happened.

Christiana defied the grip he had on her hips and leaned

back down to kiss the corner of his mouth. "Yes."

"You're supposed to be sleeping."

"I woke up. Then I felt like waking my husband up."

He sent a scandalized glare her way. "Your husband is very worried about you right now, *krasavitsa*. He would prefer it if you laid back down and rested, while he found someone with the talent to tell him you're fully recovered."

She licked the center of his lower lip. "Or you could figure it out on your own, Milo."

His grip only tightened and he pushed his head deeper into the pillows in a vain attempt to escape the teasing of her tongue. "What are you doing, Christiana?"

"I'm trying to seduce my husband, but he's not being very cooperative."

"I'm worried."

Hearing the grim truth in his voice, Christiana stopped trying to tempt him. She bracketed his head with her arms, her hands braced on the mattress just below the pillows, and pinned him with an exasperated stare. She was leaning low, her hardening nipples sliding over his chest as she breathed, but he was so much taller that even in this position, it required a lifting of her gaze to meet his.

"I was scared, *really* scared, Milo. And I need you right now, inside me. I need to feel you filling me and moving within me, with your arms around me and your mouth on mine. I just need you, Milo."

"You were hurt."

"And you'll be gentle." She put her lips to his, her plea becoming a caress against him. "Please, make love to me."

His lips softened under hers. But they only parted enough to take in her bottom lip, giving her quick lick before he released her to breathe over the dampness he left behind. His big hands left her hips and came up to cradle her skull, his long fingers tangling in her hair and making her scalp prickle deliciously.

There was such care in his touch, in his hold. Christiana felt cherished, for the first time in a very long while. She felt loved, worthy of love and willing to accept his love. The warmth of that knowledge swirled all the way down to her toes.

"I was scared too, *krasavitsa*. I thought I lost you."

"I'm right here."

His hands tightened but she didn't tense. He wasn't trying to hurt her—it was simply a reaction of his fear. Immediately, he gentled and stroked her hair, following its length with one hand until his palm smoothed down the skin of her back. Christiana would never have thought that just the soft sweep of fingertips along her spine could feel so good.

Milo's hand trailed down until he gripped her ass. Christiana shoved his shirt up higher, but could only make it so far with her breasts in the way, and she wasn't ready to sit up and lose the wonderful friction of cotton against her needy nipples. So she rocked against the narrow strip of belly she'd bared, painting her husband's skin with the cream brimming from her body.

His eyes glittered. "That feels very nice, *krasavitsa*. Your pussy is so warm and wet already, where you slide against me."

"Because I want you. I want you inside me."

"Ah, but I'm still dressed in all these clothes. How can I make love to you when I'm completely covered?"

She huffed a laugh and licked his lips. "It is a problem."

Reluctantly, Chris dismounted, but her efforts were rewarded with a sexy striptease. She hadn't known her husband had it in him, but she was impressed when he rolled to his feet and gave her a show.

He lifted his shirt to his nipples and pointed to the wet streak just below his navel. "Evidence of your pleasure, *krasavitsa*. Maybe one day, I'll leave evidence of mine on your soft belly."

Kneeling on the rumpled sheets, she gave a shake of her head, denying him. "No, I like it when you come inside me, filling me up until your pleasure runs of out me."

Milo's lips quirked. "But you trust me now, remember? That gives me free reign to fulfill some of my fantasies."

Milo whipped off his shirt and she took a moment to appreciate the sight of him. He wasn't bulky, but his chest was well-developed for his body type. Lean muscles, a dusting of pale hair and dark nipples that were sensitive for a man. Packed with subtle power and a dancer's grace, Milo's average looks became beautiful when unclothed.

"What fantasies?" But her words were hard to say, as Milo reached for the ties of his sweat pants.

All too slowly, he pulled and the knot came undone. The pants only sagged a little, but where they caught when they dropped highlighted the muscles carved out from his hips and the top of his groin. She licked her lips as Milo started tugging the pants lower in a blatant tease.

"I like to make you hotter than you can stand, Christiana. Even our first time together you were so responsive to me. A little patience, a lot of control, and you opened up so sweetly."

She shook her head. Their first night together had been awkward, the thickness of Milo's cock faintly frightening, and she'd been filled with post-wedding jitters. But he'd taken his time, touched her, stroked her and brought her enough pleasure for her to relax as he'd entered her. Then he taught her what glory was.

"I'd never had it like that before. You were sweet, Milo, to take all that time to make it good for me."

"I want to give you more. And I want to take more."

Milo gripped his freed dick and stroked. Christiana was riveted, her eyes glued to his fingers where they curled under his shaft, taking in every tiny shift as he dragged his palm toward the tip. He moved slowly, and the deliberate eroticism of that act had her catching her breath.

"I like the look in your eyes," he whispered darkly.

"I like what I'm looking at. You should come back over here so I can look closer."

"Is that all you want to do?"

Her belly pulled tight, a lick of heat curled down through it. She shook her head. "I want to touch. I want to feel you."

"Feel me where?" Milo's voice dropped into such a low octave it was more like a rumble Christiana felt roll over her nerves. "Show me."

She blinked. She was surprised, nervous and curious. He was showing her another side of himself, playing games and demanding she play too. But he'd stop if she wanted. One word from her and he'd return to the bed and touch her, fill her, pleasure her. She took a deep breath and gave serious thought to what she wanted to do.

Christiana wanted to play. She wanted to tempt her husband, seduce him so thoroughly there would never be another doubt of whether or not he desired another woman. She wanted to meet the challenge sparkling in his eyes, because even though he'd dared to give her a command, it still felt like she wielded all the power.

She put her hands to her chest and met her husband's smoldering gaze with only a little hesitation. Watching him closely, she dragged her fingers down to her breasts. Cupping them, she pressed harder than Milo had done in months—since they became so sensitive—and eased the faint ache within. Then she continued her downward slide as she shifted on her knees, parting them so he could see her intimate flesh.

Down her ribs, past her navel—she almost faltered but pushed on, sliding two fingers into her short curls and beyond. She circled her clit as Milo watched, hungry and intent, then dipped lower.

"I want you here," she breathed.

His face was carved from granite, but the heat sparking in his emerald eyes nearly set her on fire. He stared at her hand, watched it play between her legs and took a ragged breath.

Milo's voice was gravel in his throat as his cock flexed in his hand. "Where is *here, krasavitsa*? I can't see."

Heat flooded her face. Then it flooded the rest of her body.

"In my pussy, Milo."

"Lie back so I can see what you mean. Right now, it's all too hidden from my sight."

The longing in his voice captured her full attention. Confidence rushed through her, wound around her nerves and muscles and made her lightheaded. She did as he asked and settled down on the mattress, spreading her legs so he could watch her touch herself.

Without taking his eyes off her, Milo released his cock and stripped off his pants. He came up on the bed with her and stroked up her calves, applying pressure until they were not only spread farther, but her feet were planted on the mattress with him kneeling between. He had a perfect view to anything she would do, and he encouraged her to do it.

"Touch yourself, Christiana, and show me what you need. Show me what you like, what you've been wishing I would do to you."

"I like what you do to me. It's already good."

"Show me how to make it better," he ordered in a dark whisper.

If her first husband had ever put her in her current position, she'd have been shaking with fear and terrified the game they played would go much too far. But everything was different with Milo and the gentle kiss he planted on her knee reminded her. Even more than the last time they were together—just hours ago, when they'd broken through the blockade Chris had tried so hard to build between them— she trusted him. Every intimate encounter they'd shared had secretly been solidifying into a foundation Christiana hadn't even known she depended on. She felt free enough to be bold in a way she'd never been.

She stroked her clit and ran her fingers over her folds. Sensation tingled through her, but even better was the heat in Milo's steady gaze, the sound of his breathing as it fractured. The feel of his big hands shaking on her knees as he held her wide. The sight of his tongue as he licked his lips.

She pushed two fingers into her pussy and lifted a little. To give him a better view, to feel her own penetration a little deeper. It wasn't enough — she wanted to be stretched as only he could stretch her, with his hard dick slamming into her, making her burn and writhe and beg for more. Just the thought, the memory, the *need*, had her moaning and bucking, putting on her own show for him.

"You are so beautiful," he growled. "If you could see what you look like, wet and hungry for my cock. I can see how those two, slender fingers you're teasing yourself with aren't enough. Your pussy wants me, doesn't it?"

"Yes. It needs you. I need you."

His eyes met hers for a heartbeat before zooming back down. "You like me watching you, don't you?"

She nodded jerkily. Goddess help her, she loved this game he'd introduced. She loved the feel of his eyes on her, his focused attention when too much of their lives were spent stealing moments between Family meetings and business deals. She loved that she stroked confidence into herself with every thrust of her own fingers and that an element of power over her husband remained, even as she followed his commands. She loved that the look on her husband's face made her feel beyond beautiful and valuable as a woman, as a wife, and not just a high ranking Davenold female.

Milo gripped his dick again, squeezing and stroking as he watched her fingers play. He shuffled forward and a wicked grin crossed his lips. He put the crest of his cock against her clit and rubbed a slow circle as Christiana hurriedly pulled her fingers free of her pussy's wet clasp.

"Here, *krasavitsa*? Is this where you need me?"

He took her breath. She'd been building heat between her legs with the slow thrusting of her fingers, setting her nerves to wriggling, sensation spreading, pleasure growing. Milo was a frustrating tease. His cock was a soft pressure when she'd touched herself harder, his flesh was a hot, smooth curve when her fingers had been a rough drag.

But his magic sizzled against her flesh. Christiana knew

it was deliberate, that he used it to heighten the sensations, and she admitted she should have let him do it long ago because Milo's gentleness combined with his magic to have every nerve between her legs drawing taut.

Chris' mind and body both concentrated fully, so as not to miss anything. She tracked his movements with crystalline devotion—every shift magnified, sharp awareness, clarity slicing through her lust and heightening the excitement. He slipped his thick head over her clit in a tortuous path and slicked down between her folds, spreading them until the soft pressure of his touch seemed exaggerated.

Christiana arched, rubbing herself against his crest, feeling the shift and slide of her flesh around him. Then Milo's cock lodged against her opening. She could hardly breathe as her body clamped down in eagerness, her inner walls squeezing against themselves as he waited, teasing her as her entrance contracted in unashamed temptation.

He pushed into her body with a single thrust that left Christiana wondering how a motion so slow could still be so intense. Then he withdrew and rocked tauntingly, two inches of his thick shaft working her inner walls until she screeched in frustration and her hips flew up to gain more of him.

Another slow, powerful surge had his whole length buried inside her. Christiana arched mindlessly, riding his cock and trying to take more. Writhing as heat worked through her and her nipples contracted violently. But when Milo pushed as far as he could, he held them both still, denying her exertions.

Eyes squeezed closed and his face inflexible, Milo's lip barely moved when he said, "I love the way you melt around me, *krasavitsa*. You're so wet, I can feel your cream sliding over my shaft."

Chris gave a moan that turned into a harsh sound of protest when Milo wrenched from her completely. He hauled her legs off the bed and over his shoulders, rocking forward to send the length of his cock shuttling over her flesh, slipping over her folds and striking against her clit.

He was wet with her pleasure, her need. The sight of his cock shining between her legs as he pushed against her called more cream from her body to slide down the curves of her ass. The way her flesh compressed under the thickness of his shaft to send sharp-edged lust spearing into her body stole her breath. Milo grunted and rocked forward hard, harder than he'd ever do inside her. Again and again, until Christiana wailed and bucked, eager to feel that same force ramming into her pussy.

The heat and the pressure of her husband's dick electrified her clit and made her need so much more. She needed *connection*, a bond as profound as any woman could experience. And Milo gave it to her. His magic called to hers until both powers swirled between them with an intimacy Christiana couldn't deny. An intimacy that heightened every pleasure as it strung sensation on cords tied directly to her emotions.

She jerked helplessly, pushing her ass against her husband's knees, loving the soft feel of his balls smashing into her. They were wet too, her pussy leaking all over him in expectant bliss as fire licked up into her torso.

"Please, God, Milo, I need you inside me. I'm empty, please, please…"

Christiana descended into incoherent pleas and shrill sobs. She rose from the mattress, tightening her legs on her husband's shoulders and using the leverage to lift against him. Undulating, she watched his thick cock rub her clit, unable to look away.

Milo's nostrils flared. The next forward thrust had him driving into her with a heavy thrust that stretched her pussy and had her screaming, flexing powerfully around his penetration. Pleasure speared through her. Sparks of sensation erupted into full-blown fireworks as her nerves exploded. He was so hot, so thick, and she was so needy. He was only halfway home when she detonated.

Shuddering, convulsing, gushing around his cock,

Christiana lost her breath completely as Milo rode her hard, driving through her contractions until they lengthened into a ceaseless wave of ecstasy. She felt as if he gained girth when her walls clamped down, tightening on him until every shift dragged his ridged cock over a new place that sent streamers of ecstasy through her body. She rocked and jerked, arched and undulated, greedy for more.

The last barriers around her heart cracked open as she came again. Magic poured into her, through her. Not just a soothing sweep against her skin, but filling her heart with a new power, one thrust directly upon her by her husband. A warm connection of safety and care in the midst of the chaos he'd brought to her, and promising her something she'd never thought she'd be given.

Milo dropped her legs and surged over her. She wrapped her shaky arms around him with all the strength she could find and held on as he shuddered over her, driving through his climax until he pushed deep and let go. His heat filled her, covered her, and soothed her. She held him close as he bucked and stilled, groaning his orgasm into the curve of her throat.

Christiana closed her eyes and reveled in the sensation of being loved.

Chapter Twenty-Nine

Silviu

Silviu's chest throbbed, but he'd gotten used to the sensation. This time, with the alien pain pulsing through his ribs, he understood what was happening, thanks to Costel's explanations. Though the feeling seemed disconnected from his own nervous system, the impressions were sharper than the pangs of sadness shared by the coven as a whole had been earlier. The ache stemmed from the physical pain of at least twenty Davenolds injured in the blast of dark magic.

Mason Davenold approached. "Any idea who did this?"

Silviu had developed a new and profound appreciation for his father-in-law. Mason was gifted with a level of organization that was hard to deny. Georgie's father had sprung into action the moment Christiana fell, setting up a makeshift triage for the injured, assessing their wounds and prioritizing them for Silviu's meager healing abilities.

Every witch knew the incantations that provided basic first aid but Silviu was terrified his magic wouldn't be enough. He could cast the necessary spells to drive out the lingering effects of the damaging hex, and his talent provided a measure of relief as it influenced and enhanced the magic of the witches he worked on, but he feared he wouldn't be able to stop the dark spell from infecting the Davenolds as it had Madeleine.

He'd give a great deal to have a gifted healer on the estate, but that was not a talent the Davenolds had in abundance. Silviu would give anything for a witch with the ability to feel the insidious enchantment that resisted discovery, because he could hardly feel it at all. The dark magic was slippery and formless, melting into the depths of a witch's soul, where it laid in wait to strike again.

"No." Silviu pushed his words through clenched teeth. "This attack felt different than what your former Mother experienced, but since I didn't make direct contact with it, I can't evaluate the magic further."

Mason rubbed his eyes. "Damn. If we knew who did this, maybe we could figure out *why*."

The spell that had caught Christiana had been meant for Silviu. He knew that fact as surely as he knew his own name, but he didn't understand why he'd been targeted. Simply because the magic felt so different than what he'd discovered in Madeleine, Silviu wondered if the casting witch was a challenger who had decided he was a better mark than Georgie. Especially considering her Bane imperviousness, and their Matched bond.

About to answer his father-in-law and explain his theory, Silviu stilled as a sudden, new idea presented itself. If he concentrated hard enough, awareness of his wife slid through his psyche, yet Georgie's presence within the bloodline's magic felt nearly nonexistent, compared to the misery of the Davenolds in the immediate vicinity.

Silviu went cold, thinking that perhaps the attack on him meant Georgie had already suffered physical harm, and needed his help.

"Mason," he ordered. "Go find Georgeanne. Christiana said she was on the beach and I need to know she's well."

Silviu couldn't go to her while the Davenolds required his help. Not with the furious tug of magic on his deepest senses causing such discomfort and pain. He was the Mother and he had to fulfill his responsibilities to his Family if he wanted to regain Georgie's trust. The gods only knew what his wife would do if she *wasn't* hurt and she found out that he'd left her Family to their injuries when he was the strongest witch in the room.

"All right, I'll check on her." Mason's lips thinned, but

he nodded. Then he pointed at a pair of witches slumped against the far wall. "They're the last. They were the farthest away from the blast, so their injuries aren't severe, but both of them are badly shaken."

Silviu looked the pair over. The two older women made a show of strength with lifted chins and set lips, but their shaking shoulders pressed together tightly and they held hands. Silviu didn't know them, but he felt them deep inside his own skin where the Davenold magic blazed with love and concern.

As Mason left, Silviu knelt in front of the women. He reached for the first and laid hands on her. Magic rose to his command, a cool, silver stream Silviu once again wished was more effective at healing. To his surprise, a papery, chilled palm fluttered onto his wrist.

"Are you all right, Silviu Lovasz?"

He looked into the eyes of the unknown cousin and saw nothing but concern for him, in spite of her shock. "Yes, ma'am. I wasn't hurt. The spell rebounded in the opposite direction. Those of us nearer the door were uninjured."

"That's not what I meant," she whispered. "I can feel the turmoil inside you. It's a gift of mine."

Silviu closed his eyes and willed his magic deeper into the woman, forcing it to twine around her magic until he could enhance the healing she'd already begun herself. Warmth bubbled up, springing from the woman's concern and adding into the resilient sense of love the former Family Mothers had infused into the Davenold power. Something twanged in his chest, and, in that moment, he could have sworn some elemental change had taken place inside him.

But he only said, "I've been healing the Family for almost two hours, ma'am. It's a difficult task."

"We're your Family too now, aren't we?"

"And I have become extremely aware of my responsibilities toward you," he agreed.

"Because you've married our girl, haven't you?" The woman narrowed her eyes, but smiled gently enough. "My talent tells me of your bond, and it is deeply entrenched."

"We're Matches, madam."

"Georgeanne will be a good Mother, but she will need a High Male at her side who understands duty, loyalty and love."

Silviu nodded. "She *will* be a good Mother. And I will be the best husband I know how to be."

"Excellent. You both may face problems with some of the cousins," the woman warned, "but I doubt any will truly challenge your bride. She has worked too hard to gain the position, and has been too active amongst both this Family and the other covens for another to believe they could do better."

"Suzette has already challenged her." Silviu opened his eyes and moved to heal the other woman. "Georgie won."

"Suzette reaches above herself. Mark my words, Silviu Lovasz, the Family will only follow Georgeanne. The cousins may test her, but no other will do to lead the Davenolds. It's unthinkable, unacceptable. Should another displace Georgeanne, our Family will descend into war."

"My wife has to prove herself, though. I know and we're prepared."

The woman huffed. "Georgeanne proved herself long ago. If she hadn't been found worthy, Madeleine would have killed her for being Bane."

The words shocked him with their simplicity. For a moment, Silviu's magic grew unsteady with his thoughts, his wishes. His fears. In spite of the Davenold woman's ability to sense his turmoil, Silviu tried to hide the emotions he struggled with by focusing his gaze on the aged hand that reached out to pat his own.

He cleared his throat. "Madeleine loved Georgie."

"Madeleine has never loved anyone more than the Davenold coven, as a whole. It's what made her a great Mother. If Georgeanne had fallen short of her expectations, Madeleine would have removed the stain from our bloodline."

"The most dangerous challenges won't come from *our* Family," the other woman added. "Protect her well, Lovasz. I believe she'll need you, in the future."

The first woman giggled. "My sister has a gift, as well."

"I intend to." Silviu resisted fidgeting. The gift of prophesy was the oldest of all talents and rare, but the Davenolds were among the oldest of Families and powerful. Taking the woman's words to heart, he offered a tight smile and wound his magic around the last of her injuries.

Finally, every Davenold witch was steady on their feet. The ache in Silviu's chest subsided for a brief moment, before flaring anew. Brighter, more connected to him, more personal than anything else he'd felt over the past two hours, the new discomfort was familiar. Without the Family drowning him in pain, Georgie's agony took up residence as if she were a piece of him. Rubbing his chest, Silviu turned toward the door, only to find Mason waiting for him.

"What did you do to my daughter?"

Silviu rushed forward. "Is she all right?"

Mason's ashen features stiffened. "No."

Silviu's blood turned to ice. Without another word, he pushed past his father-in-law and raced to the closest exit. He stumbled into the garden and flew over the path. The sound of the sea grew louder, battling his heartbeat in his ears. He staggered through a break in the hedges and slid on the rocks.

He spied Georgie a little way down the beach, lying low on the sandy flat below the rocks, wrapped in an afghan and unmoving. Silviu's heart stopped. Acid washed through his stomach and rose into his throat. Adrenaline kicked a hot flood of fear directly into his bloodstream, narrowing his focus until the only thing he could see was the still form of his wife.

"Georgie!"

She flinched and her movement was the only thing that helped Silviu slow his unbalanced descent down the rocky slope. She was just beyond the rocks, at the top of the sand, curled into a fetal position. A few yards away, the turbulent water washed the beach and drowned out every noise but Silviu's panicked scream.

He dropped to his knees at her back, barely managing to ease the pressure of his hands as they came down on her and ran the length of her tucked-up form. Her face was covered and offered no clues, with her fingers holding the blanket too tightly to dislodge easily. Instead of fighting her grip, Silviu focused on her body. He could hardly feel her through the thick afghan, but couldn't sense any trace of dark magic and her breathing was relatively even, if a little choppy. In his chest, all he felt was her pain.

"Are you hurt?" he asked frantically.

"Leave me alone."

Hearing the quaver in her voice, he stilled. His gut told him she was whole and healthy, and any pain she'd felt was at his betrayal. His magic agreed with that diagnosis.

Silviu took a moment to breathe, to calm himself. He desperately flipped through strategies and tactics, discarding each in the same moment they came to him.

While the gentlemanly thing to do might be staring her in the eyes and stating his undying devotion followed by profuse apologies, Silviu couldn't do it. Guilt ate him alive, as did frustration at Georgie's distrust and anger at her threat to dissolve their union, but he didn't regret taking the Davenold magic. He wouldn't lie and say he did. Mixed into those emotions, was a sense of victory at having gained them a powerful position, leftover panic, and raging satisfaction that she was his forever.

There was no going back, and their going forward depended on this moment. Right there on the beach. Silviu called himself a coward and sat down at Georgie's back, scooting against her until his hip pressed her spine. Twisting into an uncomfortable position, he threw a leg over hers, caging her, and leaned forward until he could plant a shaking hand in the sand by her knee in case she tried to bolt.

She didn't move. The afghan still covered her face and Silviu was willing to leave her that illusion of refuge. It provided the same illusion for him. She didn't look at him and didn't try to wrestle free of his embrace. She didn't speak either, so with no other plan appealing to him, Silviu let words tumble from his mouth — off the top of his head, hoping like hell the right ones would come to him.

"The moment I met you, I knew your strength. I knew your loyalty, and I am so sorry that what I did made your Family question that loyalty. I'm sorry they sent you away, but I couldn't have kept my hands off you if every witch in your Family had stood between me and your bed."

Silviu stared at the top of Georgie's curls, just about all he could see of her, and hoped she was listening. He took a deep breath.

"I needed you then, Georgie. I can't even find enough words to tell you how much I need you now. For me, and not any political goals my father or your grandmother may have dreamed of. For my own dreams, love, of a future and a family."

Silviu bit the inside of his cheek as she remained silent. His body rioted, hot and cold by turns, his cheeks growing chapped by the brisk wind. His eyes felt damp, but he put that down to the wind too, though it was a struggle to keep his voice even the next time he spoke.

"I'm scared that other witches will find out about your talent and come after you. And that's on top of the fears I already had. I've never been so arrogant as to think I was the strongest witch in existence, no matter what my father believed, or that a stronger witch couldn't be born tomorrow. And at the Ngozi's we did find a stronger witch."

Just the memory of how close he'd come to losing her under the dark spell at the Ngozi's had him pausing to battle fresh panic. Silviu had never known fear like that, and when Georgie had returned to life, returned to him, he'd never known rage like what he'd directed at Muso. Even now, his muscles burned with the need for violence against the Ngozi Father, just as they burned to take Georgie into his arms and force her to forgive him.

There was the slightest shift in the folds of the afghan. Silviu gripped his hope tighter and fought the constriction around his vocal cords that made his voice too thick. "However I have to do it, I need to protect you, Georgie, because I can't live without you."

Restlessness swept through Silviu in a flood of fire, burning him alive from the inside out. He couldn't take her silence another minute. He caught the edge of the blanket and pulled it off her face.

Only to be met with big eyes running with tears, misery stamped across her features. His strong bride, a woman who faced unimaginable pressure at a terribly young age. A woman who grew into her power and authority the hard way, facing down those who would kill her for what she was — both a witch and a witch without magic. A woman who rarely cried.

Silviu's heart twisted, and he knew it would stay in its new shape for the rest of his life. "Don't cry, my love. Please, don't cry."

Her words broke free on a sob. "I trusted you."

Chapter Thirty

Georgeanne

Georgie didn't know what to think or believe, or what to trust anymore. She was breaking. She could feel it — the cracks forming within her, widening until bottomless chasms yawned and supposedly solid ground tumbled into them. She was so tired.

Silviu leaned over her, staring at her with the most savage expression she'd ever seen on his face, with pain in his eyes and cheekbones sharp enough to draw blood. It only twisted the invisible knife in her chest. His voice was uneven, thick with guilt and regret, and she didn't know what to do.

"I didn't know what else to do." His thoughts seemed to mirror hers. Then he took it a step farther. "I'm sorry I hurt you, but I'm not sorry I took the power of your bloodline."

With frightening speed, he rolled over her, tugged the afghan out of her grip as he shifted into the cocoon she'd made. Steely arms wrapped around her, one hand anchored in her hair, tightening until pinpricks ran over her scalp. He gave her no time to get away, no chance to fight.

The gentle, uneven words he'd begun his unconventional apology with were gone. Lost in his savagery when he snarled in her face.

"I will fight. I will fight every fucking obstacle in our way, every witch who tries to manipulate us and every fucking scheme they try to maneuver us into playing out for them. I will even fight *you*, because I fight for *us*. For our future."

Georgie looked into Silviu's mercury eyes and saw his true self. The dominant patriarch, the Reap witch. For the first time, she saw everything he normally tried to hide from her, the core of what he was that she'd only felt when he filled her with his magic, the full extent of everything his Family and hers had tried to beat out of him. His veneer of civility was stripped away, leaving only the powerful, wild witch behind. Raw in his intensity.

"I need you to trust me, Georgeanne."

She was eased by the hard edges of his warrior side. If he'd continued with his pretty words and soft pleas, she'd have known Silviu was sweet-talking her into a forgiveness he didn't deserve. Manipulating her. Instead, his brutal, blunt declarations reached into her fractured heart and knit it back together — with scars and missing pieces, but enough to lead her past the agony of betrayal so she could think and reason.

The small, dark voice in the back of her mind rose from the turmoil and whispered that, perhaps, she'd have done something just as extreme, to keep the ones she loved safe.

His hand tightened even more in her hair and he pressed his forehead to hers hard enough to cause some discomfort. His rasping whisper still held ferocity. "It's all so fucking complicated. And I wish I could I simplify it, but I can't. We are what they made us and it's too dangerous for us to pull back from that now."

He was right. It was too complicated, and Georgie remembered a time when she hadn't understood that, when what she felt was so much simpler. When they were both young and unbearably lonely, ostracized for things beyond their control, but finding understanding in each other. Like he'd said so often, recognizing the missing pieces of themselves.

Georgie needed simple. She was so tired, so cold. Sad beyond words. Too much had happened and too much inside her hurt too badly to make sense of.

So she kissed Silviu and let all the complications burn away under the heat of his mouth.

Their previous kisses had always been a battle for

supremacy, but this kiss was a war Silviu won before Georgie even realized she'd initiated it. In one fell move, he surged deep and conquered, forcing her surrender. Her head spun as she tried to keep up with his bold licks and fierce nips. He sucked her tongue into his mouth and sent her spinning.

With his hand in her hair, he directed her, tipping her face, angling her mouth. He fused their lips together until she couldn't breathe, and breathed through him, instead. There were no slow glides or steamy seductions, only hot, desperate friction as he consumed her. Only the searing sense of his magic rushing to fill her completely.

She felt him open the floodgates and pour all his excess into her. Silviu's heat swirled up from her toes in a silver rush, beckoning her response. Demanding it. With no idea how to stop herself, Georgie met him, reached for him, and the silver exploded into gold.

In the midst of her recklessness, she felt his truth as clearly as she felt his lies. His intent to manipulate her, his determination to protect her. He would fight for them, whatever the consequences may be. He held no remorse beyond the fact that he hurt her. Because he loved her, he would destroy anything—even her—to keep her safe.

That understanding hurtled heat throughout her body. Skyrocketing lust blazed a path through her nerves, her muscles. The thoughts crowding her head with confusion and bringing pain to her heart leaped back, out of the way of the need Silviu poured over her. Into her.

She worked a hand between them, groping for his waistband. She found the button and jerked. The whisper of his zipper was lost in the hungry sounds they made as they ravaged each other's mouth, but when she caught his cock in her hand, she tasted his groan. His hips flexed, pushing his length harder into her palm.

One hand still locked in her hair, holding her mouth to his, he sent the other down her back in a hard press that lit every nerve around her spine. He forced her body to conform to his, chest to lower abdomen. His big hand kept moving down, curving around her ass and pulling her close.

Georgie tightened her fingers on his dick, stroking with short pulls, all she could manage as he soldered her to his body. She absorbed the feel of his rigid cock into her palms, the soft skin, the intriguing ridges, the pounding heartbeat. The pulse in his cock mirrored the one in her chest and sharpened her lust into something that cut deeper than his betrayal ever could.

The simple, short dress Georgie had pulled on a moment before rushing to her grandmother's deathbed was no impediment to Silviu's questing fingers. He burrowed under the hem and met her naked flesh, hot and swelling under the need he transferred with his magic. His fingers slid down, probing roughly. The time for delicacy was long past. Neither had it in them.

Heat blazed over Georgie's skin and seared her folds. She tried to arch back, greedily searching for more, desperate to take some part of him as he'd taken so much of her, but the strength of Silviu's palm against her lower curves held her prisoner. She wriggled, but there was no breaking his hold.

Intolerable. His magic coursed through her, filled her and made her need more. So much more. His touch wasn't enough to satisfy the cravings cascading through her. He wasn't low enough, he wasn't close enough.

With all the nerves near her pussy electrified and demanding action, Georgie put every ounce of strength she had into lifting her leg over his. She slid her knee up in a jerky movement entirely too revealing, but she didn't care. With her hand trapped in an awkward position, she stroked her thumb over his crest, following the curve, finding the dip in its center, as she tried to force her leg higher.

Silviu's fingers left her wet folds and locked on her thigh. With a violent yank, he pulled her knee to his hip and angled into the opening he'd made. And she was open. Spread and wrapped around him, writhing to get closer as his hand returned to her ass and helped her shift forward.

His fingers hunted for her entrance. Raw lust barreled through the magic they'd merged between them, but, for once, Georgie had no idea if it was his or hers. Maybe it was just theirs. Whatever the source, her pussy flexed and cried, weeping for his touch as he prodded.

He wasn't gentle. Gentleness had been lost before they'd ever begun. This was all-out war, and the victor would claim all the spoils. Georgie was fighting for their future as much as Silviu was—him through magic, her through lust. Anguish scented the air around them.

Silviu drove two fingers deep into her pussy. Georgie tried to break their untamed kiss to snatch a breath. He wouldn't let her.

He pumped his fingers as he sucked her tongue into his mouth. Silviu's arm tightened around her, his palm pressed harder to her ass. His fingers thrust hard, and Georgie found herself caught against his rocking hips as he drove his dick over her clit. Magic and pleasure spun together, shifting and parting as new needs and thoughts penetrated her haze. He worked her from both ends, distracting her even as pleasure piled up and shook her straight through.

Georgie clasped his cock and dragged it down. She worked his crest over her clit as she arched her hips, running the smooth tip over the swollen peak pulsing with urgency. Her entire lower body hummed at the feel of him against her, and it only grew louder, more insistent, as she pushed Silviu's tip between her folds.

Spreading around him as his flesh displaced hers, bolts of energy and magic brought emotions she never knew she had to life. His cock caressed her skin and set her on fire. She bucked until every sense she had was impressed with the feel of him lodged against her, until his crest was tucked against her entrance, trapped between her flickering flesh and his driving fingers. Wetting him in her cream.

She bit his lip hard enough to make him bleed and gained freedom from his kiss. She snarled, "In me, now, Silviu."

The last time they'd been together, he tried hard to make the moment special. He'd drawn out every caress, every kiss, every sensation—and used his magic to heighten the effects. Now, wrapped in an afghan on a cold beach, with regret, fear and grief whipping them bloody, there was too much on the line for sweetness to prevail. There was no room for devoted care or politeness, no awareness of anything beyond the intensity battering them.

They panted over each other's lips, his hand in her hair twisting brutally, forcing her face up, forcing her to meet his gaze with no way to look away but the closing of her eyes. And she couldn't do that—not with the emotions turning his to tempered steel.

She needed to see those emotions.

Silviu pressed into her. And kept going until he was fully buried. Fully merged. One stroke. A long, heavy drive to the end of her.

Georgie's eyelids fluttered, but she refused to close them. Her mouth fell open, but there was no air to be had. She stretched around Silviu's penetration, slick inner walls simultaneously protesting the forceful intrusion and flexing in relief as he filled her completely. Then he held still, seemingly more for his adjustment than hers.

"I love you, Georgeanne Davenold-Lovasz." Silviu bared his teeth, and if she didn't know the wildness coursing through him, she wouldn't have understood the intensity in his words. They were more a challenge than a promise. "I will protect you. I will care for you. *And* your Family."

He leaned down and bit her lip. Her blood mingled with his on her tongue as he kissed her savagely. Their magic trembled, waiting for her vow to complete the bond they'd begun to seal.

"I will take you, Silviu Davenold-Lovasz. All you have to give. Then I'll demand more. I want it all, everything you have, because if you're stealing it from me, I *won't* be left alone in the chaos."

"Never alone!" He yanked on her hair. "I'll always be

there, Georgie."

Magic roared and erupted, untamed and uncontrolled. And the most honest they'd ever been with each other. Lightning flashed like black flames flickering with gold. The sand around them turned to glass.

In that moment, Georgie *knew* Silviu as her Match. She'd known she was made for him, known she'd been promised to him and known she'd shared a connection with him. But in that moment, with his lust melding with hers and their magic slicing grooves into their souls, the truth shone with crystal clarity.

He was the reflection of her, and she was the reflection of him. No matter the pain, no matter the doubt, no matter the fear, there would never be another for either of them. Their blood flowed together.

Forever as one.

Magic magnified with the realization. As if the last barricade inside her fell, she wasn't just filled with his magic, overflowing like a vessel specifically created for his use — she *became* his magic. It rose and sparked inside her until Georgie was shining like molten gold, absorbing his lust and love, his pleasure and pain. Until it was hers, too.

"You make me lose my mind," he whispered.

She couldn't answer, there were no words, no breath. There was only sensation — his thick cock lodged in her body, her entrance burning around his base, her inner walls shuddering, begging him for more. True magic, not just within them, but around them, a part of them and melting them into one. Not just merging them, but making them whole, complete, for the first time in their lives.

Georgie's eyes did close then, but it didn't stop her tears from falling.

"Am I hurting you?" he gasped brokenly.

"Always." She struggled to speak. "But keep going. I need you."

His lips whispered over hers. "I need you, too, my love. I need you."

The gentleness of his tone did not communicate itself to his body. His intensity grew, descending into barbaric drives and untamed incivility. The ferocity only increased until his movements became something so primal Silviu's control seemed to break as thoroughly as Georgie's heart. Pushing instead of thrusting, pressing in instead of pulling out. It was like he wanted to climb inside her body and remain there forever.

Georgie was locked to him, unable to move as his arm tightened enough to cut off her breath. He pushed harder, grinding, not rocking, filling her over and over without ever once pulling back and leaving her to emptiness.

Because he'd promised she wouldn't be alone in the chaos.

Magic flowed between them freely. Georgie's pussy convulsed and clenched until all she knew was the hot length of Silviu's cock pulsing against her inner walls as they clamped down on him. Her leg shook where it curled over his hip, his hand became inflexible against her ass. Heat spiraled inside her, sliced through her and pulled her muscles into tight knots. She wrapped her arms around his neck and held on tight, pressing her face against his throat until his heartbeat hammered in her temple.

Silviu flexed his hips, finally pulling out, thrusting in. She gasped as a lick of fierce sensation jolted through her and Georgie detonated. He urged her closer as her pussy exploded in a series of hidden blasts, magic and pleasure shoving her beneath a brutal wave of ecstasy. She lost time and mass, spinning out as nothing more than molecules in the cold wind rushing past them, soaring up into the cloudy sky as golden light lit the world in a way the sun simply couldn't.

Hot, full, melting—Georgie was pushed into something deeper than orgasm. Something that came with low, heavy pulses in her abdomen, electric shocks between her legs and a total loss of tension in her muscles. She became pure sensation, pure magic.

His.

Silviu rammed into her, caught her mouth and roared his pleasure down her throat. He shuddered and jerked against her as magic swept them both along a torrential current washing away everything that had been planned for them, everything expected of them, leveling the foundations their lives had been built on and creating a clean space to begin again.

Razed.

Georgie was lost in a golden haze for long, long minutes. Slowly, she learned how to breathe again. Slowly, her heartbeat returned to normal and their separate magics unpeeled and settled back into their rightful souls. But she still carried Silviu's essence inside her.

She never took her face away from his throat. His shirt collar was soaked with the tears she'd yet to stem, but he only stroked her back and held his silence for a long time.

Until he finally asked, "Why do you cry, Georgie?"

She gave him the only answer she had. "Because I love you."

Silviu's lips drifted over her hair. He shifted the slightest amount, his hand brushed her lower belly, and the sound of his zipper rasped in the silence. He got to his feet and showed extraordinary strength by taking her with him. He held her to his chest with the afghan tucked around her and her face tucked into his throat, and carried her back to the house.

Chapter Thirty-One

Milo

Dinner was a quietly miserable affair. Milo led Christiana into the dining room, where the pall of grief hushed the Davenolds as they poked at their meals. The massive table, stretching the length of the room, was just barely big enough to hold all the Family members at one time, but they'd gotten used to bumping elbows after the past few days, so it wasn't as chaotic as it could have been.

Georgie sat at the head of the table, staring at her plate with dull eyes and a downward tilt to her lips. Silviu sat at her right, very close, keeping watch over her with an expression anyone with eyes could see was a touch nervous and carefully compassionate. And rabidly protective. Tulah and Adam sat next to the new High Male, so Milo helped Christiana into a vacant seat to Georgie's left before sitting at his wife's side.

Looking across the table, Milo nodded at Adam, who returned the greeting with mild respect. With the easing of the hostility between them, Milo wondered if they could start interacting on more moderate terms. Without the sniping and arguing.

Adam transferred his gaze to Christiana and searched her face. "How are you feeling? Should you even be out of bed?"

She smiled. "I'm fine. You all healed me pretty well."

Georgie looked up with a frown, her eyes traveling over the little group huddled at her end of the table. Then she locked her gaze on Chris. "What are you talking about?

What happened?"

With a grimace, Chris told her. "I got in the way of a dark magic spell this afternoon."

"It was meant for Silviu," Adam interjected. "He helped us pull Christiana through the worst of it."

Georgie turned on her betrothed with a stillness in her expression that sent a nervous flutter down Milo's spine. "You didn't tell me that, Silviu," she said.

To Milo's surprise, Silviu looked vaguely intimidated. "I didn't think about it, love. I had other things on my mind."

"This whole time? You were so preoccupied that you couldn't find a minute to tell me my cousin was attacked with a spell meant for you?"

Silviu's brows lowered. "Yes, Georgeanne, and if you remember, you spent most of the evening calling the other Davenold branches with the news of your loss. We were busy, and Christiana's health did not even once factor into my thought process. I knew she would be all right, and my focus was elsewhere."

Georgie blushed and looked back down at her plate. She blushed harder when Christiana asked, "Did you guys get everything settled between you?"

"We are still working on it," Silviu replied smoothly.

Under the table, Christiana grabbed Milo's hand. Her gaze flicked between her cousin and Silviu with a suspicious look in her eyes. Milo sensed Silviu's rising irritation, and Georgie's cheeks appeared hot enough to set the table cloth on fire. So when his wife opened her mouth to ask another question, he leaped into the conversation, keeping his voice to a low murmur that wouldn't easily be heard by the other members of the Family.

"I tried to track down Daniel Levy and ask him our questions, Silviu. I was told he left the estate after the attack."

Silviu's steely gaze worked around the table, taking in every face. After he made a full circuit of the crowded room, his stare trapped Milo. "How convenient for him."

"It's in bad taste to hang around while we prepare for Madeleine's funeral." Georgie's tone spoke volumes of her irritation at being kept in the dark "Please, enlighten me. What questions did you two have for him?"

With one look at the new Matriarch's enraged glare, Milo did as he was told immediately. "I walked in on Daniel and Suzette—"

"So I heard." Georgie's brows lifted, but her dark eyes narrowed and flicked toward Christiana.

Milo worked his jaw. "She was sucking his dick," he said bluntly. "Asked him when he was going to give her the baby he promised her. I didn't think anything of it until Daniel threatened my business, trying to keep me silent about what I'd seen."

Georgie sent a quick glance down toward the foot of the table, where Suzette sat morosely at her grandmother's side. "Why would Suzette want to have Daniel's baby? She's married to her Match and could bear him as many children as he can give her, but if she has a child with Daniel, that's the only one she'll ever have."

The rules of nature had been proven through countless generations. Magic Matches could have many children, but non-Matches were limited to one. Any witch who conceived a child with someone who wasn't their Match was doomed to sterility thereafter. Even if the baby didn't make it to birth—a thought which sent a bright flare of panic through Milo every single day—there would be no more.

Milo nodded. "I was wondering if Suzette and Daniel had conceived a plot to unite the Davenold and Levy covens through their child."

"Crossing the Schism divide." Georgie pushed her full plate away, leaned an elbow on the table and gave the matter serious thought. "The other covens would flip out. The biggest matriarchal house joining together with the largest patriarchal Family would have them all shaking in their boots. There would be no way for the other houses to gain an advantage for themselves unless they all created their own, massive alliance."

"Which would be nearly impossible," Silviu added. "Not only because they don't get along, but because other covens are locked into ironclad alliances with either the Levys or the Davenolds. Obligations must be met or they will suffer the consequences."

"There's more," Milo warned. "Daniel threatened me, and upset my wife by lying to her about who was really with Suzette. So I started looking into him, his background and his business dealings. Most people agree that Daniel is an upstanding guy, but I found some things that raised my suspicions."

"Like what?" The weight of Silviu's gaze was nearly enough to make Milo fidget—but he'd spent too many hours in Madeleine's company to be wholly intimidated.

Milo met the silver stare calmly. "He contributes to political campaigns in Matriarchal strongholds."

"He what?" Georgie straightened in her chair. "You mean he's financing policies directly affecting any *business* opportunities he has in those areas? Things that will affect any companies he's invested in?"

"Beyond that," Milo answered her. "He's throwing money at a multitude of causes, some of which are strictly societal in nature, human rights issues and policies for social change. But I have no idea where he's getting the money. He seems to be living well beyond his income, and massive amounts of money just appear in off-shore accounts tied to him."

"He has a backer?"

"Perhaps the dark magic witch," Silviu suggested.

"No," Milo objected. "Daniel owns a substantial, though minor, stake in a business I believe was owned by Graves Ngozi. An agreement was set to be signed, handing controlling interest over to Daniel a few days ago, but there's been some sort of delay. I assume Graves' death threw a wrench in the works."

Tulah perked up. "That *must* be why Constance was to

marry him. She would gain a higher position and Daniel would get money, right?"

Georgie rubbed her forehead. "Finance and economy isn't my strong suit. When I have to deal with those things for the Council, I rely heavily on my father's advice."

"Well," Milo sat forward, leaning toward her, "you can rely on my advice, now. The whole mess is very suspicious, and on top of that, Daniel's creating a primary branch residence network in territories rightfully controlled by other branches of his own Family. Secondary, fourth and fifth, straight on down the line. Just not the tertiary."

Georgie cocked her head. "He's not buying property in Poland?"

"No, and not the Ukraine, either."

Georgie stared into space, drumming her fingers against the tabletop softly. "It's because of Eliasz. He's got more magic than any other Levy male and if his father, Fredrik, noticed Daniel encroaching on his territory, especially after the drama in their grandparents' history, he'd go ballistic."

Christiana made a soft noise of agreement. "Grandmother always said Fredrik Levy was the only patriarchal man worth knowing." Realizing what had just come out of her mouth, her cheeks pinkened and she grinned in Silviu's direction. "No offense."

"Uh-huh." He glowered at her for a brief moment before setting his sights on Milo. "Economically speaking, how could his financial affairs relate to his political goals, and possible alliance with Suzette?"

"That's a great question," Georgie said before Milo could answer. "How does she fit into this? How could aligning himself with her, of all witches, bring him any benefit?"

"If he thought she would become Mother…" Adam's voice drifted off, implying more than his words stated.

Georgie shook her head. "Even if they considered the possibility my Bane status would remove me from inheritance, Christiana is still the better choice for Motherhood. It would have gone to her."

"But it didn't. The Davenold magic tried to choose Christiana." Silviu's eyes took on the faraway look of a man remembering something in great detail. Then he visibly shook himself and his tone took on a hint of secrecy. "But before it came to you, my love, it was actively working itself into Suzette. Something it shouldn't have done, if she is as weak as you all claim."

Adam lifted his brows. "She's one of the weakest of the coven."

"But the hidden witch none of us seem to be able to find has been using enhancements," Georgie pointed out.

Their little group fell into a momentary silence. As the hushed whispers of other conversations farther down the table washed against him, Milo let his thoughts drift where they would. He tried to see a path through the confusion, tried to reason out what had been happening, and even what Georgie had meant by her last comment.

Spells were not his talent, so he decided to ask. "What do you mean by enhancements?"

With their fingers linked and resting on her lap under the table, Christiana rubbed his knuckles with just her fingertips. "When Adam and I cast the locator spell, Silviu and Ileana did something to help enhance the efficacy." She stopped speaking as a distant expression crossed her face. She turned to Silviu. "In fact, you enhanced our magic in the Ngozi residence, too. You and Ileana, Eliasz and me. Remember?"

"Yes, but I simply lent you three my strength of will."

"Yeah, right." Chris' eyes narrowed. "But, when we cast the locator spell in the library upstairs, your enhancement grew stronger after Georgie touched you. And more stable."

"Matched Magic." He tipped his chin. "Georgie's strength helps mine. I have some success with manipulating the energy of magic to increase the benefits for others."

"I bet you do." Christiana's eyes became slits. "It's not you, is it?"

Georgie leveled her cousin with a hard stare. "No, it's

not him, Christiana. I have personally felt the dark witch's attacks, just as I have personally felt Silviu's magic. There is a huge difference between them. First and foremost, Silviu doesn't use dark magic."

"Unless he's trying to confuse you and can" — Christiana met Silviu's eyes — "*manipulate the energy* to that effect."

"If Silviu was trying to harm me with magic, I'd already be hurt." Georgie shook her head. "He's the only one who can push through my Bane shields."

"Unless he doesn't want you hurt, only thrown off the scent." Milo didn't back down as they all turned to stare at him. But he did raise his free hand in a gesture of surrender. "I'm just playing devil's advocate. After all, through your inheritance, he became the Davenold High Male, and now wields a great deal more influence in the world."

Georgie's face paled. "I don't appreciate the track your thoughts have traveled."

"We're just exploring all our options, Georgie." Christiana squeezed Milo's hand in support. "I already admitted that I trusted Silviu, remember?"

Their new Mother looked less than dignified as she rolled her eyes, yet her tone was as imperious as Madeleine's had been at her most commanding. "Trust *me*. Silviu didn't cast those attack spells. I would have felt it, and I would have known the truth."

Silviu stroked Georgie's shoulder, though his gaze was trained on Milo. "I would have preferred Madeleine to live. I have political ambitions beyond being the Davenold High Male, and would have welcomed the support of the Council High Seat."

"Besides," Adam tossed out, "how would he have attacked himself this morning? And I know that spell was meant for him. I couldn't figure out where it came from, but I promise it didn't come from him."

Georgie turned to Silviu, studying his face as if she saw something no one else could. "I'd been the previous target. I'm Bane, so the attacks didn't make much sense, they couldn't hurt me, but I assume it was an effort to intimidate."

He lifted a shoulder, seemingly unconcerned. "Targeting me would make a great distraction and eliminate your strongest ally—your Magic Match, the witch who can stabilize the magic everyone believes you to be lacking."

"The other spell was testing my limits." Georgie cast a glance down the table. "Maybe the dark magic witch was learning about my Bane imperviousness."

Without moving a muscle, Silviu suddenly went on high alert, exuding a predatory stillness very similar to what Milo had observed in him that morning. "They should have known it wouldn't work. Especially with a strong spell anchored with fragile magic."

"Weak magic?" Adam asked.

"No, but easily broken." Georgie tapped her bottom lip. "Too weak to do much damage, I suppose."

"Like the spell I was hit with," Christiana chimed in. "Yeah, it was very strong, knocked me on my ass and scared me silly, but it was formless. Spells without direction are less effective and more easily pulled apart. Maybe the dark magic witch just wanted to test Silviu's limits, too."

"Which seems to me," Milo said with a flash of insight, "knowledge that would directly benefit Suzette, who does, in fact, use dark magic. And is considered by your Family to be weaker than most."

"You make an excellent point." Silviu ran his tongue over his teeth. "I had an interesting conversation with Suzette this morning—"

"Did you?" Georgie's tone was icy.

Silviu took her hand and kissed her knuckles before he continued. "She grew very defensive when I accused her of trying to destabilize the magic between us, my love."

"What do you mean by destabilizing your magic?" Tulah asked. "I don't understand that."

"Magic is less successful," Silviu explained, "and more chaotic, and therefore potentially dangerous, if there is conflict between Magic Matches."

Milo shifted in his chair. "I didn't know that. But I don't doubt Suzette does. There is a huge rift in her own marriage."

"Not according to her." Christiana leaned forward in her chair. "She says her weak husband is the perfect man, willing to fade into the wallpaper to please her. He lets her do anything she wants."

Silviu made a low, rough sound. "I doubt they ever developed the type of affection that would strengthen their magic, though she's claimed her magic receives a boost just from being Matched. But that's not how it works, and many Davenolds would know that, considering how active your Family is in finding Matches for your children."

Milo shook his head. "If she was happy, she wouldn't have had an affair with Daniel."

Silviu reached out to pet Georgie's shoulder. "She implied she would challenge you, my love, and that she had allies of her own."

"Daniel, I presume," Milo murmured.

Silviu shrugged. "I asked if she was working with someone wielding the talent of enhancement. I asked her who the dark magic witch was, but she never said a word. I asked if she'd formed an alliance with Daniel, if they were in this scheme together. She neither confirmed, nor denied it."

Georgie's finger whitened when she gripped her chair arms. "You think Suzette joined some dark magic alliance, hoping to enhance her own magic, hoping to break the bond between us so our magic wouldn't be as strong, so she could be Mother and help Daniel achieve whatever goals he's working toward?"

Milo looked at Suzette. She sat at the far end, to the right of her grandmother, Margaret, the rightful leader of the secondary branch. Suzette looked neither triumphant nor angry, but sat instead with a sullen cast to her expression. She twirled her wineglass between her fingers and stared at her plate. In the midst of a crowded table, she alone had more elbow room, with her nearest neighbor having pulled his chair toward the Davenold on his other side.

Without taking his eyes off Suzette, Milo said to Georgeanne, "She does have a habit of testing limits. If another witch enhanced her talents, adding in the so-called boost from being a Match, she may have thought she could do enough damage to put you off balance, at least. When she didn't, she went after Silviu, hoping to weaken you through him."

"Because she intends to challenge me." Georgie nodded. "Hmm. Dark magic alliances, politics and the changing of the guard."

Silviu blinked. "What are you thinking, my love?"

"I'm thinking I'll challenge Suzette, instead."

Milo whirled to face Georgie in surprise. Having lived through numerous challenges in his former Family, he considered himself something of an expert. "That's not how it's done, Georgeanne. You already have the Davenold magic, what would you challenge her for?"

"The truth." It didn't take very much for Georgie to lift her voice above the low whispers of the other diners. "*Suzette.*"

Sending her challenge straight down the table, Georgie brought the entire room to a silent stand-still. She waited until every last Davenold looked her way, including her cousin at the far end. Tension soared, a palpable tremor raced through the room. Milo had felt this very thing before, and had dreaded ever feeling it again. He took a huge breath and tightened his grip on Christiana's hand, readying himself to rush his pregnant wife from the battlefield.

In a voice as clear and authoritative as Madeleine's had ever been, Georgie asked, "Tell me, dear cousin, exactly what had you thought to gain by killing my grandmother?"

Chapter Thirty-Two

Christiana

Christiana winced as Milo's hand tightened around hers. He practically vibrated in his chair, his long body completely tense. As were most of the other diners. Chris was too fascinated to feel fear.

"I did not kill Madeleine." Suzette slammed the glass she'd been spinning between her fingers onto the table. Red wine sloshed out, staining the cloth. Nobody in the silent crowd moved to offer a napkin.

Christiana immediately looked back to Georgie, who remained in her chair. Her casual posture lent her a more menacing air than she probably realized and Chris felt a thrill of excitement move through her. Goddess help her, she was having fun. There was an evil little monster in her head that cackled at the thought of Suzette finally getting her just desserts.

Georgie stared at Suzette, unblinking. "Look around you, sweetie. Do you see anyone else at this table, in this house, who plays with dark magic? Dark magic killed my grandmother."

"She was already ill when you brought her here," Suzette sputtered.

Georgie's lips thinned. "And you took advantage of whatever spell Graves had leveled her with, joining an alliance with a dark magic witch who could enhance your own abilities."

Margaret rose to her granddaughter's defense, though her protest had Christiana biting her lip against ill-timed humor. "Georgeanne, my granddaughter simply doesn't have the talent to bring down the Davenold Mother. Don't be ridiculous."

"You're correct, of course," Georgie agreed immediately. "On her own, she doesn't have the strength, but she's working with a dark witch with a gift for enhancement." Georgie's stare transferred back to Suzette. "You thought your magic would be heightened enough to take the Davenold power, too, but you were proven wrong."

Even from the opposite end of the table, Christiana could see her vile cousin's face flame as she gritted through her teeth, "I was the heir long before you were ever born! I have no need of enhancement."

"And yet," Georgie drawled, "your magic *was* enhanced, as I noticed when you attacked me the first time. I defeated your challenge. That's why you decided to try again, without magic."

Suzette's chin shot up. "And why shouldn't I challenge you? You are a Bane atrocity, defective and deformed. What makes you think you have any right to lead our Family?"

"Because I already do. Because I *am* the Davenold Mother."

Calm and composed, yet radiating lethal intent, Georgie inhabited her seat like a queen on her throne. Perfectly assured of her status and power, simultaneously terrifying and inspiring. She commanded respect and loyalty, and took it by virtue of her experiences.

For the first time, Christiana saw the real consequences of her cousin's efforts on behalf of the Asian witches caught in the hunts. Thrown into the fire at such a young age, Georgie had been tempered like steel. Love of her Family and the need for their love in return had moderated her behavior, her natural diplomacy had polished her sharpest edges, but she was what she'd been made to be.

An undiluted warrior woman, who would attack and destroy any threat to those she'd promised to protect.

In that moment, Georgie showed her true colors to her

entire Family. Her strength and determination, the hidden river of vengeance that snaked out to enclose them all within the walls of the sanctuary she extended. And Christiana was relieved that the woman she'd put her trust into, the woman she knew she'd follow to the ends of the earth, was capable of bearing the responsibility she'd lifted onto her shoulders.

Suzette alone did not see the threat Georgie personified. "You are weak, without magic. God, even today Silviu carried you through this house like a child, and you sobbing into his shoulder like a baby."

It was Lydia who jumped to her feet and put Suzette in her place. "That wasn't weakness you foolish, selfish bitch. That was grief. Our Mother had just died, and Georgie was right to mourn her passing. She loves her Family."

Davenolds all around the table nodded and murmured in agreement. Like a brushfire, whispered tales of Suzette's callousness swept through the room.

"Unlike you," Mason Davenold drawled. "Married to your Match with no children to show for it."

"Quite right," Georgie's mother, Julie, hissed. Christiana felt true shock then, as the woman was the most even-tempered Davenold in existence, mild-mannered to the point of meekness. But, as Julie mimicked her eldest sister and rose to her feet, Chris supposed any mother would be riled at the offense to her daughter. Other voices lifted in agreement, a traveling wave of noise around the table.

Georgie took a breath Christiana felt more than heard. She glanced over at her cousin's face, and saw a hint of bemusement in her dark eyes. "Georgie?" she whispered.

"They're defending me." Georgie licked her lips. "They're all defending me. They support me as their Mother."

Christiana blinked as she realized Georgeanne hadn't expected that. Her cousin's wounds went deeper than Chris had imagined — the loneliness of her youth, the knowledge of how different she was from everyone else. For all her bravado, Georgie had doubted the Family would accept her as their true Mother.

Christiana had known better. She'd always known the Family wouldn't tolerate anyone else in the position. Admiration filled her as she thought of the years her cousin had appeared so confident, when, secretly, she'd been anything but.

She leaned toward Georgie and dropped her voice. "Because they love you, honey. Because you proved yourself so long ago, you didn't even remember that you'd done it."

Georgie nostrils flared. Her chin lifted and she nodded.

Her mother stabbed a finger toward Suzette. "You had a duty to our coven. You had a duty to bring children into our house and strengthen the magic of our bloodline. You failed in the easiest task we could have given you."

"Yeah, what happened?" Christiana couldn't help but add her voice to the chorus rising up to defend Georgie. "You fuck so many men, Suzette. How big of a deal would it have been to fuck your husband too?"

"Unless, of course," Georgie's even tone sliced through the jeering of the crowd, "you expected to bear another man's baby. Daniel Levy, for example. Tell us, Suzette, what had you hoped to accomplish by bearing a patriarchal Father's child? It wouldn't be eligible to inherit either house."

Her statement struck Christiana hard. Power passed to the grandchildren. Neither Suzette, nor Daniel, could put their child at the head of their own covens. The only way their offspring would inherit naturally was to marry the heir of another house.

"Unless Daniel was interested in taking the Council High Seat," Christiana finished her thoughts aloud, without realizing she did so. "Silviu, you said something like that the day Daniel arrived."

He nodded, but made no other response, his attention obviously focused on the scene unfolding before them. Suspicion clamped down on Christiana's imagination, but she forced it aside to concentrate on what was happening

305

between her cousins.

"How dare you take that tone with me?" Suzette looked at Silviu and lifted her lip. "You'll bear a patriarch's child, yourself."

"My husband's. My Magic Match, a man born to a coven wielding more magical strength than any other."

"A *Lovasz*."

"A Davenold-Lovasz." Georgie remained calm, though Christiana saw her hand tighten around her chair's arm. "A strong witch. A hundred times more powerful than Daniel Levy, a man with almost no magic."

"You don't know—" Suzette tossed her hair. "He's an influential man. He wields more authority than Silviu."

Margaret slammed her hand on the table, staring at her granddaughter in horror. "Are you admitting to this, Suzette? Are you admitting that you've been trying to have a child with the Levy Father?"

"I admit nothing."

In the six months of their marriage, Milo had proven he had trouble silencing his opinions, so Chris wasn't surprised when he called out, "Daniel focused his sexual attention quite a bit more north of any place necessary for conception of a child. In spite of Suzette's begging, and in spite of the Levy Father's promises, all of which I witnessed with my own eyes. Unfortunately."

Christiana's lips quirked, Suzette's face blanched. Margaret emitted a sound of pure rage. "I went out of my way to find your Match!"

"He's as weak as she is!" Suzette vaulted to her feet and threw a hand toward Georgeanne. Her husband made no reaction as she screamed in Margaret's face. "I wanted a witch with strength!"

"He's your Match!" Margaret hurled her napkin onto her plate.

"And Daniel isn't," Georgie said. "Obviously, the father of any child you bore didn't have to be magically strong. But you didn't really think Daniel would elevate you to a position of power, did you, Suzette? He treats you like his dirty little secret, going so far as to threaten Milo for his silence. You couldn't have thought you'd gain influence through him, or you wouldn't have considered the position of Davenold Motherhood important enough to kill your own aunt for."

"*I did not kill her!*"

"Who did, Suzette?" Georgie crooned. "Exonerate yourself by telling me who the dark magic witch is."

But the other woman only shook her head. Christiana squinted down the table and took in Suzette's pinched lips and defensive posture. She could practically see the stubborn refusal shimmering in the air around her. A truth serum or spell would loosen her tongue, but both required a great deal of time to make ready.

And there was no time. Face twisted in hopeless rage, Suzette sent a visible blast of dark magic rolling down the center of the table toward Georgeanne. Plates and glasses shattered, the table cloth rippled in the breeze. The sheer width of the dining table saved the screaming Davenolds from harm as they hastily constructed shields to protect themselves. Chairs clattered as the diners pushed away, rushing to put more distance between them and the dangerous magic.

Milo gasped and threw himself on Christiana. His weight sent her chair skittering back and he wasted no time in trying to lift her out of it and move away. But Suzette's spell found its target before he could.

Milo stilled as the blast warmed the air inches from where Christiana sat. They both watched in shock as Georgie leaped to her feet and let the full blast of Suzette's magic slam into her Bane imperviousness. The attack fizzled out in a soft display of purple sparks. Christiana peeked over Milo's shaking shoulder and glanced at Silviu, whose face was rigidly blank, though his eyes promised painful retribution.

"I challenge you, Georgeanne Davenold, defective Bane

bitch and thief of the bloodline's power."

It was difficult to tell if Suzette fully understood what had just happened. If she'd realized that her spell had absolutely no impact on her cousin. Christiana wondered if Suzette felt that she'd painted herself into a corner, and had no other option than to brazen it out.

"Decided to try again with magic, did you? Come on, then." Georgie crooked a single finger in mocking invitation.

Suzette screamed in rage. "You have no right to be Mother. I was *first*, and you should have been killed at birth. I challenge you for the position."

She sent another spell winging the length of the room. Milo planted a slightly hysterical laugh in Christiana's hair. "So formal. I suppose that's better than Suzette leaping on Georgie's back and braining her with some heavy object."

"I think Silviu would kill her mid-leap," Christiana told her husband as a lavender flash of light reflected off a broken plate. "Milo, please get off me, I want to see what's happening."

Hulking over her, protecting her with his own body, her husband curled his neck into an awkward position. It gave them the opportunity to look each other directly in the eye. His were only millimeters away when they widened and filled with pain. His body jolted, purple light flared. Suzette's spell had gone wide.

Panic snapped through Chris. She bared her teeth in pure outrage. Clutching at her husband, Christiana shot him full of magic to protect him from the worst of the hit. She snarled in pure rage. "I'll kill that bitch myself."

"Please…let me take you…from here."

She stared at her husband as she jerked her fingers. Emotion lent her magic strength as she formed a barrier around him, encompassing them both. Her determination to protect her husband made it an effortless endeavor, not even requiring words.

But she couldn't leave.

"I need to see this, Milo." She redirected a cooling stream

of her magic over his spine, easing the injury Suzette's wildly aimed spell had caused.

Magic upended a fork and stabbed it into the table. Milo glanced at the quivering utensil and bared his teeth. "No, I can't allow—"

"Don't stop them!" Chris shook him by the shirt. "You can't calm this down. It needs to be done."

Another flash of light sent a salt shaker flying past their heads. "No, I won't use my magic. Georgie must accept all challenges. I can't calm the situation, but I can't allow you to stay. We must go."

Christiana's hair streamed out behind the chair as another spell passed by. She laid a quick kiss against her husband's temple, then strained to look over his shoulder. "Not a chance."

"Christiana, please let me take care of you."

"I *need* to see this, Milo. I need to see that bitch fall." She let her eyes fill with truth. It was the final portion of the unexpected therapy that had commenced at her Family's secondary estate, the final thing required to end all her pain and let her move forward with her new husband. "Suzette deserves an ass-kicking, and I plan on cheering Georgie on."

With a frustrated sigh, Milo swept Chris into the flow of Davenolds who moved to ring the walls—out of the way, but not out of the room—as Suzette sent bolt after bolt of magic down the table. Christiana let her husband put her behind him without protest She wrapped her arms around his waist and peeked around his ribcage, trusting in her protective spell to keep them both safe.

Silviu moved to stand at Christiana's side. Georgie remained at the head of the table, drumming her fingers on the tabletop and staring at Suzette with a bored expression on her face. "I can do this all night, Suzette."

Milo groaned. "It's a challenge for magic. Magic must be used."

"Who says?" Chris tightened her arms around him. "Who

says a Bane witch has to play by the same rules as everyone else?"

"Look at your Family, *krasavitsa*. They are starting to wonder why Georgeanne isn't using the Davenold power to fight back. Being Bane has drawbacks. Doubt grows as tall as trees, over time."

"He's right," Silviu whispered. Chris watched him as his eyes scoured the crowd. "She needs to use magic. *Georgeanne*, lower your shields."

"Fight me, you defective bitch!" Suzette's taunts were uncannily close to Milo's warning. "Or has your Bane magic swallowed the Davenold power? Has your deformity weakened us? Is our Mother even capable of using the magic she's stolen?"

"Reach for the magic the way I taught you to." His tone low at first, Silviu then raised his voice. "Prove your Motherhood."

"Why should I?" Georgie tilted her head, contemptuously staring at Suzette. "She can't hurt me."

"Look at them, love. *Look*." Once again, Silviu's words dropped into a low register. "Your Family needs you to prove your magical capability."

"You have no magic!" Suzette screamed. "Your weakness will destroy us. It will consume the Davenold power until we are all like you. Bane and pitied!"

Davenolds along the wall turned to Georgie with a look in their gazes that suggested they were fighting their suspicions. Christiana felt real fear surge through her, but her emotions were nothing compared to what she saw in Silviu's mercurial eyes.

Then a whispered sigh swept between his lips. Silviu's hand rose to press against his sternum and he staggered back a step. Chris reached for him instinctually, surprised at the glimmer of pain that pulled the skin over his cheekbones taut.

"Are you all right?" she asked.

His throat worked. "Georgie's pulling strength from me.

It's how it should be, but something's wrong. Not the way it was before."

Suzette laughed maniacally and shot a bolt of violet magic from her fingertips. The magic blazed around a thick, silver candle holder, lifted it and sent it soaring. It crashed into the wall next to Georgie's mother's head. In spite of her protective shield, the woman flinched and screamed.

Christiana's mouth dropped at the sheer rage that overtook Georgie's features. The warrior woman emerged again, all pretense at boredom dropped. She took on a golden glow, a radiance that seemed to shine from every pore until the room was saturated with so much magic that Christiana's bones creaked under the pressure. Everyone stumbled against the walls, leaning against the wainscoting and bracing their feet. Margaret lifted a hand to her chest.

Then the gold light turned jet black.

Silviu grunted, a hard expulsion of breath that sounded loudly in the silence of the room. His free hand caught his weight against the wall, the other fisted against his chest.

"What the hell is that?" Milo asked in a strangled yell.

"Black magic." Christiana tried to define the terrifying, dark glow in her mind, but failed. "Is that what hid behind her shields?"

Milo curled his body around Christiana's. "Is it Suzette's? Is Georgie breaking it?"

"No, it's Georgeanne's magic. This is my fault." Silviu bared his teeth as a twist of onyx light flicked out over the table. "It's unstable."

Georgie lifted her arms and snarled, "Bind her."

Black magic raced to her command. Thick ribbons snaked through the dining room, coiling around obstacles and chilling the air. They wrapped around Suzette and pulled tight. Georgie's hair thrashed in a gust of power. Christiana lost her breath as she watched her cousin steal her rival's magic, violet light absorbed into the black.

A matter of seconds, heartbeats.

An explosion of gold stole everyone's sight. Silviu

pushed away from the wall and gritted his teeth, the golden radiance around his body reaching for the black around Georgie's. With bright tracers streaming through her vision, Christiana saw Silviu clutch his wife, and his magic sent hers scattering.

"Bane witch to Reap witch." Silviu met every terrified gaze in the dining room, pausing as shocked gasps swept through the crowd. "Let our strength be known to all in our Family, and let it be known that we will do everything in our power to protect our Family."

Christiana snatched a shaky breath and healed what damage she could. "If that's what you two can do together, I'm glad you're on our side."

Milo put his lips to Christiana's ear. "What the hell just happened?"

"Justice. Georgie broke Suzette's magic." Chris cleared her throat. "Now that bitch is Bane, too."

Chapter Thirty-Three

Silviu

They buried Madeleine in England. Before the primary line had immigrated to America and the English estate had passed to the secondary branch, it had been the Family's ancestral home, a fitting place for such a beloved leader to find her final rest.

Silviu adjusted his hold on the umbrella he shared with Georgeanne, surreptitiously surveying the Davenolds gathered at the graveside. He didn't trust the matriarchal witches. He'd seen the growing consideration on their faces when his wife had fought Suzette and knew they'd wondered if Georgie's Bane magic would weaken the Davenold power.

They had an answer now, regardless of the truth. As far as he was concerned, Georgeanne was the Mother, no matter who hosted the magic. He would never admit otherwise.

As Georgie stepped forward to join the twins next to the casket, Silviu took careful note of the expressions on every face and the emotions in every eye. The Davenolds seemed to have forgiven Georgeanne for her overwhelming display of magical strength. The few he'd spoken with had voiced their agreement with Christiana, who he could have kissed for her timely pronouncement. They were all pleased the Bane witch belonged to them, and not another coven.

In spite of the fact that it appeared the new Davenold Mother wielded black magic.

At least the entire coven knew how much Georgie loved her grandmother, and so they did not suspect her of

Madeleine's murder. In Silviu's opinion, that was another deadly bullet dodged.

Georgie placed a wreath of lavender, periwinkle and dogwood on the casket. Silviu took another look around the mourners and a flashback made him relive his horror again. He struggled to push it back, he fought to keep his hands where they were and not press a fist to his chest in remembrance, but the memories would haunt him forever.

Fear had rifled through his gut with cold fingers and panic had squeezed his lungs, though he trusted Georgie's shields to keep her safe from physical harm. He'd been more concerned at the Family's reactions—they'd *wanted* to support her, but they'd needed reassurance. Silviu had been pushing his magic at his bride, but she hadn't been open to him, hadn't accepted their joining. He hadn't wanted to risk his Reap power being revealed—not that it mattered anymore—and without Georgie's cooperation, Silviu hadn't known how to make a strong connection.

The moment Georgeanne had registered that she would have to meet her cousin's magic with her own, Silviu had felt a small tug near his navel. He'd had thrown open the gates and Georgie had taken advantage, but the tug became a discomfort difficult to ignore. Still, Silviu had sent his magic out in a fierce wave.

All she had to do was let it.

Georgeanne had blazed with an unholy fire, pure black and flickering with onyx flames. Her magic had consumed Silviu's and demanded more. And he had more to give—with a mind of its own, his magic wanted to fill the void inside Georgie—but her distrust in him had muted the true power they could wield, preventing control.

Then she'd sent it back, closing the circuit, making a loop. Silviu's pain and fear were destroyed under the flow she redirected back into him. Magic rebounded, doubled, tripled. The pressure in the room had become lethally intense, but it could have been worse.

"Are you all right, Silviu?" Georgie stepped back from

the grave with an odd, watchful look in her eye.

Silviu clutched her cold hand in a grip he feared would leave bruises as the mourners began to disperse. He waited until they were alone before tugging his wife back toward the coffin. Placing his hand on the top, he vowed, "I will take care of your Family."

"Are you telling me, or my grandmother?"

Silviu turned and pulled Georgie closer. "Both of you. This...*thing* between us needs to be resolved."

"What thing?"

"Your distrust of me." He dipped the umbrella, using it as a shield against the watchful gazes of the others, waiting for them by the line of cars. "Our magic is unstable. I could feel it when you fought Suzette."

"It felt fine to me."

"Georgeanne!" He stopped, took a breath. Gripped the handle of the umbrella in an effort not to shake his stubborn wife. "Their terror beats at my senses. You are the nightmare witch they've all feared. You are the creature of legend others will rise up to destroy."

"And you are Reap," she growled. "The Match to the *horror* I am. My Family does not fear me, Silviu. They know I will protect them."

"Yes," he admitted. "But they love you. What will others do—"

"That's your problem, remember?" She lifted both her chin and her brows, facing him with taunting defiance. "You're the one who's set on *protecting* me, though clearly, I'm capable of handling myself."

"The magic raged out of control, Georgie. I had to pull it back, showing my strength, revealing our secrets. Whatever you used was completely unstable, and if you can't find a way to trust me again, others will notice that. Others will fear that, and they will come after us to eliminate the threat."

"I am the Davenold Mother, remember?" She lifted her chin higher. "I will do whatever I must to keep my Family safe."

She turned down the path before he realized she would walk away from him. Gritting his teeth, Silviu rushed to catch up. It wouldn't do to show everyone else so much evidence of their troubles.

"We'll work on it, my love. And we'll regain what we lost."

Without responding, Georgie rushed toward the limo waiting to take them back to the house. Milo and Christiana huddled under their own umbrella next to the rear door.

Georgeanne reached for Christiana as Milo started to assist her into the vehicle. "Chris, are you okay?"

Christiana snuggled back into her husband's embrace, looking up at him with a watery, but loving smile. "Yeah, we're going to be okay. Milo and I are going to be just fine."

"*Krasavitsa*," their umbrella shifted as Milo pressed a kiss to his wife's forehead and placed a hand over her belly, "we will be more than fine. We will be in love, and perfectly happy. I have gotten everything I wanted from life."

Chris' eyes went misty. "I think I have, too."

Silviu was pleased to see the distance between the couple was gone. For some reason, now that he was Mother, he was anxious for everyone under his protection to be happy. He slid a glance at his own wife and vowed they would get there too, one day soon.

"Are you certain you don't want the secondary branch?" Georgie asked her cousin.

The other woman shuddered. "No. Besides, with Suzette out of the running for inheritance, Margaret's been focused on the next in line. I don't want the job, and refuse to cause any more rifts in the Family by pretending otherwise."

"No, no more drama because someone felt they'd been passed over." Georgie wrinkled her nose. "That's how this whole thing started, with Graves. He was denied inheritance, too."

Silviu tucked that reminder away and asked, "Has Suzette spoken yet?"

317

Chris shook her head. "Not a word. Before she goes to her new home, far away from the Family, I'm going to try a truth serum on her. I'm just waiting for the spell to mature."

"Almost all the loose ends are tied up." Silviu wrapped his arm around Georgeanne's shoulder. She didn't pull away, but he couldn't help feeling as if they were back to square one, as they'd been in Poland, putting on a show of affection for others.

"There's still so much to do." Georgie took a deep breath as she watched Chris and Milo get into the limo. "The Council will need to be convened to elect a new High Seat. We need to start making phone calls to our allies."

"Costel is already there, along with Ileana and Eliasz. I am hoping they are playing well with Bijoux Laurent and persuading her to be a friend for our cause."

Georgie climbed into the car. "You want Bijoux's help?"

"Yes," Silviu stated. "Very much."

"I'll call her when we get back to the house, then. Grandmother used to send me anytime she needed Bijoux's input on Council happenings. She can't read my mind."

Silviu looked down at his bride. "I would appreciate your help with her."

"Well, we're a team now."

Something in Silviu's chest eased. He'd broken Georgie's trust, but he would do whatever he needed to earn it back. For now, she'd admitted she loved him and was ready to face down the Council for him.

For now, it was enough.

"What will you do next, Georgie?" Chris asked.

Silviu answered for her. "We'll go to the Council, and fight for the right to lead them all."

Outrageous Offer

Excerpt

Chapter One

"Dang, woman, I can hear your caterwauling all the way down at the post office."

Only vaguely hearing him through her sobs, Hyacinth didn't recognize the deep male voice, but that wasn't surprising. After all, she'd only been in Creek Bend for thirty minutes—just long enough that the stage coach had departed. Just long enough to have fear tearing holes through her stomach as the prospects of her future turned darker than they'd ever been before.

"Oh, leave me alone!" Hyacinth turned her back on the male voice at the same time she shot to her feet, but a low whistle kept her from leaving—not that she had anywhere to go.

"God have mercy, woman. You here to work in the saloon? Tell me when you start and I'll scrape a few dollars together to visit you."

Hyacinth collapsed back onto the rickety bench as a new wave of terror tore her legs out from under her.

"But I've got to be your first customer, darlin'," the stranger continued, "because them other ladies are all diseased, so it's only a matter of time before you are too. It's a shame, but unavoidable. For them, that is. I just forego their company, but it's been a while and if I could be your first—"

"Oh, dear God! I can't work in the saloon." Head lowered into her hands, she cried harder.

"You waiting to go home, then? Because someone should have told you that the next stage won't come through here for another two days."

Home. No, she couldn't go home. Not with all the nasty— though admittedly true—rumors going around. Not with her parents in their graves and the money they'd left her gone. Not with the man she'd thought to marry starting a family with another woman.

Hyacinth was beyond hopeless. Her sobs turned uglier, racking her body on the bench set along the splintered wall of the coach depot.

A sigh reached out to her and heavy steps crossed the shoddy boards half-buried in the muddy aisle the backwater town in the armpit of the American frontier insisted on calling a street. Through her tears, worn leather toes and ragged dungarees came into sight.

"You all right, ma'am?" The tone of the voice didn't imply that its owner cared.

"No!" She answered his question in a shrill wail. "Does it look like I'm all right?"

"Don't know. Can't hardly see you anymore, considering the way you're all hunched down over your own lap. What I did see was nice, though. That's a real fine drape to your skirts, ma'am."

Hyacinth pried her fingers off her brow, but she didn't raise her head. Having seen enough horrified shock cross

320

men's faces to last a lifetime, she didn't want to let the stranger see her eyes. She made an effort to control herself, but tears still tracked down her cheeks and dripped off her chin.

A frayed bandana was thrust into her newly-unoccupied hand.

"Thank you." She crumpled the handkerchief against her nose. "Your kindness is appreciated, seeing as how I've been abandoned."

The boots in her line of sight rocked back on their heels. "Well, give it a few more minutes and I'm sure somebody 'round here will claim you. Women are in short supply."

Hyacinth shook her head and let another sob break from her throat. "Oh, no man's going to claim me. Not after the scene Ernest Horsham just enacted."

"Hmm, tough luck then. So, you're waiting for the next stage?"

"I don't have the money to go back home. I don't even have a home to go back to." Hyacinth took the briefest moment to wipe her nose then continued as if the stranger had asked for further explanations. "I was supposed to marry him—Ernest, that is—but he has rejected me. I have no money, no place to go, no way to get back East. I have nothing and after the things he said, no one will help me."

"That is too bad, ma'am. Good luck and all that." The boots turned away and took a step. Then they stopped and did an about-face. "You're the mail-order bride?"

Hyacinth nodded and plastered the handkerchief over her eyes. "It was a terrible idea."

"It sure as hell was," the man agreed. "Jesus, woman, he posted that ad in a hearts and hands catalog. Butt of the town's jokes for quite a while, but then he got all puffed up when you agreed to come on out here. I'm surprised he rejected you, considering both his pride and the way your back end looks."

"Please don't be vulgar!"

"I've been accused of worse. Why did he tell you to take

321

a hike?"

The man's words struck deep and bounced off a steely core Hyacinth wouldn't have guessed she had. Abused pride flooded her, finally stopping her tears as her chin shot up. She whipped the bandana off her face and jumped to her feet, bracing her fists on her hips.

She raked the man with her gaze, not that he noticed. His eyes were busy burning a path up her body, leisurely perusing the heavy skirts hiding her legs, lingering on the wide curve of her hips, which were unfortunately emphasized by her short jacket. He dragged his scrutiny higher but seemed to get caught on her chest. Hyacinth fought not to cross her arms over her bodice.

More books from
Lola White

She has little choice – she swore she'd never trust a man again, but she needs his help.

In witching society, magic and politics are the only things that matter.

In witching society marriages are arranged for advantage rather than love.

About the Author

Lola White

I've always been a storyteller, just as I've always been an avid reader. I love stories that twist reality at its edges, and adore new takes on old myths and legends. I've travelled extensively, which has given me the opportunity to hear many legends from many cultures and I make use of these in my stories as often as possible.

Lola White loves to hear from readers. You can find contact information, website details and an author profile page at https://www.totallybound.com/

Home of Erotic Romance